WHO'S SORRY NOW?

WHO'S SORRY NOW?

HOWARD JACOBSON

Jonathan Cape
London

Published by Jonathan Cape 2002

6 8 10 9 7 5

First published in Great Britain in 2002 by
Jonathan Cape
Random House, 20 Vauxhall Bridge Road,
London SW1V 2SA

Random House Australia (Pty) Limited
20 Alfred Street, Milsons Point, Sydney,
New South Wales 2061, Australia

Random House New Zealand Limited
18 Poland Road, Glenfield,
Auckland 10, New Zealand

Random House (Pty) Limited
Endulini, 5A Jubilee Road, Parktown 2193, South Africa

The Random House Group Limited Reg. No. 954009

A CIP catalogue record for this book
is available from the British Library

ISBN 0–224–06286–7

Papers used by The Random House Group Limited are natural, recyclable
products made from wood grown in sustainable forests; the manufacturing
processes conform to the environmental regulations of the country of origin

Typeset by Palimpsest Book Production Limited,
Polmont, Stirlingshire
Printed and bound in Great Britain by
Mackays of Chatham plc, Chatham, Kent

To Jenny – with love

The sacred lowe o' weel-plac'd love,
   Luxuriantly indulge it;
But never tempt th'illicit rove,
   Tho' naething should divulge it:
I waive the quantum o' the sin,
   The hazard of concealing;
But, och! it hardens a' within
   And petrifies the feeling!

Robert Burns

The fuck it does.

Marvin Kreitman

BOOK I

ONE

Y OU CAN LEARN a lot about a man from the sorts of bedtime
stories he tells his children. Marvin Kreitman, archivist of
himself, put his daughters to sleep – when he was at home – with
reminiscences so painful to him, they might have been designed
to hurry the girls out of childhood altogether.

This was one of them:

Every Thursday, Friday, Saturday night, come wind, come
rain, small squishy-hearted Marvin Kreitman – that's me –
watched his father, the Purse King – that's your grandfather
– shake from his leather apron, like rats from a rat-catcher's
sack, the takings from his market stall. Spellbound, he
watched the crumpled notes creak like sand crabs in a
huddle, slowly open, move sideways and come apart. Every
Thursday, Friday, Saturday night the same. And every
Thursday, Friday, Saturday night, small squishy-hearted
Marvin Kreitman was excluded from the count.

'Go up to your room and do your homework.' Your
grandmother talking.

'I've done my homework.'

'Marvin, you can never do too much homework!'

'Can't I just stay to straighten the fivers?'

'Fivers! Fivers!' Theatrically, like a woman concealing a
terrible secret, a crime or a deformity, Mona Kreitman

interposed herself between her only child and the contents of the sack. 'Do you know what my dream for you is?' she asked. I did, but I waited for her to tell me anyway. 'My dream for you is that you won't ever have to touch money. My dream for you is that you will be above money. Look what money does to you.' She showed me how dirty money was, how it got into the grains of your skin, how it stained the palms of your hands and blackened the tips of your fingers the way newspapers did, only worse. Had she been able to tear open her chest for me, and show how money discoloured the soul as well, of course she would have done so.

'So why do *you* touch it then?'

'Ha!' A bitter laughless laugh, full of narrative promise. Once upon a time . . . But a grown-up story with no good fairies in it. Unless the good fairy was her. She lowered herself into the notes, a mermaid in a sea of creaking crabs, until we were the same size. 'We do what we do, Marvin,' she sang to me, on her knees, making 'we' a tragical and lonely word, 'because we have no choice. You, on the other hand, have a choice. We have given you that choice. You ask me why we touch money? So that you won't ever have to. Now do your homework and become Prime Minister.'

Not to be argumentative, but because I wanted to stay swimming in the warm pools of her eyes, I said, 'Prime ministers get to touch money.'

'Oh, do they now! So what do you think the Chancellor of the Exchequer is for?'

'Then I'll be Chancellor of the Exchequer.'

'See! There only has to be money on the floor and already you're thinking small. Listen to me . . . A little boy as clever as you are doesn't ever have to settle for second-best. You just do your homework and become

4

Prime Minister.' Whereupon she put her arms around me and kissed me, more as if I were a little king than a politician, the king Cophetua and she, with her blazing black Caspian eyes, her gold hooped earrings and her filthy fingertips, the beggar-maid.

'If you want to count something,' my father chipped in, a croak from the house of the dead, 'count your blessings.'

But blessings are less easy to count than money and Marvin Kreitman never did learn to count his.

'Not even us, Daddy?' the girls were too young, in those days, to have asked.

Which might have given him pause for thought. As it was, determined to be a better parent than his own father, loving if a little absent, at his most comfortable with them once they'd actually gone to sleep, he rose from the tiny toadstool chair by their beds, put his cheek to each of theirs, smelled their hair, as sharp as Chardonnay, kissed the tangy gristle of their ears, and wished them sweet dreams.

'And tomorrow night, if you're good' – and if he happened to be home – 'I'll tell you what they did to Daddy next . . .'

Charlie Merriweather, on the other hand, a father who was always at home, sprawled on the bed with his children and invented stories calculated to make them splutter into each other's necks and slither about all over him like sea lions.

For example:

One day, Timmy Hyphen Smelly-Botty Farnsbarns, brother of Kitty-Litter Farnsbarns, was hiding in the school lavs reading the *Financial Times* – as he did every morning in summer, preferring to keep the *Daily Telegraph*, which, as you know, is warmer, for the winter months – when suddenly the headmaster, who also happened to be his father, the Right Reverend Doctor Arty-Farty Farnsbarns, hammered at the door with a dire warning. 'If you don't come out of there in the next seven and a half hours, Timmy Hyphen Smelly-Botty, you won't only end up being flushed away along with your dooh-dahs, you will miss the school outing to Feelgood Hall. And you know what that means, don't you?'

Timmy Hyphen Smelly-Botty knew only too well what missing the school outing to Feelgood Hall meant. It meant missing a ride in the school bus, singing 'Ten Green Bottles'. It meant missing sitting next to his girlfriend, Dymphna No Hyphen Droopy Drawers and stealing dolly mixtures from her socks. It meant going without isosceles triangles of cucumber-and-cream-cheese sandwiches, and trapeziums of treacle tarts, and rhomboids of hot rhubarb crumble drowning in lumpy-dumpy custard, to say nothing of his favourite – lemon meringue pie, served in crystal icosahedral dishes with the arms of Feelgood Hall engraved into their bottoms. But above all it meant not seeing the First Lord Felix Very Very Feelgood, who also had the family coat of arms engraved into his bottom, and who was often to be found by the lily pond with one leg tucked under him like a duck, reciting the poem Timmy Hyphen Smelly-Botty Farnsbarns loved best in all the world –

> I'll tell thee everything I can:
> There's little to relate.
> I saw an aged, aged man.
> A-sitting on a gate.

But then Charlie Merriweather was a professional, one half of the team who wrote the much-loved (if these days . . . but to hell with these days) C. C. Merriweather books for children. Whereas Marvin Kreitman, despite all the eloquent interventions of his mother, only sold purses.

Why Kreitman saw selling purses as an 'only', considering the number of them he did sell – his father's boy, after all, the luggage baron of south London in his own right now, with not-quite-prime-site shops all the way from Battersea to Peckham – only someone who has been groomed to be Prime Minister, but has never stood for Parliament, can understand.

And as he had once tried to explain to his children, lying stiff and startled, if not downright terrified, in their beds, he was not a man gifted with the grace to count his blessings.

TWO

WHICH IS NOT a reason for our refusing to count them for him.

Handsome, clever and rich, white, male and whole, a sperm-tank heterosexual, though not a heave-ho heterosexual, youthfully middle-aged, with a comfortably over-furnished home, an only middlingly cheerless disposition by the suicidal standards of the age, and, as of his most recent precautionary Wellman going-over, entirely clot-, cholesterol- and cancer-free. Prostate firmer than a green mango and a colon so clean he could have invited his mother to take tea in it. Put your ear to Kreitman's squishy, wire-haired chest and you'd hear the engine purring nicely. Forty-five thousand on the clock and who would dare say there wasn't another forty-five thousand left in him. For Kreitman is of the generation that might just live for ever.

But let's not go overboard. Handsome only if you like bruised summer-berry lips and eyes that appear permanently – and painfully to the person who must look at them – punched out; clever, if you don't too much mind assertive, though not so assertive as to have done anything worthwhile with his PhD, such as become the Prime Minister he was meant to be, or Chancellor, or even, as many of his contemporaries *had* become, ball polisher, language juggler, or brave-face artist to one or to the other; and no more than moderately rich given what everybody else was earning, south London only being south

London – so not eat-your-heart-out or *Hello!* magazine rich, not a multi or a funky millionaire, but certainly well-enough-to-do to have fulfilled the first of his mother's ambitions for him, and to have kept his hands free of the stain of paper money.

To complete his happiness, he loved – without much thinking about them – four women: his mother (of course), his wife (which was more unusual for a Kreitman), and his daughters Juliet and Cressida. And was *in love* with – that's to say he thought about them every second of every day, except for when he was lying whimpering in the arms of any individual one of them, during which time, as a matter of erotic rectitude, he thought only about *her* – five more. His mother's second husband's nurse, his wife's interior decorator, the curator of his daughter Cressida's first mixed show, and the mothers, unsuspected of course by their daughters or daughters-in-law, of his wife's interior decorator's ex-husband, and of a window dresser with whom he'd been in love in earlier times.

It isn't necessary to memorise all these. Kreitman didn't.

That's bravado, of course. Though he was sexually squeamish and shrank from being thought dissolute or lecherous – anyone less lecherous than himself he had never met – Marvin Kreitman did entertain a nostalgic affection for many of the old discredited categories of masculinist swagger. He would have liked to cut a swathe. He would have liked to leap from balcony to balcony, the edge of his sword a flash of silver lightning in the Venetian night. But he wasn't enough of a blasphemer to be a rake. Had any frozen statue confronted Kreitman with his misdeeds, he'd have cried 'God help me!' and run a mile. In fact, he was just a serial faller-in-love, a sentimental maker of goo-goo eyes like Thomas Hardy or H. G. Wells, rheumy, sad moustachioed men in frock coats and tight Edwardian trousers. Kreitman could do sad and rheumy as well as anyone, but because he was dark and shiny, with a complexion as polished as the carapace of a beetle, people took him to be a hunter and a carnivore. He was the victim of his appearance. He looked the way men were no longer supposed to look.

Which might explain why he got on well with women of an earlier generation. Mothers of the girls he went out with always liked him more than their daughters did. And mostly he felt the same about them. Give him a mother and he'd forget the daughter, any time. There was a quality of disappointment or disillusion in mothers that agreed with him. Offered the choice, he would rather have sarcasm in a woman than sweetness. Maybe he felt he could do something for sarcastic women; console them or compensate them. Maybe he felt that their bitterness exonerated him in advance: at worst he would only confirm what their experience had already taught them. Or maybe, if this isn't altogether too simple an explanation, he could never be on the end of too much mothering. Whatever the reason, one way or another, he went in for mothers.

So how come he had made such a dog's dinner of relations with his wife's mother?

The very question Marvin Kreitman put to Hazel Kreitman (then Hazel Nossiter) at the time of their engagement, more than twenty years before. 'So what's wrong with your mother?'

What could Hazel Nossiter say? 'She doesn't like you.'

'I know she doesn't like me. *Why* doesn't she like me?'

And what could Hazel Nossiter say to that? She doesn't like you because your father sells purses on a street market in Balham? She doesn't like you because you're sulky and never look at her? Instead she said, and this was also true, 'She doesn't like you because you've never let her like you.'

Kreitman's mother-in-law kept a photograph on her dressing table of her daughter with her arms around a man. The man was not Kreitman. The man was a soldier in the Israeli Defence Forces. Yossi. A grinner with more teeth visible than Kreitman had in the whole of his mouth. Hazel had met Yossi on holiday the year before she met Kreitman. She had been travelling with a student

Christian group to the Holy Places. She wasn't Christian in the Christian sense, but it was something to do. Hazel was like that: people asked her to go somewhere with them, so she went. As witness Yossi. He had stopped the bus Hazel was travelling on, ordered her off at rifle-point, walked her into the Negev and strip-searched her.

It was love at first sight. As soon as Kreitman's mother-in-law saw Yossi's photograph she fell in love with him.

That Yossi was no more than an outdoor version of Kreitman, Kreitman without his shirt on, only made it worse for Kreitman and for Hazel. 'If you're so hot for Yossi, how come you aren't hot at all for Marvin?' Hazel asked.

'Because Yossi smiles,' her mother explained. 'And because he doesn't have a pleading expression in his eyes. And because he doesn't look as though he thinks he's done something wrong. And because his father doesn't sell purses on a street market in Balham. Are those enough reasons for you, darling?'

This was why Kreitman had never let his mother-in-law like him enough for him to fall in love with her. She was already in love with another man. And Kreitman only fell in love with women who were already a bit in love with him. Which shows, as Mrs Nossiter had shrewdly noticed, how little confidence in himself he had.

Despite which, or more likely because of which, he was head over heels in love with five women and not insusceptible to a sixth. For once you start falling in love with women it is impossible to stop.

And once you start counting . . .

But Kreitman had to count something. No one can get through life indifferent to numbers. Money, blessings, lovers – we are too ethereal to do without the material world, and too indeterminate to tell ourselves apart without measuring how much material we've commandeered. Call it ballast, call it markings. So many tons, so many stripes. The God-fearing count their beads, and even the most self-denying anchorite tots up what he's relinquished at the end of every day.

Making a distinction between those he didn't think about and those he thought about all the time, between those who were so conjunctive to his life and soul he didn't need to think about them and those who renewed him with the novelty of their affections, Kreitman counted to five. When his life made no sense to him he would try counting backwards, to include every woman he had ever loved, and every woman who had ever loved him, but there was something pathetic about that. He'd save retrospective accumulation for when he was an old man. For the time being, five (plus four) would do. Not too few. Not too many.

Though of course any number can be too many for some people. Take his friend, Charlie Merriweather . . .

'I get nightmares after talking to you,' Charlie told him over their weekly pretend-pauper dim sum lunch in Lisle Street. 'I dream about waking up in bed with someone whose name I can't remember.'

Excluding his daughter, whom he could never not think of as his little girl – for ever the wriggly Kitty-Litter Farnsbarns – Charlie loved just the one woman. And her name he had no difficulty at all remembering in bed, seeing as it was the same as his. Charlotte Jane – the other half of C. C. Merriweather, the composite writer of children's stories – known as Charlie since before she could remember. A tomboy name. And a tomboy she had looked, protruding like a sheaf of wheat from her wedding dress, unconfined and boisterous, even as she and Charlie exchanged their marriage vows. 'Charlie Juniper, do you take Charlie Merriweather? Charlie Merriweather, do you take Charlie Juniper?' Both unprotected, lacking eyelashes, big-boned and trundling, with the air of having been left out in all seasons, like the Cerne Abbas giant and his wife. Did the Charlies take? Of course the Charlies took. 'I now pronounce you . . . You may kiss . . .' And they'd been kissing each other, to the exclusion of all others, ever since. Bone of my bone, flesh of my flesh. Just fancy, Marvin Kreitman thought, wondering if it was like kissing yourself.

'I'm interested to hear,' were his actual words, 'that when you go to bed what you dream about is going to bed.'

'Only after seeing you.'

'I wouldn't think that one through, Charlie.'

Charlie Merriweather laid down his chopsticks and sighed one of his big sad cheery sighs. 'Not the homo routine, Marvin.'

'I can't help it. I'm homophobic.'

'You *affect* to be homophobic.'

'Only because I'm a latent homosexual.'

'You're not a latent homosexual. And anyway, no homosexual would have you.'

'That's why I'm homophobic.'

'All this,' Charlie said, trying to change the mood, 'to disguise the fact that you think *I'm* the bent one.'

Kreitman laughed. People liked getting Kreitman to laugh because his laughter always seemed to take him by surprise, as though it was a sound he didn't know he had it in him to make.

'Charlie, not for one moment have I ever thought of you as bent. To be candid with you, and I'd like this not to go any further than these four walls, I don't believe anyone is bent. Not really. Not in their hearts. My theory is that they're all pretending. But *you* . . . Why are you shaking your head?'

'Because you *aren't* being candid with me. Why won't you admit you're not able to come up with any other satisfactory explanation.'

'For what? The mincing way you pick at your food? You don't have to be gay to burn your fingers on pork-and-chive dumplings.'

Charlie Merriweather inspected his fingers, velvety and padded like a dog's paws. He appeared to be thinking about licking them clean. 'Now that's homophobic,' he said.

'Tell me about it.'

'You think I'm peculiar, Marvin, because I don't have affairs.'

'Charlie, it's not my business whether you have affairs or not. Besides, for all I know you have hundreds. I've seen you at book signings.'

'You've seen us *both* at book signings. And the people we sign for are all under twelve.'

'Twelve going on seventy. They're getting older, your readers, I've noticed that.'

'Your usual point is that they're getting younger.'

'The old are getting younger – I think that's my usual point.'

'You'll also have noticed, since you notice so much, that I haven't had an affair since I met Charlie.'

'When I first knew you you were complaining you hadn't had an affair *before* you met Charlie.'

'Oh, Lord, was I? Then that just proves it. I'm not an affair person. That's why you're starting to wonder about me.'

'People who wonder whether people are wondering about them are usually wondering about themselves. But I'd leave being gay out of it. Doesn't the received wisdom have it that gays tend more to promiscuity than the other thing?'

'Not the happily married ones, Marvin.'

'Ah!'

Kreitman finally let the hovering Chinese waitress take away his bowl. She'd been eyeing it from the minute Kreitman started eating. But that's the way of it in Lisle Street, where the restaurants tend to be tiny and the clearing-away matters more than the cooking. What Kreitman and Merriweather both liked about this restaurant was having to step over the yellow plastic slop buckets at the entrance. It gave them the feeling of being in Shanghai.

'*Ah* what?' Merriweather wanted to know.

'Just *Ah*,' Kreitman said. He wiped his mouth with his napkin and closed his face down. Not another word until the quarters of orange arrived. And the hot barbers' towels, exploding out of their hygienic wrappers. Bang! Bang! Untouched by human hand. (There was a joke, in the backstreets of Shanghai, W1 – fastidiousness!) Only after he'd exploded his towel did Kreitman explain himself. 'Are you on an errand from Hazel via Charlie? Is that what this is all about? Are we raising questions of sexual irregularity so that you can steer the conversation round to mine?'

'Charlie and I don't discuss your marriage, Marvin. Much, no doubt, as you would like us to. You've been trying to wring disapproval out of me for twenty years. Sorry – no can do. I have no attitude to the way you live.'

'*The way I live?*' Unbidden, the face of Shelley, his mother's second husband's nurse, invaded Kreitman's thoughts. They had been to the theatre the night before where Kreitman had been struck by the prettiness of her concentration. He had told her so, whereupon, without changing her expression, she had called him a patronising bastard. He was remembering how prettily she said that.

'I have no attitude to you and women other than maybe some sneaking envy. I think you're a lucky devil . . .'

'Luck doesn't come in to it, Charlie.' Unbidden, the long unshaven legs of Ooshi.

'I don't mean I think you're lucky because of what you get. I mean you're lucky to have the temperament you have. Lucky to be able to do it. I couldn't. Can't. Don't want to, either, in the end. I think I've become used to nice sex . . .'

'Run that by me again.'

'Nice sex . . .'

'You mean tired sex.'

'I mean nice sex. Same person, same place, same time – I like that. But that doesn't mean I disapprove of your way. It's not for me. I just don't have the balls.'

15

'Fairy!'
Followed by the bill.

Two old friends, one steadfastly in love with the same woman all his married life, one not, meeting regularly to decide who is the unhappier. And then losing their nerve.

Some days, so engrossed were they in not getting round to having the conversation they would like to have had, they couldn't part. They would idle about Soho, back through Chinatown, across Shaftesbury Avenue and into the wicked warren of Berwick and Brewer and Broadwick, where every window was suggestive of deviance, even those with only cream cakes or rolls of calico on display. Then they would cut back through the street market, past the fish and veggie men playing furtive stand-up poker with the barber outside the King of Corsica, past the fruiterers offering 'A pound a scoo' 'ere!' – three tomatoes, five lemons, seven onions, take your pick, pre-weighed in stainless-steel bowls, scoops, like winnings at a fairground – then out via suppurating Peter Street, where the pimps pick their teeth with match ends, into Wardour, dog-legging through Old Compton, getting gayer, into Dean and Frith, scenes of some jittery escapades in the skin trade when they were students, or at least when Kreitman was, but sorted out and hardened now, pedestrianised, masculinised, production company'd, cappuccino'd. What they were waiting for was a decent interval to elapse between lunch and afternoon tea. They needed to go on sitting opposite each other, eating and drinking, skirting the issues of their lives, *almost* saying what they wanted to say. Space allowing, they would crush into Patisserie Valerie where it was too public to break down and weep, failing that one of the new coffee houses, though preferably not one that was too exclusively or too hostilely butch.

Genuinely bothered by gays, were they? No. Yes. No. Yes.

16

No, not *bothered* exactly. More destabilised. How could they be otherwise? The public hand-holding was so new and so challenging. And intended to be destabilising, was it not, in the way that a protest march is intended to shake the convictions of those happy with the status quo. Of the two, Kreitman was more agitated by gayness than Charlie, for whom the hetero life was baffling enough. The beauty of monogamy is that nothing outside its magic circle impinges on it; it has its own worries to attend to. Kreitman, though, was in a sort of competition with gayness. He felt seriously undermined by it. Challenged on the very ground where he had planted his colours. He meant it when he said he wasn't sure he believed anyone really wanted to mess around in his own sex. Other, other – that had been his driving force since he could remember. As much other as you could muster. They had even called it other, he and his friends. 'Cop any other, last night?' Other when life was ribald, other when it grew more serious. The nobleness of life is to do thus . . . He being Antony, the other being Cleopatra (blazing black eyes, gold hooped earrings and dirty fingertips). But apparently not. Not necessarily so. What about the nobleness of life is to do thus – he being Antony, the other being . . . well, you tell me? Was that the great love story of our time – *Antony and Antony*? In which case where did that leave him, toiling at an activity no longer prized? Carrying home the cups and pennants no one else wanted or could be bothered to compete for?

Only recently, while sitting at a bar in an exhibition hall in Hamburg – off buying purses – he had fallen into conversation with a couple of Biedermeier gays from Berlin. He had liked them, found them handsome, found their neatness transfixing, enjoyed the musky smell of them, got drunk and allowed his tongue to run away with him. 'This gay business . . .' He was speaking as a man's man himself, he hoped they understood. Which they did, perfectly. The only thing they didn't understand was why a man's man chose to spend so much time – so much quality time, they laughed – in the company of women. 'What?' He was surprised by his own surprise. As were they. Had he really never stopped to ask himself before today what it said about his masculinity that it shied so nervously – they were only taking him at his own word here – from masculinity in others. They didn't put it to him like this, of course, they were altogether far too urbane, but if anyone were to be called a sissy . . .

Was the cyclist who shouted 'Honk, honk, urgent delivery' and deliberately all but ran Kreitman down on the corner of Broadwick and Poland Street gay? He rode as though dozing in an armchair, not remotely urgent, his head thrown back, his hands insolently off his handlebars, wearing green bulging lunch-pack shorts, a thunder and lightning sleeveless vest, a pink and purple nylon baseball cap reversed, with a matching pink and purple nylon backpack scarcely big enough to hold an eyeliner pencil and a couple of tightly rolled condoms – what did that say?

'My fucking right of way!' Kreitman yelled after him. 'Try that again, you moron, and I'll have you in the fucking gutter!'

Almost out of sight by now, for Kreitman delivered long sentences, the cyclist put one of his free hands behind his back and showed Kreitman his finger. Was it painted?

'Make me Mayor of London for just five minutes, Charlie,' Kreitman fumed, 'invest me with the power and I'll have every sanctimonious fucking faggot cyclist in the capital in clink.'

'Only the faggot ones?'

'What gets me is they think they've got some God-given dispensation, the lot of them, just because they're not punching holes in the ozone layer. I've seen the future, Charlie – we fetishise these arseholes and they run us down! Serves us right.'

What amazed Charlie was how furious Kreitman had become, how quickly and seamlessly furious, given the smallness of the offence and the number of reasons (five plus four) Kreitman had to be happy.

This didn't happen every time the two men lunched late in

town. Mostly they would plunge back peaceably into twilit Soho, enjoying the nightly handover, the silver cans of film spilling stardust as they skipped between production houses, the workers leaking home and the theatregoers nosing out, the shops shuttering, the rubbish piling, the bars starting to fill, the daytime beggars leaving with their sleeping bags over their shoulders, ceding to the night shift, and the mobs of inflamed teenage boys from penurious countries, bound in a sort of helix of indecision, drifting apart but always attached to one another, like the arms of a kindergarten mobile. In their different ways, both Marvin Kreitman and Charlie Merriweather felt at home here; nothing to do with the film and television industry, or the wholesale jewellery trade, or the silk merchants, or the Lithuanian lowlifes; what they enjoyed was the peculiarly English early-evening melancholy, the sensible damped-down expectancy, the scruffiness taking from the excitement, unless scruffiness happened to be what excited you . . .

'What I can't decide,' Kreitman said, 'is whether it's like peeling off an expensive whore and finding cheap cotton underwear, or undressing a scrubber and finding La Perla.'

'I wouldn't know,' said Merriweather, setting his big chin. 'I wouldn't know either way.'

Whereupon they would decrease their pace, ring their wives on their mobiles, and decide on somewhere to have dinner.

Tonight, and it was to be a night different from all other nights for both of them, they chose a big noisy Italian which Kreitman's window dresser had told him about and where, therefore, he couldn't take her mother – one of the new steel-cool New York Italians, sans napery and sans space between the tables, in which, supposing they let you in, you were laughed at if you asked for *fegato* or *tiramisu* and waitresses as touchy as grenades took you through pastas named after eminent Mafiosi.

'Christ, Charlie, what's *cavatappi*?'

'Ask the waitress.'

'I'm frightened to. But it comes with a sauce of smoked turkey, seared leeks and brandied shallots. Nice and light. I'll have that. You?'

'*Elicoidali* with five cheeses.'

'What's *elicoidali*?'

'What it sounds like. Italian for coronary.'

'Then don't have it.'

'Too late to start worrying about that.'

He rubbed his great dog's-paw hands together, daring death. Charlie the high-risk voluptuary. Around food he was still the prep-school glutton, smacking his chops and popping his cheeks to cram in one more lolly. Be the same around the you-know-what, Kreitman thought, deliberately courting ugliness, not himself yet, not recovered from the affront of being almost knocked down by a cocksucker. And lectured to by his best friend – was it a lecture? – about nice sex.

'And a bottle of Brunello di Montecello,' he told the waitress. It was time to start that.

Had they not eaten Chinese for lunch they might well have gone for Indian tonight. Not the poncy stuff. Not cuisine vindaloo, served on big white plates – two dry lamb chops presented with their legs in the air, like Soho pole-dancers, in a baby-powdering of fenugreek. By Indian, the two friends still meant stainless-steel bowls of blistering brown slop, suddenly called balti. They had lived in Indian restaurants in their student days, shovelling down old-fashioned bhunas and madrases in Camden High Street before and after going to see Jack Nicholson movies. Kreitman's choice; Charlie Merriweather didn't care for movies and only went to have somewhere quiet to sleep off one curry and dream of the next. Kreitman (who could have passed for an Indian anywhere but in India – Sabu, they had called him at school) even got around to learning to cook festive Indian dishes, sitting cross-legged in the kitchen of his too expensive digs, crumbling saffron and separating sheets of vark, the edible silver leaf of which angels' tongues are made, with a view to transforming the humble pilau into an offering to the gods. And Charlie? He rubbed his hands and watched. Sometimes he rubbed his stomach and salivated. 'Knives and forks, Charlie!' Kreitman would shout. 'Bowls! Pickles! Spoons!'

Considering their upbringings – Charlie left to fend for himself at an unheated minor public school near Lewes, Kreitman encouraged to run riot at a progressive in Farnborough and never once to make a bed or rinse a toothbrush if he wasn't minded – you would have put your money on Charlie turning out the housemaker. But Charlie had been awed by university and fell helpless the moment he got there. His bulk embarrassed him. When he went to lectures, he felt his head was too big and annoyed the people behind. He tried slumping, but that only drew sarcasm from the lecturer who told him that if he was as tired as he looked perhaps he ought not to have got up. He was ashamed of his voice which was too public school for the crowd he had half fallen in with, and too loud as well. 'Don't boom at me,' a girl from Newcastle had told him on what couldn't quite pass for a date, and that had made him more ashamed and somehow, as though to compensate, more booming still. By the end of his first term he was racked with confusion, a person who was too noisy and too shy, who was too much there and yet not there at all. He drooped disconsolately, like a puppy who had grown too big for its owner and been thrown on to the streets. 'I'm just waiting for someone to take pity on me,' he told Kreitman. 'I've taken pity on you,' Kreitman reminded him. 'No,' Charlie said, 'I mean a woman.' Someone to take pity on him, adore him, cook him breakfast and give him a good home.

Whereas Kreitman was putting mileage, fast, between himself and the idea of a man instanced by his father, the Purse King. Sullen at work, sullen back from work, whisky from the cut-glass

21

decanters on the solid-silver tray on the walnut sideboard, scoff without a thank-you, empty apron, count, curse, packet of Rennies, five spoons of Gaviscon, half a gallon of Andrews Liver Salts, gallstones, ulcer, cancer, heart attack, swear, snore, stroke. Maybe at first the decanters weren't cut glass, or the tray solid silver, or the whisky single malt, but Rome wasn't built in a day; by the time the purse empire had extended to two markets, then to three, then to the first of the shops in Streatham High Street — KREITMAN THE RIGHTMAN FOR SMALL LEATHER — nothing conducive to Bruno Kreitman's well-being, not that he ever enjoyed any well-being, wasn't of the best. Why did Kreitman hate his father so intensely on account of those whisky decanters? Because they bottled up curiosity. Because they denied the random mess of life. His father could have come home from the markets with funny stories, anecdotes of the pedlar's life, traveller's tales. Guess what happened to me today . . . ? Who do you think I ran into . . . ? Listen, you'll enjoy this . . . But he didn't see himself as a pedlar and therefore wasn't able to avail himself of any of the pedlar's consolations. The fact that it was small leather he was peddling only made it worse. You can't distance yourself from the public when you're flogging them small leather. Purses and wallets infect mankind with a distraction close to madness. But he could have made a virtue of that, couldn't he? Could have come home expert in the rich insanity of his trade — 'You should see them at my stall, like perverts loosed into a playground. Fingering, poking, probing. Sniffing the leather. Rubbing the suede against their cheeks. You're the clever dick, Marvin, you explain to me why every woman over fifty, whether she intends to buy a new purse or not, feels she has to show you the contents of her old one.' Marvin Kreitman, growing into a speculative boy, would have enjoyed putting his mind to that. 'Could it be love they crave, Dad? Could purse-buying be like exhibitionism, a cry of sexual loneliness?' Bad luck, in that case, if you happened on Kreitman

Senior. Nothing doing there. He rebuffed all cries for help and told the punters not to finger his goods if they weren't buying. Swore at them, too, if they persisted or grew tetchy or had the effrontery to haggle. Take it or fucking leave it. Sambo! Yes, Sambo as well, under his poisoned breath. Anybody call Bruno Kreitman a kike and he'd have had the Haganah in and instigated another Nuremberg. But Sambo awakened no consciousness of equivalence in him. He would still be swearing when he got home, reliving the mortifications of his day: the bleeders – curses aimed at his own chest, blows to his own heart – the bleeders! Turning Kreitman's soul to ash. It amazed the boy that with manners as gruff as his, his father ever managed to sell anything. But there's the mystery of the purse. In the end it will sell itself.

So if he didn't see himself as a pedlar, what did Kreitman's father see himself as? Simple – a man with a round stomach and a bald head who wore silver-grey waistcoats and black mourning ties and drank whisky from cut-glass decanters. A sort of *maître d'* in his own house. Everything else took from his dignity. Kreitman went buying with his father sometimes, accompanying him in silence from warehouse to warehouse in Stepney and Stamford Hill, where it upset him to see how cheerfully other purse sellers embraced the ups and downs of purse-selling, and how much they reciprocated his father's icy loathing of them. There was always laughter in the warehouses, exaggerated comedy even when expected lines had not arrived, or returns were being dealt with, or someone was accusing someone else of pinching from his trolley. Everybody, from the smallest tuppenny-ha'penny stallholder in Brixton to the owner of the biggest bag arcade in Hammersmith, everybody including the person in the mobster suit and expensive wig whose warehouse they were in, rejoiced in the rubbish around which their lives revolved. 'Look at this! Henry, look at what you're asking me to buy. The clasp doesn't fasten. The lining's hanging out. The zip's the wrong colour. And the dye's coming off in my hand.' 'It's fashion. It's what

23

the kids want.' 'Henry, you've been stocking this same bag since the Coronation. And it wasn't in fashion then.' 'Morris, you know what your trouble is? You're a short-term merchant. If I've been stocking this bag since the Coronation, what does it tell you?' 'That it's such drek you can't sell it.' 'No, that it's such drek I can't get enough. So how many do you want?' 'I'll take a gross.'

Everybody making the best of the worst except his father, Bruno the Bagman, known to his fellow bagmen as Bruno the Broygis – that's to say Bruno the Bad-Tempered, Bruno the Taker of Umbrage, Bruno the Bilious.

'You're not a bad kid,' one of the bagmen took Marvin Kreitman aside to tell him once, 'but if you want to know why we can't stomach your old pot and pan, it's because he acts as though there's a bad smell under his nose all the time, and we get the impression that the bad smell is us. He's a *gantse k'nacker*, you understand? He acts like a big shot, like he's superior to us. But there's something we all want to know. You tell me. What exactly is your father superior at?'

Marvin Kreitman, blushing to the roots of his hair, shrugged his shoulders. 'You'll have to ask somebody else that,' he said. But he had no idea who that would be.

It also upset him to discover that his father stole from the warehouses, removing the newsprint and tissue-paper stuffing from briefcases and overnight bags when no one was looking, and filling them with key fobs and billfolds. Were they so badly off that his father needed to do that? No. His father stole as an expression of umbrage. He did it to spite. And who knows, perhaps to besmirch himself in his own eyes; to confirm his fall from a grace he hadn't attained. And was he never found out? Years later, buying on his own account, Kreitman learned that his father's petty thieving had been common knowledge, tolerated because he bought big – thought big, bought big – and also, it seemed, because those he stole from knew that Kreitman's father was thereby slowly poisoning himself, and were content, for the price of a few key fobs, that his death should be as horrible and protracted as possible. Which it was. Not gallstones or ulcers or cancer that claimed him in the end. Strictly speaking there was no end. He just went on being himself until his constitution had had enough. Cause of death – if that which has never lived can die – gangrene of the personality. Unable to support it any longer, the body coughed up black bile streaked with black blood, collapsed in a bucket of Andrews Liver Salts and was gone. Six weeks after the non-event his mother took up with a man who didn't think the world owed him deference because he looked like a Hungarian waiter, and cleared out the previous incumbent's things. The market stalls she gave away. Washed her hands of them. The shops she sold. Kreitman got the decanters, which he donated, without unwrapping them, to Oxfam.

These were some of the reasons why Kreitman tried to remember to smile if he possibly could, did his best to memorise and tell jokes, cooked curries, never thieved a single book from the student bookshop, and became interested in Francis Place, the radical, a journeyman breeches-maker who had reason to believe he could have been better employed, but never repined, never turned his back on self-improvement, never stinted himself in a cause, never acted as though there were a bad smell under his nose and, as far as Kreitman's searches could discover, never set much store by what he drank his whisky from.

Kreitman's eventual turning of his own back on Francis Place, as good as abandoning all his researches into the great puritani-cal tradition of English radicalism, forsaking a university career and forswearing radicalism itself in favour, once and for all, of purses, was not to be ascribed, in Kreitman's own view, to genetic or moral backsliding, but to the times. He had meant to be high-minded and disinterested at a historical moment unpropitious for any motive except advantageous low-minded selfishness. He remembered the hour everything he valued flew out of the window, the hour hobbledehoy Thatcherism blew its first triumphalist fanfaronade, sending disinterestedness orphaned into the night, where for years it could be heard shivering and scratching at windowpanes, like the ghost of a relation no one dared claim. It didn't feel like cynicism, his abandonment of his projects, his reversion to family form – cynicism never does. Nor did it feel like defeatism. What it felt like was getting pissed. Just giving up on being sober for a night. There is no such thing as society, proclaimed Mrs Thatcher – always looking suspiciously pissed herself, sozzled more the word, her patent heels never less than precarious, like Minnie Mouse's – and Marvin Kreitman, along with most other people, was mightily relieved to hear it. Three cheers for ourselves! It was like the lifting of an oppressive burden. Society, society! Was there to be no end to it? Society, the societal, the socio, the sociogenic, the sociographic, the sociosocio . . . Give us a break already! And she did. For even the most industrious won't say no to a holiday when it's the boss's suggestion. Drinks all round on Mrs T! That was what it felt like to Kreitman, anyway – time off; not a greedy going to work at hard-heartedness, but a needful holiday from soft; in his particular case, a needful holiday from squishy. Though as it turned out, not even G&T and don't spare the ice Thatcherism could prevent the tears from rolling down his cheeks whenever he had to remove himself, if only for a weekend, from the company of a woman he loved.

He remained a romantic, then, through all the every-man-his-own-island (every man *own* his own island) years, opening one shop after another, branching out from small leather to large luggage, hiring and firing and fucking in between? Oh, yes. Romantic, sentimental and, as night follows day – for where else can sentimentality lead? – perfidious. As loose as careless talk.

Leave the guy alone. His head banged and falling in love incontinently gave him some relief. He had climbed back into his father's shadow scarcely before he'd left it – easy to do: he knew where all the warehouses were – and he couldn't blame it all on

Mrs Thatcher. He had married young and fathered two children, neither of which was her fault. And he had expensive habits over and above fathering, which weren't her fault either. Not *all* her fault, though of course had she paid academics better . . .

False reasoning, and he knew it. All the money in the world wouldn't have kept Kreitman in the academy. He felt wrong there, a traitor to something in himself. Maybe even a traitor to his father, to what his father did and should have done better. He felt ashamed, catching his reflection in leaded windows, striding through quadrangles with his books under his arm and students clinging to his gown, as though teaching even at that level still smacked of the servility of domestic service, like being a governess or the tutor to a rich man's children. And even if it didn't, what pride could a mature man take in being King of the Kids? Stay doing that till he was fifty and he'd have grown that parchment skin, neither old nor young, that mask of squandered sempiternity, which is the reward for passing all your days in the company of eighteen-year-olds. Yet those of his university friends who went into commerce fared no better in his estimation either – slaves to some corporation, dirtying themselves not with notes but with the principle underlying notes, which was even worse. Whichever way you committed yourself you were demeaned; so better not to commit at all, to step outside and have a leg in both camps, and in that way to be fully recognisable to neither, a thorn in the flesh of each (as if either cared!) and a continuing puzzle to yourself.

Besides, in abandoning Francis Place, Kreitman wasn't entirely abandoning Francis Place's example. Place himself had opened a shop, improving his mind and doing much to improve the country's on the back of a flourishing tailoring business. 'I had three things continually in my recollection,' Place wrote in an autobiography too unwieldy ever to be published in full. 'The first, and by far the most important, was to get money, and yet to avoid entertaining a mercenary, money-getting spirit; to get money as a means to an end, and not for its own sake.' And the other two things continually in his recollection? Kreitman knew them off by heart. Not to allow the 'contumelious treatment' he had received in his breeches-making days to make him a 'sneaking wretch' to those above him or a 'tyrant' to those below; and to be forever on guard against presumption and arrogance.

As a matter of more than passing interest to Kreitman, Francis Place went on, in the course of a long public life, to campaign for birth control and free love. Though not, of course, in any sensual spirit. And his second wife was an actress, named Mrs Chatterley. Though not, of course, Connie Chatterley.

Kreitman didn't know why the chill wind of self-congratulatory integrity that blew through nineteenth-century English radicalism, utilitarianism, Moral Chartism and the like, appealed to him as it did. His hatred of his father explained it partly. He revered everything his father wasn't. Principled Englishness, above all. He didn't know where his father was from. It was never discussed. Kreitman assumed Hungary, but it could have been somewhere equally horrible. Romania. Bulgaria. Albania. The Balkans. One of the thin-skinned, contumelious countries. Not England, though, of that he could be sure. And for his own part, perhaps because of his mother's example, he felt at home with long-winded moralists, loved the rapaciousness of their restraint. Give him a page of sententious prose, the gluttonous elaboration of the principles of self-denial, that tireless puritanism of the intellect which mowed down every frivolity in its path, and Kreitman was a happy man. Throw in a sentimental fuck with the mother of one of his lady-friends and he'd have called himself delirious.

He also liked selling purses. Proving it could be done, partly; proving it could be done with a good heart. But also he enjoyed testing his taste against the market. Seeing whether, in purses if in nothing else, he could harmonise himself with the spirit of the age. And he loved playing shop. The money part was necessary but not interesting to him. For accumulation for its own sake he had even less enthusiasm than Francis Place had. What interested him was what he already employed staff for – unpacking cartons, stacking shelves and making sales. Like Christmas, the physical excitement of taking receipt of stock. Like all his Christmases and all his birthdays rolled into one, counting the boxes, getting down on his knees and ripping open the cardboard, cutting his hands on the staples, breaking his fingernails in his impatience to snap the tape and see what was inside. Yes, yes, he knew already – obviously he did, since in those early days he was the one who did all the buying – but it pleased him to take custody of the new lines, to recall and reaffirm his original enthusiasm, expressed at some trade fair months before, and now to touch and smell it. Intoxicating, the cheap Moroccan wallets, squashed and flattened in their elasticated dozens, which he eased apart like squeeze-boxes, releasing their scent of oxhide, of urine, of all the dyes and spices of the kasbah. And more voluptuous still, the squeaky-tanned Italian handbags in smoky colours – brandy, Armagnac, blood-spot cognac – individually wrapped in branded, rustling paper, sometimes boxed, sometimes in linen shoebags (bags in which to keep your bags), ornamental as the Florentine bridge on which they'd been stitched, as still as works of art, answering as they never would again to the philosophical idea of handbag – the Platonic bag to which all other bags aspired – prior to the gross contingencies of use.

And then into the window with his sleeves rolled up, engineering his display on the simple joyous principle of ascent, the stock rising in vertiginous tiers like an Umbrian hill town. Why did he love that effect so much? One set of rooftops rising behind another. The purses and wallets first, then the handbags, then the vanity cases, then the sports bags, then the travellers and shoppers, and at last the suitcases. Infinity; was that it? Was he building a graduated Tower of Babel to the heavens, leaving no space for God to express His indifference? It looked shit, anyway, as his first manageress found the courage to tell him. Nobody had dressed a window like that since 1930. She was wrong, as he showed her, walking her up and down Tooting Broadway. *Everybody* in travel goods dressed their windows like that. She wrinkled her nose like a money pouch. Wasn't that her point? Did that make it any less shit? He took her meaning and shortly after took her to bed. Mixing business with pleasure? No – mixing pleasure with pleasure. Do that wrinkle thing with your nose again. Make your loose change clink. But on the question of window-dressing he knew what he knew, the great lesson learned from his father – purses sell themselves. And cases too.

He surrendered in the end. Had to. Other people opened the cartons and other people designed his windows. He didn't get it. One bag in a window – what kind of come-on was that? But the times were changing around him. He was an inordinate man, dumped into an age of minimalism. Little by little the smell of rutting camels faded from his nostrils. Purses grew plainer. Handbags more coldly sculptured. The briefcase with its once mysterious vertical recesses, its deep suede slits and dark concertinaed divisions, was now a moulded shell which opened horizontally with an empty-headed click. Even the lovely creaking leather satchel of his childhood had given way to the nylon sportsbag with ARSENAL printed on the side – more capacious, he granted, but less redolent of the hot, serious adventure of learning. Over time, fearful of his pertinacious taste for the bazaar, his staff began to dread his appearances; all he had to do was take off his jacket and start to roll his sleeves up and he'd hear them groan. What choice did he have but to leave them to it? He looked away, distanced himself from the fun of shops and just opened more. A reluctant tycoon. And because his head banged and his heart squelched – accept that a man must somehow express the inordinacy of his emotions – a sentimental votary of love, looser than gossip.

Tonight, though, by one of those queer reversals incident to an old intimacy, it was Charles Merriweather whose eye was squeaking loosely in its unprotected socket, pending the arrival of his coronary *elicoidali*. 'She's gorgeous,' he said, meaning almost anyone.

Almost anyone, thought Kreitman, shaking his head, who happens not to be his wife. He didn't bother to follow his friend's gaze. He knew its promiscuity. Anything on two legs. Fewer, if fewer were all there were. No pattern, no coherence, no discernible predilection, nothing that answered, say, to Kreitman's refined and, when you thought about it, wholly consistent preference for mothers of women he liked. Simply skirt. Not for the first time, Kreitman was almost ashamed to be seen out with Charlie Merriweather. These constant husbands! Christ! These unispousal gallants! Daring to pronounce the phrase nice sex with a mouth full of dim sum one minute and then to be up for every other sort the next. So what kind of sex was this which Charlie couldn't deny himself, squirming around in his low-backed steel chair, lapping at everything that clattered past – not nice or nic*er*?

'Charlie, she's young enough to be your reader.'

'Oh, crikey, is she? Nice, though.'

So there – not nic*er*, not not nice, simply nice, simply *as nice*.

After more than twenty years of veering from the straight and narrow, Marvin Kreitman wondered if he had only now touched the bottom of betrayal. *As nice*. Eeny meeny miny mo. Shall it be you or shall it be you? True, the cesspit of sameness of which poor Charlie had vouchsafed him a glimpse was only in his head, but was that what the insides of the heads of all good husbands necessarily looked like? In which case which of them *was* the better husband – Charlie, who would do unto others (if he could) exactly what he did unto his wife (if she still let him), or himself, Marvin the Cad Kreitman, who knew what he liked but never, on principle, felt the same way (tears apart) or spoke the same words twice?

Kreitman gave in to a twinge of concern for the other

31

Charlie. He was marginally responsible for their marriage, having introduced them, on a hunch, at a student party. Charlie, meet Charlie. He had pulled her out of a chair for himself at first, liking her long lolloping milkmaid's body, her boxer's jaw and her unexpectedly tiny hands. 'Oh, God, I don't think I can,' she had laughed, meaning do the dance of the hour, the Bump. 'Nonsense,' Kreitman had said, 'you're built for it.' And she was. When Charlie bumped you you stayed bumped. 'Try to be more rubbery,' he suggested. 'Try to bounce off the other person's hip, and also not to put the other person in hospital.'

'Oh, God, I'm sorry. I did tell you. You can put me back where you found me, if you like. I don't mind if you pass on me.'

He didn't do that, but he did decide to pass her on. She was a happy find, a lovely girl, brimming over, beyond the common, exciting at some level, maybe potentially exciting, exciting in the bud, but she was just too raw for him. The vegetable in her seemed to outweigh the animal. He smelled parsnip on her. She made him think of the frost-hard earth. And of those English counties he found least congenial. Given the choice, he went for women who evoked the inside rather than the outside world, women who whiffed of chemical things, perfume rather than sward, and who had shiny surfaces like him, who reflected light rather than bled it out. But he believed he knew the very panting puppy to go snuffling after her skirts as she traipsed across the golden glebe. And he was proved right. It worked. They adored each other from the off. No sooner were the Charlies an item than she was dressing him, not altering the way he looked exactly, for he was close enough already to perfection in her eyes in his shambling cords and thick all-season lemon socks, but actually doing the buying for him – comprehensively, *cap-a-pié*, not just the handkerchief for his hacking jacket, or the knitted ties for his Vyella shirts, but the shirts themselves, the big parsnip-tramping shoes, the loose vests, the floppy pyjamas, the vast underpants. Look under the table this very evening and there were Charlie's sturdy limbs encased in chinos Charlie chose for him from a catalogue. They went from strangers to familiars, knowing everything about and concealing nothing from each other, coining nicknames – she Chas, he Charlemagne – in a matter of hours. He became her child, yes, that was easy to see. And even Kreitman, as a rule squishier hearted about himself than his friends, could not begrudge him that. Poor Charlie had been subjected to the freeze of sensible parenting, ordered about and made downcast by a mother who believed she was failing of her maternal responsibilities if she didn't remind her children at least twice a day that she believed them to be nincompoops. 'Doesn't do for a person to have ideas above his station, or for a child to think he has brains when he hasn't,' she told Kreitman when she met him for the first time at Charlie's wedding. 'What do you think of this girl, then?'

Though of an advanced age, Charlie Merriweather's mother was so remotely beautiful, so flintily elegant and straight-backed in the abstemious manner of that last generation of the genuinely colonial English, those who still remembered careering about the globe in boats, attending to one international botheration after another (because who else if not them?), and who to this day bathed in great rusting rectilinear tubs, practising the self-denial they preached – what is more she was so attentive to *him*, as though he were her beau, a shipboard romance on the way to Cape Town or Aden – that Kreitman would have fallen in love with her on the spot had he not, only an hour earlier, fallen in love with the mother of her new daughter-in-law's bridesmaid. He took it that her beauty was one of the reasons she had mothered so unsympathetically. There never was a beautiful woman yet who didn't think her life had turned out less sensationally than her beauty merited, or who didn't blame her children for every ravage. 'I'm a widow, you know,' she told Kreitman. 'You can write to me, if you like.'

'I'll write to you,' Kreitman agreed.

'What? Speak into *this* ear. I'm hard of hearing.'

'I'll write to you,' Kreitman repeated.

'Well, that's what I said.'

'Then I will.'

'But you must promise you won't write rubbish.'

'I'll try not to.'

'Charlie used to write me the most stupid letters from school, always complaining about being cold and hungry. As if I wanted to hear any of that. He never had any news. Unless you call an ailment news. Or being bullied. Aren't you a bit big to be bullied, I wrote back. But he said that was why they bullied him – because he was so big. I told him to put his head down and charge like a rhino, the way I did when girls bullied me at school. But I doubt he took any notice. Bullying one week, cold and starvation the next. Utter rubbish. I used to toss his letters in the bin the minute I'd read them.'

'As long as you didn't toss them in the bin *before* you read them,' Kreitman said.

She threw him a baffled look. 'Why would I do that?'

The other certainty about beautiful women, especially the flinty ones – they didn't comprehend the rudiments of play. Or at least they didn't comprehend Kreitman's.

'I'll make a point of not writing to you about being cold or being hungry,' he said.

'Why? *Are* you cold and hungry?'

'Some of the time,' Kreitman heard himself saying.

'Then come up to Twyford and see me. I can't help you if you're cold, my husband was always cold and I couldn't help him – I think people just imagine they're cold most of the time – but I can feed you up. I'll give you fish pie, Charlie's favourite. Do you like fish pie? Charlie used to eat so much fish pie when he was small he started to look like a fish. Finnie Haddock, his sisters called him, whenever they wanted to make him cry.'

'What did you call him?'

34

'Who?'

'Charlie.'

'The same. Finnie Haddock.'

'And did Charlie's father also like fish pie?'

'I'm not sure I ever discovered what Charlie's father liked. He was a headmaster, you know. Only of a miserable little state-maintained grammar school in the wastes of Leicestershire, to which I dutifully followed him and for which I was never thanked, but he loved it. Used to stand on his head outside his office on the first day of term, reciting Lewis Carroll. Then they changed it into a comprehensive overnight. That finished him. Never once stood on his head again. He was a weak person. Like Charlie in many ways. He cried a lot. Wouldn't go out of the house. Just hid under the table in his raincoat, holding his briefcase, sobbing like a housemaid, the poor man. We sedated him in the end. Filled him full of happy pills. He turned the colour of fruit salad and sat grinning like the Cheshire cat. But at least that stopped the crying.'

'I'm sorry,' Kreitman said,

'Why should you be sorry? It wasn't your fault. I hope you're not going to write me letters saying you're sorry all the time.'

But Kreitman wasn't able to reassure her because the hour to make the speeches and cut the cake had come.

'Very clear,' Mrs Merriweather told him when he'd finished his eulogy to the happy couple. 'I heard every word.' But throughout Charlie's speech, she talked in a loud voice to Kreitman. 'I'm amazed where he's found the courage,' she said.

'To get married?'

'Of course not. Doesn't take courage to do that. Any fool can marry. To stand up and talk, I mean. He wouldn't say boo to a goose when he was small. Not that he looks particularly confident now. Shaking inside, I suppose, like his father. I hope *he* doesn't end up underneath the table.'

So, no, Kreitman didn't begrudge his friend a second attempt at filiality. Besides, his own penchant for women his mother's age hardly put him in a strong position to pass judgement. The two cases weren't identical. Kreitman didn't do helpless mutt. Kreitman did saucy whelp. He liked making a gift of his friskiness to women who had forgotten what friskiness looked like, or at least had not expected to have it chewing up their carpets again. Soon enough, to be sure, the eyes drooped and the chops fell and the young pup was moping about the house like an old dog. But dogs do that. They age. And bore easily. Either way, the short of it was that both men landed panting in their loved ones' laps, but Kreitman moved more.

Up and down, side to side – not playfully but restively – then off . . .

Whereas Charlie stayed . . . And practised nice sex.

Pleasing to Kreitman that the match he'd made had worked well, if only in the still-together sense, which, when all is said and done, is probably the only measurement there is. Otherwise, he hadn't paid much attention to it. A happy marriage in the still-together sense wasn't a drama that beguiled him. And he didn't suppose that his fractious marriage to Hazel – though also working well in the still-together sense – was of consuming interest to the Merriweathers. Occasionally his nostrils would fill with the parsnip odour of Charlie Kate's kitchen-garden disapproval of 'the way he lived', but nothing was said. The nearest she came to a declaration wasn't over women at all, but over Cobbett, the Kreitmans' cat. Kreitman was at war with Cobbett on account of the way he arched his back against Kreitman's shin bone the second Kreitman got out of bed. Until Cobbett hit upon this method of ingratiation, Kreitman had not thought of himself as a man with unusually sensitive tibia; but now his shins were like blackboards awaiting the shiny squeak of chalk. That there was an emotional no less than a physical aspect to this shrinking from the feather pressure of his own cat Kreitman didn't doubt. Cobbett caught him out in an insufficiency: among all the other dishes on his menu of cravings, the cat wanted affection, and Kreitman, knowing his was not a nature that could turn affection on as from a tap, even supposing it had affection to give, felt as though his soul, with all its inadequacies, was being tickled open. So when Cobbett came asking on the stairs, quivering and death-rattling and making a horseshoe of his back, Kreitman did what he was not able to do when any human asked affection of him, and kicked. Hearing about this brutality from Hazel, who made a brave show of seeing the funny side of Cobbett taking the quick way down from the top of the house to the bottom, Charlie Merriweather threatened to turn Kreitman in to the RSPCA unless he either give her his word he would learn indifference, if love was beyond him, or better still give her the cat. Without discussing it with his daughters or his wife, Kreitman gave her the cat. Other than that, he wasn't sure what Charlie thought of him as a paterfamilias or husband. In so far as the Merriweathers and the Kreitmans argued their couply differences out, they did so as it were by proxy, taking advantage of the mishaps of third parties.

'I can forgive the wilfulness, the selfishness, even the conceit,' was one of Charlie's most recent pronouncements on her older sister's erotic leap, at the age of forty-seven, into the arms of a man half her age, 'but what I can't turn a blind eye to is the silliness.'

'Silliness?' Kreitman wondered.

'It's silly of Dotty to go running round one day telling everybody how blissed out she is, and then to go running round the next slagging off Angus for acting unreasonably.' (Angus being the husband who, partly for that reason, was proving to be every bit as pissed off as Dotty was blissed out.)

Over the years, Kreitman had met Dotty many times at the Merriweathers' and had always been a little bit in love with her, firstly on account of her being an assistant to the deputy literary editor of a small-circulation journal – and Kreitman gorged on any company he could find that wasn't purse- or luggage-yoked

– and secondly on account of the heat of imminence she gave off. Anyone with a brain in his head, Kreitman thought, would have noticed that Dotty had so far not leapt for her erotic life only because no man of her acquaintance had so far opened his arms and shouted 'Jump!' A pity his own had been so full whenever he met her . . .

Among the other things he liked about Dotty was coming upon her in one of the Merriweathers' bathrooms doing mouth exercises in the mirror. Dotty had read that in order for her jawline not to go wrinkly-custardy she had a) never to smile and b) to put in as many hours in front of mirrors as she could manage, curling her lips inwards like little Swiss rolls and tensing her neck. Since this seemed to Kreitman to be exactly what lizards did and lizards had the most wrinkly jawlines in creation, he wasn't confident Dotty was following the best advice. He loved catching her doing it, however, and seeing through the mirror if he could get her to forget injunction a). This too – Dotty's facial exercise regime – Charlie considered silly.

'Silly? I'd say it was desperate.'

'Call it what you like, she's behaving like Madame Bovary.'

'And you'd like her to behave like who? Old Mother Riley?'

In fact, if she was behaving like anybody, Kreitman thought it was Anna Karenina. The last time he'd met Dotty was at a grand publishing party to mark the Merriweathers' twenty-fifth work of collaboration, a sort of silver wedding of true minds. All very well for Kreitman to be ironic, but the truth was he clung to the Merriweathers' literary and artistic connections like a shipwrecked sailor to a plank from the captain's table. Being the retail luggage baron of south London had its social compensations, and Kreitman was careful not to go his father's way and turn his nose up at them: trade fairs in Italy and Germany, the hospitality of wholesalers and importers, visits to manufacturers in Israel, Morocco, India, and sometimes, if he could get in when his staff weren't looking, just serving in a shop and meeting customers. To this day, against the grain though it was, singing the praises of a purse he'd seen made in Rajasthan and then selling it in Camberwell – count the compartments! look at the stitching! feel how soft! – filled Kreitman with the purest satisfaction he knew, though of course he left it to others to handle the money. But he had loved university, revered people whose professions were their minds, and missed just hanging about, having time, talking over matters that need never be put to any practical or commercial test. Mental irresponsibility – that was what he craved and what the Merriweathers' social circle gave him. And of course better sex, because as everyone knows, women in ideas deliver more imaginatively than women in business. As witness, *maybe*, Dotty Karenina.

Against her sister's wishes (because there was no way Angus couldn't be invited), Dotty brought along her beau, a surprisingly sweet-faced boy, considering his reputation for malice, who was famous for the number of books on any subject he was able to review in one week, and for the number of mentions of writers other than the ones reviewed he was able to squeeze into six hundred words. As a person meticulous about shirts, Kreitman disliked Dolly's boyfriend because he purposely let his frayed cuffs hang out of his jacket sleeves unfastened, and didn't always wear collars – a look Kreitman took to denote honest and even old-fashioned labour of the mind. Kreitman could easily have been wrong about this, but he believed the person you were meant to be reminded of was George Gissing, slave to Grub Street. 'In your dreams!' Kreitman thought. But he should have been more understanding. Although he dressed like Frankie 'the Hat' Lampeggiare now, at one time he had aspired to look like Francis Place, the radical. It was at this party, anyway, that Angus finally lost his nerve, abusing his wife in a loud and clanging voice, calling her a cradle-snatching, name-dropping adulteress, attempting to slap her face but missing, and subsequently leaving, slamming doors. A wound in the celebrations which healed no sooner than it was inflicted. Adulteress? Big deal! Except that it *was* a big deal to Charlie Kate who was looking for less silliness all round. And also a big deal to Kreitman, who could never commit enough adulteries of his own to feel easy with the idea of them going on elsewhere. For him, no less than for Charlie, adultery was a disturbing concept and an adulter*ess* a dangerously inflammatory personage. Why wasn't she committing adultery with him, being the first of many flaming questions she inspired. Hearing the word, Kreitman immediately sought Dotty's crinkled eyes. Twist eyebeams with one of the parties to an adultery and it can be almost as good as the real thing. Nothing doing, though, at least not this time round. But an hour later, still observing her from across the room, Kreitman watched as Dotty, in a black linty woollen skirt and matching short-sleeved fluff-fraught top, inadvertently (or not) trailed her forearm through a platter of coleslaw. Was she watching him watching her? Slowly, she raised her arm to her mouth, sent out a tongue whose length and coloration were foreign to Kreitman on account of his only ever having seen her with her jaw set, and licked herself. Three darting probes followed by one wet lingering caress. Then she flushed, threw back her head and laughed like one of those humourless princesses in Ukranian fairy stories, finally tickled into gaiety by the antics of an uncoordinated peasant boy. Was Kreitman that peasant boy? Was the laugh a gift to him? He decided not. Dotty had turned crimson for the room. In that moment at least, she was whore to the universe.

Of all the things he thought about Dotty in the immediate aftermath of this, it never once occurred to Kreitman to ask how come the whore of the universe could be Mrs Charlie Merriweather's sister. And you pay for omissions such as those.

'When somebody you're not sure you know seems to be smiling at you but might not be,' Charles asked, after the meal, 'what's the sophisticated response?'

'Keep your eyes down and your face straight,' Kreitman answered. 'Why? Who do you think's smiling at you?'

Charlie Merriweather nodded in the direction of a woman whom Kreitman thought he recognised as someone his daughter admired, a sculptor like herself, only of a seriously older generation, say twenty-six, whose pieces were much in demand by public galleries though not, needless to say, by private buyers who couldn't run the risk of their cleaners doing what Charlie's mother used to do with Charlie's anguished letters from his freezing school and throwing them in the bin. 'I'm not going to fall into the trap of asking by what aesthetic this is art,' Kreitman had joshed his daughter, 'but why call it sculpture when she doesn't sculpt?' To which her reply was, 'Oh, Dad, just leave it.'

'Well, if she's who I think she is,' Kreitman said to Charlie, 'she's one of Ooshi's.'

'Ooshi's?'

'A dealer. I'm not sure but I think her name's Nicolette Halliwell and she does things with trash.'

'What does she do with trash?'

'Conceals speakers in it, I think.'

'Then what?'

'Then she arranges it to look like trash again. Talking trash. You have the air of a man who would like her to do something similar with you.'

'I wish,' Charlie said.

'You don't,' Kreitman said. 'You don't wish anything. You're happily monogamous and even if you weren't, why her?'

'The slut thing.'

'Oh, for God's sake, Charlie! Those are just cold sores.'

But Charlie was beginning, in a general way, to smile back. 'Don't you think she's sexy?' he said, more to the air and its angels than to Kreitman.

'Not to my eye,' Kreitman said. 'To my eye she looks seasick. Queasy, like a half-drowned rat.'

41

'Then there's something wrong with your eye,' Charlie said. 'To mine she's drop-dead gorgeous.'

'Do me one favour,' Kreitman said, 'don't talk like your children. Dangerously close to whose age, incidentally, she is. So do you know her or not?'

'Not.'

'Then she isn't smiling at you. Turn away.'

Try telling that to Lot's wife. Still convinced her radiance was for him, and dangerously woozy now, Charlie Merriweather shone his countenance across the distance of three tables and gave Nicolette Halliwell the benefit of that trample-me expression which had served him so well with Charlie several decades earlier, and no doubt continued to prove useful, Kreitman thought, in keeping him in her favours.

In their day a mistake was a mistake and everyone was careful to help one another out of an embarrassment. Things were different now that there was no such thing as society. Public personalities come and go quicker than a burning match, but ideas take longer to blow out and reignite. Thatcherism had fallen off its patent heels, an absurd memory today, like trying to recall Mr Pastry; yet society hadn't, as a consequence, been fanfaronaded back inside. It suited everyone, even the new socialists, *especially* the new socialists, to pretend it had gone away of its own accord and wasn't coming back. Without it, we could be as charitable or as hurtful as we felt like being, for we weren't on any journey together. Hence Nicolette Halliwell's too loud snort, her dismissive wave of her bejewelled fingers – funeral rings, she collected, trash from the past, one on each finger – and her zonked ejaculation: 'Not you, saddo!' And then, to her company, but for everyone in the restaurant to hear – 'The leery old prick thinks I'm smiling at him.'

Sozzled? Freaked out? Who could say. Kreitman couldn't tell who was on what any more. His daughters came home not themselves for different chemical reasons every night of the week.

One of his lovers had taken to laughing during orgasm. Another to weeping on the lavatory. Only their mothers seemed to be together. For two pins he'd have marched over to the artist's table and beaten an apology out of her (his second imaginary assault that night), however forcefully the stubbly beards that grinned approval round her might have tried to stop him. But why draw even more attention to Charlie's mortification? He was drained of blood, the colour of mozzarella, and didn't seem to know what to do with his face.

'Let's go,' Kreitman said. 'We'll pay at the desk.'

But Charlie couldn't, or didn't want to move. 'Coffee,' he said. 'I think coffee. And I think another bottle of wine. Oh, God!'

And over coffee and wine and more coffee and more wine he asked Kreitman what he thought the matter with him was, why he was so unhappy, why he was so prone to make a fool of himself these days, why he was forever catching his children giving him long anxious sideways looks, as if they feared he was going to run away or fall over or fall away or be run over the moment they took their eyes off him, why he was sleeping badly, why he seemed to be getting on Charlie's nerves, why he was rattled by what was going on in his sister-in-law's love life, why he wished sometimes that it was he who was knocking her off, except of course that he didn't, and why, in short, his life was fucking falling apart.

Kreitman put his fingers together. 'Well now . . .' he said.

'Don't take the piss out of me, Marvin. We've been talking about nothing for ten hours. Let's be honest, we've been talking about nothing for twenty years. Just this once, eh? Eh?'

'All right, Charlie, then it isn't your life that's falling apart, it's your marriage that's fucking killing you.'

'Well, you would say that.'

'In that case don't ask me.'

'You've been wanting to tell me that my marriage is fucking killing me since you first met me.'

'You weren't married when I first met you.'

'You know what I mean.'

'Charlie, I don't know what you mean. I promoted your marriage. I would even say, were I given to like marriages, that I particularly liked yours. But this conversation has got nothing to do with what *I* want to say, or even with what I happen to think. I'm just watching you. You're behaving like a man whose marriage is fucking killing him. You've not stopped looking at women all day. Not even women, Charlie – *girls*! When a man of your years can't take his eyes off every under-age bit of skirt that flounces by, that hasn't even grown tits yet, it's fair to deduce his marriage is in trouble.'

'That's different. Marriage in trouble is not the same as marriage killing me.'

'Then go fuck one of these titless girls and get your marriage out of trouble. Give yourself a little leeway. I'll get up and have a word with the trash queen for you. I doubt she holds to any position for very long . . .'

'If I were to "fuck one of those girls" Chas would never forgive me. It would break her heart.'

'Don't tell her.'

'She'll find out.'

'How will she find out, Charlie?'

'She finds out everything. She knows me backwards. I can't dream about a fuck without Chas knowing.'

'There you are – your marriage is fucking killing you. And I'll tell you which part of it is killing you – the nice-sex part. Fantasy, Charlie. Sex isn't nice.'

'Maybe not for you, Marvin.'

'Leave me out of it. It isn't nice for *you*, otherwise . . .' Kreitman made a weary, exasperated gesture with his hands, taking in the waitresses, the sculptor and every other damn distraction that had made a monkey out of Charlie Merriweather this night. Made a monkey out of him as well, because even late

44

and in the company of men he hated marriage talk, wife talk, love talk, fuck talk. For he too was a good husband in his way, and believed he owed it to Hazel not to discuss her. Or her interior decorator. Or his daughter's curator. Or his one-time lover and her mother. 'Look, Charlie,' he went on – in now, in for a penny, in for a pound – 'why don't we have this nice-sex thing out once and for all? You think I don't get it. OK – I certainly don't get it. And if I don't get it we can't talk about it. You started this. You said your life's falling apart. I'm saying you can chalk that down to nice sex. So you go ahead and prove to me why I'm wrong. You explain to me what I've been missing all these years.'

'Deprivation.'

'Paradoxes now. I could surprise you, Charlie. I've done plenty of doing without.'

'Yes, but not systematically. Nice sex is about *agreeing* to do without. It's a trade-off. In return for relinquishing everyone else – and that doesn't mean not having an eye for everyone else, Marvin – you enjoy a closeness you wouldn't otherwise have. I'm not talking about trust only. Partly the closeness is contingent on the sacrifice . . .'

'You get hot thinking about everything you both haven't done? It's like talking dirty, is it? Only it's talking clean? Tell me about it, darling, whisper it in my ear – Who didn't you fuck today?'

'Is that what you think?'

'I don't think. About nice sex I have no thoughts. You're the expert.'

'You might not remember this, Marvin, but when we were first married and living in Market Harborough you and Hazel used to stay with us for weekends. You two weren't married yet. It's possible you weren't even thinking of getting married at that stage. One night we gave you our bedroom. I can't remember why, maybe you'd just got engaged or something, maybe it was Hazel's birthday. Maybe it was mine. Anyway, you slept in our bed. We were both astonished by the noises you made. Like creatures in pain, Charlie said.'

'You were *listening* to us?'

'No, we weren't listening, we heard. We couldn't not hear. The dead would have heard. And when we got our bed back in the morning we couldn't believe what you'd done to it. You'd ripped the sheets. You'd mangled two pillowcases and somehow shrunk a third. You'd torn the headboard off the bed. You'd bitten chunks out of the mattress . . .'

'I'll buy you another mattress.'

'Marvin – just once in your life, shut up! Believe me, there were bloodstains on the ceiling. If that's what your friend does to someone he loves, Charlie said, I wouldn't want to be in the next room when he's with someone he hates. I know, I see it on your face – what right did we have to sit in judgement on sex Marvin Kreitman-style? But we weren't sitting in judgement. We were just frightened for you.'

'Oh, come on, Charlie, *frightened*!'

'You didn't hear yourself. Anyway, whatever the rights of it, whatever you meant by half-throttling Hazel or letting her half-throttle you, and whatever we were doing having any sort of attitude to it, *that* wasn't nice sex. I trust you will at least agree to that. Nice sex, Marvin, isn't about finding another form for murder. I couldn't have raised a hand to Charlie even in play, nor she to me. What is it Hamlet says about his father's lovingness to his mother – 'he might not beteem the winds of heaven visit her face too roughly'? That was me. That was us. Even a vulgar slap and tickle would have been impossible between us. *Is* impossible between us. It's not for me to enquire about the hows and whys of it now, but you and Hazel used to make no bones about it – you fought like tigers, and then you fucked like tigers. Your own phrase, Marvin – the clash of mighty opposites. Well, Charlie and I didn't *feel* opposite, we felt the same. We weren't reconciling differences in sex, we were

46

confirming congruences. In bed together, sometimes, I wouldn't have been able to tell you where I ended and she began. My cock, her . . . What's wrong, Marvin. Why are you gagging?'

'You know darn well why I'm gagging.'

'Of course I do. I've drunk too much and you hate sex talk that isn't adversarial.'

'You're wrong. What I hate is the word cock. Watcha, cock! Use dick, it's more respectful.'

'Yes, yes, the famous Kreitman niceness around the organs. Nice around the nomenclature, less nice around the usage.'

'You're the nice one, Charlie.'

'Well, you're certainly not. Listen, you asked, so I'm telling you. Nice sex – it means what it sounds as though it means. Sex that is all consideration. Smug too, if you like. An expression of how much you like each other and everyone else can go to hell. And that's why I've always found it impossible to do anything if I'm away from home, in a foreign country or wherever – I know I wouldn't be able to think of anyone but Charlie. So what would be the point? Then when I got back I would be guilty, and when we made love I would be unable to think about anything but my guilt, lying there lewdly between us like a third party each of us thought the other had invited. Three in a bed. Something you're not averse to, I know. But not me. I don't judge it, I'm not against it, I just can't do it. So that's something else about nice sex – it's sex strictly for the two of you. Sex you don't go round experimenting with . . .'

'Sex that's not sex, you mean?' Unbidden, Erica, his wife's interior decorator, sitting on his chest in nothing but black hold-ups, her hands crossed on his throat, saying 'Make me!' Unbidden, but he bade the apparition go. 'Sex that's no fun, you mean?'

'Wrong. That wasn't fun you were having with Hazel all those years ago. That wasn't even play, Marvin. That was hang, draw and quarter. And you both looked like you'd narrowly escaped the mob when you came down to breakfast. You've always looked like that after sex. Another close shave. Got away with my life again – just. Don't forget how many times I've *seen* you after you've been fucking. And you never once looked as though you'd been having fun. People smile when they're having fun. When did you last smile at Hazel, Marvin?'

'This morning.'

'After sex?'

Marvin Kreitman put his elbows on the table and supported his chin on his fists. 'Charlie,' he said wearily, 'Hazel isn't the person I do the deed with these days. Decent men don't badger their wives of twenty years for sexual satisfaction.'

Charlie waved away any imaginary imputation that he might be curious who, in that case, Kreitman *did* badger for sexual satisfaction these days. 'The last time you smiled at anybody post-coitally, Marvin? Or even pre-coitally, come to that?'

Kreitman thought about it. 'Do you want the year or the day?'

'The year will do.'

'Nineteen seventy-three.'

'Then that was the last time you had nice sex.'

And in such a manner, had the discussion been about Kreitman's misery and not Charlie's, would the evening have ended. Go home and sleep on that one, Marvin. He was quite prepared to. Nice sex, eh? Well, why not. Two in a bed, no thought of a third, and a smile before and after? Thinking of the smile worried him by virtue of its unlooked-for allure. Forget the rest, but a smile wouldn't have gone amiss. Nineteen seventy-three was a lie. Kreitman had never smiled before or after sex. Or, if he had, he had forgotten, and where was the point of a smile you couldn't remember?

He sat with his chin still on his fists, staring into the blood-red lake of his wine glass, listening to the long silence of Charlie's triumphant refutation. He was head over heels in love with five women – discounting the other four he loved in a calmer fashion – and he couldn't drag from the bottom of the wine-dark Brunello sea a single recollection of a sex-related, sense-drenched smile. Not on his part anyway. What he could see, if he concentrated, were sometime smiles directed to him. A fatalistic but comradely creasing of the eyes only the day before yesterday from Bernadette, mother of his wife's interior designer's former husband, registering the black folly of life. A playful grin after the theatre, because she scarcely knew him yet, from Shelley, nursing Kreitman all of a sudden when a violent cramp threw him howling off her. Did they count? If you inspired a smile did that mean you were the reason for nice sex in others, even though you were not a participant in it yourself? Could just one of you have nice sex?

What do you think, Charlie?

No, was what Charlie thought. No way, no how. Just as nice sex couldn't be for more than two, so it couldn't be for less.

'You're a stickler for numbers,' Kreitman said.

'Rich, coming from you,' Charlie said.

'You know what this is all about?' Kreitman said, as though struck by it for the first time. 'Sentimentality. Masculine sentimentality. We both love ourselves in the love women bear us.'

'Wom*en* don't bear me anything,' Charlie said.

'It comes to the same thing,' Kreitman said. 'You love the image of yourself as a nice man which Charlie reflects back to you. I love the image of myself as a bastard which Hazel and the rest reflect back to me. That's why you can't betray Charlie – she has a sentimental hold over you. She is the monster guarding the labyrinth where your other selves are hidden.'

'So I have to behead her to find out who else I could be?'

'That's only if you want a fuck, Charlie.'

'I want a fuck, Marvin.'

'Then behead her.'

'And you?'

'I'm happy as I am.'

49

'You aren't. You've let me see you aren't. You'd like to smile before you die.'

Would he? 'Then who do I behead?'

'That you must tell me. I don't know who's guarding your labyrinth.'

'I have told you. They all are.'

'Then behead them all.'

'Ah,' Kreitman said, 'I can't do that.'

'Then choose one,' Charlie said, 'and give her to me.'

Kreitman threw his head back and laughed. A waitress in a short black leather apron, whose pants you could see when she cleared a table, whose pants she was no doubt contracted to *let* you see when she cleared a table, came to check how they were for wine. 'Gentlemen?'

'We're all right,' Kreitman said. 'But my friend's in love with you.'

'I'm not,' Charlie said, 'I love my wife. I only take advantage of other women. And we'll have two brandies. Any. The best.' Then to Kreitman he said, 'So?'

'So what, Charlie?'

'So which are you going to sacrifice?'

'You're drunk, Charlie.'

'Maybe, but I'm clear. If it's the women who are stopping us from doing what we'd like to – in my case from fucking someone else; in your case from finding out what it's like to be fucking only one – then we change the women. *Ex*change the women. What's wrong with that? You have Charlie, I have whichever one you're prepared to part with.'

'I have *Charlie*!'

'You don't want Charlie?'

'What do my wants have to do with anything? Do you honestly envisage Charlie leaping into bed with me? Have you forgotten that she nearly had me arrested by the RSPCA? She blackmailed me out of my own cat. She thinks I'm a brute.'

'You *are* a brute, Marvin. But I'm not offering you the cat . . .'

'No, that's right, you're offering me Charlie. Who is of course renowned for her easygoingness in matters sexual. Look how she's taking Dotty's indiscretions. If she finds those silly, how's she's going to react to this? Sillier still, Charlie. A lot sillier still.'

'Why don't you just leave Chas to me. I have a feeling you'll be surprised by her. Now who do I get? I'd be happy with Hazel but if you're not fucking her and she's not expecting you to, there might not be any point. I want whichever one will best reflect back to me the image of myself as bastard.'

'Oh well, in that case, any one of them would do,' Kreitman said. 'They all know about bastards. Why don't you take the lot?'

For the first time since the quick consumption of his *elicoidali*, the ever hungry prep-school boy with a gob full of lollies appeared in Charlie Merriweather's place. But only fleetingly. 'No,' he said, after giving Kreitman's offer a decent period of consideration, 'I think it's important you should choose. Make it equally costly. Who's it going to be, Marvin?'

'Charlie, enough.'

'Come on, play the game. Which one . . . ?'

And so out at last, brandied, into the roaring Soho night, remorseless with clubbers, boys bald as missiles, girls gashed red across the face as though with razors, and Kreitman exclaiming, 'Christ, these kids!' and Charlie swaying off the pavement, agreeing, 'Yes, beautiful, aren't they, so much more sure of themselves than I ever was, splendid really, so come on, Marvin, who's it going to be?' and then the cyclist – *that* cyclist! – with his hands off the bars, pink and purple luminous under the street lights, crying, 'Honk, honk, urgent delivery,' and Kreitman's chance, come sooner than expected, to unseat the cocksucker before he mowed down his jabbering friend, and the next thing flat out under the vomiting moon with tyre marks across his chest.

★   ★   ★

Not liking anything about the world when he came to in it, with a fright more nauseating than birth, back as though from hell with all its devils, only to find more of them waiting to pitchfork his soul, and Charlie not sobered, still with his big white jaw hanging open, wanting an answer to his crazy question – 'Which one, Marvin? Who are you going to give me?' – Kreitman went to sleep again on the street.

When he came to a second time it was already another day and he was lying on a castored metal trolley in a corridor off Emergency.

'Is this where they are laid who tangle with a faggot?' he enquired.

Whereupon someone smoothed his hair and said 'Shhh!' And strike him dead – strike him dead again – if that someone wasn't Charlie, not Charlie his old chum but Charlie his old chum's wife. Charlie otherwise known as Chas.

That Charlie!

THREE

S O WHERE WAS Hazel?

More to the point, *who* was Hazel?

'I might not be anybody,' she warned Kreitman on their first date. 'I have never had a father. And girls who have never had a father never really learn how to turn themselves into a resistant force.'

'Then don't resist me,' Kreitman said. Though even he knew she wasn't talking about that.

They were sitting in a curry restaurant near his digs in Camden. They had noticed each other in lectures for months but their paths hadn't otherwise crossed until they'd met in a picture queue for *One Flew Over the Cuckoo's Nest*. Neither was alone, but neither exactly looked tied up either. Kreitman decided to ignore the feelings of their respective dates and gave her his card. No other student at the university had his own card. Hazel laughed when she read it –

Marvin Kreitman
B.A. Pending

– and the squishy-hearted Kreitman immediately fell in love with her because her laughter had such sadness in it. 'Ring me,' he said in a dark voice, and she did. That was partly what she meant by having no resistant force. When somebody asked her to do something she did it. And now here she was letting him choose what she ate, how many poppadoms, which sorts of pickle, not because she couldn't resist, but because she couldn't see any logical reason why she *should* resist.

She tried. For weeks after this first date she refused to see Kreitman, actually washing her hair every night for a month and once even sleeping with another man she hardly knew in order that she shouldn't have to lie to Kreitman when she made the usual excuses and said she was seriously seeing someone else. She was terrified of her own quiescent nature. The year before, holidaying in Israel at a friend's suggestion, she had let a soldier take her off the bus and strip-search her in the Negev. Yossi. She even told her mother about him. 'Handsome devil,' her mother said, 'I can see why.'

She lacked moral guidance. Her mother had worked in the House of Commons library in the fifties (the last good-naturedly fancy-free decade of the English twentieth century), where she dressed in pencil skirts which showed off her calf muscles and satin blouses which made her breasts float like pillows, and where she became intimate with any number of Cabinet ministers, all of them Tories (the only ones she liked: a social confidence, sense of humour thing), one of whom – though if anybody knew which, nobody was saying – had fathered Hazel. Given Hazel's mother's predilection for men who looked like Hazel's Israeli soldier – tiers of teeth, no-smoke-without-fire eyes, shoulders bristling with wool, moustaches like a sea lion's and a bazooka in his belt – it oughtn't to have been too difficult to whittle down the number of Tory ministers in contention; but Hazel never felt she'd got close (Harold Macmillan, no; Selwyn Lloyd, no; Anthony Eden, hardly) and maybe her mother was never dead sure herself. Whoever he was – or at least whoever he was *told* he was, and that did not preclude his being a cartel comprising every suspect on the list – he left the women well provided for, with a flat giving out on to a Juliet balcony overlooking the British Museum, a blue-grey Austin A40, an inexhaustibly stocked drinks cabinet and a sufficient allowance to make Hazel's mother think twice before selling her story or asking for more. Which outcome, viewed all round, hardly disposed her to bring her daughter up a bundle of maidenly compunctions. She put Hazel on the pill at thirteen and advised her to let impulse be her judge. The only trouble with that being that Hazel could never decide which her impulse was or what it was telling her.

Enter Kreitman, spouting determined views. Later on, they both decided, he must have smelt fatherlessness on her, given how wide he opened his paternal arms – Come to Marvin! – and also given how much space he tried to take up in her company, filling all her needs; but at the time of his first wooing her she made him think more of the forest than the orphanage. There was some quality of feral shyness about her that fascinated him; she seemed to peer at him from behind trees, startled, wanting to snuffle him before she would come out. Even her face was snouty, pointed like a deer's, with piercing grey forestial eyes, suggesting indolence no less than timidity, and maybe not timidity at all so much as cruel reserve. In her dressing she chose to give the impression of floaty impermanence, tying her cascading lion's mane in ribbons too insubstantial to contain it, and favouring flighty dresses in filmy colours over the wintry denims most girls wore for lectures.

One warm spring day she turned up for lunch in the union twirling a damson-coloured parasol. And matching damson-coloured ribbons in her hair. When Marvin saw that he thought his chest would burst with love. A parasol!

'You remind me,' he told her on their third curry date, 'of a tropical butterfly.'

'Oh, please!' she said.

'I'm not spinning you a line. I feel that as long as I keep my palm open and absolutely still you will stay on it' – he demonstrated his meaning with a hand as steady as he could manage – 'but as soon as I try to close around you' – snap! – 'you will fly away.'

Maybe that was the moment, she told herself much later, when I should have fucked him off. She tried a second time. She wrote to him after their first essay at lovemaking, suggesting that they leave it, that they weren't suited, that whatever he may have thought he was making with her, it wasn't love.

'What was it, then?' he phoned to ask.

She took her time. 'Moan,' she said, at last. 'You made moan.'

He took his time too. He was upset. And genuinely bewildered. In the end the best he could come up with was, 'I thought you were meant to moan.'

'Not like that. Not like a soul in torment. Where was the joy?'

Joy! He didn't ask what the fuck joy had to do with it. But he did say that for his part he thought it had gone rather well.

'Exactly,' she said. 'Like a social occasion. Like a difficulty negotiated. You laboured over me, Marvin. You sorted me out.'

'Nerves. Just give me another chance. I know where everything is now. Next time I won't moan or labour. Next time you can labour over me.'

Too much trouble to resist. She accepted his invitation to visit his mother when his father was away selling purses at a two-day bank-holiday fair. There was an upright piano at the Kreitmans', dark and heavy and over-ornamental, like all their furniture. Kreitman's father hated music but believed any house he lived in should have a piano. Mona Kreitman was able to play a few tunes on it, all of them of a sort to arouse confused longings in her son. 'Jealousy', 'I Wonder Who's Kissing Her Now', 'You Always Hurt the One You Love', 'Who's Sorry Now?' – songs like those. At first she waved away the suggestion when he asked her to play for his new girlfriend. She couldn't. She had no aptitude.

Whatever noise she made on the piano was not meant to be heard outside the family. Finally she played and sang 'I'll Never Smile Again' in an arrangement by the Ink Spots, then closed the piano lid and went to boil the kettle.

Hazel felt unliked and tried to make a better impression by sitting at the piano herself.

'Oh, you play, do you?' Mona Kreitman enquired, rattling the cups.

'Not really,' Hazel said. She essayed the first movement of a late Beethoven sonata, taking care not to essay it too well, then sang 'Drink To Me Only With Thine Eyes' in a voice more thrillingly purple than Kreitman had any idea she possessed.

Had Kreitman not been in love with her before, he would certainly have lost his reason over her now. A woman with a tawny mass of startled hair, who twirled a damson-coloured parasol and sang Ben Jonson! He saw his life extending through its middle years and into old age, serene and comfortable, the French windows open to a fragrant garden blessed by butterflies, wine the colour of Hazel's hair on a silver tray beside him, and Hazel herself, his wife, untouched by time, playing the piano for him, Schubert, Chopin, Debussy.

Mona Kreitman, a psychic in the matter of her son's heart, closed hers to Hazel. 'You should hear Marvin sing,' she said. 'He has a lovely voice.'

That was the moment, Hazel told herself much later, when she should have fucked Kreitman's mother off too. With me you will hide your light under a bushel, Mona Kreitman had as good as told her. And Hazel, the fool she was, agreed. Whatever you wish, Mrs Kreitman. Whatever will make you and Marvin happy. And so she had hidden and shrunk herself. And did it make Mrs Kreitman happy? Not on the surface, it didn't. On the surface Mona Kreitman gave the impression of a mother who couldn't understand what her son saw in a woman who had so little to offer, who shrank from conversation and seemed to wilt in company. 'She's such a mouse of a thing,' she told her friends. But then being able to say that is a species of happiness for a mother, isn't it?

As for whether it made Marvin happy – of course it didn't. But then what did make Marvin happy?

In the end she got the hang of his way of doing it. Labour, sorrow, pain, talk – 'Tell me, tell me' – excruciation, vehemence, violence even – each of them out there spinning in a separate universe, striving, at best, for collision. Not uninteresting once you gave away the girlish dream of reciprocated romance. And she was programmed not to hang on too tenaciously to anything if it got in the way, even though in this specific instance her programmer advised her otherwise, not liking Kreitman's bolshiness or his antecedents, and of course considering Yossi, who still occasionally sent postcards of the Negev, the dishier option.

So no, not uninteresting, sometimes very interesting indeed, for she too had a place of pain for Kreitman to labour to locate – who doesn't? – a loneliness to graze, buttons of uncertainty and dread to press; and besides, it was all atoned for, Hazel thought, by Kreitman's lovingness away from the lovemaking that wasn't. He showered her with his time, she who had grown up without male company; he went shopping with her, took her to the pictures, cooked for her, expatiated in her ear, discoursed on the evils of money, showed her how dirty money made you, and when they had to be separated, let it be only for a weekend, only for a day, he wept over her. She had never seen a man weep so copiously. She had never seen a man weep full stop, but even had she, she was certain he would not have wept as Marvin wept. Off to the country to see an old school friend one Friday at the end of their second month together, she kissed him on the platform at Paddington and was shocked by how desperately he clung to her, how sorrowful he looked, how haggard and hollowed suddenly, a shadow of his usual brash self, hiding his grief-deformed face from her, unable to speak, his heart spilling from his throat. He didn't run after the train, as she'd seen some men do, but waved her off with a hopeless hand, like a little boy's, and blew her gentle kisses, and stood as though he meant to remain in that very place until her train pulled in again on Sunday night.

If that wasn't what you called being in love, what was? Away from the brutalised bed, he loved her for herself, loved her to distraction, bought her presents – mainly lingerie, high heels and sex toys, but still presents – made exorbitant declarations, couldn't bear to be without her, and surprised her again and again by the delicacy of his feelings for her, whatever the sex toys seemed to say to the contrary. Once, when he came upon her laughing with a bunch of male students at the union bar, exchanging embarrassing lavatory experiences, fart jokes, turd jokes, overflowing-cistern jokes, then clapping a monologue, her hands full of rings he'd given her, the monologue a droll explanation of why dogs lick one another's arseholes (because originally they'd gone to a dogs' convention and left their own arseholes outside on hangers – so it's Platonic, you see, each dog forever searching for his own lost self), he pulled her away by her hair then dissolved into tears. He couldn't bear to see her defiled like this, ensnared in coarseness, compromised by smut. And laughing at what wasn't laughable. 'Dogs' arseholes aren't funny, Hazel!' Promise him, promise him, never again. He loved her to distraction, and her gratitude for all those unexpected proofs of his distraction felt very much like distracted love in return.

'Don't tell me this isn't the real thing,' she told her mother, 'because it's the nearest I'm ever going to get.'

'Not true, darling,' her mother said. 'Remember the Negev.'

'Oh, Mother, that was just the hots,' Hazel said.

'Exactly!' her mother told her.

And she *did* have the hots for Kreitman, or at least would have had the hots for Kreitman had her hots not called out his hots – oh, God, *those*, his dreaded inflexible stage-managing, his iron-grip ritualising, this way not that way, say this but not that, beg for me, deny me, open yourself, close yourself, cheap whore it, expensive mistress it, hurt me, hurt me more, ensnaring her in coarseness, defiling her with smut, before away they went again, labouring and moaning, spinning centrifugally, lost in their separate immensities. After which, as predictable as dance steps, her dark forebodings – 'He's wanking into me,' she thought, 'he's doing something on his own, I might as well be a bucket' – followed by his breezy day-to-day devotion, prodigality with his company, anguish at the merest mention of an absence, followed by her line-of-least-resistance conviction that if that wasn't proof of love then nothing was.

She liked him, liked the idea of herself with him, high-principled woman on the arm of high-principled young man, loved it when he called her 'his girl', his romping girl, came alive in the role of a companion-wife if not in the role of a harlot-wife, came to think that she was cut out, after all, to do socialising and give dinners – though not in the presence of her mother-in-law – to remember birthdays and have babies, but still she should have fucked him off when she had the chance. Now, a score or more years on, she could not remember when she first discovered that his desolation on the platform of every railway station in London did not stop him sleeping with another woman as soon as he could find one, 'as soon as' meaning within the hour sometimes, within the half, should another train luckily disgorge someone of the same mind. He was as broken-hearted as a man could be for fifteen minutes, then he wasn't. It was as subtle, morally, as that. As subtle as one dog sniffing after another. Was he looking for succour, for consolation, a replacement only while she was away, *because* she was away? Frankly, she didn't give a damn. He had tried to flatter her with that one, when first caught out: No, no, *no*, not what it looked, nothing like what it looked, in truth he was merely dipping into the general pool of her sex made fragrant by her dear self, and therefore – didn't she see? – only gazing after temporary reflections of her. Loving her made him alive to *all* women. The only men who didn't love all women were those who were not lucky enough to love one. She flooded him with vitality, energised him, replenished what she took, made him feel as powerful as a god. Should it be any surprise, then, that he *acted* like a god? Looked down out of his lordly superfluity and plucked whatever took his fancy? As for what it meant: nothing. Passing fancy, that was all. There was only her . . . she must believe him, her alone, and her reflections . . .

'Whatever,' she said, instituting separate beds.

'Whatever' – was she the first person, she wondered now, to have coined the new nihilistic usage of that word? Watching daytime television, sick to her soul, watching the victims of failed love affairs and marriages, the betrayers and the betrayed, the liars and the lied-to, agree for the sake of ten minutes of telly notoriety to turn their unhappiness into a free-for-all freak show of the emotions, Hazel noted the increasing frequency, month by month, year by year, of 'Whatever'. Tired of listening, tired of reasoning, tired of lies, that's all there was to say – 'Whatever.' The rest was silence. 'You murdered my feelings, you stole from me and cheated me, you trashed my home, you corrupted my children, you turned my friends against me, you made me loathe myself . . .'

'Whatever.'

But she'd said it first and, she believed, she still said it best.

She blamed herself at the time. No will power. Of course he took advantage. *Anyone* would take advantage. She'd have taken advantage of herself if she'd known how. No point then, in her middle twenties, with one child had and one child coming, making empty gestures. She didn't want the gift-wrapped life her poor mother lived, unaccompanied in a silent flat overlooking the British Museum, waiting to be strip-searched by the Israeli army. And she wasn't up for starting the whole shebang again: 'Hello, I might not be anybody', followed by another seeming-softie weeping buckets on the platform at Paddington. And at least now she could be free of Kreitman fucking with her head. Drop the 'with' – actually fucking her head was what he'd done. 'My lower parts were never the problem,' she told her friends, 'though of course he talked cunt until the cows came home. But it was head he really wanted. And I don't mean what you think I mean. What my husband liked to do with head was fuck it. Show me what's in yours and I'll pretend to show you what's in mine. He fucked my brain, girls, but now at last, I am pleased to tell you, I am able to think for myself again.'

For which they applauded her and ordered more champagne.

Easy to be brave, out with the girls. Easy to believe it might all be a charade and when she got home where there were no girls to cheer her on – no big ones, anyway – all would be well again. 'Let me be wrong,' she told herself, she couldn't bear to remember how many times. 'Let me have made a mistake.' But when she got back and saw his face, saw his own disappointment with himself on it – that was the clincher every time: what she couldn't hide of what he couldn't hide, his consciousness of his crookedness – she knew there'd been no mistake.

She cropped her lion's mane, expelled everything floaty from her wardrobe, bought tailored suits and turned her home into a business. Files, folders, drawers of paper clips and drawing pins, appointment books, wallcharts, timetables. Theatre tickets bought months in advance, another holiday booked before they'd had the last, wallpaper changed annually, ditto carpets, children's teeth checked every quarter, ironing woman Tuesday, sheet-changer Wednesday, dust-mite inspector Thursday. Kreitman could come home, or not, when he chose, provided he gave Hazel three weeks' notice of any variation from the usual and pinned details of same on the board in her office. 'All I ask,' she said, 'is the consideration you show those you do business with. You don't break appointments with your wholesalers or manufacturers, or with your manageresses or window dressers – ha! – you won't break whatever appointments you have with me. And of course you'll pay me an annual salary and make adequate provisions for my pension.'

Her mother all over again, after all.

Sometimes her heart almost failed her, so close was this to the chill she'd always dreaded. Let me be anything but this. But he had already damaged her heart beyond repair anyway. Her own fault. No resistance. Well, that had changed at least. Now she was *all* resistance.

No bad thing, either. She breathed in the thin brave air of independence, filled her lungs with it, strode out into the world in shoes that didn't kill her, made choices without reference to another person, heard her own voice ring out loud and clear. Was that really her she heard? It was. Hazel Nossiter – forget the Kreitman – speaking for herself. And people listening. Yes, Hazel. No, Hazel. Right away, Hazel. No bad thing? A fucking wonderful thing, that was the truth of it. If only she hadn't been brought up to believe that being one of two, one half of someone else, and the quiescent half at that, was what life had up its sleeve for her. Strong one minute, she fell back the next, going over it and over it. Not *getting* over it, but *going* over it.

It could have turned out differently, even allowing for the inevitable bitterness of marriage to a man who couldn't walk straight. Had she pursued her own academic interest, followed up her work on the noble savage with a full-blown study of the unseen Negro – the Negro implicit or concealed, actual or mythic – in English life and letters in the eighteenth and nineteenth centuries, she'd have been where the university was at. The very centre of the turning world. And to hell with Kreitman's now you see me now you don't. But she was a mother in the making, and anyway, Kreitman was the academic one. Now it was too late. The university is unforgiving of anyone who leaves it for a while, even though its only subjects are post-colonialism, new historicism and women in distress and she was the perfect post-colonial new-historicist woman in distress. Blink and the professors speak another jargon. Alternatively, she could have demanded that Kreitman take her into his firm, once he too parted company from the university, make her chief marketing director or something like that, and have her accompany him to trade fairs and on buying trips to India and Morocco. But she didn't want the humiliation of seeing him around women. He was beyond any appeal, beyond all reasoning, beyond help. He had no choice in the matter. It was like an illness. A woman moved into his field of vision and Kreitman went as still as a hare on a wintry common. 'They're the only things in life that interest you,' she'd accused him once. But that was wrong. For Kreitman women existed below the level of interest. It was umbilical. He was joined to them in some unfathomable way. A woman had only to stir the air in Peking for Kreitman to become seismic in Brixton Hill.

Best to stay away. In the early days when he came home full of shops she thought she might kill him. Did he not grasp how much she would have liked to be a part of that, the fun of starting out and making anxious progress, like Hansel and Gretel before the big bad accountants got them. She couldn't pretend she saw what he saw in purses, she didn't share his passion for narrow openings and suede clefts, but novelty was novelty and she liked their original silly idea that she keep an example of every bag they stocked, a little museum of the heart for them to visit when they were old, the story of their joint adventure. First, she seized upon every new exhibit herself, bringing the children to the shop – look! Daddy on his hands and knees, a bigger baby than both of you, now which bag shall Mummy take? – then she left him to it, less and less curious to sample stock, until at last she ceased caring altogether and bought her own fashion bags, as and when she wanted them, from Fenwick's. As an act of bitter acrimony she keeps the museum illusion up, keeps receiving the latest styles which he religiously presents as though in honour of some saint whose name they have both forgotten, but now she feels she is building a sarcophagus, collecting memoranda of her own death. Week after week, year after year, she opens the door to their museum and shoves another reliquary inside.

Over it and over it. Only now she *is* over it.

So Hazel sits in her office supervising the installation of a new joyless Jacuzzi, the relaying of her lawn, inspecting plans for a loft conversion in which, in time, she will resituate her office. Most of her working day is spent airing grievances on the telephone. Should any of her friends need to know the name of someone to complain to they ring Hazel who might even, if they are lucky, do their complaining for them. She has the number of everyone in charge of every conceivable service operation in London. 'Good morning, Hazel Kreitman here,' is all she has to say, and you can feel the phones going cold all over the capital.

Of her daughters she said, 'They get their mental restlessness from their father, their political nous from their grandfather the Cabinet minister, and their determination not to be fucked with from me.' Anyone meeting Hazel for the first time now would readily have believed that. Not-to-be-fucked-with Hazel. Some laugh that was. When never a day went by when she didn't catch herself mourning for what she'd been – a lustrous, nervous girl, susceptible, trusting, with all her gifts clutched to her chest like a trousseau, the little fool, in waiting for something terrific to happen to her.

Kreitman, passing her office, catches her in the act of remembering, sees the girlish trousseau she sees, sees her twirling her parasol, sees her at the piano, and apologises. She puts a hand up to stop him.

'I know this isn't adequate,' he says.

'It isn't about you,' she tells him. 'Are you ever going to understand that? It's about me.'

About me. Hold on to that. About me.

Over it and over it. Only now she *is* over it. As her daughters somehow prove.

65

Though neither was yet twenty, her daughters were already little corporations, bristling with rumour and negotiation, offers and counter-offers, supporting their own websites and employing their own lawyers and accountants. Cressida, at eighteen, with a whole year of art training under her belt, a skylit studio in Hoxton, a studded dog collar round her neck and a mouthful of steel braces she'd designed herself, looked certain to those in the know to spearhead the next generation of Young British Artists. While Juliet at nineteen and three-quarters, and therefore already a has-been to Cressida and her friends, was taking a year off from Oxford to complete (courtesy of her mother's old research) a socio-sexual history of the Negro woman in the British Isles, with case studies and a section dealing with the iconography of 'black' in popular porno, on the strength of a couple of chapters of which she had secured an advance equal in size to the wage bill of a small hospital, though on the tacit understanding that she'd be willing to raise her skirts for the photographers, with or without an iconographic Negro servant in attendance, on the book's release.

'Over my dead body!' Kreitman had protested, but none of the women in his family took the slightest notice of anything *he* said.

Hazel liked her daughters and got the point of them. They were her without her mistakes, her as she would have liked to be. When Kreitman saw Cressida's first show in what looked to him like a whore's bedroom on Old Street – 'Well, you'd know,' Hazel said – his first impression was angry bewilderment and his second impression was the same. 'What the fuck does a daughter of ours know about hand-me-downs?' he whispered to Hazel.

'It's amusing. Just laugh and be proud,' Hazel told him.

He was proud but he didn't get the joke. Or, as he would have preferred to put it, he got the joke but didn't find it funny. He belonged to another time. He thought art had to be big, grand, declamatory, significant, serious, mined from the soul and loaded with meaning. And that you ought to want to spend a long time looking at it. But how long could you spend in front of Cressida's rickety coat-stands of reach-me-downs and tattered heirlooms? Or in front of the accompanying chromogenic prints on paper, showing little kids looking lost in big kids' coats? What was there to penetrate? And again he wanted to know what his pampered daughter had ever experienced of hand-me-downs. Under Hazel's unvarying regime, all items of suspect clothing went into different-coloured baskets, waiting for the sewing woman who came on Thursdays or the Oxfam and sundry charities woman who came on Fridays. If she wanted to 'sculpt' clothes, why didn't Cressida look into her heart and 'sculpt' new ones?

'You're a fossil,' Hazel advised him. 'Go to work.'

Unlike him, she saw the world the way her daughters saw the world. She liked things now. Pity she hadn't been born a quarter of a century later herself, and grown to be eighteen in the year 2000. Oh, to be quick and slick, whoever and wherever you wanted to be simply on your own say-so. And to be brittle. And astringent. In her day you melted when a fellow took you in his arms. Now any man chancing his mouth with one of her daughters risked ammonia or metal poisoning. Death by a thousand ironies. No wonder Marvin didn't get what was going on. What was going on was a consequence of him, a rebuttal to his however many thousand years of supremacist patriarchal certainty. 'Significance,' he called it. Ha! Hazel knew the significance of 'significance'.

And not a twinge of jealousy that Juliet (named, of course, after her mother's sad little balcony overlooking the British Museum) was making hay with her research? All right, a twinge. But you can live through your children, and Hazel was squaring her accounts through hers. Good for Juliet if she'd done a deal with a publisher on the strength of someone else's thoughts and her own good looks. According to Juliet every girl in her college that wasn't

67

an out-and-out dog had a book deal. Historians with big tits were particularly voguish, but a philologist with a nice arse or even just a pretty face was also in with a shout. 'Bad luck if you happen to be George Eliot,' Kreitman had said. 'But, Daddy, I'm not George Eliot,' Juliet had reminded him. Hazel had listened to that exchange while sitting airing grievances on her office phone. Inexpressible, the satisfaction it gave her. *But, Daddy, I'm not George Eliot.* What a long way back that went! What a merciless stripping down of however many thousands of years of male hypocrisy in the matter of beauty and intelligence. Now deal with this – the beauty you commodified we are commodifying back, so what was that about our not being intelligent? Daddy, our beauty *is* our intelligence. The thing has happened that you always dreaded: we have learned to exploit your weakness for our weakness. Only this time not in a whorehouse. And you can't be certain whether we are laughing at ourselves or at you.

How wonderful, Hazel thought, to have put such a creature into the world. Her very own consolatory act of vengeance. And Cressida made two.

And was anything else making her happy? Some spicy little intrigue independent of her daughters? Some gentleman?

'Oh, please,' was her automatic answer to any enquiries of that sort. 'No more butterfly chasers, thank you very much.'

'Go into the bottom drawer of my bureau,' her mother told her, 'take out the round Fortnum's scented violet creams box, untie the ribbons and help yourself to as much cash as you need for a fortnight in the Negev.'

'Mother, he'll be dead by now. They'll have shot him. Or he'll be fat and living in Haifa with a wife in a long dress and ten children.'

'Then you should spend more time standing with me on my balcony. Such distinguished scholars you get to see from here.'

'Not any more you don't, Mother. They've closed the library.

Those are tourists, you're looking at. And most of them are Russian Mafia. Not that that makes any difference to me. I've done men. I've done being blubbered over.'

But that was before she met Nyman, an Anglicisation of Niemand, as he made no bones about explaining. Niemand meaning Nobody. Not merely Man with No Qualities but Man with No Prospects of Qualities. The cocksucking cyclist who knocked her husband flat in Old Compton Street. Except that he wasn't a cocksucker. Unless he was. The point about having no qualities and no prospects being that you don't know who or what you are. And a little ambiguity, in the meantime, gets you by.

No wonder Hazel liked him when she talked to him in Emergency, while Kreitman lay comatose in the corridor. He reminded her – startled yet aggressive, at a bit of a loss really, but no pushover – of her old unindividuated self. Charlie Merriweather had rung her, telling her not to worry and not even to come to the hospital if she couldn't face it. Marvin was out cold, sleeping rather than unconscious, and not seriously injured. A quick tetanus jab when he woke and they'd probably send him right home. In the meantime he'd stay to keep an eye on him, since in a manner of speaking it was his fault. Chas was driving in to keep him company, no doubt preparing a flask of hot tea and wrapping the runny egg baps in silver foil as they spoke. On top of that, the cyclist who'd done the damage was seeing the vigil through as well, feeling pretty bad about it, although the worst you could charge him with was posing while in control of a pedal bike. So Marvin wasn't exactly short of well-wishers.

'Did you say *pedal* bike?'

Charlie was not able to see the importance of the word, but yes, pedal bike.

Hazel roared with laughter. 'God, can't my husband even succeed in getting himself knocked down by something decent? I thought we were talking a Harley-Davidson at least.'

'Does that mean you *won't* be coming?' Charlie asked.

'Lord, no, I'm a wife. It's a wife's job to be at her husband's side whatever he's knocked flat by.'

As for where she was when her husband finally came to – she was across the road in Waterloo station, enjoying a hearty English breakfast with the pedal cyclist in question, the Man with No Anything.

FOUR

No SOONER HAD Charlie Merriweather rung Hazel Kreitman than he regretted it. What if he'd done the wrong thing? What if Kreitman was expected somewhere else in the early hours? What if Hazel was the last person Kreitman wanted to open his eyes and find? Too late now, but if he'd thought of it first he could have gone through the call list on Kreitman's mobile, which he'd actually caught as it flew from Kreitman's pocket in the fracas, and checked if it really was Hazel he had rung earlier in the evening to say he'd be late home. Home? Where *was* home? And how *many* homes did Kreitman have?

Sexual curiosity can be a terrible affliction when it gets its teeth into a grown man. Charlie Merriweather believed it was slowly separating him from his reason. No, not slowly – rapidly! How long does it take to go mad? Overnight, if you've been putting in the groundwork for thirty years.

When he was a boy Charlie had wondered along with every other boy how things worked, where things went and when he was going to get his turn to find out. They were in it together. It was all part of the fun. He remembered one boy who was more precocious than everyone else, who had a moustache when he was eleven and was locked into a serious relationship with a girl when he was barely thirteen. Simon Lawrence. He wore a locket containing his girlfriend's picture round his neck and was reputed to have inside knowledge of oral sex. The others envied him crazily, as goes without saying. They stole the locket and put shoe polish on his balls so that his girlfriend wouldn't like the taste, though there was some controversy in the matter of whether tasting balls formed a part of oral sex. Charlie Merriweather had thought not. Why would any girl want to taste Simon Lawrence's balls? Simon Lawrence sealed his own fate on that one. 'Why shouldn't she?' he said. So on went the polish. They also wrapped a turd in silver paper and hid it in his schoolbag. With a bit of luck his girlfriend would find it and think it was a gift to her. End of relationship. That much they *did* know about girls. But their envy was equivocal. Simon Lawrence's experience put him offside, excluded him from the group. He seemed to spend every break reading letters, biting pencils and then composing answers. It was like extra homework. He looked sad most of the time, frowning, burdened by his dark knowledge. It was better to be with the others and know nothing. Knowing nothing was at least a laugh. But now Charlie felt he was the one cast out, the last one left standing in the playground in the freezing dark, wondering what hilarity drew the others to the pavilion. And kept them there.

He had been a shy boy. Up to a point they had all been shy boys. Being a boy is a shying business. Over and above that, though, he'd been an unlucky boy. He was the child of odder than usual parents. The son of a more handsome than usual mother. And of a sadder than usual father. Few of his friends went home to happy households at the weekend, but Charlie knew of no one else who went home to find his father quaking under the kitchen table in his raincoat.

Long before then, when Charlie was little, his father used to embarrass him by turning cartwheels in public places, standing on his head while reciting 'You are old, Father William', and otherwise playing the eccentric English schoolmaster. Sometimes, for garden parties or village fêtes, he wore a mortarboard, sometimes plus-fours and a shirt with a frilly front. '*Mon jabot*,' he called it. '*Mon jabot du Jabberwock.*' Who was he being? Charlie didn't know. Just someone from the past. Someone harmless. Someone curiously learned. And ineffective. Charlie's father had golden hair and a cherub's face. Even the wrong way up he looked angelic. Outside the family, Charlie noticed, everybody acted as though they adored his father and couldn't get enough of him upside down reciting nonsense. But a child takes his cue from his mother in matters of embarrassment, and Charlie Merriweather's mother was abashed, therefore so was Charlie.

Back home after another spontaneous recitation in the park –

> O My agèd Uncle Arly!
> Sitting on a heap of Barley
> Thro' the silent hours of night, –
> Close beside a leafy thicket; –
> On his nose there was a Cricket, –
> In his hat a Railway-Ticket; –

– Edwin ('Teddy') Merriweather would submit to his lovely wife's latest ultimatum. 'Humiliate me like that again and you'll be *sleeping* on a heap of barley,' she warned him. 'What you do the rest of the time is your business, but I insist you remember you are a headmaster when you are out with me. Having brought us to this hellhole, I consider it the least you can do.'

> But his shoes were far too tight,

Teddy Merriweather concluded wistfully, by way of reply.

'Grow up, Daddy,' his daughters told him.

Even when he was annoyed with his father for not remembering to act like a headmaster, Charlie loved the precise and yet irresponsible way he spoke, as though nothing was either serious or funny but somehow both. Charlie had heard somebody called the Archbishop of Canterbury speaking on the wireless, and he thought his father's voice was a cross between the organ pipes of the Archbishop and the burbling whiffles of that Jabberwock whose jabot his father wore.

In his heart, Charlie felt sorry for his father, going from applause to vilification in the time it took him to cross the threshold of his own house. It would have made sense, he often thought, for his father never to have come home at all. But then who would Charlie have looked to for forbearance? In his hurry to please his mother, before it dawned on him that he would never succeed, not ever, not ever ever, Charlie was constantly being flustered into mixing up his words and saying the opposite to what it was in his mind to say. He said yes when he meant no; he said up when he meant down; when she offered him her glacial cheek at bedtime, barely bothering to look up from her crossword, he would sometimes get so flustered he would call her Dada and wish her many happy returns instead of good night. Once she flew into a rage and boxed his ears, leaving him listening to silence for a morning, because he wouldn't stop going on about the mats and rice he'd seen scuttling about the garden shed, chewing paper and disappearing into bags of plant feed. 'What in God's name are you talking about?' she railed. 'How can mats and rice chew paper? Is this some cuteness?' His father understood. 'It's no wonder the boy makes such a hotchpotch of his sentences when you keep flummoxing him,' Charlie thought he heard him say. 'Anyway, it's perfectly clear to me what he means. The Reverend W. A. Spooner would have understood him.' 'Then you and the Reverend W. A. Spooner talk to him,' Mrs Merriweather said. 'Nonsense is your medium, after all.'

But being frightened imposes its own obligations, and being understood was no compensation for being shamed. What Charlie gathered from his mother was that his father's engagingness outside the house degraded all of them. A man in his position had no business turning himself into a jackass for other people's amusement. If she'd wanted a clown to be the father of her children, she'd have gone looking for a husband in the circus. Listening to her, even with his ears ringing, Charlie was convinced. Somehow his father was wasting something that belonged to them.

Once, when Charlie was six, his father took him to a stately home in Derbyshire. Just the two of them. They had tea together – triangles of cucumber sandwiches, chocolate cake, slices of lemon on a little plate – then walked by a lake where Charlie's father taught Charlie the names of different breeds of duck, showed him how to make stones skip across the water and, balancing on one leg with the other leg hidden behind his back, said:

> I'll tell thee everything I can:
> There's little to relate.
> I saw an aged, aged man,
> A-sitting on a gate.

And Charlie thought how wonderful it was to have a funny father who could rhyme and recite to him and who held his hand and didn't hurry him. But in their leisurely wanderings they hadn't noticed a sign saying PRIVATE and suddenly there *was* the aged, aged man, only he wasn't a-sitting on a gate, he was a-standing behind it, holding back two barking dogs with cheeks as pouched and furious as his were, and he was brandishing a walking stick and shouting, 'Be off with you, can't you read?' and instead of shouting back, 'I'm a headmaster, of course I can read! I can read a damn sight better than you can!' or standing on his head, or reciting a funny poem, Charlie's father flushed scarlet, lowered his eyes, stammered out an apology as flummoxed as any of Charlie's own, and hurried away, breathing audibly and holding Charlie's hand so hard he thought it would burn up with the heat. Charlie could not remember ever having felt so sad. It wasn't just that a perfect day had been ruined; Charlie felt that this incident would stay with him for the rest of his life and that there would never again be a day when he would not feel sad on account of it. Propping up his sadness, like poles supporting a rotting pier, Charlie recognised two distinct sensations. Firstly, he was hurt on his father's behalf by the telling-off. How much it hurt his father he could tell from how tightly his father held on to his hand. Secondly, he felt let down, that his father hadn't stuck up for them both and told the aged, aged man what he could do with his stick. A boy doesn't want to see his father disgraced, whatever the rights or wrongs of the case. Was this what his mother meant when she accused her husband of lowering himself, and of lowering her and her children with him? Well, Charlie could now vouch for that with his own eyes. He had seen his father talked to like a servant. And he had seen his father bow his head and accept the talking-to, as though a servant was all he was.

Those were the happy carefree years. The blithe times, when Charlie's father still had his powers of recovery, could take a rebuff one day and could spring back upside down in his knickerbockers the next, before comprehensivisation did what his wife had never quite been able to do, and drove him under the table.

Charlie was eight or nine, growing taller, growing lonelier, growing shyer, when the table-shrinking started. Although his father was on a pension and there were uncles to help with mortgages and school bills and the like, the change in circumstances moved his mother to the sort of action countenanced by women of her class only during times of national crisis. She went out to work! More exceptionally still, she went out to work as a dental receptionist! It occurred to Charlie that although his mother gave as her only motive money, the real reason she went out to work was so as not to have to look at his father curled up on the floor with his briefcase. An explanation contested by the remains of the person in question who, during one of his periods of lucidity, crawled out from underneath the table to accuse his wife of taking a job as a dental receptionist only in order to be close to people in pain.

'In which case,' he shouted after her, 'you might just as well have stayed home with me.'

But she was buttoned up in her National Health blue uniform by then, belted and badged as though there were a war on, and already in the street.

Once a week a lady with a mutating mole on her neck and no flesh on her bones visited the house to do the cleaning. Catherine. 'Ah, Catherine, Catherine – and would that be Catherine Wheel or Catherine the Great?' Teddy Merriweather hummed when he was apprised of her appointment. 'Catherine the Great Unwashed,' his wife corrected him with a snort. Charlie was frightened of Catherine because of her mole, because poverty had ingrained her skin with soot, because she called him 'Sonny Jim', and because she seemed to find the height of him amusing. Once she pushed open the door when he was sitting on the lavatory. Once she found him leaning out of his bedroom window, throwing lead soldiers at the garden shed to see if he could frighten out the mats and rice. Another time she sneaked up on him when he was lying on his bed, talking to Pobble, the bear he'd owned since he was a baby. She moved so silently about the house, on slippers which must have been distributed charitably to the poor, for he had never seen any but poor people wearing them, that he was never given warning she was coming. It seemed to Charlie that she was spying on him, deliberately seeking him out in compromising positions so she could wag her finger at him, call him Sonny Jim and laugh in his face.

But he had been brought up to be a little gentleman, albeit a little tall gentleman, which meant going to the rescue, sometimes, even of people you didn't like. So he knew what to do the day he came home from school early on account of a teacher committing suicide and found a man with no clothes on pressing Catherine to the floor, presumably with a view to robbing her or murdering her or both. Entirely against his instinct, which was to leave her

77

there and let the man rob and murder her as often as he had a mind to, Charlie grabbed an umbrella from the umbrella stand and began striking the man's back with it. Only when the man turned around did Charlie realise it was his father. Charlie recognised the expression on his face. The last time he'd seen his father with a face like that was when the person with the two angry-cheeked dogs had accused him of being unable to read and ordered him off his property.

Charlie was right. Thanks to his father he was never not going to feel sad again. Never.

Although he had no words for what had happened, Charlie knew it was wrong in some way that would upset his mother. 'I won't tell that you were robbing Catherine,' he told his father, who was back under the table now, holding on to his briefcase and sobbing like a child.

But Catherine too must have needed reassuring, because she sat him on the sofa and snuggled up to him not long after and thanked him for saving her and asked him to name his reward. Charlie couldn't think of anything he wanted. 'How about an introduction to Miss Cuntalina Fuckleton?' Catherine asked. When Charlie said he did not know who Miss Cuntalina Fuckleton was, Catherine roared with the sort of laughter Charlie associated with witches and took his hand and introduced him, whereupon it was Charlie's turn to begin sobbing like a child, though he at least had the excuse of *being* a child.

He was an unlucky boy. Unlucky in his parents, unlucky to have been carted off to Leicestershire and then sent back down to Lewes to finish his schooling, unlucky in his encounters with the lower classes and, until he met Charlie and his luck changed, unlucky in love. He couldn't find anybody. One by one the other boys caught up with Simon Lawrence. Oral sex? Nothing to it. Straight sex? A breeze. Now they were all biting pencils and wearing lockets. All except Charlie. He bought a locket of course, but put his mother's picture in it. 'Miss Cuntalina Fuckleton,' he would have said, had anybody enquired. Some love charm! – the chain gave him a neck rash while the locket itself smacked into his sternum whenever he moved. Small wonder he continued to be lacking in the necessary confidence. They can smell it on me, he thought, I must stink of everything I haven't done. He did. At school dances girls shied away from him, put off by the avidity with which he stared at them, frightened of his big hungry face, repelled by the odour of his virginity. He believed it was his penis that stank, and washed it in a basin a hundred times a day. He thought he had some disease, he thought his penis was putrefying. He thought his sperm smelt off. But of course it had nothing to do with his penis or his sperm. It was his attitude that stank. Marvin Kreitman pointed that out to him when they met in their first week at university. He emptied a bottle of Givenchy over Charlie, advised him to keep his drawers and cupboards open for a year, recommended he stop wearing vests and change into clean underpants every morning, put it to him that he might consider circumcision, but above all ordered him to stop looking so needy.

'How do I do that?' Charlie wanted to know.

'You put your tongue back inside your mouth for a start.'

'Do you know what the worst of it is,' he told Kreitman, 'legs and nipples.' He longed for legs and nipples. Ached for them. It was an Indian summer and all the girls had their legs bare and their nipples pushing at their shirts and cardigans, like eyes in the wrong place. 'Why eyes in the wrong place should get to me the way they do, I don't know,' he said, 'but they do and I'm going mad for a pair.'

'Your nipples are fine,' Kreitman told him.

'Listen to me, Kreitman,' Charlie said, 'if I don't get to walk out with someone with nipplissimus erectibissimus before this term's out I'll shoot myself.'

Soon after, rather than let that happen, Kreitman introduced him to Charlie.

And guess what? She had tiny introverted nipples and wore brassières and men's jackets.

And long canvas skirts.

And woolly winter tights.

But Charlie fell in love with her for all that.

And should have lived happily ever after, if there were any fairness in the universe. Yet here he was again, at the beginning of another century, wondering to what end those shadows on the walls of the school pavilion leapt and cavorted.

As a general rule other people did not have as much fun as you feared they were having; he had learnt that as he'd got older. The grass isn't always greener. Your neighbour is invariably as dissatisfied with his ox as you are with yours. Figuratively speaking, he wasn't the only one who had worn his mother's portrait round his neck. Everybody added a little to the truth. 'No one ever goes to as wild a party as you throw for them in your head, Charlemagne,' his wife used to tell him when she feared he was growing restless. Some such calculation of human sameness is necessary to keep us all in a passable state of contentment and it had been enough for Charlie for twenty years. Nice sex with Chas twice a month – and Charlie in his peroration to Marvin Kreitman had not exaggerated how nice sex between them was, sex so nice he sometimes wanted to cry while he was having it – nice books to write about children who were only comically not nice, nice sales, nice house on the river at Richmond, nice friends. He even sent off self-effacing articles to fogey journals in praise of his lifestyle, joys of suburbia, charm of the old-fashioned, what you don't know you don't miss, better a buffoon than a bounder, as if he'd clean forgotten what it was like to fear you had a putrefying penis. And it *was* enough. It did. More than that, it was true. The rest was lies. Silliness and lies. Then suddenly it wasn't. Suddenly the rest was truth and he was lies.

What had happened? Nothing in his relations with Charlie, he was sure of that. Dear Chas – they still worked as they had always done, on ancient clitter-clatter typewriters at opposite ends of a large pine table with a vase of freshly cut flowers between them, and he still had only to raise his eyes from his machine and see her engrossed in hers, poking her little fingers into the keyboard, as conscientious and unworldly as a head girl at a convent school; still had only to catch her looking quizzically at him over her bifocals, ascertaining whether he was genuinely listening to what she was reading ('Charlemagne, attend!' she would say when she thought his attention was wandering), and his soul would leap as it had always leapt to nuzzle into hers. So, no, nothing to do with Chas. Nothing to do, either, with his son getting his nipple pierced (talking of nipples) and showing up without a word of warning on *Blind Date*. 'My name's Tim Merriweather and I'm from *Rich* . . . mond!' Nor with his daughter getting *her* nipple pierced and informing them that while she wasn't once and for all committed and they mustn't think that that was her settled for the duration and that she wouldn't be giving them grandchildren eventually, she did fancy having a tentative stab at the other thing. 'Kitty's a bulldyke!' Charlie announced with a wail, during a party for grown-ups on the lawn, and all their friends roared with laughter. Strangers boating on the Thames roared with laughter too. Not at the daughter's waywardness but at the father's drollery. Who cared if there was or wasn't another bulldyke in the world? It was all regulation Richmond. As was, when all was said and done, Dotty with her frayed-sleeved toyboy – yawn, yawn. Respectable Middle England which had never, in truth, been in the slightest bit respectable at all, simply opened its insatiable maw and swallowed the lot. No, none of Charlie's externals had changed. Something had just switched on in his body. Or in his head. Maybe he'd banged himself. Walked into a wall or ricked his neck rolling off Charlie. Smack, rick, switch – behold, a pervert! *No one was ever having as much fun as you feared they were having?* The hell they weren't! Look at Kreitman. Well, don't look at him just this minute, with blood in his nostrils and tyre marks on his shirt; but in a general way, look at him.

How many houses did Kreitman have? How many love nests? With how many lovers in each? A new woman every night, was that his routine? Two new women? Two together? Should he have asked for two before Kreitman walked into the cyclist? Would Kreitman remember anything of the conversation when he woke? Would he know if Charlie told him that the deal was *two* – his beloved Chas for any two of Kreitman's? Or three? Would he remember enough to know that three had never been on the table?

He was parting company with his reason but there was nothing he could do to reverse the process. He *wanted* to be parted from his reason. The poison had entered his body. Never mind Kreitman, he was the one they should be jabbing against tetanus.

Contrary to what moralists tell you, an excessive preoccupation with sex makes you serious. Or perhaps that should go the other way round: only the serious are able to brave wholeheartedly the repercussions of sexual thought. The young are excepted from this. Sex in the young is another matter, unphilosophical, a necessity not a luxury, the fulfilment of an instinct not an illness. Thought to be a jolly person in the past, though tinged of course with that melancholy incident to any man who has looked about him or been sent to public school, Charlie Merriweather was now possessed of so much of the gravitas of unsatisfied desire he barely recognised the weight of his own limbs.

The other burden he had to carry, of course, was that of treachery, and treachery's twin brother, loneliness. He didn't feel he was acting against Chas in his heart, but of course he was. They had done everything together since he was a young man. When he'd been unhappy or uncertain he'd told her and she'd kissed him better. His unhappiness was her unhappiness. They were a couple. They shared. But she couldn't share this one, could she? He was acting against her, thinking against her, by simple virtue of the fact that what he was thinking he couldn't tell her. *There* was the betrayal – not the imaginary other women themselves, but his having to exclude her from all knowledge of them. For the first time since they'd become a pair, he had reverted to being single. And the cruelty of that, for him, was that he had no one to talk to just when he needed someone to talk to most.

So it wasn't with any idling lightness that he sat looking at Kreitman's rescued mobile and thought about the contents of its databank. Pick a number, press a key, and that lurid world of which Charlie Merriweather had for so many years denied the very existence would at once dance into lunatic life. He turned it about in his fingers, picking at the stitches of its leather case (everything Kreitman owned came in a leather case), while he waited for Chas to turn up with the tea and egg baps. Nyman wasn't watching; fearing he may have killed a man, the cyclist slumped with his head between his cycling shorts, intermittently leaping to his feet to make another desperate representation to the receptionist.

'Nyman, why don't you go home?' Charlie said. 'Nothing's going to happen.' But the minute he said it he realised his mistake. By his own confession – 'I am Nyman,' was how he had introduced himself while they were watching Kreitman being stretchered into the ambulance, 'I am no one in particular' – Nyman had been waiting for such an evening all his life. Nyman the Killer – so that's who I am!

'I will get some air,' he said. 'Please to call me if there are developments.'

Charlie wasn't certain he believed the cyclist was Austrian or German, let alone, as Kreitman had insisted, a faggot, however many German faggots on bicycles Kreitman said there were in Soho. He watched Nyman's back recede, in its pretend athletic vest, then went like a thief into the phone book of Kreitman's mobile and pressed a key.

The name Erica appeared on the display. He pressed another

key. Bernadette. Then Jane. Then Ooshi. Then Vanessa. Then Dotty. Then Shelley . . .

Then *who* was that? He went back a number. Dotty? Kreitman was in the habit of ringing *Dotty*?

He felt the blood run into his neck. Was Kreitman already halfway to enjoying both sisters? The thought sent a sewer of bile into Charlie's stomach. A man should not fuck sisters, whatever attitude the Old Testament took to Jacob fucking Leah and Rachel. A man should not fuck sisters. In a decent world a man would not even *think* about fucking sisters. Not Chas *and* Dotty. Not Dotty *and* Chas. So where did that leave him? Up in flames, longing for abominations and going madder by the minute.

Hope and pray it was a different Dotty. Kreitman must have known a thousand Dotties. Charlie did not recognise the number, but then Charlie did not recognise *any* number. In his house Chas did all the ringing. She had even programmed his mobile for him – just as she still put together his outfits for the day, which socks with which pants – showing him how to operate the phone book, though the only number he could find in it was his own. He checked his watch – fast approaching two in the morning – then pressed the yes key anyway. If this was Dotty's number and she was asleep she'd either have her phone off or switched over to answering machine, the way Chas did theirs. Anyone else, well, what the hell. His own needs came first. The phone rang four times, then someone picked it up. The voice irascible with broken sleep – 'Who's that?' Dotty! Dotty, for sure. Remembering to pinch her lips together, even though barely awake, lest words made the muscles round her mouth collapse. 'Wh's tht?' Dotty without a doubt. 'Oh, Lord!' Charlie said, whereupon Dotty said, 'Charlie, is that you? What's the matter? Is everything all right? Has anything happened to Charlie?' And all Charlie could think of saying in return was, 'I'm losing my mind.'

★   ★   ★

The first thing Chas and Hazel did after Charlie rang them to say he was sitting in St Thomas's waiting for Marvin to wake up after being run down by a cyclist but not to worry, was to ring each other. If Chas was driving in from Richmond, then Hazel would take a taxi to Wandsworth where the girls had gone to a friend's house to rave, from which Chas could pick them up without seriously going out of her way and deliver them all to St Thomas's. Had any man been party to this arrangement he would have pointed out its logical and geographic flaws and come up with an alternative suggestion. Such as, 'Go separately.' This was the joy, for Hazel at least, of having no man party any longer to anything.

In fact, the girls pointed out the chief flaw as they saw it when their mother came to collect them, to whit: if Daddy wasn't dying, why did they have to see him this very minute when this very minute they were enjoying juggling little, graven love tablets on the tips of their tongues and dancing with bottles of Evian water? Shit, Mummy!

'He *is* concussed, darlings,' Hazel said. But could think of nothing further to add when her daughters smiled sweetly back at her and said, 'But, Mummy, so are we.'

That being the case, Charlie picked Hazel up from Wandsworth and the two women motored in on their mercy errand without the hindrance of other company.

'Kind of you to do this,' Hazel said.

'*De nada.*'

Chas and Charlie had recently been to Seville for a children's literature festival, and now Chas was speaking joke Spanish. In the Merriweathers' world you weren't expected to be very good at anything, especially languages. A conviction of the propriety of lightness, which Hazel secretly envied. Oh, to be not very good at anything and see it as a virtue!

'The last time I did anything like this,' Chas said, moving up the gears, 'was when Timmy's headmaster rang to say he'd fallen from his dormitory window while trying to launch himself back into it from a drainpipe.'

'What was Timmy's headmaster doing on a drainpipe?'

The two women laughed. They felt like the mothers of small children again. Suddenly bruised knees were back in their lives.

'So how come yours didn't get hurt and mine did?' Hazel asked.

'Yours will have been doing something wilder.'

'To a pedal bike?'

'Even an argument with a pedal bike's beyond Charlemagne. He's too big a baby to get into any real trouble. He walks through danger unaware. He'd have walked through the Russian Revolution without getting a scratch. No one notices he's there. It's his height. He seems to be above it. But I bet he's as jealous of Marvin as anything. He'd love it to be him we were charging in to see with champagne and flowers.'

'You've brought champagne and flowers?'

'Well, egg sandwiches anyway.'

Chas the provider. Because there was never any room in the boot or back seat of Chas's car, taken up with umbrellas, wellingtons and anoraks, Hazel had to sit with the Glyndebourne picnic basket between her feet. Hazel knew what would be in it. Not champagne, but rather more than just egg sandwiches. Hand-raised pork pies, which Charlie loved. Cold potato salad with lashings of mayonnaise, which Charlie loved. Taramasalata and thin wheat crackers, which Charlie loved. A bottle of retsina, which Charlie loved. Runny raspberry cheesecake, which Charlie adored. Lemon meringue pie in which Charlie would have bathed, had he been allowed. Why doesn't she simply fill it with jars of mashed rhubarb and strained peach and have done, Hazel wondered. Chas the mother of Charlemagne the big baby.

Although she liked and admired Chas in the abstract, positively revered her when she didn't see her, idealising her capabilities and her appearance, loving her pretend-clumsy handsomeness, the way she seemed to get her face tied up in her spectacles, the way she looked as though she were at any minute going to trip over her own legs, or lose her way in her own kitchen, even while she was single-handedly catering for thirty – although Chas, in absentia, had been her best friend ever since their glory days, when they'd been the girlfriends of that inseparable duo, Charlie Merriweather and Marvin Kreitman – in the *flesh* Hazel wasn't sure she liked Chas very much at all. What she forgot, when Chas was not in front of her very eyes to remind her of them, were the notices she hung on all their conversations. 'Don't touch my baby.' 'Don't harm my baby.' 'Please don't take my baby away from me.'

As if, Hazel thought.

It wasn't that she hadn't noticed Charlie's charms in the time she'd known him. Or that he hadn't let her know he'd noticed hers. He took you in all right, Charlie Merriweather. He shot you sudden penetrating glances, along the beams of which you had no choice but to send him penetrating glances back. In this regard, if in no other – and in the end what other is there? – he was a man in working order. Big too, unthreateningly strong, and lovable in the bumbling manner of men of that class and generation. A sweet man. But she didn't know of a single woman, all questions of hurting or not hurting Chas apart, who viewed him as any sort of proposition. A pet was for life and so was Charlie. You couldn't quickly let him in on the understanding that he'd quickly let himself back out. Which she suspected was exactly the quality women liked in *her* husband. Marvin Kreitman would cry over you longer than you might find easy, but he'd be gone fairly smartly thereafter. She could vouch for that. It was very nearly a matter of wifely pride. In fact, in Chas's company, it *was* a matter of wifely pride. For there was ultimately something unforgivably insulting about the protective playpen Chas constructed around Charlemagne – insulting to the people the playpen was constructed to keep out, never mind to the big baby it was constructed to keep in – as though one had so few consolations of one's own that one was bound to want to snaffle Chas's.

I know what it is she makes me feel, Hazel thought – she makes me feel as though she pities me for having a collapsed womb or lazy ovaries. And she makes me feel as though she fears me for the same reason. Beware! – unnatural, unreproductive woman about.

For her part, though she never much cared for Hazel in the abstract, positively hating her when she didn't see her, denigrating her for never having made her own career, running down her second-hand stylishness, her reliance upon outside help – architects, landscape gardeners, designers, personal trainers, party chefs, wine waiters – and satirising her transformation from frightened sylvan creature to huntswoman of the savannah, in the *flesh* Chas admired her, felt calmed by her compact presence and relieved to be in the company of someone who appeared to be as cynical about the sort of silliness upon which Dotty had embarked as she was. In short, though she had been challenged if not affronted by Hazel's part in those first overheard acts of sexual mayhem and murder with Kreitman, and then alarmed by the cold marital accommodation she'd subsequently come to with him (which still, somehow, did not take from the idea one had of her as his accomplice), these days she did not feel that Hazel was capable of dropping down on her from the trees and sinking her jaws into her defenceless family. If anything, Hazel had given up and gone middle-aged before the rest of them. Which of course made her excellent company.

Only one teeny-weeny anxiety remained. That orphaned stuff that Hazel had once gone in for, all that business about how not having a father robbed you of resistant force – Chas had never believed a word of it. She hadn't seen much of her father herself while she was growing up. Most of the time she'd been as fatherless as Hazel, but that hadn't made of her a feather to every breeze that blew. Quite the opposite. In Chas's view, not having a father on whom to practise the arts of pleasing had made her independent and strong-willed. She was father to herself. What had made Hazel weak was not fatherlessness but spinelessness – if spinelessness was the word for always needing a man to lean on and to blame. Not that Hazel was spineless any longer. But you never knew with weaknesses of that sort, whether they were ever completely gone.

Chas drove as if driving were a romp, like climbing over stiles in a high gale. She wore special glasses for it which she peered over comically, and kept getting her feet, which were far too big for the pedals, in each other's way. And the more entangled her feet became, the faster she drove.

'Do you want me to take over?' Hazel asked. 'It's tiring driving in the lights with all these late-night lunatics around.'

'What you could do,' Chas said, 'is help me off with my jacket, thank you, and pull my skirt up between my legs, it's so I can find the brakes.'

As long as Hazel could remember, Chas had dressed in a man's double-breasted navy jacket, usually buttoned over a top that might have been knitted out of cucumbers, and a long canvas skirt resembling a spinnaker, always (even on the hottest days) worn with thick ribbed tights. It was a blue-stocking get-up – sensible, rural, droll – which was partly forced on Chas, Hazel understood, by the longness of her limbs and the flatness of her chest, but she wore it so unapologetically that Hazel wondered if it wasn't also provenly a vote winner, that's to say arousing to someone – some person or persons – other than her husband. Marvin, an individual of such refinement he had pulled his wife weeping (he weeping) from the contamination of smutty jokes, had once offered it as his opinion that Chas was unfuckable to anyone but Charlie, and for all he knew unfuckable to Charlie too, because no man relished the prospect of a mouthful of hot woolly winter hosiery. 'You fuck with your mouth now, do you, darling?' Hazel enquired. 'There was a time when you knew perfectly well how I fucked,' Kreitman responded. And for the briefest of moments, as they both thought 'joylessly', they were more together than they'd been for years.

And had one asked Chas whether she thought she was fuckable to men other than her husband, whether she wore what she wore because she knew something about what men liked that Hazel in her tailored MaxMara suits did not, and which might or might not have been a mouthful of hot woolly winter hosiery, what then? Would she have turned crimson with anger or embarrassment or both – would she have said she didn't care whether she was fuckable to other men or not, that she was a woman of the twenty-first century who had better things to think about, and that the question, anyway, if it had to be asked at all, was whether other men were fuckable to her – or would she have lengthened her face and looked over the rim of her comical glasses and very loudly said nothing, like a woman whose soul was her own secret?

She was a virgin when she met Charlie, which made two of them; and from the solemn hour she had been asked if she took Charlie to be her lawful, and she had replied 'I do', she had never once committed, or so much as thought about committing adultery. Are we to take it, therefore, that on the night she drove Hazel Kreitman to the hospital, so recklessly she almost ploughed into a queue of kids waiting to get into a club at Clapham Junction, and then had to suffer the ignominy of a breath test on Albert Embankment, Chas Merriweather was a woman who could put her hand on her heart and swear she had carnally known no man who was not her husband? Yes and no.

Adultery is violation of the marriage bed, and though she had already met Charlie she had not yet given herself in marriage to him, nor had her professor given himself in marriage to anybody, when midway through discussing her essay on Chekhov (which, incidentally, he thought magical), he had pulled her to him, thrust his little pink tongue into her mouth, suggested his little pink penis into her hand and told her that he loved her. Not an unusual academic event in those days, but unusual for her, unusual for Chas, in that she neither spat out the tongue nor suggested the penis back inside the professor's pants. Unusual or not, leaving everything where it was hardly constituted adultery, surely to God, regardless of the marital state of either of them. Indeed, in Chas's view, as it was happening, it didn't even constitute sex.

Years afterwards, a president of the United States of America would cause an etymological storm by defining fellatio as a performance of something or other entirely non-sexual, and therefore entirely unblameworthy, in its nature. Did Chas beat the president to it? Was this an earlier (if less controversial) instance of not-sex she was having with a man old enough to be her father, whose brain she revered, and whose translations of the Russian masters she knew by heart? Charlotte Juniper, as she was then, was subtler than the president. She thought kissing and holding on to her professor just the once, and not allowing him to come in her hand – though it alarmed her to remember that he came on her essay – both was not sex and yet was not something she should have been doing either. She felt terrible about it and she didn't. And the reason she felt terrible about it later was that she hadn't felt terrible about it at the time.

In another corner of her mind, however, for even a good wife keeps corners which her husband never gets to visit, Chas was exhilarated. She had been mistress of events. When she encountered the professor coming in and out of lectures she perched her sunflower head even prouder on its stalk than usual and smiled an adventuress's smile, while he slunk past, hidden in the folds of his gown, not knowing whether she thought him a lecher, not knowing whether she thought him a fool, not knowing whether she was going to tell on him to the authorities or to other students. It was a time for women to prove they could be as insouciant as men, and Chas believed she had passed the test.

Sex wasn't supposed to matter to men, and now she had shown it needn't matter to her. Except, of course, that it wasn't sex.

So what was it?

She had a feeling it ran in the family. She didn't mean Dotty. In Dotty's case it ran away from the family. But discounting Dotty, who was the anomaly, there was, she fancied, a proneness to minor quasi-sexual mishap (if that wasn't putting it too strongly) extending matrilineally she did not know how far back. Her mother and her grandmother were countrywomen of unassailable propriety, the wives of successful public men – the first a surveyor, the second a doctor – but eminent in their own right as well, both serving officers of their respective parish councils, both voluntary educationalists, conservationists, preservationists, indefatigible charity egg-beaters and National Trusters against whom not a breath of malicious rumour was ever raised. Let a working man tip his hat to Charlie's grandmother too familiarly and he ran the risk of being elbowed on to the road. Charlie's mother, too, bore herself sternly, wearing corsets as impregnable as armour long after such protection had gone out of fashion, even in Shepton Mallet. And yet to Charlie's eye they both appeared vulnerable to solicitation of an absurd or accidental nature. There was something of the pantomime dame about them both, now starched and forbidding, now capable of ending up on the straw with their skirts raised. It was almost as though, in proportion as they armed themselves against direct assault, they courted compromising surprise. Not because they hankered for adventure, quite the opposite – because being compromised proved how gauche and therefore how unfitted for adventure they were. Like her? Well, she wasn't sure about that. But an entry in her grandmother's diary, bequeathed to her on that formidable lady's death, only months after her own inconsequent interlude with her professor, certainly rang bells.

'Sunday evening, rained all day,' the diary read, 'drenched to the bone and glad to be home. Spent an unlooked-for hour sheltering under *a tree with Mr Leonard Woolf, whose gardens I had gone to inspect. The poor man wretched on account of the recent suicide of his wife by drowning. The sight of all that falling water would not have helped much, I imagine. Whether I should have acceded to his requests in other circumstances I very much doubt. But there was a charitable side to it. And it was only a small favour he asked. Besides, my own curiosity as to the matter of his Jewishness – never having encountered the phenomenon before – spurred me on a little. For myself, cannot say it was a pleasure, cannot say it was not. For him – definitely not.'*

Like her? The same droll obligingness, not devoid of a sense of duty? The same passive recipience of what was and yet was not erotic liberty? Maybe the same. Or, if not the same, similar.

As for Charlie's mother, Dotty on the telephone to Charlie in London swore blind that she had seen the coalman position himself a hot breath behind her at the Shepton Mallet street party for the Queen's Silver Jubilee and manoeuvre her hand into his flies.

'I don't believe you,' Charlie said. Though she could quite picture the pantomime. Lawk-a-mercy, Mr Brotherton!

'Then don't believe me. But if you'd seen him bulging in his best suit you'd have wished it was your hand.'

'Dotty! What did Daddy say?'

'Daddy? Daddy was away surveying, as usual.'

'So what did Mummy do?'

'She kept it there, silly.'

Well, I suppose it *was* a party, Charlie told herself. And in a small, cold community you don't hurt the feelings of the coalman.

She pursed her lips for the traffic cop in Vauxhall, thought about a joke since Hazel was with her, then thought better of it and blew into the bag.

And despite the family susceptivity she truly only opened her mouth for her professor, and never moved away her hand, on that one occasion?

Truly.

And never ever, post Charlie, with anybody else?

Never ever?

Well . . . just the teensiest time. But that wasn't anything of vital importance either.

'Shhh!' she ordered him, smoothing his hair.

Kreitman loved nothing more than having a woman's hand in or near his hair. Had someone told him that God was a woman and would stroke his brow and run her fingers through his hair on his arrival in Her presence, he would gladly have gone to Her at once, and to hell with all the others.

Now more than ever. A woman to blow cool air across his brain, that's what he needed. A woman to blow women *out* of his brain.

The cruel paradox of Kreitman's life, as he saw it: he was ill with women, but only a woman could make him better.

He felt a little less ill, opening his eyes this time, than when he'd first come out of his faint on the Soho streets. For Kreitman, fainting was the proof that he would die badly, and that life was an accident, without meaning or purpose. He had been a congenital fainter as a boy. The sight of blood did it. Horror stories did it. Hot food did it. His father did it. Being struck did it. Seeing a hand raised in anger, even if not to him, did it. Nietzsche went mad on the streets of Trieste, seeing a man beating a horse. Marginally less unstable than the philosopher, Marvin Kreitman fainted at the zoo, seeing a parrot, crazed with being caged, denuding itself of its feathers. Kreitman knew how the parrot felt. Not the being caged, but the futility. Sometimes he plucked at himself, ripping out his fingernails and toenails, tearing the skin from his knuckles, pulling out individual hairs from his scalp. And fainting. Told by the doctor that this was merely a phase Marvin was going through, his mother took him to be examined by a specialist. Several thousand pounds of tests later, Marvin was diagnosed 'sensitive'. Money well spent. 'My son is clinically sensitive,' she informed friends. 'I could have told you that and saved us a fortune,' his father croaked. Whereupon Marvin fainted again.

The fainting itself he could live with. Sometimes it was even pleasurable just to vanish from the scene. What he could not bear was the coming-to. When Kreitman came to after fainting it was as though he were being reassembled. So why wasn't there satisfaction in that? Reunification is meant to be a happy event. Things coming together which have been apart – friends, lovers, nations, ligaments – are deemed to be fortunate. Occasions for a party. Fireworks. Not in Kreitman's case. When Kreitman came to after fainting, he felt he was being reassembled out of parts that were not his and did not fit. There was physical pain in it, the agony of bones going into sockets that would not take them; but the mental anguish was the hardest to support, the nauseating certainty that the mind you'd been given back was not *your* mind, that it was of another colour and configuration from your mind, that the patterns you saw were not the patterns you were accustomed to seeing, that there was a music to the objects you woke to which bore no resemblance to any music you knew, or to any rhythmic pattern or system of notation you recognised or liked. He had been reassembled randomly, thrown together, a stranger to himself, without consideration of suitability or match, and that proved there was no meaning or purpose out there. Kabbalists argued that the Godhead who had once presided over a unified and harmonious universe had become alienated from himself, and as a consequence we were all so many scattered sparks, shaken as through from a falling torch. Fine by Kreitman. There had been meaning once, but there wasn't any now. Unfortunately, he was living now.

Among the scattered sparks that comprised this latest disgusting composition of what wasn't himself was a fiery recollection of loose talk with Charlie Merriweather. What he thought he could remember couldn't possibly be the actual event. Another person's conversation had been confused with his. As for how he'd spent his own evening, some poor insensible bastard elsewhere on the planet was waking with a dream of that.

But he was still alarmed to find Charlie Merriweather's wife, standing like Florence Nightingale in a spinnaker, by his bed.

'Where are the others?' he asked her. 'Or are you here on your own?'

Because Kreitman noticed such things, he noticed that she didn't say, 'Why, would you *like* me to be here on my own?' But he also noticed that she also didn't say, 'And what, Marvin, would I be doing here on my own?'

'Charlemagne's asleep on a bench in the waiting room,' was what she did say, 'and Hazel's having breakfast with Nyman.'

Here we go again, Kreitman thought. Wrong parts. 'Nyman?'

'The cyclist.'

'Which cyclist? Not the faggot who ran me down?'

Charlie shrugged and shook her head, as though Kreitman's bad language were a poisonous insect that had flown into her hair and she wanted to be rid of it.

'And he's called Nyman, you say?'

'Yes. An Anglicisation of Niemand.'

'How the fuck do you know that?'

'He tells you.'

'A German?'

'I don't know. An Austrian, I think.'

'There are no such things as Austrians. All Austrians are Germans.'

'Hush, Marvin.'

'I don't have to hush. Germans I can say what I like about. That's their function for the next thousand years – to be the butt of everyone who isn't German. Especially when they're faggots who run me down in the street. And Hazel's having breakfast with him, did I hear you say?'

'Yes.'

'Loyal of her. And would you have any idea how Hazel happened to run into this Nyman?'

'He was here. He's been here all night with Charlie.'

'I'll tell you what,' Kreitman said, 'why don't you join them for breakfast and leave me to have another little faint. Maybe when I next surface the world will make more sense. It's kind of you to have come, Charlie.'

'*De nada*,' Chas said.

FIVE

Neither quite awake, nor quite unconscious, impressionable Kreitman drifts through Spain.

Schlock Spain, but then what other kind is there? Castanets, garlic, warm nights, a dusty bar in a dusty *calle*, beaded curtains rattling like snakes, and a pregnant whore, older than his mother, fingers hotter than hell, thrumming out a malagueña on his thighs.

(Surprising, really, that Kreitman never recounted this experience to his young daughters, lying stiff as lozenges in their beds. For it contained everything he liked in a story – expectation, sensuality, disappointment, failure.)

'*Todos los otros son fríos*,' the pregnant whore sings – not to him, to the other whores, but it is music to his ears.

All of the others. All cold. All except him cold.

And not just cold as in the opposite to hot. But *fríos*. Which sounds icy to his Spanish. Arctic. Freezing in the blood. Frigid and frigidaired with fear.

But not him.

'*Gracias*,' he says.

She smiles at him. '*De nada*.'

He is thirteen, on a school trip to Barcelona. 'Don't go off the beaten track,' the teacher tells them, so they do. Old Knotty with his twisted teeth. 'Careful, boys.' So they're not. But it's only beer the five under-age boys are after, *cerveza* in a shady bar where they can practise their Spanish and get a taste of what it will be like to be men in a foreign country. Sooner than they think.

'*Aqui!*' the barman orders them. He is wonderfully blind in one eye and lame in one leg. Everyone in Spain is either half blind or half lame. The legacy of the Civil War, according to Knotty. So there's the smell of killing in the *calle*, too. You don't argue with killers. The barman rattles open bead curtains – '*Aqui, aqui!*' – to a bare anteroom with a single bullfight poster on the wall. Here, confessions will have been beaten out of traitors. Kreitman has seen the films. Cruel hands shaving the heads of young girls who consorted with the enemy. A scrubbed table awaits them. A jug of beer is slid in. And some colourless liquor in an unlabelled bottle. Did they ask for that? 'Clip joint,' they all think, their five little hearts beating as one. But they don't know what a clip joint is yet.

After the beer, the whores. One after another they enter, like aunties bearing birthday gifts. A fat one, a thin one, an old one, a young one, and his, the pregnant one, not too far gone, only a blip where her belly is and eyes that dance at him. Older than his mother, but otherwise could *be* his mother. The fat one sits on Gerald Barnish's lap. The thin one inclines her head on Hugo Feaver's shoulder. The old one and the young one carve up the Dorment twins. And Kreitman's drums her fingers on his thighs. Call it the beginning of his life, call it the end. Everything is decided for him at this moment. Whatever it is I'm feeling now, he tells himself, is what I was put on earth to feel. Blood runs like honey through his veins. His bones fold. Tremors skate across his skin as though on a field of melted butter. Now he knows.

And the others? Frightened and wanting to go home. *Fríos.*

He is so whatever the opposite to *frío* is himself, the bottom of his mouth has welded itself to the top. '*Cuánto?*' he manages to ask.

'*Diecinueve.*' Her voice is harsh and alcoholic. A bicycle chain lubricated with aniseed.

'*Pesetas?*'

Could it be pesetas? For that many pesetas he could have her a hundred times that night and still leave with money in his pocket.

She laughs a gypsy laugh, her drumming fingers scaling heights he did not know were there. '*Años,*' she says.

He knows she isn't nineteen *years*. But if lying is to be part of it, he's up for that as well. For lies, too, taste sweet.

'*Muy hermosa,*' he says.

'*Quien?*'

'*Usted.*'

She laughs at him, the little red-faced fiery formal boy. '*Gracias, señor,*' she says.

'*De nada.*'

But he never does find out how many pesetas. Suddenly, Knotty with his twisted teeth is asking for them at the bar. Five boys, in blazers, seen disappearing into a disreputable bodega much like this. Yes, those five. And now, out!

Must he? He feels the tears rise. Will he never see her again? Never, never, never, never?

Relieved to be rescued, even by Old Knotty, the other boys file out. But not Kreitman. Kreitman feels his life is over. The whores shrug lazily. Kreitman shows his tear-torn face to his. She smiles and raps one final melody on his leg. '*Adiós,*' she says. '*Adiós, mi héroe.*' And then in gargled English, 'Till the next time.'

And now the next time is all he can think about. Confined to his hotel the following day. Out of town on a bus trip the day after. Musical theatre the evening after that. Something about bells in a village in the Pays Basque. Ding–dong, ding–dong. The clanging of his heart. For he is in love as well as on heat. On his last night, clutching all the pesetas he owns, he gives his frigid school friends the slip and goes looking for her. Down this *calle* and up that. But how to tell one disreputable bodega from another? He has no luck. Every barman has one eye. Every bar a beaded curtain to a naked anteroom. And because he doesn't know her name he cannot ask for her, even were desperation to give him the courage to shape the sentence. Towards the end of the night, sad and footsore, he thinks he sees her ahead of him. He runs to show her his pesetas. It will be like showing her his heart, for he is not at all dismayed by the element of transaction in this, his first passion, whatever his mother would have said. Not at all. The pesetas define his excitement. In some important way, they *are* the excitement. It was exciting just counting them out. But the woman he overtakes is only a ghastly simulacrum of his woman, respectable and half her age.

In bars he cannot find, women sing with the voices of men. The smell of melancholy, now and for ever, is garlic prawn. Hot nights in cobbled alleys will always remind him of desire gone begging.

He never does find her. Never, never, never, never. But for a whole year he thinks about her all the time, and for the rest of his life he thinks about her some of the time. *Todos los otros son fríos* . . .

It helps to have that said in your hearing. It explains your difference from other men.

And now he knows that he never is and never will be happy unless he is suffering the pain of hope gone begging, of thwarted desire and of unbearable loss.

SIX

ORDERED TO GET some rest, Kreitman agreed to let Hazel drive him down slowly to a hotel they both liked, though Kreitman less than Hazel, on one of the softer edges of Dartmoor.

It wasn't just being knocked down he needed rest from. He needed rest from Charlie. All week, as though ducking flying bullets, Kreitman had been dodging his friend's calls. You know when someone's desperate to reach you. You hear it in the way the phone rings. And every time Kreitman's phone rang he knew it was Charlie, demented, ill with fidelity, pushing for the swap.

You also know when someone's avoiding you. Conversing with his women, Charlie thought. Making assignations even while his bones ache. Talking dirty. Three on a phone. The couple of times he did get through, Kreitman cut him short. 'Up to my ears, Charlie. Let's have another day in Soho again soon. Yes, exactly – on the principle that a man who crashes his car should start driving it again without delay. This Thursday? Love to, but let me see, let me see – no, can't.'

Wouldn't, more like. He'd been trying not to think about Charlie, but when he did, he understood that the best reason for denying him – sanity and decency aside – was that he didn't want him in so close, didn't want to forgo the experience of having him out there as a dumbstruck spectator of his irregularities. Everything else was pointing to the conventionality of Kreitman's routines. Twenty years ago he'd been a wild man, the Casanova of University College, now what he did his own daughters considered too naff even to tackle him about. Yuk, Daddy, adultery? Get a life! But Charlie at least was still bulging his eyes. Shame to lose that. And lose it he would once he and Charlie became, so to speak, brothers in arms.

'What about Friday?' Charlie asked.

Kreitman pretended to rustle his diary. 'Same again. No can do. I'm just hellishly pushed right now.'

Well, who *wasn't* hellishly pushed right now?

Not that Charlie honestly believed anyone had pushed him. This time, Charlie in his calmer moments reflected, I've gone and jumped. Christ!

He couldn't believe the hammering his chest was taking. Was this what not-nice sex did to your ribs and diaphragm? And he was only *thinking* about it!

As yet.

He held on to that. *As yet*.

A one-time shooting and fishing hotel, then a murder-mystery weekend hotel, then a white-water rafting hotel – a briefer incarnation, this, on account of the absence within a radius of five thousand miles of anything that could reasonably be called white water – and latterly a string quartet and dance alternating with a book club hotel (in which form it was at last returned to the earlier hush of its shooting and fishing days), the Baskervilles had been a favourite of the Kreitmans and the Merriweathers during that brief opportunity for liberty which comes between courtship and children.

Kreitman was still the idealistic historian of English radicalism in those days, and not yet the luggage baron of south London, else he would have shown up at the Baskervilles for his first ever walking holiday on Dartmoor – if truth be told, his first ever walking holiday *anywhere* – accoutred in rucksacks and map holders and water bottles and walking sticks all finished with the softest leathers. As it was, he arrived looking smarter by a country mile than any of them, though he never got to walk a country mile because of the weather. 'I don't care what these boots are built to do,' he told Hazel, 'they're brand new and I'm not going out and putting them in puddles.' So he sat in the lounge and read *Country Life* and played with the odd jigsaw while the others experienced the exhilaration of rocky landscape and teeming rain. Come night-time he was the only one with energy and didn't want to hear that they'd seen eagles. 'Please, I'm exhausted,' Hazel said, 'I can't even bend my knees.' But no day was a holiday for the young Kreitman that didn't end in a fuck. Lying in the stag-wallpapered room next door, the two Charlies listened as Kreitman ground his will out pleasurelessly and Hazel uttered not a sound.

This trip Kreitman wasn't taking walking boots. By now he knew himself. It was a hot early May, an oasis of hot in a month of showers, too tiring for walking – it was always either too hot or too wet, too misty or too glaring, for walking on Dartmoor – and he had his heart set, since he'd been ordered to turn off that nicely purring engine of his, on sinking into a winged armchair in the mini-palm-court lounge, reading newspapers, smiling at lesbians, consuming pots of tea and anchovy sandwiches, thinking his thoughts and, so long as Hazel kept her distance, ringing up the other women in his life. There was, as Charlie had surmised, though he had overestimated the heat, a fair amount of ringing up and putting right to do. A man actively in love with five women can't just disappear on holiday when the fancy takes him. Leaving the shops was easier. He had managers and manageresses to tend the shops. But nobody tends your mistresses when you're not there to see to them yourself. Mistresses? Hardly. That wasn't the tone of the times. He was more their mistress than they were his. It entailed duties, anyway, whatever it was all called. So he'd said no to the idea of a break at first. 'I've got responsibilities,' he told his doctor. 'I've got matters I can't leave,' he said to Hazel. But two days after his night on the town with Charlie, though his collision with the cyclist had barely left a scratch on him, just a few throbbing aches in the ribs, he fell asleep at his desk in the middle of the afternoon and missed an appointment. He was dead tired, he had to admit that to himself. And among the things he was dead tired of were the women.

Number itself wasn't the problem. Of course you had to organise your time intelligently if you weren't to end up with angry women all over town. But Kreitman employed a driver to help him get around, a discreet semi-liveried Kenyan who laughed at everything and for whom Kreitman had provided a ruby-red Smart, manoeuvring and parking being of the essence. And of course lightness of touch – for what could be lighter than a laughing chauffeur with leather patches on his navy polo neck driving a car the size of a bedbug? Men like Charlie who were driven nuts by the fewness of women in their lives were wont to scrutinise Kreitman's face for signs that he was on overload. 'Sheesh, Marvin!' they would say, shaking their heads, meaning, 'Can't you see they're destroying you, man?' Wishful thinking. Confining himself (and his driver) to those parts of London where he already had business to attend to, he could have coped with any number. What was tiring in five was what was tiring in two – the pity you expended.

Actively love two women, attend to them as you are able only when you're fucking them (fucking *with* them, Kreitman tried to remember to think, in deference to his own daughters) – though the truth of it was that they were fucking him, using him like some tart they'd picked up on a street corner in Streatham, for that was the way of it between the sexes now – actively *love* two women, anyway, the sociology of it apart, and you are forever adjudicating between the hands life has dealt them. Lying with Erica, whose skin seemed made of Christmas-cracker crêpe, so quiveringly taut and percussive was it, he would suddenly experience a revulsion on behalf of Vanessa, who each day collected another purply bump on her shins and thighs, not a bruise, though of course a woman of her age walked into more table edges than Erica did, but marks of inner deterioration, signs that veins were popping with overuse and blood forgetting where to flow. Too cruel that such was the reward, in Erica's case, for lolling on couches half the day, reading *Homes and Gardens*, while Vanessa's blue-black bumps were all the thanks she got for having racked her brains in the service of *Book at Bedtime* before succumbing to the BBC's unspoken horror of the un-young, collecting her pay dirt, and turning herself into a teacher of the intellectually impaired. Not fair, either, that the lucky one should have rocked him sensuously in the cradle of inconsequence, and given him sweet dreams, while the solemn one left him agitated, tingling to his fingertips with purposiveness, unable to find rest. By sleeping with them both, Kreitman brought them into moral juxtaposition and felt the universal unfairness of things on their behalf.

Unlikely that these revulsions from beauty and good fortune helped those who had neither, but they deepened the picture. To the simple pleasure which being fucked by women who were beautiful and exuded confidence gave him, he now had to add the complicating fact of his betraying them in his heart. And it was the pressure of this constant ethical refereeing, combined with the conviction that such conscientiousness was enjoined upon him by the amount of fucking he was doing, as though sex were like inherited wealth, entailing greater social responsibilities the more of it you had – it was this that was knocking him out.

Not a cheerful fucker at the best of times, he was now grown heartsore. He seemed overburdened, a bearer of grievous history, an implanter of sorrows, rather than the fun, gag-a-minute guy – lightsome Kreitman – he would have liked to have been.

Take what had happened with Bernadette only the night before the drive to Devon. Ten years his senior, Bernadette was an architect with a deep voice, fearsome cheekbones and a strict manner, the kind of woman you saw from a distance and felt immediately reprimanded by, a woman you put up scaffolds to approach and ascended gingerly, in a harness and a hard hat. Circumstances had taken a swing at Bernadette – the lover before Kreitman pinning a letter to her drawing board saying he couldn't bear seeing her beauty succumb to age and so was running off with her youngest daughter, take it the right way, Geoffrey. Taking it the wrong way, Bernadette had rung Kreitman, who, as the husband of the woman who employed her ex-daughter-in-law to redesign her house, she had once or twice encountered at dinner parties. 'My daughter's fucked off with my lover,' she told him, 'and since she doesn't herself have a lover off with whom I can fuck in return, I thought I'd try some other woman's man. Are you busy?'

Kreitman loved fucking her because *she*, even more than all the others, over and above what the times insisted on, fucked *him*. Ironically and with her steel-grey eyes wide open, waiting for him to make her laugh. That was all she wanted from him, exactly what he'd wanted from his father – jokes, anecdotes, messages from the breathing world, the blacker the better. Any sign of his losing himself on her breast or otherwise thinking about ecstasy and she stopped moving. Sometimes, before visiting her, he'd have to go cap in hand to his own staff, to beg for the latest joke. It was like feeding a monster. Entertain her harshly and she was his. Bore her with sweet talk and she'd be gone. Then, the night before Devon, he lost her in the bed. Simply couldn't find her. Called her name and she didn't answer. Nothing on the pillow. Nothing under the duvet. When he pulled all the bedclothes back, there she was at the bottom of the mattress, flattened like her own shadow, extruded as though flayed and thrown away and only the outer skin of her remaining. 'What are you doing?' he said. 'Where've you gone?' She didn't know what he was talking about. 'I'm lying here waiting for you to amuse me,' she said. 'But you've made yourself vanish,' he said. 'It's too upsetting, seeing you do that.' She sat up with her knees against her chest and lit a cigarette. 'I think it's time we took a rain check, Marvin,' she said. 'I think you're getting a trifle tragic for me.'

He was.

Looking forward to the rest, he was disappointed, when they checked in to the Baskervilles, to discover that Hazel had planned him a surprise. This weekend the hotel book club was addressing the subject of children's literature as adult literature, and in attendance to address it with them were the C. C. Merriweathers, Charlie J. and Charlie K. So for the Merriweathers and the Kreitmans (when the Merriweathers weren't discussing their craft) – this was Hazel's cute, recuperative idea – it would be a little bit like old times.

That was the first part of the surprise.

The second part of the surprise concerned Nyman. Guess what? He was here too.

'So tell me about yourself,' Kreitman said over dinner. 'I missed out on the introductions and the breakfasts. What do you do when you're not biking urgent deliveries around Soho?'

Sitting on his hands, Charlie Merriweather gave thanks that Kreitman hadn't asked him what he did when he wasn't being a faggot.

What everybody found personable about Nyman was his absence of personality. Nyman too found this personable about himself. 'There is nothing to tell,' he said. 'And I don't even deliver packages any more. I only pretend to do that.'

'To make yourself interesting?' Kreitman wondered.

But killingness was wasted on Nyman who had long ago embarked upon the course of killing himself. Finding if he had a self first, then killing it. 'Exactly so,' he said. He had a round blank floury face, the texture of one of Charlie's baps, but angled to look sad, like a white-faced clown's. And a small, perfectly circular mouth, shaped as though to receive slender rolled-up magazines, the *Spectator* or the *New Statesman*.

'Then tell us all some of the other things you do to make yourself interesting,' Kreitman persisted.

'Well, for example,' Nyman said, 'I can bend my thumbs to meet my wrist.'

'Show us,' Kreitman said. Then, when Nyman had showed them, 'And is there anything else?'

'Well, for example,' Nyman said, 'I can make my eyes squeak.'

'I don't think we want to see that,' Hazel said.

'Oh, I don't know,' Kreitman corrected her.

So Nyman put his knuckles in the sockets of his eyes, and ground them until they squeaked.

Chas and Hazel looked away.

'That it?' Kreitman enquired.

'Well, for another example,' Nyman said, 'I have bicycled down here.'

Chas gasped. 'You've cycled here from London?'

Hazel also gasped. 'Today?'

'No, I left first thing yesterday morning. Last night I slept under a ditch . . .'

'*In* a ditch,' Kreitman corrected him, 'or *under* a hedge.'

Because he had had less opportunity to talk to Nyman than the others, Kreitman continued to work on the assumption that he was German. That was why he took the liberty of correcting his English. Kreitman regularly attended trade fairs in Germany, Germans having an atavistic love of leather – *echt leder*, how could you put it better? – and he knew that Teutonic longings to overmaster the English persisted, also atavistically, in a dream of mastery of the English language. Help them with idiomatic expression and they would spare your family. But there was every possibility that Nyman wasn't German at all. Not even foreign.

Just foreign to the English tongue.

'Yes, under a hedge. Then I began again early, with the birds, and got here as you see me now.'

'You must be whacked,' Hazel said.

'Well, I am pumped, certainly,' he said, rolling up a trouser leg and inviting Hazel to inspect his calf muscle.

Fluttering her hands like a princess about to feel her first frog, Hazel bent and made a stab at Nyman's muscle. 'I should say so,' she laughed, her voice ringing with little girlish bells, as though still not sure whether pond life agreed with her. 'Pumped's the word!'

You can tell, thought Chas, that she has never nursed a boy child.

Some instinct for propriety had told Nyman not to come to dinner, nor to come near Kreitman at any time, wearing cycling gear. Instead he wore a crushed sandy suit, which went with his colouring, a crushed sandy shirt, a crushed sandy tie and sandy shoes. His general appearance was crushed, of course, as a consequence of being folded in a saddlebag for two whole days and one night under a ditch, but there was no questioning its muscular conformability.

Why is the little prick wearing camouflage on Dartmoor? Kreitman wondered.

How variously he dresses, Hazel thought, remembering the elasticated green lunchbox shorts and sleeveless thunder and lightning cycling vest he had on when she first met him. How nice it is to see a man prepared to experiment with his appearance, unlike Marvin with his invariable sharp suits, declaring this is the man I am, this is the man I am, this is the man I am. How pliant and gender-undemonstrative Nyman is, for a man with so hard a body, and how he starts when I look at him.

How she starts when he looks at her, Chas noticed. Yet how pointedly he averts his eyes from mine. What is it he wants me to see he doesn't want from me? Alternatively, what doesn't he want me to see he *does* want from me?

Chas was wearing a Butler and Wilson dragonfly on the lapel of her jacket. From time to time she fingered it, changing its position so that it might catch the light and maybe dazzle him. And did he dazzle her? Of course not. No man could be less dazzling than Nyman. He did not emit light, he absorbed it. He was a black hole, and by the magic of physics, all sources of light sought their extinction in him.

A mystery to Kreitman, this, even as the blackness drew him to it. Kreitman was of the generation that believed you had to be brilliant to win a woman's attention, that you had to sparkle conversationally, that you had to make wisdom fall from your lips like rubies, while your eyes danced like showers of falling stars. You laboured at your coruscations and the woman was the reward. He could not conceive that a woman might find attractive what *she* had to labour to win.

Flash, flash, went Chas's glittering dragonfly.

Of the group, only Charlie was incurious about Nyman. But then Charlie had his mind on other things. From where he sat there was a view through the hotel window of one of those warty tors for which Dartmoor is famous. He wasn't sure whether he could see people on the tor, or merely sheep, but the distant prospect made him melancholy. Distant prospects always did that for Charlie, especially when they were of tors and the tors were pink-tipped by the sun, like the nipples on a flat-chested girl stretched out on a beach or, more melancholy still, asleep in a summer meadow buzzed by flies. He gazed out of the window absently, tying his linen napkin into love knots, unaware of Nyman.

Unaware of Hazel too, it appeared, though it might reasonably be supposed, given the time he'd spent trying to raise and remind Kreitman of this last week, that his absent-minded love knot was for her. But Charlie wasn't counting his chickens. For the time being it was some lovely glorious nippled nothing he was seeing. Miss Cuntalina Fuckleton.

'But apart from cycling,' Kreitman persisted with Nyman, 'what is it you want from life? Presumably there isn't much of a living in cycling . . .'

'My husband is always curious to know what there is or there isn't much of a living in,' Hazel interrupted.

'I see,' said Nyman. 'A businessman.'

'A captain of industry no less,' Hazel said. 'The luggage baron of south London.'

'Your husband has a title?' Nyman marvelled.

'They say his father was a king,' Chas threw in.

Kreitman bridled. No one in Charlotte Juniper's family had ever worked a market stall. They had survived genteelly, on charity when necessary, for however many hundreds of years, but no stain of any market stall to darken their good name. 'Who am I dining out with here,' Kreitman asked, 'the Tunbridge Wells chapter of the Communist Party? I am making small talk. I am asking Nyman what he wants from life.'

'Marvin's idea of small talk,' Chas threw in again – '"And how do you explain creation, young man?"'

To her enormous satisfaction, Nyman laughed. A curious ripple that ran up his chest and shook his shoulders, before dying in his face. She wasn't sure, but wasn't this, in their company at least, Nyman's first ever laugh? Discovering that she could coax a sound, or at least a sight, suggestive of mirth out of a person as ruthlessly mysterious, and therefore mirthless, as Nyman heated Chas's blood. It was a joy comparable to gardening, like watering a parched bed and watching the flowers open. In her excitement, she danced her dragonfly and watched it disappear into the colourless immensity which was Nyman.

For no reason she could put a name to, Hazel dropped her napkin and while retrieving it accidentally effected a second graze of Nyman's well-pumped calf.

The quick look Nyman shot her – two pale points of Arctic light – was perceived by Chas at the very moment it was perceived by Kreitman, who believed he noted a similar roundelay of exchanges beginning with Hazel and ending he wasn't certain where. Only Charlie remained outside the circle of infatuation.

'Somehow, in all this merriment,' Kreitman said, 'my question has been lost. I suspect you're going to tell me you're an artist. Everybody seems to be an artist at the moment, all our children, all our wives. The only person I know who isn't an artist is me, though even I sometimes design a handbag or a suitcase with something approaching artistry, let my daughter insist all she likes that artistry is not to be confused with artisanship. But if you are an artist, please don't tell me that the art you make is yourself.'

'No,' said Nyman, 'the art I make is not myself. I do not have a self.'

'So I understand,' said Kreitman, 'though to me you have a very distinct self – I still feel the bruises from it. But you are, then, an artist? Do you blaze a trail or do you leave a path?'

'Jesus, Marvin!' Hazel said. Then to Nyman she added, 'You are not obliged to be interrogated, you know.'

'Unless you happen to enjoy it,' Chas said, putting her face on a slant, as though the world of abstruse enjoyments were her oyster.

'No, it's all right,' Nyman said. And that was when Kreitman noticed he was being aped, that Nyman was twirling his wine glass between his fingers exactly as Kreitman twirled his, and that he was making a fist of his other hand, rubbing it absently into the tablecloth, as though kneading dough, as though killing dough, again as Kreitman did. Kreitman's rigid fist was infamous among his women, each of whom began by hoping she would be the one to get him to open his fingers and release his murderous grip on himself. Now he could see what it looked like and why, as a discrete object, like some tiny meteorite humming with unearthly tension, it upset those who had to eat and drink in its vicinity. But what was Nyman up to? Was he making merry with Kreitman's mannerisms? Was he learning what Kreitman was with a view to doing him some damage? Or was he just being Kreitman because Kreitman was a good thing to be? Had the little cocksucker chosen to admire him suddenly?

Whatever the answer to those questions, Kreitman found himself wanting to go on holding Nyman's attention and winning his approval. If the boy had a yen to be like him he wasn't going to be dog in the manger about it – he would *show* the boy how to be like him. The first consequence of which was that he was unable to remember how his own voice worked naturally and started to shout.

'Shush,' Hazel said. 'They don't want to hear you at the far end of the room.'

'You don't know that. They might very well want to hear me at the far end of the room,' Kreitman boomed again. And he twinkled at Nyman who, for a black hole, made a pretty good fist, since we are talking fists, of twinkling back.

Over coffee in the lounge, for the Baskervilles remained one of those hotels that could not bear to serve coffee to its patrons until they were seated too low down to drink it comfortably, Nyman finally told them what he wanted out of life. He wanted to be on television.

A moment or two of silence greeted this revelation. All of their children wanted to be on television. Sardonic as a matter of generational principle though their children were, and doubly sardonic when it came to television, they had no other medium for appraising worth, and no other measure for knowing whether or not a thing existed. If it didn't flicker it didn't count. But until now neither the Kreitmans nor the Merriweathers had quite thought of Nyman as being of their children's vocational kith and kin.

Then, 'You'd be good on television,' Hazel said.

'You think so?'

'Yes, yes I do. I think you'd make people sit up.'

'But then it's always possible,' Chas put in, 'that Nyman doesn't want to make people sit up. He might want to make people sit down. That's how we normally watch television.'

'My guess,' said Kreitman, 'is that Nyman wants to go on television to do neither. My guess is that Nyman wants to go on television simply to subvert the form. I think when Nyman says he wants to be on television he's taking the piss. *Nicht wahr*, Nyman?'

They waited, husband, wife and someone else's wife, for the stranger with no character or prospects to tell them who was right. Kreitman saw that Nyman was making a white-knuckled fist with the hand that wasn't raising the coffee cup, and felt confident. Hazel sank lower in her chair and showed Nyman her neck.

'I think I don't know yet what I want to do on television,' Nyman said. 'I think I just want to be on it.'

'Aha!' Kreitman said.

'I think I want to show that I am . . . What is the word?'

'A humorist,' Kreitman suggested.

Nyman shook his head. 'I believe I have no humour.'

'Palpable,' Chas tried. 'You want to go on television to materialise yourself. We all do.'

Nyman looked evenly at her, almost granting her what he had granted Hazel, those two pale points of distant Arctic light. '*Palpable* . . . That's not so bad.'

But Hazel had not yet had her go. 'A winner,' she said. 'I think you want to show that you can win.'

'Win at what?' Kreitman wanted to know.

'It doesn't matter,' Hazel said. 'Specific achievement is out. You're so stuck in the past, Marvin, with your winning at what. With television you win simply by being on it. You exceed the common.'

'And how do you do that?' Kreitman asked. 'By being even more common than everybody else?'

'It is not a sin,' Hazel replied with heat, 'to be unexceptional.'

'Thank you, Hazel,' Nyman said. 'You have found my word. I want to go on television to show that I am exceptionally unexceptional.' He was so pleased he actually clapped his hands together like a seal. 'It is you, Hazel,' he continued, letting his blank barm-bun stare, with its distant snowy reflections, last long upon her, 'who understands me best.'

At this, Chas did something which no one who was watching had ever seen her, or come to that anyone else, do before. She threw up her canvas skirts. Outside of a Victorian novel, Kreitman thought, I have never *heard* of a woman throwing up her skirts. He tried to think of Peggotty, but it wasn't Peggotty Chas reminded him off. It was someone more French.

Realising how her action could be misconstrued, Chas affected to be worrying about crumbs, and exaggeratedly shook herself out. But a raised skirt is a raised skirt, and her cheeks blazed.

'And now can we play croquet on the lawn?' Nyman asked.

'Too late,' Kreitman said. 'Croquet is a daylight game.'

'Doesn't have to be,' said Hazel. 'There are floodlights.'

Kreitman closed his face as though closing a door. 'It's not a floodlit activity. You can't measure the distances right. The shadows interfere with your judgement. And with your safety. You'll end up cracking your shins, or cracking someone else's, with the mallet. And anyway, the lawn will be starting to get dewy. The balls will skid.'

'How good it is,' Hazel said, 'to be married to an authority.'

But instead of edging her one of his glances of blank complicity, Nyman suddenly turned to Charlie. 'Charles,' he said, 'I think of you as the authority on all things English – what do you think? Is it your opinion that croquet is out of the question?'

And had Kreitman been wearing skirts himself, he too might well have flung them over his head.

'So what's this all about?' Kreitman asked.

They were lying on their backs in their separate beds, like a lately deceased Pharaoh and his queen, waiting to be embalmed.

'What's all what about?'

'Come on, Hazel. It's called Nyman. What's it about?'

'You mind your affairs, Marvin, I'll mind mine.'

'It's an affair now, is it? You only met him a week ago, isn't that a bit soon?'

'We don't discuss these things, Marvin. Your rule.'

'If you don't want the boy discussed then you shouldn't have brought him here. *Your* rule.'

'What is it about him you want to discuss? The way you've been trying to woo him all night.'

'Woo Nyman, me? Why would I do that?'

'Because you're a wooer, Marvin. Because you have no choice. People have to notice you, be fascinated by you, then love you. Women, preferably. But if no new woman happens to be present, you'll make do with something else. It's the way you operate.'

'Not with Nyman it's not,' Marvin said. 'You're lucky I'm civil to him. The faggot put me into hospital, in case you've forgotten.' He was staring at the ceiling from which, if he could trust his memory, a dusty chandelier used to hang. Now it was downlighting. Twenty years ago they made hay in a four-poster. Now mummified in twin beds.

Hazel got out of hers and went to the window. She was wearing a straight white Victorian shift she had bought in an antique shop. Shapeless and innocent, with lace on the sleeves. Kreitman noticed her feet, like a little girl's. From his experience it was an unvarying truth about women – even the oldest of them had feet like a little girl's. It was the one part of them, at least that you could see, that stayed young. No wonder he was upset all the time. The more you had to do with women the more sadness you encountered.

Once upon a time I could have gone over to her, Kreitman thought, and slid my hands around her through the sleeves of her nightgown, and she would have leaned back into me with all her weight, utterly trusting. He had loved that, the trust, the weight of her, and the way her leaning into him raised her breasts infinitessimally, their undersides softer than peeled fruit. Brand new skin, never before touched, never before seen.

How long now since he'd touched or seen?

She stood at the window, looking out in silence. Moonlight on the moor, Kreitman thought. She is probably thinking what I'm thinking. How long it's been. How much we've lost. But what he didn't know was that she was watching Nyman crouching on the lawn, inspecting the croquet hoops, and the Merriweathers bent over him, presumably explaining the rules.

'You'll get cold,' he said.

'It's not in the slightest bit cold,' she said.

Then he noticed she was crying. Dry tears, not sobs, the dry tears every faithless husband fears he is the reason for. I have dried up even her accesses to sorrow, the swine I am.

'Why can't I ?' she said. 'Why can't I ever?'

Kreitman's ears pricked. 'Why can't you what?'

She wasn't really talking to him. 'Why can't *I* ever have what *I* want? Always so hard, always so much soul-searching, always such a fuss. This to consider, that to consider. What the girls would think. What you would think, as though I'm obliged to care a tinker's damn what you would think. Why can't I be more like you? Want something? Take something. A click of the fingers – Here, you!'

'Here who?'

'Why do you think I can't do it, Marvin? Why do *you* think I can't take him, have him and be done with him, Kreitman-style?'

If it wasn't cold, why was he cold? 'Why can't you have whom?'

'*Whom*! Don't *whom* me, Marvin. You know perfectly fucking well *whom*. Why can't I fuck him without you fucking with my head? Why do you have to have an attitude? Why do you always have to be there? I've kept out of your way, why can't you keep out of mine?'

'Hazel, you brought me here. You organised this.'

Outside on the lawn, Chas was standing closer to Nyman than the rules of croquet, let alone the etiquette of explaining the rules of croquet, demanded. Hazel turned from the window and showed her husband her distraught face, furrowed with tears which wouldn't flow. 'I'm not crying for the reason you think I'm crying,' she said. 'I'm crying because it's so demeaning to be back feeling all this again.'

'It's so demeaning to be back feeling what?' (Tell me, tell me.)

'It's so not what I wanted.'

'Then stop feeling it,' Kreitman said.

For a moment he thought she might come over to him and hit him. 'How dare you say that to me!' she hissed. 'How dare you, of all people, make it sound so blithe – you who have never denied yourself a feeling in your life. Except the feeling of loyalty.'

He withdrew his face, as though frightened for it. But he couldn't withdraw himself. Too interested. Too interesting, all this. 'Then if you want to fuck him, fuck him,' he said.

My fault, Hazel thought, my own stupid fault for introducing the fuck word. Introduce the fuck word to my husband and he'll shake its fucking hand off.

'Don't!' she said.

'Don't what?'

'Just don't! The spectacle of you putting your mind to the rights and wrongs of anything is too horrible to contemplate. I'm ashamed to be married to you. *If you want to fuck him, fuck him.* Where did you pick up your code of ethics, Marvin – in a cat house?'

'Do you think you might be a little bit in love with him?'

'Stop it, Marvin!'

He began to cry himself, the full waterworks she remembered so well from the platform at Paddington, and after that every station you could name. She knew what they were worth. She could price the downpour, tear by tear. Nothing was what they were worth. Not a farthing. But she was lonely and horrified by herself, to be feeling what she was feeling, to be at the mercy of all that old pestiferous stuff again – desire of so little consequence it made your stomach turn, but still, somehow, desire. 'Move over,' she said, 'and let me in.'

He folded her in his arms, surprised, as he had always been, by how small she could make herself. 'It's all right,' he said. 'It's OK.'

'It isn't OK,' she said.

He knew what she meant by that. A dread clutched his heart. When women who had loved you lay in your arms and said it wasn't OK it only ever meant one thing. It meant that they were in the grip of an uncontrollable longing for someone else. A melodramatist of sex, as are all dedicated adulterers and fornicators, Kreitman conceived such longing as a force so irrefutable and destructive that nothing could possibly survive it. Not duty, not home, not decency, not reason, not God, not him. The dread that clutched his heart was a foreboding of his own obliteration. No half measures for Kreitman, when it came to the gains and losses of sex. You won everything, you lost everything. What was marvellous was how alike those two extremes could be. Embracing his obliteration, shutting his ears to every sound except his lurching heartbeat, Kreitman felt desire for his would-be faithless wife race like poison through his body. 'How bad is it?' he whispered. 'How much do you want to fuck him?' At once, as though she were some washed-up shell creature, poked at by a callous boy, Hazel closed and went rigid in his arms. Kreitman knew what he had to do. He had to shut the fuck up. Not say another single fucking syllable. But he too was at the mercy of an ungovernable longing. 'Tell me,' he said.

'Speak to me. You can imagine I'm him, if it will make you feel better. Call me Nyman. I am your husband's enemy. Beg me to fuck you . . .'

And this time Hazel did hit him.

SEVEN

T HE FOLLOWING DAY, Kreitman sat in a metal chair – one of
thirty or forty arranged in book-club formation around the
Moriarty Room – and listened to the Merriweathers taking
questions from their fans. The usual: where do you get your ideas,
how do you find a publisher, how are you able to work together,
do you try your stories (sorry, *did* you try your stories) on your
own children, what would you like to be if you weren't writers.
Sour for all sorts of reasons, but at his sourest in the presence
of book readers and their providers, for he had imagined such a
life for himself once, touring the world discussing Francis Place
and the glory that was once the English mind, Kreitman allowed
his own mind to turn against his friends. *What would you like to
be if you weren't writers?* Excuse me – what the Merriweathers,
Charlie and Charlie, did was not write. Writers wrote for adults,
not for children. As for where they got their ideas – ha! The
Merriweather books did not contain ideas. Kreitman did not
know that for a fact. He hadn't read, properly *read*, any of the
Merriweather books. But he knew it as an intuition. He didn't
approve of children's books. He had not read children's books as
a child himself and to the degree that he had been allowed a say
in the matter he had not permitted his own children to read them.
What was wrong with *The Mill on the Floss*? What was wrong with
Jane Eyre? What was wrong with *A Tale of Two Cities*? What was
wrong with lying listening to Daddy telling you about himself?

If John Stuart Mill could be enjoying Herodotus in the original when he was three, Kreitman was not going to give his children *Thomas the Fucking Tank Engine*. It was sometimes put to him that John Stuart Mill suffered a nervous breakdown in later years, as though that negated the Herodotus, as though readers of *Thomas the Fucking Tank Engine* didn't also suffer nervous breakdowns. Nothing makes us sane, Kreitman believed, but some things make us smart. *Smart* – what a word of now! In his head he took it back. Not smart, intelligent. And that most definitely was *not* a word of now.

I am the sole guardian of the culture, Kreitman thought, and I sell purses.

An attentive observer will have noted some ambiguity in Kreitman's feelings about his friends the Merriweathers. As a professional couple at the soft end of the writing profession, and he a mere bagman, they kept open a number of doors to his idealised past which would otherwise have creaked closed. But Kreitman was a puritan who loved art for its strenuousness and history for the stories it told of struggle. Whatever came easy was of no value to Kreitman. And that that included fucking we already know. The problem with the Merriweathers, viewed solely as a couple now, considered only as a literary entity, was that they had neither struggled to find their *métier*, nor struggled *with* it once found. A niche opened for them and they fell into it. The same of course could be said for him, but in his case the casket of riches that fell open was not prized by the *Kultur*. The more money Kreitman made, the further into the background of the nation he felt himself recede. Money ruled, without doubt. The catch for Kreitman, though, was that the way you made it also ruled, and except in so far as it showed him in a picturesque costermonger light, the way he made his (dirty fingers, Kreitman) did him no favours precisely where a favour would have been appreciated. 'Ah, purses!' an academic philosopher with a boy's brow and a soldier's back had once repeated, meeting Kreitman on the Merriweather lawn, and the Thames flowing sweetly, and the blackbirds melodic, and the shadows lengthening. 'Ah, handbags and the like!' And he had remained with his pale hand to his cheek and his Mekon head thrown back in contemplation for so long, that Kreitman wondered whether his profession had turned the thinker to stone. His own fault for caring? Decidedly. No one knew that better than he did. But what could he do? He'd gone out and got *Kultur*, and for *Kultur* when it infects the un-*kultured* there is no known cure. With the Merriweathers, though, it all went, as it had always gone, swimmingly. He had not been able to imagine how the Charlies were going to survive leaving university. He remembered waving goodbye to them when they drove off on their honeymoon, immediately after graduating. To this day he could see their big unsheltered eyes receding, seeming to plead with him to call them back. It was like watching Adam and Eve leaving the Garden. It all but broke his squishy heart. But he had got it completely wrong. They weren't leaving the Garden at all, they were entering it. The one excluded from the Garden was him, Marvin Kreitman. Thereafter, there always seemed to be someone giving one or other of the Charlies something. This one bought them a house. That one bought them furniture. Another paid their first child's school fees. Not relatives, either. Not even friends, as far as Kreitman could make out. Just people. Folk. Personages of the *Kultur*. Until the Merriweathers in turn became personages of the *Kultur* themselves, ready to assist whoever came passing the hat round in the Garden next.

Some friend, that Kreitman! But what choice did he have? There was never an orphan yet who did not envy a big family. And the truth is, *he* would have bought them a house if no one else had. And furnished it for them. And paid for Timmy the Pierced, latterly of *Blind Date*, to go to Bedales. It was possible to feel concern for those you loved and to feel resentful of them at the same time. Possible? In Kreitman's estimation it was a universal law.

He slipped away from the book readers as soon as it was respectable to do so and took a stroll around the gardens. Sitting on a sun-bleached bench, she in linens, which he'd watched her steaming with her travel-steamer after silent breakfast, he in *heimat* urchin mountain pants cut off halfway down his legs, she animated, he not, she the watering can, he the flower, were Hazel and Nyman. Kreitman turned and walked the other way. Finding a bench of his own, he took out his mobile phone, scrolled through the names in his phone book, paused at one he fancied and punched OK. There was a time when Saturday imposed the most arduous obligations. On sofas and daybeds all over London, Kreitman's lovers pining for their prince. And he, with his pockets full of change (what would his mother have said!), darting into every phone box he could find. Oh, for a mobile phone in those days. Now he had the technology, the occasion for it was gone. Wasn't that always the way. Five numbers, and not a one of them was answering. Five women, and not a one of them was home.

No one on the planet more lonely than me, Kreitman thought. It wasn't self-pity, it was self-punishment. For Kreitman understood loneliness as a species of failure. It disgusted him to be alone. It showed him to be incompetent in the art of not being alone. It shamed him. It angered him. And he turned the anger on himself.

Crossing the lawn, oblivious of him, careless of the sun except as it illuminated each for the other, a young couple entwined, he in a loose short-sleeved shirt with his arm around her shoulder, she in a clinging strawberry-patterned summer frock, as undulant as the sea, with her arm around his waist. Be happy for them, Kreitman thought. Be happy for humanity, of which you are no less a part than they. Share with them. Share *in* them.

Fat chance of that. The fact was, other people's erotic happiness took from his. Their absorption in themselves excluded him. Which of course was exactly what it was meant to do. But that was no consolation. It was beyond reason and beyond cure, but he could not stroll through a garden, he could not cross the street, he could not enter one of his own shops, he could not wait at a carousel for his luggage or at a counter for a sandwich and see a woman with her hands on a man without the sight diminishing him. Talk was even worse. Conceal Kreitman where he might overhear dalliance or description, a woman declaring her love, a woman confiding her love, a woman no more than wondering if she might be in love, and let the lover not be him, not be Marvin Kreitman, and he would suffer convulsions of jealousy. What did that man have that Kreitman did not? What business had those women, anyway, falling in love with another man, *any* other man, before they had met him? He was in sexual competition with everybody, not only those he knew and had already challenged, but with men he had never seen and never would see, men already dead and men still waiting to be born, men who had no shape or appearance in his eyes, men whose age he could not guess and whose intentions he could not fathom, but who were vividly alive to him by virtue of nothing but their being the object of a girl's devotion.

All biological, no doubt. Kreitman's genes seeking their perpetuation to the exclusion of all others. But what did knowing *that* solve?

Mid-afternoon, a light rain falling, Charlie came looking for him. The two men met between pots of foliage, on the steps to the lounge. Afternoon teatime. 'Join me,' Kreitman said. Devonshire tea – jam, clotted cream, the works. Charlie bit the air, which Kreitman took to signal assent.

He had seen Charlie crossing the lawn to him and was struck by how deranged he looked, his mouth open and closing, yammering wordlessly like a madman. He was dressed peculiarly, too, in a heavy jacket with green and yellow squares, a ribbed cricket sweater and a scarf thrown around his neck. Winter towpath clothes, for Dartmoor in May.

'I see that something is the matter,' Kreitman said, pouring.

'I've beheaded the monster,' Charlie said.

'I don't know what you're talking about.'

'I've beheaded the monster guarding the labyrinth where my other selves are hidden. I'm free. The swap's ready.' Kreitman could hear his breathing.

'I thought we'd agreed to say no more about all that,' Kreitman said.

'Did we? I don't remember any agreement of the kind. I haven't agreed to stop anything.' His jaw was trembling. 'Are you chickening out on me now?'

'Charlie, there's nothing to chicken out on. We were pissed.'

'Oh yes there is. You get Chas, I get Hazel. You get to taste fidelity, I get to taste the opposite. That's what we agreed.'

'It's not my recollection that you were to get Hazel, Charlie. I thought we hadn't decided who you were getting.'

'Ah! So you *do* remember!'

Kreitman thought of Chas throwing up her skirts for Nyman. 'I remember that we behaved like clowns,' he said. 'But how come you've decided on Hazel suddenly? Because she's been slobbering up to Nyman?'

Charlie thought of Hazel, rooting under the table to steal a second marvel over Nyman's pumped-up calves. 'Everyone's been slobbering up to Nyman. *You've* been slobbering up to Nyman.'

'He seems to make one do that,' Kreitman agreed.

'Not me.'

'No, not you. But then your mind has been on other things.'

'And not yours? I've watched you, Marvin. I've watched you eyeing Chas. Well, now's your chance. She's ready.'

Kreitman laughed. 'You've prepared her for me, have you?'

'She's prepared herself. She'd do anything to pay me back.'

'For what, Charlie? For staying out late on a Friday night with me?'

'Nothing to do with you. To do with me. To do with me and women.'

Kreitman laughed at the incongruity of the phrase 'me and women' on Charlie's lips. Charlie as bastard. 'You're not telling me you've fucked Hazel already?'

Charlie's mouth started to move silently again. A diadem of sweat appeared from nowhere on his brow. 'Not Hazel,' he said. He wasn't eating anything, Kreitman noticed. Not rubbing his hands over the fruit scones. A bad sign. 'No. Not Hazel.'

Kreitman sat up in his chair and wiped all trace of Devonshire tea from his face. For what he was about to hear he wanted to look dignified. 'Then who, Charlie?'

'It's not who I've fucked, it's who I've propositioned for a fuck.'

Kreitman appeared to mull that over. 'Go on,' he said.

Charlie took a deep breath. 'I've been seeing Dotty,' he said.

'Dotty!' Now it was Kreitman's turn to yammer like a madman. 'Dotty! What do you mean you've been *seeing* Dotty? You didn't tell me you were *seeing* Dotty when we last talked.'

'You didn't tell me *you* were seeing her when we last talked.'

'I wasn't. I've taken her out to lunch once, for God's sake. That's it.'

'Me too. I took her out to lunch once – only that *wasn't* it.'

'Taking your wife's sister out to lunch isn't *seeing* her.'

'Maybe not. Why are we arguing over the meaning of *seeing*? Seeing her or not, I took her out to lunch and asked her to sleep with me. Do you want to correct me over the meaning of *sleep*?'

'You took your wife's sister out and asked her to sleep with you? I hope this was a very long time ago.'

'What difference when it was? But it was last week, if you want to know.'

'And she said no?'

'Of course she said no.'

'Then everything's all right,' he very nearly said. Good job Hazel wasn't there to hear him very nearly say that. *The spectacle of you putting your mind to the rights and the wrongs of anything, Marvin, is too horrible to contemplate.* He tried to do better. Everything wasn't all right. Not intelligent to proposition your wife's sister, and not nice, either. Not something you should do and not something you would want your wife to get to hear about. But then why should she get to hear about it? Good job Hazel wasn't there to hear him very nearly think that. Cat-house morality. But it was a conviction written into the lining of Kreitman's soul – a lie was always better for everyone than a confession. Better in the sense of more humane. Suddenly he remembered what Charlie had told him of his fear of guilt, lying like a garrulous third person in his marriage bed. 'Oh, Charlie,' he said, 'you haven't been owning up?'

Charlie shook his head. 'Hardly had the chance,' he said resentfully, a man for whom never being given the chance was the story of his life.

'Dotty told?'

'Not in so many words.'

'What does that mean?'

'Dotty didn't tell Chas. She told her under-age boyfriend.'

'And he told?'

Charlie nodded.

'The little shit. Never trust a reviewer, eh?' Both men pondered that truth, then Kreitman said, 'But hang on a minute. If Chas knows that you've been propositioning her sister, how come she's been behaving so calmly down here?' (Leaving aside the throwing up of her skirts.)

'She's only just found out.'

'The little shit rang her here to tell her?'

'Not exactly. The little shit sent a fax.'

'To the hotel?'

'No, to home.'

'But you're not at home.'

'No. But Kitty and Tim are.'

Kreitman covered his face. Through his fingers, he said. 'Oh, Charlie, no! Please don't tell me Tim and Kitty found it.'

Charlie nodded. Timmy Hyphen Smelly-Botty and Kitty-Litter Farnsbarns found it. The end of innocence. He kept nodding. The biggest, saddest nods Kreitman had ever seen. Kreitman rose from the table and put his arms round his friend's shoulders, squeezing them, then lowered his lips to Charlie's head. The hair was wet, smelling of trampled leaves and panic. How heavy his head is, Kreitman thought. How hard it must be, sometimes, for him to carry it.

'And Tim and Kitty,' he deduced, 'rang Chas? That was sweet of them. I wonder if mine would have acted with the same consideration.'

'They didn't actually. They rang me. But they must have rung while I was talking to the book club. They left a message warning me. Threatening me, too, I suppose. Warning me off. But giving me a chance. The trouble is . . . Chas always goes through my messages for me.'

Kreitman returned to his seat and made fists of his hands. 'Ah, the beauty,' he said, 'of a trusting marriage.'

Charlie looked at him. 'Not any more.'

The silence of the grave between them. Had the earth opened there and then, sucking down the table and all its tea things, neither would have been much surprised. Ruination comes quietly, picking off the china, emptying the mantelpiece first. Kreitman heard a clock ticking, which ten minutes before he would not have been able to tell you was in the room. He felt that universal sadness of the sentimental man, slightly bleary as though alcohol had played a part in it, but long anticipated and familiar, as though it were the fulfilment of the very fear with which one comes into the world. Here it is then, the distinguished thing. Or rather – for he had refamiliarised himself with the forestaste every time he waved goodbye to a woman he loved – here it is *again*. Was this all his fault? Had the example of his looseness, his loose tongue, destabilised Charlie? He felt guilty, too, that even as Charlie's children were leaving their fatal message on his phone, he, Kreitman, had been begrudging Charlie his life-pass to the Garden of Eden. Choke on your own bile, Kreitman, Kreitman thought.

'So, the coast is clear,' Charlie suddenly said.

Kreitman had forgotten that this was where they'd begun. Sex and death. Contemplating the destruction of his marriage, Charlie sought redemption through sperm. What a wonderful thing life is!

'Wait a bit,' Kreitman said.

'What for? Seize the hour, Marvin. I've beheaded the monster, I claim the maiden.'

Not a time for Kreitman to be saying he didn't care to be Chas's revenge on her husband, or that he did not desire her whatever the conditions. 'She'll come round,' he said. But he didn't believe it; some crimes against the marriage vows are capital.

'If you think that,' Charlie said, employing the logic of the insane, 'then just do the swap while I'm waiting. Just lend me Hazel.'

To tide you over, Kreitman thought. Among the other things he could not say was, Hazel isn't mine to lend, not mine in that she was never mine to *lend*, for God's sake, Charlie, not mine to give or lend, but also, simply, just not *mine*. Not now. Not any more.

'The bugger!' was what he said instead.

'The bugger what?'

'The bugger Nyman has got there before you, Charlie.'

Kreitman did not go down to dinner. He left the room when Hazel came in to change – left quickly and silently, before she could order him out – and returned once he was confident she had gone. Whatever was happening out there would not make for the sort of dinner party he enjoyed. He couldn't imagine the Merriweathers making a joint showing. Chas may well have driven home by now. Charlie may well have been lying at the bottom of a trout stream. At least he was dressed for it. Or, energised by death, propositioning one of the waitresses. Which left Nyman for Hazel to enjoy unhampered.

He lay on the bed and rang room service. Red wine was what he wanted, red wine as bloody as it came and a thick rare steak, also bleeding. The remote was broken so he had to get up to turn on the television. Shit on every channel. He watched a desolating programme about people who wanted to sing like other people, obscure people who imitated famous people, though he didn't know who the famous people were either. His daughters would have known. And Nyman of course. For wasn't that what Nyman was doing, first on his bike and now down here – impersonating some other person in the hope of been recognised for someone he wasn't? Stars In His Eyes. Dreaming of being famous for reminding people of someone else. Maybe right this minute Nyman was on a high being him, being Kreitman. Big mistake if he hoped thereby to make a favourable impression on Hazel.

But that wasn't his business.

He fell asleep watching shit and woke up only when his steak arrived. Not bloody enough. But then when ever was it? He ate it sitting up in bed anyway and polished off the wine. Then he got out of bed and turned off the television. Then he got back into bed and rang his mother.

Whenever he was at his lowest, Kreitman rang his mother. He had been doing that since he was small, ringing her from school, ringing her from camp, ringing her from Barcelona, ringing her from his honeymoon hotel, so that she should hear the melancholy in his voice. The blotting-paper effect, partly. You're my mother, suck up my sorrows. But more than that, Kreitman rang his mother when he was low in order to blame her.

Your fault! Nothing specific – she had done him no wrong, other than being his mother. But that seemed to be sufficient reason.

Your fault!

Kreitman admired his mother. He admired the way she kept herself youthful – black-haired and jingling like a gypsy still – and he admired the way she rose above her circumstances. Barely one year into her second marriage she found herself having to support an invalid. There was money over from husband number one, the bitter little key-fob thief who had been Kreitman's father, but she wasn't sure how much of that Kreitman was going to need (for he was still bound for Downing Street in those days), and it was important to her that what was left of husband number two should be cared for decently. Young Kreitman didn't believe it behoved him to look too closely into his mother's personal life, but he was of the opinion that she had fallen in love in a big way the second time around, even though the object of her devotion was a mouse-man called Norbert who found his fulfilment stamping books and refolding newspapers in a small public library in north London. A person of such quiet deliberation that you could hear the sound his pink-whorled fingers made when they touched a page – a soft, hypnotising, papery phttt which acted voluptuously on Mona Kreitman's nervous system – Norbert Bellwood was nature's refutation of Kreitman's father, the least dyspeptic, most unaggravated man on the planet. Where Kreitman Senior used to dash his food down as though he were getting rid of the remains of someone he'd murdered, the police hammering on his door, Norbert Bellwood ruminated on every morsel until it liquidised into his stomach without his even so much as swallowing. 'It's uncanny,' Mona Kreitman told her friends. 'No Rennies, no Gaviscon, and not a rumble in the night. He is the answer to my prayers. And you should hear him clean his teeth! Except you can't. He's like a ghost with an imaginary brush.' No need for anyone to call Quiet! in Norbert Bellwood's library. The unruliest children, the noisiest readers, felt Norbert's presence and fell silent. The only disturbance, the inking of his rubber stamp and his long gingery eyelashes fanning the air as he read. Even the stroke which made him an invalid and broke Mona Kreitman's – now Mona Bellwood's – heart came quietly. One minute he was at his desk calculating a fine, the next he was out on his back on the library carpet, looking up unseeing at a grubby bust of an old philanthropist of the borough. And nobody had heard him moan.

Enough of what Mona had found lovable in Norbert remained for her to want to make it supremely comfortable. A large garden for him. A heated pool for him. An aviary for him, for he had always loved the music small birds made. And to finance all this Mona Bellwood became a sort of bird herself – a vulture, hovering over the remains of the dead. Every community newspaper published in north London was delivered to her door, and no sooner was a family's sorrow announced than Mona Bellwood struck. Something her job taught her – something her marriage to Kreitman's father had taught her – people wanted the wardrobes of the deceased emptied quickly, unemotionally, without a word, and whoever came offering, in a van with its engine turning over outside the front door, was as though sent by God, however small the offer. Out of the house and good riddance before the tears dried, the old suits and dresses, the shoes, the handbags, the shirts, the ties, the furs, the whisky decanters and, more often than you would expect, the jewellery – most of it rubbish, but not all, never *all*. 'I could claim I perform a service,' Mona said, 'but it's a business. I do it for Norbert. Not that Norbert knows.'

Kreitman imagined Norbert in a second childhood not unlike Kreitman's first, excited by the takings, fascinated by the sight of the sand-crab notes creaking eerily apart. 'Why can't I count?' And Mona denying him, showing him how money filthies everything it touches, the palms of your hands, your fingertips. It crossed his mind, sometimes, that she was making not a sou out of raiding the houses of the dead, and was doing it only as a sort of penitence and abasement, seeking out and subjecting herself to the contamination, just so that Norbert shouldn't have to, even though there was no possibility now of Norbert doing anything. Sacrificing her immortal soul, dirtying it so that he could keep his clean. Just as she had done for Kreitman's.

Was he grateful to her for that? Yes and no. She'd been an example to him. Made him not a radical but at least a student of radicalism. Indirectly put him on to Francis Place. But he blamed her for it as well. Nothing had come of him and Francis Place. He had not known *how* to make anything come of it. Maybe if his mother had let him dirty himself he'd have grown up better equipped to live in a dirty world.

Her fault.

It wasn't all punitive. He wanted her to hear on the phone how bad he felt, but he didn't begrudge her feeling good on that account when the reason he felt bad was a woman. In that sense he was always going back to her, like a faithless lover returning to a forgiving wife, showing how little the infidelity had ever counted. But whereas the most forgiving wife would always insist on knowing why, if it counted so little, he had bothered in the first place – 'Then why do it, Marvin, why demean yourself and me?' – his mother was content just to have him home.

No one knew better than she did, after all, what refinement of feeling beat in his breast. She had taken him to the specialist when he fainted. She had told all her friends she had a son who was 'clinically sensitive', which was the next best thing to having a son who had won the Nobel Prize. And who was to say he wouldn't do that next? 'And this year's prize for Clinical Sensitivity goes to . . . Marvin Kreitman!'

Sometimes he felt that she was expecting his call, knew to the hour, maybe to the minute, when he would phone. Had he not inherited his sensitivity from her? When he was a boy she claimed powers of sympathetic prescience, a bodily intuition of his pains that was nothing short of supernatural. At the very moment Marvin took a tumble off his first pair of skates in Regent's Park, Mona Kreitman's knees went from under her as she was standing at the kitchen sink. The night he woke with burning tonsils on his honeymoon in Rome, Mona Kreitman fell out of bed clutching her throat. She knew when something was amiss with him, wherever he was. And that included romantic despondency, despair, satiation, boredom, even disgust. So she had a pretty good idea when the phone was going to ring.

'I'm in Dartmoor,' he told her.

'Tell me something I don't know,' she said.

'Ma, I bet you couldn't find Dartmoor on a map.'

'You're right. But what's that got to do with anything? Unless you want me to come and collect you. Then I'd find it on a map. Is this business, family or pleasure?'

'You are cynical, Mother. It's family.'

'Then I hope you're managing to have a good time.'

'I'm having a lousy time.'

'Well, you've always known how to have that. But Hazel likes it down there, doesn't she?'

Ah, yes. Hazel. Mona Bellwood was too subtle ever to risk an explicit criticism, but there hung over every conversation she had with her son an awareness, as fine as mist, of what might have been called the Hazel problem.

'God knows what Hazel likes,' Kreitman said. 'But you're right, she does enjoy it here. She believes the air agrees with her . . .'

An intake of breath and then a moment of silence, during which Mona Bellwood could be heard measuring the qualitative difference between her son's sensitivity and her daughter-in-law's. Egregious, the condition of Hazel's nerves; insufferable, how needy and on edge she was, the little mouse. Dartmoor! Air! What next – the pollen? But not a word, not a word.

'Well, just try to get a rest,' was all she said. 'We thought you looked tired when we saw you last.'

The 'we' constituted an unholy little bond between them. 'We' meant the women of the house, his mother and Norbert's nurse. 'We' acknowledged that she knew all about his affair with Shelley and, more than that, reminded him that she may have been the one who had promoted it in the first place.

Your mother, your pimp. Kreitman couldn't decide what he thought of this, ethically. When he was hers alone, his mother wouldn't have dreamed of putting him in the way of women. When he was hers alone, she filled his ears with dire warnings of the ruses of the other sex. They would say anything, do anything, to get him. And the first thing they would do was turn him against her, the best if not the only friend he had. 'If you really love me, you will rip out your mother's heart and bring it to me in a plastic bag.' And Kreitman, because he was a man, would do their bidding. 'No, Ma!' 'Yes, Marvin, yes, you will. You'll see. You'll see how they'll make you dance.' But after Hazel became his wife, the world, or at least that part of it which Mona inhabited, was suddenly filled with interesting, selfless, lovely women to whom she couldn't wait to introduce him. Sometimes, at a family get-together – a birthday party, a golden wedding, a funeral, it didn't matter, and it didn't matter either whether Hazel was in attendance or not – she would actually deliver some girl into his hands, go find her, go fetch her, lead her in by the wrist and hand her over clanking to her son, as though into captivity. Nah, have her, enjoy!

Should a mother do such things? Kreitman's ethical considerations were inevitably coloured by his sentimentality, but no, generally speaking a mother should not do such things, though in this instance the mother was mindful of the specifics of her charge – a clinically sensitive boy who had never enjoyed the advantages of a decent father, who worked hard to support his family, who had not quite fulfilled what had been expected of him, who was easily upset and influenced by women, who was married to one with frayed nerves (never mind who'd frayed them), and who was therefore exceptionally in need of recreation. So whatever came to him, as it were, gift-wrapped by his mother – here, have, take, don't make a fuss – he could hardly throw back in her face.

But when he was in depressed spirits this was one more thing he could ring her up and blame her for. Another fine mess you've got me into, Ma!

In this instance it pleased him to think of his mother and one of the women he loved discussing his health. If he existed primarily in the solicitudes of women, then he doubly existed when two of them were worrying about him together. And yes, they were right, he was looking tired.

'I've got this headache that won't go away,' he said, in corroboration.

'Where?'

'In my head, where do you think?'

'Don't be smart with your mother, Marvin. It matters in which part of your head you have it. Don't forget I know about headaches. Norbert began with headaches.'

'Well, this one's in every part of my head. It's vague. It's sort of all over. But listen, don't worry about it. I shouldn't have said anything. It's nothing. It's probably just a spiritual after-effect of the accident.'

Oops, the accident!

He had promised himself not to trouble her with that. Once upon a time he'd have rung her from the ambulance, let her hear the sirens at close range. 'Here, Ma, talk to the paramedic while he's pressing on my heart. What's that trickling sound? My blood, Ma, my blood ebbing away, what do you think it is!' But he was a grown man now, older than she was when he went to university, older than she was when he married Hazel even. And there are some things a grown man spares his mother, such as being knocked down in the middle of Soho by a crazed bicycling faggot-impersonator whom his wife must now reasonably be presumed to be fucking. His mother didn't need to know any of that, did she? And he didn't need to tell her. An impressive decision or what? And he'd done well. For eight whole days he hadn't breathed a word. Until oops, the accident. After which he had absolutely no choice but to spill the beans.

And with such immoderation of language and vehemence of feeling that anybody listening would have thought it was the poor woman's doing.

Which it was, really, for having set him on the road to seriousness.

Her fault.

When he next awoke it was dark. He looked at his watch. It was almost one in the morning. And Hazel not back. The light rain was still falling, but that hadn't deterred some mad fuckers from playing croquet. He heard the chock of the mallet on the ball. That queer colonial sound. Then whispering. Then another hollow chock. Not an urgent game, whoever was playing. Then nothing. He got up and went to the window, much as Hazel had the night before. And saw the watery outline of the moon above the moor, and saw the silhouette of a hermit's chapel on a tor, and saw Nyman leaning on his mallet with a stange expression on his floury face and his *heimat* pants down round his ankles. And on her knees, somewhat abstracted, like a washer woman rubbing shirts upon the pebbles in a river, or a half-hearted nun in her devotions, looking somewhere else, not Hazel, definitely not Hazel, unless the darkness were playing tricks on him, but Chas.

Chas? Chas of Charlie and Chas?

Chas.

Whereupon it all came back, an event of no special coloration in the aftermath, though surprising enough at the time, shoved away with other matters of little consequence or sin in the sock drawer of his marital memory. He and Chas of twenty years ago, on that very lawn, drunken, idle, irascible, impatient suddenly of the others, giving them the slip and larking about to the extent of his offering her his tongue, and her taking it. Taking his penis in her hand as well was her idea, her defiance, if you like, of him. Who cares . . . anything you can do . . . that sort of thing.

Had he enjoyed it? Had she? Had it *meant* anything?

God knows. Certainly it had never cropped up conversationally between them since. They hadn't alluded, hadn't colluded, hadn't smiled over it, hadn't fretted over it, hadn't worried that the other might blab or want more, hadn't anything. Wonderful, but there it is. In certain circumstances a woman might link her thumb and forefinger and make a hangman's noose around a perfect stranger's dick (for he might just as well have been a perfect stranger as far as contact of that kind was concerned) and neither of them think twice about the matter again, thereby reinforcing what Kreitman had always believed: that in itself the flesh of man and woman is entirely neutral, that neither morality nor magic inhere in it, until a decision is made to invest it with one or the other, or with both.

And since neither he nor she had invested the other's flesh with anything at all, nothing at all had happened.

In which case, why did the sight of her playing hangman with Nyman's penis affect him so powerfully? Sourness flooded into his throat, as though a bag of sherbet lemons had exploded in his stomach. That was how jealousy tasted, but what was he doing being jealous? Of all possible permutations of their little party, this was the very one, perhaps the only one, that should have left him cold. Chas and Nyman — what were Chas and Nyman to him? Come to that, what were Chas and Nyman to each other?

Here was the question, natural enough in the circumstances, that finally threw a bridge between curiosity and desire. Nyman was nothing to Chas, yet there she was on her knees kneading him. And he, Kreitman, was nothing to Chas, and yet there she'd been, on her knees — the tall woman's recourse — kneading *him*. He'd tried it on with her twenty years ago in a spirit of supreme male carelessness, and she'd matched him every inch of the way.

You don't care, I don't care. Nothing to you, nothing to me. In the mood for disconnected sex? Then let me show you just how disconnected sex can be.

Was that, then, why it had gone into the sock drawer – not because it hadn't counted but because *he* hadn't counted, and, thank you very much, he didn't care to recall that? Was Kreitman such a conventional Don Juan that he chose to remember only encounters that flattered him? No, that cannot be right, for Kreitman was a devotee of pain. A sexual insult to Marvin Kreitman was more rousing than any flattering come-on could ever be to men who like their pleasures straight. And Chas had insulted him, he saw that now. He had put it down to inexperience and forgotten about it because he couldn't afford not to forget about it. He was in love with Hazel. Charlie was his friend. There was nothing to be gained by his dwelling on Chas having out-bravado'd him one scratchy night on a manicured hotel lawn in Dartmoor. Better to call it gaucherie and have done.

Now, in the light of the queerly conventional scene being played out before him, he could mentally renegotiate what had passed between them. Yes, it hurt watching. Yes, it stung. Yes, he found himself dreading that the kneading would lead to something else, that Chas's lips would take over from Chas's tiring hands. Dreading, or hoping? Like rip-raps fizzing about a school playground, the sherbet lemons went on exploding in his gut. But then no one gets to renegotiate the past without paying for it.

Any third party knowing the players and observing them through a window must have felt some of what he felt. C. C. Merriweather – how could you! For sure, your husband has been out and about propositioning your sister, not to mention, did you but know it, bartering you for another man's wife, but even so, C. C., how *could* you touch that! Kreitman, though, was not merely experiencing that universal jealousy which assails sentimental men when they see a virtuous wife and mother throwing away her good name, whatever the provocation, on a wretch. No. Kreitman understood that Chas was playing a deeper game. She was returning feelinglessness for feelinglessness. Nyman in his ignorance may have thought he was picking up a handjob on the cheap; in fact he was having his characterlessness dismantled by an expert.

Kreitman knew. It had been done to him.

And now he wanted to see if he could dispossess Chas of her irony and make her love him for himself.

Nothing cold about that premeditation. Nothing of his daughter's calculated installations. And nothing of the elegantly symmetric quid pro quo urged by Chas's demented husband. Heated at the coolest of times, Kreitman's body exhaled its own silhouette upon the moor-chilled window of the hotel. Suddenly alive to every sexual rebuff Chas had delivered him over half a lifetime, including turning up her nose at purses and threatening him with the RSPCA, Kreitman burned with an old and yet pristine desire for her.

Nice sex?

Finally he was convinced. Nice sex? OK, he'd try some.

Only when he got back into bed and tossed aside the bedclothes did it occur to him to wonder where – since he could definitely locate Chas and Nyman – Charlie Merriweather and Hazel had got to.

Any fool could have given him the answer to that. They were in another county, on another coast, consoling each other for their several cruel rejections, entwined like unhappy children frightened of the dark, engaging in some nice sex of their own.

At least that's how it felt to Hazel.

For Charlie, on the other hand, it was wildness come at last.

BOOK II

ONE

CARNIVAL IN JERMYN Street.

The July sun shining, the cheese shops boisterous, the SALE signs up in every shirtmaker's window, and on the footpaths trestle tables behind which girls in regatta boaters, blouses striped gayer than a barber's pole, and skirts red enough to madden half the bulls in Pamplona, pour strawberried champagne for whoever has the time to stop.

Inside, clutching nine SALE shirts to his chest – three for one hundred pounds, nine for two hundred and seventy-five – Charlie Merriweather watches two shirt-sharp black Gatsbys snapping up phosphorescent ties – three for fifty. One of the men gathers the ties he wants in his fist, like flowers. The other drapes them over his arm, periodically pausing to inspect the colours, as though his aim is to complete the prismatic spectrum. Occasionally he shakes his head and puts a tie back on the rack. Charlie smiles at them over his shirts. He is a bit of a black man himself right now. Juiced up. Flamboyant. The lover of a woman who shows her legs, another man's wife whose nipples jab at her cardigan, an incontestable statement – *two* incontestable statements – that she is a woman roused.

Are nine shirts enough? More to the point, are they the right shirts? 'You'll buy your own,' she's told him. 'I'm not doing any of that mothering nonsense you've been used to. You'll choose your own, just stay away from purple and yellow stripes. You were never a member of the Conservative Cabinet and you've never looked after pigs. And see if you can find some ties that don't have regimental insignia on them.'

He can. Phosphorescent ties. The colour of blood and wine. Three for fifty, nine for one hundred and thirty-five.

They're dressing each other from scratch. She's got him out of farm clothes and he's buying her lingerie. Neither wants the other to own anything from before. It's like a rebirth for both of them. 'Take off the lot,' she told him the first time, in sight of the Porlock sea. 'And your wristwatch. And your wedding ring.' He'd never been more naked. He shivered. He wanted to cry, and wondered whether that would make him more naked still. He asked her permission. 'No, not tears,' she said. 'I don't like tears in men.' She wanted to cry herself, so long had it been since any man, clothed or naked, had trembled in her presence.

She touched his chest lightly. His skin was so tight she feared she might put a hole in him, pierce him and blow him apart. The poor man! She was careful only to lay the flats of her hands on him. Nothing sharp. Nothing sudden. And he pushed into the flatness of her hands like a dog, showing how trusting he was, and how grateful.

She imagined he would feel guilty when it was all over, reach for his clothes and jam himself back into his wedding ring. 'Oh, God, Chas!' she expected him to say. 'What have I done! My poor wife!' She had as good as kidnapped him, after all. Found him, after dinner – after a dinner from which Chas had for some reason excluded him, leaving just the two women to slurp soup in company with Nyman – bundled him into her car, not told him where they were going, because she had not known where they were going, just somewhere as far away as possible from a husband who disgusted her and a boy who was playing mind games with her and who disgusted her with herself. God knows, Charlie would have been within his rights to take what she was offering and then go into the usual male revulsion routine. Maybe she even hoped he would. Be guilty and be gone. In and out in the manner favoured by her husband. Not that she could imagine Kreitman ever saying, 'My poor wife!' But then come the event, neither did Charlie. Not a word of it. Could such a thing be? The phrase 'Poor Chas' hung in the air right enough – whether or not she had got her comeuppance for flirting like a mad thing with Nyman all evening – but strange to say the only person who was thinking it seemed to be Hazel!

Sisters under the skin, suddenly. 'Poor Chas!' Hypocritical of me, Hazel thought. But there you go. I have stolen your husband, I have betrayed our friendship, I have ruined your marriage . . . Whatever! Back to thinking about the man.

So much of what Charlie did and said was unfamiliar to her that she felt she had stumbled upon a hitherto undiscovered gender. He beamed, for one. Did men beam after sex? He glowed. He gave out light. He put his hands on her face and kissed her eyes. He told her she was lovely and that she'd saved his life. That was extreme, wasn't it? Then he leaned back on the pillows with his hands behind his head, the hairs under his arms soft and gingery – not wiry, not man-hard – and said, 'I can't tell you, I just can't tell you. I feel like a blind man who has had his sight restored.' Then he kissed her eyes a second time, told her he loved her – which was certainly extreme – and started to shiver and tremble again.

That was when she realised they might be able to do something for each other, beyond this one night.

You fool, Hazel, she thought. But hope swept through her like a fire and she didn't want to put it out.

When he moved in with her, a few days later, she burned all his clothes except for one outfit in which he could go out and re-wardrobe himself. They had a sacrificial bonfire on the lawn – stoking the flames – with the girls watching from their bedroom windows. Juliet put a finger to her brains and twisted it. Screwy. Cressida put two fingers to her brains and blew them out. But neither of those gestures, of course, was meant to be judgemental.

Charlie wanted to throw a reciprocal bonfire for her clothes, before Hazel explained it wasn't so simple for a woman. And anyway, some of *her* clothes were worth keeping. But she allowed him to do the new-underwear thing. That his taste turned out to be identical to her husband's didn't come as any shock to her. Underwear sorted the men from the boys, allowing that there *were* only boys. Charlie may have been of a hitherto undiscovered gender, but all genders have their young and Charlie was still a stripling. She said no to an ankle chain but otherwise went along with his wishes, whistling through her teeth (to keep up her courage) at the sight of herself trussed like a Christmas bird again. Do I look ridiculous? she wondered. Can I trust him to tell me if I look ridiculous? Does it matter?

The girls couldn't help her in this. The girls belonged to a generation that had skipped lingerie, leaving Hazel with the strange sensation that she had been a tarty piece twice over, and her daughters never at all. Then she remembered – her daughters had irony. You can have lingerie or you can have irony. It is not out of the question to wear lingerie ironically – over your clothes, for example, postmodernly, as a joke against itself – but something told her Charlie wouldn't have wanted that. Pleasing a man again, was she? Back to floaty? Hair soon to resume the halo of a startled lion's mane? She shook her head over what she saw in the mirror. The recidivist I am! Hopeless, I am a hopeless case. I have not learned a single lesson. I might as well be seventeen still.

But something was different. She racked her brains to find it. Happy, that was it – she was happy. Which meant that this time she could forgive herself. Leave herself alone. She was who she was. And she hadn't been who she was for a long time. Maybe she hadn't been who she really was *ever*. Careful, Hazel, she told herself. No fool like an old fool. But what could she do? She was happy. She had hope. And if hope makes a fool of us, then let us all be fools.

★　　★　　★

148

Deciding that twelve shirts will give him a better percentage chance of getting at least a couple right, Charlie Merriweather goes looking again for his collar size – double cuffs, long sleeves, no purple and yellow stripes – and all but knocks over Marvin Kreitman labouring under a dozen of his own. The two men open their mouths simultaneously, simultaneously flush scarlet and simultaneously turn away. Fuelled by champagne, a hysteria has gripped the shirt-buyers; they are not quite pulling garments from one another's hands, as the hair-netted harridans of popular culture did in the first great January sales of post-rationing Britain, but you don't dare take too long to make a decision, or you lose out. Who would have thought that men, with their philosophic indifference to goods, would become more obsessive sales addicts, more ferocious squirrellers and snatchers, than women ever were. Nothing to do with saving money, either. The sales just an excuse to acquire. What a gas! If we were still friends, Kreitman thinks, we would pretend to fight each other for our shirts; we would see the funny side of this. Charlie Merriweather thinks the same. But they are fighting each other for their wives, or they have fought each other for their wives, and though in a sense both might be said to have won, or at least to be winning, there is no funny side to it for either of them.

The swap has not worked out the way they wanted it?

Difficult to say, given that they wanted it differently, and that one of them believes he never really wanted it at all. And these are early days yet. They are both nursing tender shoots. They both *are* tender shoots. But having done the deed, having murdered their marriages where they slept, the two men have no more to say to each other in the aftermath than those who took a dagger to King Duncan.

On top of that, Kreitman is not amused to see Charlie Merriweather shopping where he has always shopped.

Bravado, again, of course. What Kreitman would like to do

is put his arms out and wind Charlie into them. But he doesn't know how to do that.

It is working out easier for Charlie and Hazel than for Marvin and the other Charlie. Perhaps Charlie and Hazel were always the needier, if only in the sense that they'd been growing the crazier – Charlie with sexual curiosity, Hazel with sexual grievance. And because they initiated what happened, taking what happened to date from the hour Hazel kidnapped Charlie from the grounds of the hotel, they are not the ones left looking, ever so slightly, the victims of event.

Over a funereal breakfast at the Baskervilles the morning after, Kreitman had put it to the remaining Charlie that charlies were what they'd been made to look.

She had shown him a steely face. 'He's been putting the hard word on my sister,' she'd said. 'What is more my children know about it. That's the unforgivable crime. Where he is now and who he's charvering is incidental. I don't care. I never want to speak to him again.'

'It might not be incidental to me,' Kreitman informed her. Then, so there should be no mistake, '*I* might care who he's charvering.'

Charvering? Not a word that came naturally to him. But then what did nature have to do with any of this?

Charlie laughed a bitter laugh. 'That'll be the day,' she said.

Kreitman sought her eyes and swallowed back his answer, as though to let her glimpse a corner of his caringness she knew nothing of. 'And you too,' he said, 'care more than you're pretending.'

She shook her head. 'No, I don't. A little silliness is one thing, asking Dotty for a fuck so publicly the whole of London knows about it, is another. I thought he was happy.'

'He was happy and he wasn't. Fidelity does that.'

'Your company does that.'

Kreitman touched her hand. 'Don't lay it on me, Charlie. I wasn't instrumental in this. It wells up every now and then, that's all. You can't stop it. It spills over. It isn't personal. You of all people should know that.'

'Me of all people?'

Too soon, Kreitman decided. 'I mean, you've seen it with Dotty. There just comes a time.'

'Then let him have his time with Hazel . . . if Hazel's the best he can do now that Dotty's knocked him back.'

Kreitman made a halt sign with his hand. Go no further, Chas.

She ignored the warning. 'This morning of all mornings, Marvin, you can't expect me to be respectful to that tub of lard you call your wife.'

'Chas!'

'Don't Chas me. A wronged woman has her rights. If Hazel wants him, let Hazel handle the spillage, that's what I'm saying. But he's much mistaken if he thinks he can come waddling back to me when his time's up. I no longer want him. You can tell him that when you next have one of your fourteen-hour lunches.'

How upset was she? How *cataclysmically* upset? Kreitman couldn't tell. She was furious − *that tub of lard you call your wife* was hardly calm or just, God knows. But then who's ever measured in their views of the trollop humping their husband? And she was fraught, though that could just as well have been the aftermath of the other thing. The thing that had kept him up half the night and her up he didn't know how much longer. Sex interfered with upset, he knew that. It skewed it temporarily. First, you have to have no sex, then you can think about being upset. First, she had to get the taste of Nyman's tongue out of her mouth, assuming it had got that far. But when she'd done *that*, how upset would she be?

'I don't believe you really think you can live without Charlie,' he said.

'Can't wait. Just watch me.'

'That's braggadocio.'

'Is it? I don't think so. He's been weird for so long it will be a relief. I always thought life without Charlie would be insupportable. But maybe what I was actually thinking was that life without me would be insupportable for him. Well, fuck him! Now I need to think about me. It wells up, Marvin, as you say. It spills over.'

Kreitman considered that. 'How will you write your books?' he wondered, after a decent interval of time.

She looked at the chandelier. 'Balls to our books!' she said.

Amen to that, Kreitman thought. Let's drink to that. Balls to all baby books!

'I think I've had it with collaborations, anyway,' she went on.

'It's served you well.'

'Depends how you measure. I don't feel well served. Anyway, the money's not in our sort of books any more. Lower-middle-class magic's back. '

Kreitman wasn't thinking about money or magic. 'Then again,' he persisted, 'you could always collaborate with someone else?'

'Oh, yes . . . ?' For a moment she wondered if he was thinking of himself. 'Who would that be?'

'The faggot.'

'What faggot?'

'Nyman.'

'Don't be absurd.'

'It's surely not that absurd. You've been collaborating with him fine for most of this weekend.'

She decided against putting marmalade on her toast. 'From you . . . From you, Marvin Kreitman,' she said, pointing her knife at him, 'I'd have expected better!'

'Better?'

She met his eyes. Hers viridiscent, a little like the burnish on a spring onion, a little the colour of cheese mould, his blacker than squashed berries, and too crooked, you would have thought, to see straight with. They both looked terrible, sleepless and bedraggled. Kreitman unshaven, in a collarless Hindu shirt that didn't suit him. Chas in something from Kathmandu, tighter than a pea pod, and with too many toggles. And clown's trousers. And woollen socks.

'I'd have expected you to be a little more sophisticated in the matter of a man and woman going for a midnight stroll,' she said.

A midnight stroll, was it? 'Well, you know what they say −' he said, although nobody he knew had ever said it − 'sophistication nips out the back door once jealousy enters through the front.'

She made a playground face. 'I'd like to see you jealous, Marvin Kreitman,' she said. 'I'd like to see you trying to work out which facial muscles to pull. I bet you wouldn't even know which colour to turn.'

'Green.'

'You've mugged up on it.'

'Not so. It came to me in the night.'

'While you were sitting up waiting for Hazel to return? Ha! Serves you right. I'd say good for her for getting her own back, if she didn't happen to be getting it back with my husband.'

'Nothing to do with Hazel. To do with you. I was at my window, playing gooseberry . . .'

She flushed, red on gold like a little fire in the hayrick. 'Marvin! You had the bad manners to watch?'

His turn now to make a playground face. Naughty Marvin. 'No choice,' he said.

'Of course you had a choice. You could have drawn the curtains.'

'And missed the moon on the moor?'

Still burning, she laughed. No, she essayed a laugh. 'You're a pervert.'

'I try to be. But it wasn't pervery. That's to say it wasn't *primarily* pervery.'

'What primarily was it?

'What do you think?'

'Idleness.'

'Nostalgia.'

She wouldn't rise to that. She wouldn't go that far back. One night at a time. 'It wells up,' was all she'd say.

'So how come he isn't breakfasting?'

Nyman? She shrugged. How should she know? Was she her lover's keeper? Not that Nyman was by any manner of means her lover. 'I suspect,' she said, 'that he left early. It's a long way to cycle.'

'You didn't spend the night together, then?' The minute he heard himself put the question, Kreitman realised how infantile the question was. No more baby books, but any amount of baby curiosity.

Charlie pushed her plate aside, put her elbows on the table and clasped her hands. She might have been interviewing him. 'Look,' she said, 'I am in some distress. I am not always responsible for what I do when I'm in distress. You of all people' – she made little quotation marks with her fingers – 'should know that.'

Kreitman inclined his head, baring his neck.

'I don't know why you're pretending to be jealous,' she went on, 'or even interested. You never have been before. But you too, I know, must be in distress. You'll pretend otherwise, but you must be. If you want to know about Nyman, I'll tell you. He happened on me at the wrong moment – wrong for me, right for him, you might say. Afterwards he asked if he could come back to my room. I told him I had a husband. He told me he thought I probably didn't. Then he told me he had no home to go to and asked if I'd put him up in Richmond for a while. I told him no. Then he asked if I would loan him money. I told him no. Then he asked me if I thought Hazel wanted him. I told him I had no idea. Then he asked me if I would mind if he went to Hazel. I told him he should check with Hazel's husband not with me. He said he thought she probably didn't have a husband either. I told him I didn't care what he thought or what he did. He told me he just wanted to be sure he wasn't hurting my feelings. Jesus, Marvin . . .' Here Charlie ran her fingers through her hair, as though all her vexations might be there and she couldn't wait to comb them out. 'Jesus Christ – your sex! '

'My sex? Nyman isn't *my* sex.'

She waved away his blustering. 'I'll tell you something, Marvin, he's more of what I understand by a man, more rattishly and motivationally a man, more stripped down to the bare bones of a man, than you and Charlie rolled together. Don't be insulted by that. It isn't so terrific to be a man.'

'Isn't it?' Kreitman wondered about that. Wasn't it? Maybe it wasn't. Then, not quite sequentially, he said, 'I thought he was a faggot.'

She shook her head, this time meaning to cause pain. 'He's not a faggot,' she said. 'Let me assure you, the one thing our friend Nyman is not, is a faggot.'

To the universally jealous Kreitman, the only person on the planet to have gone without contact with the opposite sex the night before, not counting his conversation with his mother, it was as though she had thrust her fingers in his eyes. He could see only blood, falling like rain blown against a window.

Charlie discovered the true depth of her upset when her husband turned up in Richmond after three days of being denuded of his wedding ring in Somerset and asked her to be happy for him retrospectively.

She was sitting at her old manual typewriter, at *their* table, pecking at the keys. She did not look up.

'Why should I be happy for you, Charlemagne? For shitting on our marriage?'

He was astonished she saw it like that. 'I haven't been shitting on our marriage,' he told her. 'I haven't been doing anything to our marriage. I've just been away from it for a while.'

'Doing what?'

What had he been doing? 'Having a sabbatical,' he said.

'You never wanted a sabbatical before.'

'I never needed a sabbatical before.'

'I see – we're talking needs, are we? Do you really think I'm the person you should be telling this to?'

'Who else? You're my best friend.'

'I'm not your best friend. I'm your wife.'

'It's possible to be both, Chas.'

'Is it? I doubt that. I think it's possible to be neither, but I doubt it's possible to be both. Not in the sense of being a wife *and* a best friend who is happy for you when you sleep with other women. I think you might do better with Dotty. She'd make a good best friend. Try talking to her about your needs – oh, sorry, you already have.'

Ah, Dotty. Charlie Merriweather had forgotten about Dotty.

'I was dying, Chas,' he told her. 'I was this close to being a dead man.'

Still refusing to look up, she missed seeing him measure with his fingers how far he'd been from being a dead man. But then nobody knew better than she did how close to being a dead man he remained.

This close.

She was curious about one thing, though. 'Tell me what you thought you were dying of, Charlie.'

He racked his brains. It wasn't that he didn't know. More that he didn't know how best to put it. For two pins, had circumstances been different, he'd have rung up Kreitman. Help me with this one, Marvin. You know women.

In the end, his belief that honesty was always the best policy prevailed. 'Nice sex,' he told her.

And that was when she began to cry, great wailing cries which he had no idea she had it in her to make, cries which were more like an animal's than a woman's, howls beyond the hurt or bafflement of the conscious mind, gasps and eructations of brute bodily pain, as though sealers who had already claimed her young ones were now unleashing their fury upon her with wooden clubs.

Had he done that? Just by taking his clothes off, staying away for a few days and giving himself a little leeway, had he caused *that*?

It was when she began banging her head on their table, on their old sacred space, dashing her own brains out now, hammering herself free of him, hammering him out of her skull, that he started to howl himself. Nothing compared to hers, even he could hear the difference. Mere schoolyard blubberings – cold, lonely, hungry, bullied, far from home. Help-me-mummy cries, uttered without the slightest expectation of success, because his mother had never helped anyone. But at least they quietened Chas. She caught her breath several times, made a fist and banged her chest, pushed her hands up under her chin, behind her ears, pressing into her head. That was where the pain was. There.

'Are you all right?' he asked her through his tears. 'Are you going to be all right?'

'Get out!' she shouted. 'I've wasted my life on you. You're a moron – get out!'

An hour later he brought her tea. She hadn't moved. 'I thought I'd told you,' she said.

An hour after that he brought her a brandy. She still hadn't moved. 'Do I have to plead with you?' she said. 'Give me back my life. Get out of the house.'

'Chassyboots,' he said, putting out his hand to touch her hair.

'Don't make me wish you were dead,' she said. 'Don't drive me to want to kill you.'

And that was when he moved in with Hazel.

★   ★   ★

Nothing comparably upsetting happened in Kennington. Far more civilised, the Kreitmans. Get the betrayals over early in a marriage and you spare yourself the seal-clubbing. Kreitman was out of his house, in all the essentials at least, before Hazel was back from her extra-marital escapade in the West Country. What more was there to discuss? Their marriage came to an end, what was left of it, on the night he vampired in on her distress and tried to sucker her into tell-me sex. 'Fuck me, Nyman' – that stuff either lands you the big prize or lands you in big trouble. No mistaking where it landed Kreitman. Never mind the punch on the nose; the coldness of Hazel's turned back was the coldness of finality. Kreitman was attuned to finality. He knew it from his mother's dismissal of his father, despatching all memory of him, along with his cut-glass decanters, in a matter of weeks.

He had never thought he would leave Hazel. The French windows open, butterflies on the lawn and Hazel at her piano – that had been how he'd seen his life, extending like a sunlit country road for miles and miles and miles, before vanishing off the edge of the world. Yet he had also known he would leave Hazel, because he foretold just as vividly the turning of her back. No scenes, no sad goodbyes – if there had to be goodbyes he'd never go – just a leaving of the house as on any other day, except that this time he would never return to it. Not his doing, her doing. Not what he wanted, what she wanted. He granted women this – the primacy of their desires. He just did what he was told.

But in truth he'd closed his own doors. Had he been able to summon a single rousing image of Hazel in the arms of Charlie he might have tried to salvage something. Not a nice way of gauging how much you did or didn't love somebody, but that was Kreitman. He was an incorrigible sentimentalist of anguish. Where there was jealousy there was life. And there was none. He couldn't put his imagination to work. He could see no picture.

He could hear no talk, not even talk derogatory of him. This was partly because he could not take Charlie seriously as a rival. Charlie of the putrid penis? Impossible. For all it excited or upset him, Hazel might as well have been sleeping with Donald Duck. Nyman on the other hand, Nyman of the putrid disposition, Nyman who was everywhere and nowhere, who was everything and nothing, Nyman had piqued him. Nyman he could think of as the enemy of his soul. How much that was to do with the faggot himself and how much to do with Hazel wanting a piece and Chas taking it was the big question. Whatever the answer, it was Chas who was on his mind now. *Exclusively* on his mind. For the first time since he could remember, for the first time since he was Cophetua to his mother's beggar-maid, he was down imaginatively to only one woman. And that meant being returned to the torments of only one woman, because he wasn't at all sure that Chas was feeling the same way about him.

He moved into the least formal of his convenience love nests, a narrow high-ceilinged would-be warehouse, the shape of an up-ended matchbox, above his shop on Clapham High Street, opposite a nightclub. The flats attached to his other shops were all copies of the Philippe Starck hotel rooms he'd stayed in on his buying trips around the world, places to fuck quickly and cleanly in; but this one, though hardly a home, at least reflected his unsatisfied temper, housed his books, his personal papers, the things that had no place in his marriage. It had been Hazel's suggestion, originally, that as he spent so much time away, physically and mentally somewhere else, he could do worse than fix himself up an office space to store the possessions it always made him melancholy to look at, the memoranda of the intellectual life he'd abandoned, the junk of the bachelor existence he'd sacrificed (the dartboards and snooker cues and flamenco records dating back to his first holiday in Spain), all of which was just cluttering up space she could put to better use. 'Think of it as a den,' she said. 'All men like a den, don't they?'

'Yes, but usually at the bottom of the garden. Not at the other end of London.'

She threw him a look, *the* look, meaning men who want to make sentimental noises about the bottoms of their gardens would do well to know where the bottoms of their gardens *are*.

And she reminded him that Clapham and Kennington were not exactly at opposite ends of London.

By the time he had stuffed it with what mattered to him – shelves of the writings of the English radicals going up into the girders and reachable only by ladders, box files containing his old lectures and lecture notes, an old sea chest holding letters from his mother, an antique shove-halfpenny board on mahogany legs, a wind-up record player for his 78s, all his curry spices and a collection of Jack Nicholson movies on video – there was scarcely room for a bed. He was pleased that he had put the bed last. It refuted something about him. In the end he had a mezzanine floor built which he festooned with rugs. That was the bed. Opulent but hard to get to. The ladders for his books were at least made of steel. The ladder to his bed was made of rope. And how did the varicosed mothers of the women he loved negotiate that? They didn't. Without knowing it while it was happening, he now realised he had been saving Clapham High Street. For whom? For Chas, of course.

In time she would climb up to his bed and he would hack off the rungs of the ladder behind her. And that would be that.

He had made no fuss about moving out. He had peered into Hazel's bedroom and cried. Then he had opened the lid of Hazel's piano stool – Chopin and Debussy, unplayed for however many years – and cried. Then he had taken a last look at Hazel's bag museum, everything strewn around malevolently, like some holy place that had been sacked by infidels, and this time cried long and seriously. Then he did whatever else he had to do. He left a note for Hazel telling her that she'd been right all along, that a den was the very thing he needed, and cheerio. She knew how to reach him. She wasn't in immediate need of anything. She had her own chequebook and credit cards. Her own car. Her own interests. And now her own lover. For his daughters too he left a note, saying he'd take them out to dinner as soon as he'd got his head straight. They'd understand that.

It didn't enter Kreitman's calculations that Charlie would actually interpret the terms of the swap (some swap!) quite so literally: take up residence in Kreitman's house, put his shirts in Kreitman's wardrobe, sleep in Kreitman's bed. When he thought about Hazel he thought of her as he'd known her, living the same life only with him not there. Not that different from before. He had no intention of padding pyjamaed up the Merriweather staircase himself, so Charlie's whereabouts vis-à-vis Chas was equally immaterial. He was somewhere. Who cared where. Kreitman was not going to buy into the domestic farce of dodging and being dodged. The situation was already indecorous enough by virtue of its symmetry. Some men are natural born swappers, some aren't. Kreitman wasn't. He lacked the mirth.

The same squeamishness told him to keep his distance from Chas in the first days after their grin-and-bear-it breakfast on Dartmoor. She had driven him back to London in her mobile picnic basket, neither of them speaking much, silenced by the amount of Charlie the vehicle contained – wellingtons, anoraks, walking sticks, Glyndebourne umbrellas, all the tramping-in-mud and sitting-on-damp-grass gear that had been the glue of the Merriweather marriage. But this would have been a time for quiet anyway. Kreitman had said what he'd needed to say. Shown Chas that she was able to hurt him. And she had shown him that hurting was something she might come to enjoy. Eventually. Anything further, for the time being, would have been unsubtle.

He rang her only twice in the first week, alluding to as little as possible, not even telling her that he had moved out of his house. The first call was no more than a polite thank-you for the lift and a discreet enquiry as to her spirits. Nothing knowing. Just was she all right.

Her voice was like a tall building in a high gale. She was fine. Why shouldn't she be?

'No reason,' Kreitman said.

'No reason other than that my husband has just come home asking me to be happy for him.'

Kreitman said nothing. Not even, 'And are you?'

'He tells me he's been on sabbatical. I don't suppose you've ever thought of Hazel as a sabbatical yourself.'

'No,' Kreitman said.

'No,' she jeered, extending the vowel so that it took in all the women Kreitman *had* thought of as a sabbatical.

Don't rise, Kreitman cautioned himself. Don't go near it. He wondered what else Charlie had told his wife. That he had swapped her for Hazel? That she was now obliged, by the terms of the deal, to do something nice for Marvin. Surely even Charlie knew the difference between a venial sin and a capital offence. 'You'll work it out,' was what he said.

'We *have* worked it out,' she told him. 'We've worked *him* out. He's gone.'

'What do you mean, he's gone?'

'Gone. Gone gone. I ordered the prick off the premises and he obligingly packed his bags and skedaddled.'

'I'm sorry,' Kreitman said. But he was thinking how unconvincingly she swore. Had she ever called anyone a prick before? Skedaddling was pure Chas, her hand not quite in the glove of the vernacular, and ordering people off premises had something of her soul in it too, but prick . . . ?

They were both listening hard. 'You're sorry?' Was she wondering if he'd ever used *that* word before?

'I truly am, Charlie.'

'Are you?' she said. She was weeping now, walled about in tears. 'I wonder if you are . . .'

And Kreitman, alert and lonely in his bachelor pad, heard something in that that gave him hope.

When he rang again it was to ask her out. For lunch, not dinner. Somewhere casual, not somewhere significant. To dry her tears, was the implication. To offer his shoulder, in the event of Charlie still being gone, or his counsel in the event of Charlie's having returned. She said no, of course. No to Charlie's having returned, no to her ever wanting him to return, and no to lunch. But she didn't say he had a fucking nerve.

'Call me if you change your mind,' he said.

'We'll see,' she'd said. But weepily.

The next day she did call, but only to tell him how hurt she was that he had let her rave on about her husband but hadn't informed her that he wasn't just knocking off Hazel but had actually moved in with her.

'Charlie's moved in with Hazel?'

'Come off it, Marvin.'

'It's the first I've heard of it, I swear to you.'

She didn't believe him. 'Marvin, your house isn't that big.'

'I'm not in the house . . .'

He waited for her to digest that information, measure its import for herself, but she said nothing.

'I haven't been in the house since I got back from Dartmoor,' he continued.

'Aha,' she said. Pull the other one.

'Think about it, Chas. What would I be doing there? Tucking them in and taking them Ovaltine?'

'I wouldn't put that past you.'

'You think I'm a pander as well as a sabbaticalist?'

'I think you're capable of anything, Marvin.'

'Maybe, but not that. I've told you, I'm motivated by nostalgia, not pervery.'

'I'm surprised you call it pervery.'

'Meaning?'

'Meaning you might think of it as companionable – your wife, your best friend . . . and you.'

'Forget it, Charlie. That's not my scene.'

'Not your *scene*?' She let out a mock gasp. 'I don't suppose you remember the violence, Marvin, with which you once publicly dumped on me for using that expression.'

'I don't. But I apologise.'

'For dumping on me?'

'For that too. But it shows how agitated talking to you makes me. What I should have said was, "Threesomes? My thoughts do not that way tend."'

'Which is why you left the house?'

'I've told you, I'd left the house already.'

'To live alone or with some girl?'

Was she jealous?

'I don't do girls. But yes, to live alone.'

'I can't see your thoughts tending to loneliness for long, Marvin.'

She was. She *was* jealous.

'You know damn well where my thoughts are tending, Charlie,' he told her.

She paused, listening, listening. 'Well, we'll see,' she said again. But still she made no reference to lunch.

'I am ill with grief over my husband,' she told Dotty, 'and this guy keeps ringing me up and asking me out. But I'm well aware you're not the person to be saying this to.'

They had been to *The Mikado* – 'Just take me to see anything, just get me away from the house,' Chas had begged her sister – and now they were sitting in the American Bar at the Savoy, drinking burgundy, picking at olives and looking striking. The Juniper girls up from the country, smelling of hay, but with the sun in their hair.

'And who's the guy?' Dotty asked.

'There you are! That's not the question you're meant to ask, Dotty. You're so sideways. A sister shouldn't be sideways.'

'How should a sister be?'

'Straight.'

Dotty crossed her legs, rattling her sequins, and sat back in her chair, her chest out. (Incapable of not flirting, Chas thought, even with me.) 'This straight enough for you? Now what's the question I'm meant to ask?'

'Why am I ill with grief for my husband.'

'And why are you?'

'Oh, Dotty, what a question. Twenty-three years!'

Dotty opened her eyes very wide, not because she was surprised by the amount of time her sister and her brother-in-law had been together but because she had read that opening her eyes wide for long periods prevented crow's feet. 'All the more reason for accepting it's over,' she said. 'A hundred years ago you'd have been dead already. Victorian expectations of one marriage to one man no longer apply. It's mortality that decides morality. Always has been. A woman of the twenty-first century can expect to live until she's eighty-five at least. With your constitution you'll probably make it to a hundred and five. That means you'll need a minimum – a minimum, Charlie! – of three husbands. Let this one go. Divorce him and marry this other guy. Who is he?'

'You forget that we were more than husband and wife. More than friends even. We collaborated. Twenty-seven books! It wasn't me who used to say we were a marriage of true minds, it was Charlemagne.'

Dotty uncrossed her legs, winnowing with light the sequins on her antique dress. One of their grandmother's. Chas noticed that Dotty had taken to wearing these more and more often lately, as though needing to clothe her forward behaviour in the garments of a more withdrawn time. A proof, Chas believed – and this was a belief she held dearly to – that modern women like her sister only affected abandon, while in their hearts they remained as self-restrained as their grandmothers. This affectation was what Chas meant by silliness. On the other hand she could see that Dotty was looking very beautiful tonight, that she was enjoying showing the room (and the waiters) her sequins (and her legs), that the burgundy which she'd been drinking to excess had made her voice deep and that taken all round her silliness became her.

But it wasn't only to draw attention to herself that Dotty went on changing her position; she was also looking for a posture suggestive of confidentiality. 'Listen to me, darling,' she said. 'The marriage of true minds you speak of was also going down the plughole. It's not for me to pry but I bet your sales have been plummeting. What do you expect? You've been stuck in the eighties for years. Your other half was *born* stuck in the eighties – the eighteen eighties. He was making you stale, Charlie. He was holding you back.'

'Everybody's sales are plummeting,' Charlie said.

'Not true. I can name some whose sales are soaring.'

'Please don't,' Charlie said.

'I wouldn't be so crude.'

'I mean, please don't go on with this subject.' She was annoyed. Suddenly she could detect the agitating influence of the malicious boy-of-letters with the frayed cuffs, the true face of Dotty's silliness. She could hear the *Publishers Weekly* pillow talk – 'That sister of yours is on a bit of a loser with that husband, wouldn't you say? Have you seen their sales figures recently? Not that they ever were much cop as a writing team, but at least they had the ear of the market once, when every child was a Little Lord Fauntleroy. How come no one's told them the Fauntleroys have died out? No wonder the big clown is after a piece of you. You're his last chance to enter the modern world. That's if he has anything left to enter you with . . .'

Following her thoughts, part of the way at least, Dotty uncrossed her legs, her sequins hissing like a snake, and put her arms round her sister. 'Face facts, darling,' she said. 'All good collaborations come to an end. Think of . . . I don't know . . . help me . . . Dean Martin and Jerry Lewis.'

'I'm surprised you go so far back culturally any more,' Chas said. 'I'd have imagined, given the circles you move in now, that Wham! would have been the first example that sprung to mind.'

Dotty looked at the ceiling and comically pretended to tap her brow. *Actually* tapping her brow would have broken the skin. 'Who's Wham!?' she said. Then she signalled the wine waiter for more burgundy. 'Oh, Charlie,' she said, 'you don't think Wham!'s of *now*, do you?'

Charlie shrugged. 'I'm not the one who's desperate to keep up,' she said.

'And I can't help it if I attract young men,' Dotty retorted. 'It runs in the family.'

'Dotty, it does not!'

'Oh, doesn't it! And Mummy?'

'What about Mummy? You're not going to give me that coalman routine again.'

'Never mind the coalman, what about Tony Almond?'

'I've never heard of Tony Almond. You've made him up. Mummy would never have gone near a man called Tony Almond. It's a hairdresser's name.'

'Not quite. He was a wine merchant. Half Mummy's age. He had that shop in the high street with all the vintage whiskies in the window. Almond's. He used to help Mummy choose her Christmas wine.'

'Took her down to his wine cellars, I suppose?'

'That's exactly what he did. Every Christmas until she was too old to negotiate the stairs. Then he just closed the shop for the afternoon.'

'Dotty, how come you know all these things and I don't?'

'Mummy confided in me. She wouldn't tell you because she thought you were a prude. "Charlie would just say I was being silly," she said. But I can see you don't want to believe me. Suit yourself. I find it helps, knowing I'm following in Mummy's footsteps. Keeping up the grand Juniper tradition. I wish you'd do the same.'

'Mummy was a Dunmore, not a Juniper.'

Dotty inverted her lips. 'You'll go to the grave a pedant, Charlie.'

Charlie crossed her arms on the little table and slumped her head on them. Could Dotty be telling the truth? Was *any* of it the truth? Had her mother really gone down into his cellar with the wine merchant? Even just the once? Even just for fun? And did it matter one iota if she had?

Grandma too, whose coruscations Dotty did not scruple to borrow – what about Grandma and Leonard Woolf?

Not to mention herself; only think what she was capable of, simply out of incompetent politeness, or raging grief.

When she looked up she was surprised to find that her own thoughts had taken an inconsequent turn. 'Would you forgive him?' she asked.

'Tony Almond?'

'Don't be an ass, Dotty. My husband.'

'What do you want me to say, Charlie?'

'I don't *want* you to say anything. Would you forgive him?'

Dotty opened her eyes wide, made a letter box of her mouth, looked at her reflection in the wine that had just arrived, shook out her sequins and sighed. 'No,' she said. 'No. And not because he's fucking that slack cow, but because he demeaned you by wandering around looking desperate. I'm surprised it took him so long to come on to me. Charlie, he was making a fool of you. His tongue was hanging out. He slobbered over everything that moved. Who wants to be with a man who can't get himself laid?'

Charlie would have liked to be able to open her own eyes wide, *and* make a letter box of her mouth, but her eyes were small and wet with tears, and her mouth was shut fast with unhappiness. 'Was it really as bad as that?' she asked.

'Worse. I'm sorry, darling – and don't forget I was very fond of Charlemagne myself – but it was ghastly. You'd have been better off with a fucker.'

'Like Marvin Kreitman?'

The sisters exchanged a long look. 'Out of the frying pan into the fire,' Dotty said.

'Come on. You said I'd have been better off with a fucker. Have the courage of your convictions. Would I have been happier with Marvin Kreitman?'

'I didn't say you'd have been happier with a fucker, I said better off, less demeaned.'

'So would I have been less demeaned with Kreitman?'

Dotty thought about it. 'He's a bit of a throwback.'

'Meaning?'

'He's a sort we thought we were rid of. I feel a certain nostalgia for the type myself, but I can see that his was a virus we needed to knock out. Are you telling me there's about to be another outbreak of him?'

'Dotty, will you be straight! Would I have been less demeaned married to a man like Kreitman, whether or not he was fucking every woman in sight, than I was – than you *say* I was – married to a man who was visibly dying of *not* fucking anybody?'

Dotty thought about it some more. She held an olive out before her lips for so long that Chas thought she was going to scream. 'Jesus, Dotty!' she cried. 'Is this another of your facial exercises?'

'I will conscientiously answer your question,' Dotty said.

'When? Next week? Next year?'

'Now.'

'And . . . ?'

Dotty swallowed her olive and looked long into her sister's eyes. 'God help any woman who has to make that choice,' she said.

★   ★   ★

169

Waiting for her to call, Kreitman put on flamenco music – Lorca's sore-throat *cante jondo* was what he loved, not the heel-clicking tourist rubbish – and lay on his bed listening to it all the day and half the night, drowning out the club opposite, the rasping melancholy of unrequitedness. How good sex was when you couldn't get it! Why, on the night of their soul-searching, had he not frogmarched Charlie Merriweather out of the restaurant and over to Virgin Records on Oxford Street, bought him every piece of gypsy music in the store, and ordered him to go home and enjoy cultivating the exquisite art of doing without, instead of indulging his unseemly wondering and allowing it to bring them both to this pass?

When he wanted a break from flamenco he played shove-halfpenny with himself, hours at a time. Exhausted by that, he challenged his computer to chess. Pissed off with losing, he dusted down some of his old college books and grew maudlin. Beginning his early married life in the most straitened circumstances, Francis Place had cautioned against cramped living quarters. 'Nothing conduces so much to the degradation of a man and a woman . . .' Well, there was no woman living in these cramped quarters, and in Kreitman's view nothing conduced so much to a man's degradation as that.

Looking at himself in his bathroom mirror, he saw a lonely man. Was this the loneliest he'd ever been? Was he lonelier now than on that last lost night in Barcelona, heartbreak paella perfuming the cobbled streets and his hot fist stuffed with pesetas? Much lonelier. Then he could only guess what he was missing. Now he was in a position to count losses until his hair turned grey.

There is some mischief in numbers. Waiting for you in the midst of plenty, zilch. The more Kreitman counted the less he had. So was that all he'd been amassing over so many years – nothing?

Other than Charlie, who was not available to him at the

moment, he had no male friends. It's a choice you make: either you go chasing women or you have friends. There isn't room for both. Kreitman's women *were* his friends, which worked well, kept him in company, conversation and games of chess, so long as they remained his women. But he had no appetite for any of his women now, not since he'd watched Chas on her knees on the croquet lawn, in a black-mass mockery of prayer to a man for whom she had no regard. Some sights blind you to all others. Fix your gaze on Sodom and Gomorrah going up in sulphur on the Plain of Mamre and you turn to stone. Kreitman had disobeyed the injunctions of decency and wisdom and kept his curtains open. Only he hadn't turned to stone; he'd turned to jelly.

If he were tucking his grown-up daughters into bed and telling them what life had thrown at Marvin Kreitman next, they wouldn't have been much impressed with the adult content of his story. 'Now, when it's too late, you're telling us fairy stories. In the catalogue of contemporary carnalities, Daddy, touching someone's dick is not that mega.'

Where had he been, their old man? What would he say if they told him about a triple anal?

It was true. He knew it. He had stood at the window, aghast, watching not that much happening. But how much *had* to happen? For Marvin Kreitman, sitting in a cinema and waiting for the twelve-foot kiss – just that, just two lips brushing – was a shattering experience. No matter how trashy the plot, no matter how cheesy the actors, he hung on the coming kiss in palpitating suspense – was it soon . . . was it near . . . was it *now*! And when at last it did come, it was as though he'd never seen one before: it dried up his mouth, soaked the collar of his shirt, bound steel hoops around his chest. Try breathing now, Kreitman!

No small thing, a kiss, whatever happened next. And as for reaching out for body parts . . .

In the end it's all about susceptibility to shock. If it feels rude, it is rude. Call it wonderment. The wonderment of rude. Some of us never have it, some of us don't know how to keep it. Chas had it and so far Chas had kept it. That was enough for Kreitman. He had looked out on to the moor, seen consciousness of rude and gone up in flames.

Who among those he'd been fucking for dear life only a month before – he'd show them triple anal! – could lodge anything in his head to rival Chas giving wonder? Ooshi in her rubber corset, playing the dominatrix with one eye on the clock? 'Beg, Kreitman!' Erica wetting his ear with what she'd done with other women? 'Then I . . . then she . . . then I . . . after which we . . .' Forget it. Yes, he'd begged abjectly enough in his time – 'Please, Ooshi, oh God no, oh God yes, not that, yes that!' Sure, he'd urged Erica on in her flagging fantasies – 'You didn't, you couldn't, you never!' But their day was over. They were bored with him and he was bored with them. Who started it didn't matter. They'd lost the trick of rude. They were too overt, too seamlessly the thing they were. They weren't respectable *and* lewd. They weren't confident *and* gauche. They didn't have fault lines running through them, on one side of which they kicked husbands off the premises, like queens of infinite space, and on the other pronounced prick as though it were the brand name of a tuck-shop lolly. No fault line, no desire; and if he no longer desired them (or, indeed, they him) there was no point seeing them. Here was the catch in his erotic reasoning. His social life waited on his dick. His dick waited on his imagination. So if his imagination was not stirred, he ate alone.

He rang his mother just once, then put the phone down. How was that for restraint! If ever there were a blame and kiss-it-better time, this was it, Kreitman up to his ears in his own bhuna chicken juices and reduced to playing chess with a computer. All your doing, Ma. Behold the glory and the ruination of your works! But Chas was the only person it excited him to blame for his decline and fall now. She was the woman in his life – let her fix it!

He had to force himself to leave the flat. One morning he found himself being tailed by a ruby-red Smart driven by an African chauffeur. It took him ten minutes of quickening then reducing his pace, and a further ten trying to work out who would be putting a detective on him – Hazel, obviously, but why? – before he remembered that the car and its chauffeur were his.

'Maurice, I'd forgotten I had you,' he said, when the driver wound down his window.

'You should get out more, Mr Kreitman,' the driver laughed.

He got Maurice to take him the rounds of his furthest flung shops, Lewisham, Crystal Palace, Penge, swinging back towards Putney via Thornton Heath and Wimbledon. Was this his life? He totted up what he amounted to – so many hundreds of Antler suitcases, so many thousands of Manchester United schoolbags, so many hundreds of thousands of coin-tray purses, still selling though you would have thought the penny-pinching bachelor gent who shuffled his coins on to the tray to inspect them, exactly as an ailing German will inspect his stools, was a thing of the past. Was it time for him, Kreitman, to have a coin-tray purse of his own? She loves me – shuffle, shuffle – she loves me not. She loves me . . .

Because it gave him something to take his mind off himself he was pleased to walk into a staff problem at his West Norwood branch. An assistant not in the first flush of youth, nor in any sort of flush of presentableness, come to that – only West Norwood, you see – was taking a bag down from a shelf. The bag, unlike the assistant, was hard-edged, highly polished, brittle as a diamond, not cheap. 'A good choice, madam,' he overheard the assistant saying, 'I've been thinking of buying that one for myself for weeks.' He took her aside, though not aside enough, once the sale had fallen through. 'Peggy,' he said, 'I mean this in the nicest way, but ask yourself why it would be a recommendation to a woman let's say half your age and let's guess twice your height, a woman with an air (I say no more than that) of having a degree from Oxford *and* from Cambridge and a house in every road in Dulwich, that the handbag on which her attention happens to have alighted is the very handbag chosen above all others for its fashionableness and elegance by *you*?'

It came out ruder than he meant it to, but what help was there? The shop fell quiet. The grey-haired assistant blinked three times, lowered her head and disappeared into the stockroom. Kreitman followed, inhaling leather. He loved a stockroom. 'I'm sorry,' he said. 'I could have put that better.'

'You could have put it to me *in private*, Mr Kreitman,' she corrected him, sniffing.

Kreitman took her point and apologised again. He had broken one of Francis Place's three golden recollections to himself, and played the tyrant. And for no reason other than that he was love-sick and idle. In the days when he counted off his women he was considerate to his staff. Was being in love with one woman making a pig of him? He wondered if Peggy was going to hand in her notice and then sue him for unfair dismissal. Staff were no picnic any more. Hire a person to stuff travel bags with newspapers and you have taken on a responsibility as onerous as marriage. More. Easier to shed a wife than a sales assistant.

'As you were,' he saluted to the shop in general, as he left. But none of the remaining staff looked up from what they were doing or otherwise showed they thought his joke particularly funny.

'Right, Maurice,' he said, folding himself back into the Smart, 'let's see what trouble I can cause in Mitcham.'

He was better off indoors with his unrequited gypsy music and his shove-halfpenny board. Waiting for the call from Chas.

He couldn't stop thinking about her. She had turned golden in his imagination, come in out of the sun-bled fields and taken possession of the great glittering indoors, made lustrous by artificial light. Once upon a time he had not liked the sameness of her palette, her corn-stook hair, yellow to her shoulders, framing dully her corn-stook complexion; now the homogeneity of her

174

colouring seemed to him the very model of beauty, her yellow become bronze, its evenness of shading stirringly at odds with the unruliness of her character. When he heard her voice he tried to picture what she was wearing, even though he couldn't stomach a single item in her wardrobe. When his phone rang he hoped to God it was her and was unable to prevent his own voice dropping when it turned out to be someone else. 'Come on, come on, get off the line,' he muttered into his teeth, rocking on the balls of his feet, aflame with impatience, even though the caller had once whispered up all the devils of hell for his entertainment. But there you are, they were the wrong devils, not a one of them Chas in her knitted cucumber top and spinnaker skirt, down on her lavender-gathering knees on a croquet lawn, confusing the categories, mixing up his head.

He jumped when he heard his mail delivered, or the bell ring, or the door rattle. When he looked out of his window he thought he saw her in the street, reading the shop numbers, looking up for a sight of him, smiling one of those blind person's smiles of hers – fantastical because she didn't have an inkling where his flat was, but that didn't stop him imagining her coming up the stairs, knocking on his door, seeing how he was living and feeling sorry for him.

'You've reduced yourself to this for me?'

'For you, Charlie.'

And then one of them running into the other's arms.

No, not one of them, *him*. Running into hers.

Jelly. He'd turned to jelly, grown passive, become the victim of events. He never thought of going to her, always of her coming to him. Never of his kissing her, always of her kissing him. He imagined being touched by her – her hands on him, not his on her – cudgelling his brains to recall how his skin felt the one time she had touched him. But too much had happened since then, four children had been born, innumerable other touchings had taken place, and he'd been too drunk, and she'd been too drunk, and there'd been more bravado than skin in it, anyway, and more tease than touch. And more irony than he'd had the wit to register.

Ironic women had always been his weakness. He had fallen for Hazel because she'd been sardonic about herself. Of his current crop of lapsed lovers, Bernadette had been his favourite because she put up ironic buildings – libraries too dark to read a book in, old people's homes which were death traps even for the young and virile – and because she looked to him to confirm her bleak view of existence. Chas's irony, though, was different. Something to do with protectiveness. She'd mocked Charlie protectively for however many years. Become a sort of mother to him and assumed a sort of care. Ironically *sort of*. My baby, my poor weak baby. With hindsight, Kreitman now believed there might all along have been a touch of that in her tone to him too. Was it something to do with her brand of sex? The satiric half-accidental handjob, after which she was liberated to show pity? Had she been mothering him ironically for twenty years without his ever noticing? And did she therefore feel motherly to that nonentity Nyman as well? Was she nursing Nyman in a leaded-windowed bedroom with a view of the Thames in Richmond right this minute, fumbling in his pants and rocking him in her arms, even as Kreitman uncorked his third bottle of Shiraz and ripped open his second packet of malted-milk biscuits for the night?

Do I know anything, Kreitman wondered, of what has or hasn't happened?

After all, he needed to talk to his mother.

She had moved north, when she became Mrs Bellwood, to the quiet of Rickmansworth, then further north again, nudging at the Chilterns, after Norbert had his stroke. She greeted Kreitman in her garden, a cigarette in her hand. He loved it that his mother smoked. It made her raffish in his eyes.

'I'm dead-heading the roses,' she said.

'With a cigarette?'

She showed him the secateurs sticking out of her apron pocket. Secateurs he cared for less than cigarettes, then remembered he'd seen Chas wielding them in Richmond and wondered if maybe they could be rendered raffish, by association, too.

'I knew you were coming,' she said.

Kreitman, standing ill at ease on the lawn with his arms folded, laughed. 'No you didn't.'

She tapped the side of her face, just below her eye, the nerve centre of her sympathetic prescience. 'I told Norbert you'd be here, just half an hour ago.'

He met her gaze. Don't say anything, her eyes warned him. Make no comment about the fact that when you're not here I'm talking to someone who cannot talk back to me and who most of the time doesn't understand a word I say.

She walked him round the garden, showing him flowers. A new side to his mother. There'd been no flowers in the days of his father. But then Bruno the Broygis would probably have kicked their heads off on his way in.

Kreitman didn't ask how Norbert was. He knew the routine. No mention. What there was to be told, he would be told. Sometimes his mother would take him up to see Norbert, sometimes he would be wheeled out. But if he wasn't, he wasn't. And Kreitman knew not to wander round the house. A man who has had a stroke as serious as Norbert's leaves a swinging thurible of baby smell, damp and dead, in every room he's been in. Mona Bellwood showed no sign that that distressed or shamed her. If she was careful who she allowed to go where, that was to spare them.

Too cruel. Too unthinkably cruel that his mother's second crack at romance should have ended so abruptly in this. One bastard, one vegetable – where was the fairness in that?

'So,' she said. 'Love-troubles. Have you come to see Shelley?'

'Ma, I've come to see you.'

'I know, but have you also come to see Shelley?'

'No, not today.'

'Then definitely love-troubles.'

He sat on a step while she continued savaging the roses. 'I've got something to tell you,' he said, 'I've left Hazel.'

'I know,' she said, not bothering to look up.

'Ma, do me a favour – enough with the psychic powers.'

'Who's talking about psychic powers? She rang me.'

'Hazel rang you!'

'I'm her mother-in-law, why are you surprised?'

'What did she ring you to say?'

'What do you think? "Congratulations. You have your wish. Better late than never."'

'She said that?'

'Yes. Brave of her, I thought. First brave thing I've ever heard her say.'

'And no doubt you told her that?'

'No. I said I was sorry if either of you was unhappy. Are you?'

'What did she say to that?'

'I'm asking you that. Are *you* unhappy?'

Kreitman took off his jacket and folded it on his lap. Linen. He didn't want it creased. 'What I am,' he said, 'is bewildered. I can't work out why I like what I like in women.'

'Simple,' his mother told him. 'Trouble. You like trouble.'

'Yes, but that doesn't help. What I want to know is *why* do I like trouble.'

She dropped the secateurs on the lawn and came to join him on the steps. Creakily. He hadn't noticed that in her before. He thought of her as about his age. But up close she wasn't the beggar-maid any more. You can't push your husband around in his wheelchair, smelling infancy and death on him every day, and stay a beggar-maid. 'What exactly is it you want to hear from me?' she asked. 'That I did something to you when you were small? That I gave you a taste for trouble?'

'Ma, you know I'm not asking you that.'

She shrugged. 'I may have,' she said. 'Doesn't your Freud say all mothers do that. Why should I be any different? I tried to make you believe in yourself, and who can say whether that's a good thing. Maybe I made you arrogant. Maybe you thought I was the only one who could appreciate you. And since you couldn't have me – bingo! – trouble.'

'Freud in a nutshell, Ma. I can't think why you've always been so against him. But I'm not blaming you for anything. I just want to know whether I was always . . . what I am. When you took me to all those specialists because I kept fainting, did any of them say anything?'

'Like your boy seems to want trouble from his women? Marvin, you were eight at the time. We weren't looking for woman-associated symptoms.'

'But I was morbid, wasn't I? That's why you took me.'

'No one said anything about morbid. The doctors called you sensitive.'

'But what does sensitive mean?'

'Sensitive means sensitive. You're still sensitive. Look at the fists you're making.'

She put her hands on his, unlacing his fingers. What he couldn't decide was whether their eyes had met, whether she had mutely said, 'You like that, don't you, Marvin? You like me to unfist you.'

'Do you remember,' she suddenly said, 'telling me about the woman you met in Selfridges?'

He tossed his hair. Jest and no jest. 'Ma, I've met so many women in Selfridges.'

This time their eyes did meet. Hers were black and Caspian still, but the blaze wasn't what it once had been. He thought they looked sorrowfully into his – not sorry for herself, sorry for

179

him. She squeezed his hands. 'You told me you met this one in the bag department. You told me you stopped her buying something. You were excited, you said, because she was as old as I was. A funny thing, Marvin, to tell your mother.'

A phrase he would rather not have remembered came back to him. '*You don't use your mouth like other men.*'

That first. How interesting. First the phrase, then the woman.

It was just before he went to university. Out on the prowl, anywhere, it didn't matter, Tottenham Court Road, Piccadilly Circus, Carnaby Street, Regent Street. A late Saturday afternoon, the shops not yet closed, his eyes darting in every direction, then bullseye! he found one – tall, fleshy, sarcastic-looking, self-contained in the manner of a married woman not needing to be on the prowl herself – where else but in Selfridges' handbag department. 'Don't buy that one,' he'd said. 'Rubbish leather. The patent will come off in the rain. Clasp will rust and the strap's old-fashioned. This one suits you better.'

His reward a knee-trembler after lasagne and Valpolicella, up against a wall in St Christopher's Place, close to where once stood a urinal in which the downwardly mobile Victorian painter Simeon Solomon – no long-windedly self-righteous Moral Chartist, that one, but a hero of Kreitman's nonetheless – did feloniously attempt the abominable crime of buggery (so Kreitman *could* like a faggot when it suited him) upon one George Roberts, or vice versa. Though no blue plaque marks the spot.

No blue plaque for Marvin Kreitman either, but then no blue plaque was necessary – it was scarred on his brain tissue, the place where he learned he did not use his mouth like other men.

So how did other men use their mouths?

She didn't know how to put it. She'd only come out to buy a handbag when all was said and done. And she wasn't in the habit of doing this. But since he asked – well, more assertively, more animalistically, or something.

Kreitman bit her lip.

She pushed him from her. 'There's something wrong with you,' she said, before she walked away. 'You just leave your mouth there, like a baby bird's, waiting for something to be put into it. It's horrible. Then you bite me.'

What sort of mouth did a baby bird have? Soft, red, passive, blindly hungry. Not a flattering comparison, was it? Thereafter he was careful to present a powerful set of mandibles to every woman he kissed. Lock into Marvin Kreitman's jaws and you knew how a mouse felt when an eagle swooped. But the imputation stuck – there was some masculine forcefulness that wasn't his by nature.

And he'd told this to his *mother*?

Marvellous that she remembered. How many years ago was it? Twenty-five? Thirty? But more marvellous still that he'd told her.

Why would he have told her?

'Yes,' he said, 'something is vaguely coming back to me.'

'It worried you at the time, I remember.'

'It still worries me.'

She shook her head and took his hands, both remade into fists, one in each of hers. 'You've got your health,' she said. 'You have two wonderful daughters. You have never been short of girlfriends. You make a good living. What do you have to worry about?'

It always saddened and bemused him, how little his mother expected of him now. Health, for God's sake. Daughters, girl-friends, a living . . . Where had the other stuff gone? His destiny, his moral spotlessness, his genius? Couldn't she at least be a little bit *disappointed* for him?

Or was that just the mouth issue all over again? Was that why he'd told her – so that she could pity and reprimand him, in equal measure? Did he seek his mother's disappointment?

Christ!

★   ★   ★

Before he left, his mother took him to see Norbert in the lovely high-ceilinged sunlit room she'd built for him, quiet as his old library, every sound dying in deep lilac carpet, his books and papers, unread, all around him. How old was Norbert? Kreitman wondered. He looked ageless – a thousand years, a thousand days, impossible to tell – a creature washed of all his sins, only his tongue a problem to him, everything else apparently sorted, his eyes off on some unknown journey of their own.

'Marvin's here to see you,' his mother said.

'Hi, Norbert,' Kreitman said.

Not a flicker.

Because Kreitman didn't know what else to do, he waved.

Mona Bellwood went over to her husband's chair and rearranged him, lifting him under his arms, as she must once have lifted Marvin, pulling the hair back from his unlined brow, tidying him around the ears, this never unkempt man. She raised her face and saw her son looking at her. She smiled a tired smile. 'I know what you're thinking,' she said. 'But he's in here. He hasn't gone. I know that when I touch him I'm reaching him.'

And you, Mother, Kreitman wasn't able to ask, who's reaching you?

'You're a believer in the soul, then?' he said.

'I always knew where you were when you were out,' she reminded him, continuing to clean up her husband's face, smoothing away the hairs, absently stroking his cheeks, rearranging his cravat. 'I could always tell if something bad was happening to you. I don't know whether you call that believing in the soul.'

'So you know where Norbert is?'

'I do, yes, definitely.'

'And is something bad happening to him?'

She started to answer, but then couldn't. Cracks suddenly appeared across her face, like the shattering of glass. She put up her hands to hide her grief, though whether from him or from Norbert he couldn't say. Somehow, with a movement of her shoulders, she was able to signal him to leave. 'How could you be so cruel, Marvin?' she collected herself sufficiently to ask. But by that time he was out of the door.

It wasn't safe for him to go out. When he made a call to one of his shops he upset the staff, and when he went to visit his own mother he upset her and himself. Death in the house and his mother ageing, and there was he, who should have been a comfort, absorbed in the trivia of self-damage, wondering what it meant that he wanted his mother to know he didn't kiss like other men, and by natural extension – for all roads lead to the same place when you're in the state Marvin Kreitman was in – wondering what sort of kisser Nyman was. That the reason Chas hadn't taken him up on his offer – too busy kissing the faggot? *A man more rattishly and motivationally stripped down to the bare bones blah-blah than he and Charlie rolled together* – Chas's own words. Meaning exactly what? That as men, as sexual men, as users of the mouth, he and Charlie didn't add up to a hill of beans in Chas's estimation?

It had come to something that he was bracketing himself with Charlie these days. Charlie and Marvin, two absolute no-hopers with women. Except that that description didn't apply to Charlie any more, did it?

He had run into Shelley, when leaving his mother's. On her way in to take up her nursing duties, so not starched yet, still in her civvies, if you could call them that. Thirty years old and wearing a tiny ruffle of a skirt, black convent tights and dinky bovver boots, like a fairy who had come down off a Christmas tree, looking for a punch-up. Kreitman sighed. Those were the days.

He had forgotten what women were like. Was this what they did? When Shelley spoke to him she pushed her face forward, as though she wanted him to pat her head, like a cat. Little pink tongue. Little green eyes narrowed. Little cough, due to little fur ball in little throat. Lovely, Kreitman thought. So lovely he couldn't think how he had forgotten. But no fault line. That's *why* he had forgotten. No wonderment of rude.

So there he was, back to square one.

Not safe for him to go out, so he stayed in. Three calls from Chas in as many weeks, two anguished, one aerobatically cheerful, but still no lunch date. As for his wonderful daughters, they had put their various contractual obligations on hold, postponed the explanatory dinner he'd promised them – no hurry, Daddy – and gone hitchhiking around Thailand, looking for some beach. So who was there for him to go out and see?

Who was there for him to stay in and see, come to that? Sleeping without company had never suited him, even for the odd night, but this was the longest unbroken stretch of it he'd suffered since leaving school, and it was beginning to wreak havoc on his body. A man with a wife and five girlfriends showers at least six times a day. A man moping over an inaccessible woman showers less than that. Not a comment on his bachelor facilities: cramped though his Clapham hermitage was, it lacked for none of the eroticising amenities expected of a modern bathroom. Name a refinement of toiletry, Kreitman had it. Name the most powerful shower head, name a douche appliance, name a Roman bath . . . No, what Kreitman's unaccompanied life lacked for was inducement. There was no good reason to pamper his body to the degree it had come to expect. Some days he never bothered to dress. Once or twice he never bothered to get out of bed. As a consequence he was beginning to notice upon himself something that looked like mould. The skin of tramps must look like this, he thought. Or the skin of old men. Kreitman's flesh had always been important to him. Not muscles, not toning, not a tan, simply its integumental texture, its general air of lazy and maybe even absorptive, if not to say magnetic, good health. This flesh is in constant pleasurable employment, that was the notice he hung out upon his body. Now he was rotting.

Time to get a grip on himself, even if he couldn't get a grip on

Chas. A visit to his doctor, to the chemist, to the herbalist, to his hairdresser and to his outfitters was in order. Clean up the act.

Which was how he happened to run into Charlie Merriweather on Jermyn Street, loaded down with shirts, looking mighty pleased with the world and his own place in it, a man conscious of not having anything putrid anywhere about *his* body.

TWO

ONE NIGHT CHARLIE dreamed that Chas turned up and found him in his dressing gown with Hazel. Chas was carrying a teapot and smiling, but when she saw the dressing gown and then saw Hazel she burst into tears. The cruellest sort of tears, not tears that stream but tears that spurt out as though the eyes have sprung a leak. As she cried, she let the tea spill from the teapot on to Hazel's carpet. 'What's *she* doing here?' Hazel demanded, and although Charlie knew the answer he didn't want to say.

Unable to decide to whom he owed his loyalty, Charlie woke up with a pain in his heart.

But he would have been better advised not to tell Hazel about his dream.

'If you're having second thoughts,' she said, 'I'd prefer you acted on them now, before I get too used to you.'

'Second thoughts? I've never been happier,' Charlie told her.

'Exactly. Guilt.'

'Why should being happy make me guilty?'

'Don't be a baby, Charlie. I didn't have the dream, you did.'

Sometimes Hazel understood why her husband had been so scathing of the C. C. Merriweather books. Morally, Charlie lived in Tiggy-Winkle Land. He had learned no hard lessons from experience. She could hear Marvin's explanation: 'Hazel, he's *had* no experience; he's been happily married for a quarter of a century.'

But then morally Marvin lived in the lowest circle of Dante's Inferno. And what sort of a companion did that make *him*?

It touched her to be the person who was bringing experience to Charlie, she who had never believed she had anything to bring to anybody, least of all knowledge. Suddenly she realised it was all in the luck of the draw. Some people needed you to be the grown-up one, so you mouthed wisdom; others wanted to reveal life to you, so you hung your bottom lip like a dunce. So far she'd encountered only teachers. Not like that, Hazel, like this. The curse of Kreitman. Even Yossi in the Negev had unpeeled her as though instructing her in how to eat fruit. And she'd extended her hands obediently, limply, like a little girl being helped out of her blazer. Until she stood in the desert without an item of school uniform left on her, waiting to be told what next.

Now she felt as old as Oedipus, discovering the riddles of the Sphinx to the frightened inhabitants of Tiggy-Winkle Land. She'd had to explain to Charlie why his children were having difficulty with what he'd done: why his daughter had told her mother she'd never speak to her again if she ever spoke to Daddy again; and why his son was rumoured to be clubbing till all hours, stuffing powders up his nose and not answering his father's phone calls. 'They must be able to see for themselves that I'm happy,' Charlie had said. 'It's not as though they're babies, for God's sake. Kitty-Litter's a bulldyke and Timmy's been on *Blind Date*.'

'Daddies are meant to stay with mummies,' Hazel reminded him.

'At *their* age?'

'No, at *your* age.'

'Chas must have said something to them.'

'That's very likely.'

'No, I mean she must have turned them against me.'

'Instead of what? Convincing them how sweet you are?'

'Is that beyond the pale?'

'It's beyond human nature, Charlie.'

'I hope I'd do better.'

'If Chas ran off with someone?'

'Sure.'

'And if I ran off with someone?'

'That's different.'

She shook her head over him. 'What the fuck am I doing with you?' she said.

When she wasn't Oedipus she was Jocasta. Barely a month's difference in their ages, but she felt she'd carried him in her womb. Not only that, but whenever he wanted to crawl back whence he'd come she had to show him the way. A gazetteer of her own body suddenly, Hazel Kreitman née Nossiter, who until now had been a mystery to herself, an unmapped continent for intrepid mariners to chart. In their early days Marvin had drawn a verbal picture of the parts of her she couldn't see. Which made her feel as incidental as a feather on a breeze. Was she there only by virtue of Marvin's descriptive powers? If he lost words would she shed tissue? Not any more. This way, Charlie, throw a right, no a *right*, and now straight on . . .

Same with *his* body. Hands in the air, feet together, not her coming out of her clothes this time, but him. 'I have the urge to sew labels into your shorts,' she told him.

His eyes brimmed. 'My father had to do that for me,' he remembered. 'And buttons. My mother wouldn't risk pricking her pretty finger.'

The sad, motherless boy, unlabelled, unbuttoned and unloved. Once upon a time, Charlie Hyphen Smelly-Botty Farnsbarns found himself all alone in a big wide field with no labels in his shorts. How am I possibly to know who I am, cried Charlie Hyphen Smelly-Botty Farnsbarns, if I don't have labels in my shorts . . . ?

Lost, love-lorn, without the first clue who he belonged to. Now found a home for at last.

'But Chas must have done your sewing . . .'

Chas? Oh God, yes. Chas. Yes, of course, Chas *had* done his sewing, now she came to mention it. But he was emotionally skipping Chas. Chas hadn't happened. In the context in which he was now living, Chas had no measurable existence. There'd been loneliness and then boom! – in a flash – Hazel.

When Charlie asked Chas to be happy for him, on account of his enjoying a satisfactory sabbatical from their marriage, he may not have known what he was about but he knew what he meant. I am not a complete fool, he would have told her had she only given him the chance. I know that you cannot *really* be happy for me. I know that such selflessness as I am asking for does not exist. But I am trying to mark a difference between you, the woman I have always loved, the mother of my children, the companion of my labours, and Hazel, the mother of someone else's children, the companion of someone else's labours, a woman I have never loved and, to be frank with you, barely noticed. She is so unlike you, she is circumstanced so dissimilarly, that she is not so much another woman as another species. Therefore I find it impossible to think of her as an infidelity to you. Yes, yes, I grant you, Dotty *would* have been an infidelity. Dotty I regret. Dotty was wrong. Dotty *was* a choice against you. But then Dotty was a suicidal act and she didn't happen anyway. Only Hazel happened, and Hazel isn't a betrayal of you because she isn't an alternative to you. Hazel's from another planet. So now will you be happy for me?

What Charlie meant by Hazel being from another planet was that she made him feel *he* was on another planet. The planet Impurity. The planet Wrongdoing. Some nights the planet Filth. Some mornings the planet Bliss. But never, Chas, absolutely never, the planet Nice.

He was not, whatever anybody thought, a *complete* fool. He knew he couldn't tell Chas he was now domiciled on the planet Sensuality, a place he'd never set foot on with her, not even for the weekend. And what was the planet Sensuality, when all was said and done, if not a satellite of the planet Wrongdoing? Hazel was all wrongdoing. She was his best friend's wife. She was among his wife's best friends. She was the mother of children his children had grown up with. She was a middle-aged woman whose appeal he had never much registered, almost a sister to him. And he had won her in a sort of wager. How many wrongs was that?

He could season most of that wrongdoing, if not with right, at least with a pinch of something morally neutral. For example, Hazel might have been his best friend's wife but his best friend didn't deserve her, had spares galore and probably didn't even notice she was missing. Nor was Hazel really Chas's friend; the two had only tried to get on for their husbands' sakes, and left to their own devices would have despised each other, *did* despise each other most of the time. As for his children, why invoke them? They were behaving strangely – badly, in his view, selfishly – and didn't have much to do with it one way or another. In the matter of Hazel's having been a sort of sister to him, sort of is only sort of. And finally, he hadn't really won her in a wager; rather she had come to him, coincidentally, of her own imperious volition, as a consequence of a train of events which certainly originated in that evening of wild talk in Soho but which no one could have calculated.

Then why, in that case, did he go on shaking with a sense of wrongdoing whenever he approached her? After the first time Charlie slept with Hazel he never believed there was going to be a second. After the second he never believed there was going to be a third. A hundred and one days of Sodom later, he still submitted to the turning-out of the lights, descended into the mouthing dark, resigned to the likelihood that she would not be there in the morning. He almost did not want to wake, he so dreaded putting out his hand and finding a note on the snow-cold pillow next to him, or seeing her sitting up in one of her round-backed leather boudoir chairs, fully dressed, in the belted-up Alida Valli trenchcoat he'd bought her (war-torn, though a little on the short side), with her bag on her lap, waiting to tell him it had all been a mistake. So that when he did open his eyes to discover her still there, smiling, pleased to see him, leaning on an elbow willing him to wake, her breasts all about her like a tray of canapés, or up and about in the kitchen in high-heeled slippers, making him his bacon and tomato breakfast, he couldn't believe his good fortune. Another day, then, in which she wasn't going to give him his marching orders. Another day stolen from propriety and probability. Was it really out of the question for Chas to recognise how little this had to do with her, or with their old life together? It's the desperation of it, Chas. It's the head-hurting uncertainty. Not like us, not like you and me in our bedsocks, Missus, Chasser, Mrs C. C. Chassyboots . . .

There was another way of putting this. In the only story not for children he had ever dared to write, Charlie Merriweather, then twenty-six, had set about trying to describe, in unflinchingly adult yet tender language, the fondness he and the other Charlie felt for each other. 'And you tell me this is the first grown-up story you have written?' Kreitman asked him. Charlie nodded. He was keen to know what Kreitman thought. Not least as the story had grown out of the fears the two Charlies entertained for Kreitman in the light of what seemed to them his sexual cruelty not just to Hazel (that part was obvious) but to himself. In a sense the story was as much about the Kreitmans and damage as it was about the Merriweathers and healing.

'Then my advice to you, for what it's worth,' Kreitman said, 'is not to write another. I doubt you have the gift of addressing the over-twelves. Few do. It's a calling, Charlie.'

Ouch! A thousand lances in the beanbag of Charlie's self-esteem.

Deflated, he nonetheless knew where the offence actually lay. It lay in his description of the protagonist's penis. The 'instrument of friendliness'. He had watched Kreitman come to that passage and seen his jaw drop. The instrument of friendliness would be an obstacle between them for as long they lived. Recalling it over dim sum lunches sometimes, Kreitman would put his finger down his throat and pretend to throw up. Now, years after the writing of the offending tale, Charlie understood why Kreitman had baulked. An instrument of friendliness was not what a woman like Hazel made you feel you possessed. Because she appeared to be shocked by Charlie's penis whenever and no matter how often she beheld it, Charlie began to feel differently about it himself. A weapon of terror, was that it? A battering-ram of tyranny? Not exactly. He hadn't been away from home that long. Enough that its distinguishing feature was no longer an innocent amicability. And that was the other way he might have put what was not like his life with Chas about his life with Hazel. These days, if his poor wife could only grasp it, he walked about with something dangerous between his legs.

For her part, though she was no more hooked on the specifics of a man's anatomy than any other woman, Hazel Kreitman would not entirely have demurred from this. Against all expectation, Charlie Merriweather was possessed of what she'd heard her mother call a 'fearfully big thing', a brute of a penis whose weight had impressed her from the off, and though Charlie had been altogether too embarrassed initially – too embarrassed, too broken and too grateful – to wield it with anything like the expertness it merited, he wielded it with enough for Hazel. Before Kreitman, whose maleness was too mental for you ever to concentrate much on body parts – big brain, that was what Kreitman wanted you to feel inside you, the hard-on of his intelligence – Hazel had encountered two or three fearfully big things. They were always a disappointment in that they were always attached to soppy men. Whether this was an evolutionary imperative, or an unseen consequence of one – the male of the species sad to be reduced to mere functionalism – she didn't know; but as sure as night followed day a man with a big penis sobbed on your breast after orgasm, idealised you until you wanted to puke and begged you to try to love him for his gentle qualities.

Charlie was a sentimentalist right enough, overdid the gratitude and gazed at her as though nothing like her had ever existed in creation, but he didn't pull back from the obligations of his size. He enjoyed being a big man, enjoyed towering over her when they went out, his hand on her shoulder or even sometimes Latin lover-like on her neck, enjoyed being able to change a light bulb without a chair, understood what she wanted when she asked him to lie on top of her, letting her feel the full length and weight of him, crushing the wind out of her if that was her desire and not too apologetic when he hurt her. She could read that old butterfly shit in his eyes, the same ephemerality crap with which Kreitman had wooed her – 'When I open my hand, will you be gone, I wonder?' – but he didn't want to be gone himself. Unlike Kreitman, he didn't fuck in order to make himself disappear.

'I like it that you don't seem to be going anywhere in your head,' she told him once, reclining like a girl in the strong sour crook of his arm.

'Where would I be going that's any better than here?'

'I suppose I shouldn't be telling you this,' she said, 'but in my experience men are always on a journey somewhere else. Even in the early days when he was happy just to be with me – unless I got that wrong, too – Marvin used to maraud me, ransack my body as though he'd lost something. Is it here? No. Is it here, then? No. It was like being Treasure Island, like having Long John Silver stomping across you with a spade and bucket. That was before he decided the treasure wasn't anywhere to be found on me and went looking for it on some other island.'

Charlie listened. 'And why shouldn't you be telling me this?'

'In case it puts you off me.'

'Nothing could put me off you.'

'Or gives you ideas.'

'There's only one idea you give me,' he said, wanting to break into her sadness, booming his big bedtime laugh and rolling her on to his chest, tapping his broad, straightforward intentions down the taut xylophone that was her spine.

What would Chas have said? 'Charlie! Stop it, Charlie, you'll break the bed.' With Chas it had been all panto. Dames in bloomers, giant sausages, sticky sweets for the children, oops-a-daisy, he's behind you! With Chas the sex had been continuous with family, a funny misadventure ending in a picnic and a roll down a grassy bank with his arms round Kitty or Timmy. Whereas with Hazel . . . with Hazel it ended in itself.

Undoubtedly, it helped that in Kennington, all five Georgian storeys of it, there was nobody else at home. The Merriweather house had always been in a state of preparation for invited guests or unexpected droppers-in; it was a cooking house, centred on the kitchen, the latest holiday snaps and newsy postcards affixed under magnets to the refrigerator door, the subject of conversation warming in the oven. A child was always on the phone or waiting to be driven somewhere. But Hazel frowned on fridge-magnet culture, ate out more often than she cooked and had never encouraged her daughters to treat home as a club house. Both girls had their own places to live, and though they popped in as a matter of course normally, they weren't popping in at the moment because they'd fled to Thailand. Fled? In a manner of speaking.

'Not me, is it?' Charlie asked. 'Oh Lord!'

'Of course not,' Hazel reassured him, pinching his cheeks. 'Why would anyone want to flee from you?'

And it wasn't him. It was her. Her and him. *Them*. Hazel knew her daughters. Had Kreitman brought a woman into the house they'd have hit the roof. But for Mummy to be shacked up with a new bloke was cool, even if the new bloke was only soppy Uncle Charles. So disgust wasn't what motivated them to go to travelling. Not moral disgust, anyway. Aesthetic disgust was nearer the mark. They were not keen on how their mother was dressing for Charlie, and vice versa. Too short, the skirts. Too whispering, the dresses. Too pink and white, Uncle Charles's chest, scarcely covered by his blue candlewick dressing gown, and too white and blue his unshod feet. Kreitman had been a model father as far as the decorum of the domestic wardrobe went: he wore leather slippers with a crest on them, silk pyjamas and a sort of pasha's robe that tied around him twice. Sometimes he wore a smoking jacket. And on rare occasions a braided fez. Whatever was uncomfortable. As far as his daughters were concerned this made him a prize old fart, but a prize old fart was how your dad was meant to look. Uncle Charles on the other hand was getting about like a disreputable lodger their mother was knocking off on the side. That dressing gown! The one item in his wardrobe he had not let Hazel burn. At any moment, the girls feared, this appalling ancient garment was going to fall off his shoulders, unravel or undo, or he would simply omit, one fine morning, to wear it at all. And they were sufficiently Kreitman's daughters not to want to be there when that happened. Gross – that was their verdict on the new situation. Gross and sad. But as they didn't want to upset their mother by telling her that, they upped and left. Fingers crossed that by the time they returned Uncle Charles would have gone home to Aunty Chas and Mummy would be back wearing trousers.

This couldn't have suited Charlie better. With the girls gone, it was as if they had never been. No trace of them. How did some families do that? To remove the atmosphere of offspring from his house – his *old* house – you would have had to flood, earthquake and firebomb it. Twice. And even then a little dolly with a missing arm would surely have survived the flames.

Wonderful, no matter how the effect had been achieved, to move about a space free of consequences. Free of memories as well, for there was no sign that Kreitman had once been here either. Every impression of him upholstered over. So non-repercussive did the place feel, so without recall or aftermath, it could just as well have been a brothel – not that Charlie had ever been inside a brothel – as a home. What was the opposite to nice sex? Nasty sex? No. Just sex from which nothing flowed or issued except more of itself. As long as Hazel wasn't planning to flick it all away from him, Charlie believed he could at last count himself a happy and disreputable man.

Whereas Hazel – what Hazel loved about Charlie was the aura he gave off of being domiciled. Had anyone charged her with upholstering away all memory of Kreitman she'd have flown into a rage. 'Excuse me – he upholstered away all memory of himself. He was like a ghost, my husband. When he rose from a chair he left not a dent behind. When he looked in a mirror there was no reflection. He wasn't here. He never lived here. Tell me I dreamed him and I'll believe you. The only person you'll find to vouch for Marvin Kreitman's existence is his mother, and she's a ghoul.'

Charlie, on the other hand, left his imprint on everything and smelt of every chair he'd ever sat in. Kreitman had scoffed at Charlie for living bodilessly, for being embarrassed by his own skin. But Kreitman's judgements were all erotic, and since the erotic life for Kreitman was situated between his ears, he was the last one to talk of incorporeality. Kreitman didn't need a body; he propelled his penis with his mind. Poor Charlie may have been a bit behind the door sexually, but there was a body there to call on right enough.

'I'm a fatherless girl,' she told him. 'I find it marvellous that when I wake up you're still there.'

So they both felt it. Wonder of wonders, they each disappeared dreading into the dark, and each woke grateful and relieved that the other had not gone.

'Do that thing with your eyes,' Charlie said.

'What thing?'

'That thing when you sneak a look across at me with everything upturned. That sly, peeping thing. Ascertaining that I haven't crept away, but not wanting me to see that you're checking. Like a child on Christmas Eve, keeping a lookout for her presents.'

'Do I do that?'

'Often.'

'I don't.'

'You do. I promise.'

'That's because I had no dad. No one to dress as Father Christmas. I always knew it was my mother creeping in.'

'I'll be your dad.'

She looked alarmed. Like a child waiting for her presents to be taken away from her. 'Don't say that, Charlie.'

He put his arms round her, folding her inside him. 'I only mean that it touches me, the thing you do with your eyes.'

'It doesn't frighten you off?'

'God, no. I love it. I love the way your eyes hold the light when you do it. I love the way they seem to steal all the light that's in the room.'

'They are lit with the light of you,' she told him.

Whereupon he kissed them, making them better.

Wonder of wonders.

Then, out of the blue, 'Hey, why don't we' – Chas ringing Kreitman to suggest – 'meet up at my health club?'

Kreitman's first instinct – to smell a rat. 'I thought health clubs were single-sex institutions,' he said.

'Those are health *farms*. I'm talking about my gym.'

'I didn't know you had a gym.'

'I have now.'

'Why do you want me to meet you at a gym? Do they serve food there?'

'I wonder why you associate seeing me with eating, Marvin.'

'I associate seeing anybody with eating.'

'I'm just "anybody", then?'

'If you were just anybody, Chas, I wouldn't be in the state I'm in.'

'What state are you in? Have you gone to pieces over me?'

She's hysterical, Kreitman thought. 'I'm a wreck,' he said.

'That's exciting. Tell me more.'

More than hysterical. Hyperphasic.

'About as exciting as an unweeded garden,' he said. But he decided against mentioning the mould.

'Then it sounds to me that a gym is just what you need.'

'What will I have to do there?'

'Don't tell me you've never been to a gym.'

'Not since school. Gym then was something everybody dreaded. It astounds me that these days people pay to go somewhere they once avoided like the plague. Will I be required to do handstands against wallbars?'

'You can if you want, Charlie.'

Charlie!

'Marvin,' he corrected her.

She laughed her mistake away with a carillon of little bells, making nothing and everything of it. 'Come tomorrow at ten,' she said. 'It's quiet then. Do you have things?'

'Things?' Did she mean condoms?

'Shorts, trainers . . .'

'Those I'll buy,' Kreitman said. He had already mentally picked the bag he was going to carry his things in – South American leather, very soft, lots of zip pockets, with a tartan lining, on sale in his own shop right below him, a snip at three hundred and fifty smackers, but then it came to him at half that.

She gave him the address. 'Ten o'clock, then.'

'Ten o'clock then. Oh, and Charlie, how will I recognise you?'

'Has it been so long?'

'An eternity.'

She laughed, but didn't hesitate. 'I'll be wearing a scarlet leotard.'

As I dreaded, Kreitman thought.

He slept badly. No man sleeps well before a prizegiving. Now that she was almost within his grasp – he didn't mean that in any predatory sense, but her confusing her husband's name with his did seem to signal some significant mental changing of the guard on her part – it was natural that he should consult with himself on the question of whether or not he really prized or wanted her. What if he didn't? *If* he didn't, there was no explaining why he'd been moping about without the consolation of company all these weeks – but *what* if he didn't? She seemed a responsibility, suddenly. A burden. You don't take on lightly a woman whose husband has left her, a woman whose husband has left her for your wife and whose voice has risen to perilous heights. Chas normally had a loamy, vegetable contralto – soothing rather than thrilling, like being tucked up in a warm bed. Now her voice was skidding about the upper register, as though it were on ice skates. She sounded like a woman in need of support. Remembering his cat Cobbett, Kreitman wondered whether support was something he had it in him to provide.

He was at the gym shortly before ten, his driver unable to resist a joke about the location. 'You decided to take up bodybuilding, Mr Kreitman?'

'Time to get a bit of fat off, Maurice,' Kreitman said. He thought he caught Maurice grinning Africanly at his new overnighter.

Chas wasn't waiting for him in reception. They told him at the desk that she was already upstairs in the gym, but it wasn't going to be as easy as nipping up to find her and having a quick run-around. First he had to enrol as a temporary member, choosing a full-peak, off-peak or semi-off-peak tariff, then he had to fill out a questionnaire about his health, then he had to have his photograph taken, then he had to swap a credit card for a key to the locker room and a towel, and even then they wouldn't let him up in case he intended getting on to one of the machines prior to medical assessment and without supervision. An insurance thing. 'I've got plenty of insurance of my own,' Kreitman said. 'But anyway, I promise I won't go on anything. I still have a note in my pocket from my mother, forbidding me to climb on to anything mechanical. It's held good for over thirty years. Trust me, I just want to talk to Mrs Charlie Merriweather. So far you've relieved me of the best part of three hundred pounds – that must buy me ten minutes of conversation. Please let me go up.'

The unilluminated women at the desk – he would not have employed them, not even for West Norwood – took pity on themselves, rather than on him, for gyms are wordless places and Kreitman had already spoken more sentences in a minute than they heard here in a month. 'That way' – pointing him in the direction of the locker rooms. Not like school showers, no echoing tiles, no rotting timber draining boards for feet, none of that hot badger's-lair smell of what, before the advent of trainers, they used to call pumps; but still the old discomfort around undressing in the company of people of the same sex. The woman didn't exist before whom Kreitman wouldn't, in the blinking of an eye, display his genitals. How many had seen them? How many hundreds? How many thousands, even? *In Ispagna . . . mille e tre*. But men, no. To men he remained a secret. Nor did he want to see theirs. Nor their buttocks, though that was the way men generally made it easy on one another, effecting a three-quarter turn so that any genitalia you got, you got in profile; otherwise innocuous rump. Except it never was. Very shocking to Kreitman, the plump wire-haired backside of a man. Naked with one another, men were *too* naked. Kreitman found them frightening. What they found him was another matter. A man who did not use his mouth like other men? Automatically, he undressed as he'd last undressed as a schoolboy, keeping his shirt on till last, then sliding his shorts on under that.

Chas laughed when she saw him. Pressed polo sweatshirt, socks with a horizontal blue stripe in them pulled halfway to his knees, clumping snow-white trainers the size of moon boots. And still carrying his leather overnighter.

'You look ready for anything . . .' she noted, '. . . except exercise.'

'I haven't come here for exercise,' he reminded her, going over to where she was langlaufing like a mad woman, beating eggs with both hands.

She pushed buttons on her machine and slowed down. A bank of numbers appeared on the dial, followed by a heart, lit up and pounding. She had high colour in her cheeks, no doubt from the exertion. But also, Kreitman thought, from hypermania. He was surprised to recall that he hadn't seen her since she'd driven him home from Dartmoor in a knitted hat (*her* in a knitted hat), with so much left unsaid between them. So how was she looking after all this time, other than perfervid? Was he still in love with her, after weeks and weeks of imagining, now that she was flesh again?

The other and perhaps more important question to ask – was she at all (never mind still) in love with him?

One phrase will suffice for both: Who knows.

What counted was that from this moment they felt locked into it: they had talked of meeting, they had toyed with meeting and now they had actually met – to go backwards from that would have been more tiresome than to go on.

'I'm sorry about the way I look,' Kreitman said, offering to read her mind.

'Is that another way of saying you're sorry about the way *I* look?' Chas said, reading his.

He took her in. Hair pulled up in a fairground-coloured alligator clip, cheeks on fire, chest flat under a taut white body garment whose manufacturer's label was out and which must have stud-fastened under the crotch, given how lumpy the crotch appeared to be, legs spidery, with too much space between them, and that superabundance of gusset and seam that makes you avert your face when you see it on little girls kitted out for the ballet.

How did she look? Shit was how she looked. But who was he to talk? They both looked shit, just like the last time they'd met. Was that their fate, always to look shit for each other?

But if he'd wanted smart he could have stuck with Erica, couldn't he. Not a fold or seam awry anywhere on Erica. Not a label showing. Ditto Hazel, who went to the gym once in a blue moon, carrying a little too much weight certainly, grown top-heavy over the years (though definitely no tub of lard), but always nicely coordinated and zesty, still capable of turning heads. And Ooshi in running shorts – taking it as read that unshaven legs kindled wild desire in other men as well – was a sight to make an atheist believe in divine purpose. But Kreitman wanted none of those. Kreitman wanted Chas.

'You look the way I hoped you'd look,' he lied, and when she peered down her nose at him quizzically, as though over spectacles, though she wore no spectacles for the gym, then extended her long milkmaid's arms (at the end of which her little afterthought hands, denuded, he noticed, of all rings) – a handshake was what she gave him, not a kiss, her pumping cheesemaker's handshake – he realised he wasn't lying at all. He *did* like the way she looked – she, Chas, as opposed to what she had capitulated to, her unspeakable end-of-civilisation aerobic-wear – liked her because she was contradictory, droll and solemn, stern and wicked, capable of everything that was opposite to her nature. The old fault line.

And she?

Terrified.

Terrified of what she was doing. Terrified of herself, of her own temerity. Terrified of him.

Hard to credit, watching him on the treadmill while she flailed for another fifteen minutes across Norway, a man so unrhythmic, so unaccustomed to any bodily exertion except the little of it imposed by lovemaking, that the slightest unevenness in the revolutions of the rubber tread he toiled along, like Mother Courage, made his head spin and his balance precarious – hard to credit that such a man could inspire terror in anyone. But yes, she was afraid of him. It was possible she had chosen to meet him in the gym precisely so she could put him at a disadvantage and see him at his least fearsome. If so, it didn't help. His reputation came before him. He was unreliable. He was a man who let you down, whatever he looked like on a treadmill. He made promises he couldn't keep. 'It's not as though I don't know what I'll be letting myself in for,' she e-mailed Dotty, only the day before she asked Kreitman out, supposing you could call this 'out'. 'And I am not so naive as to suppose I can be the one to change him.'

'Which doesn't stop you from supposing you just might be,' Dotty e-mailed back.

'Are you laughing at me?' Chas typed.

'No. I think you should have a good time and hang the consequences,' Dotty promptly replied.

'Which are bound to be dreadful?'

'Dire, darling. Have fun.'

So fun was what Chas had logged off and decided to have.

THREE

H E TOOK HER to a trade fair.
Fun? He'd show her fun.

'We can drive or we can fly or we can get the train,' he told her.

'Where are we going?'

'Harrogate.'

'Then let's turn it into an adventure. Let's go by train.'

'What you have to understand,' he explained, over a Great North Eastern breakfast, 'is that there are trade fairs and trade fairs. Some I go to are dedicated leather goods and luggage shows – the hard-core, big-name stuff, Globetrotter and Constellation cases down one row, Longchamps, Picard, shocking-pink Pollini clutch bags made out of ostrich up another. Some are fashion events which also do accessories – good for off-the-wall items, copper-mesh evening bags, chain-mail belts, silk purses made out of sows' ears. Where we're going is more of a gift fair, which encompasses just about everything, even arts and crafts.'

'Are those sops to my rural origins?' Chas asked.

'Not at all. They are calculated insults to the memory of my cosmopolitan father. He made it a point of honour never to have anything handmade on his stall – "You call it handmade, I call it drek," was how he charmingly put it. So I make it a counter-point of honour to dabble in a little tooled leather when I can. It sells sometimes, as well, amazingly enough. Even in Wimbledon you get the occasional backwoodswoman. And now, of course, there's line dancing.'

'It astonishes me just to hear you say the word craft,' she said, 'let alone to discover you actually stock it. I thought it was a point of honour with you that everything you sold had to have the stitching *inside*?'

'And cost a million pounds?'

'At least.'

He smiled sourly at her. She thought him slick. Glitzy. A pedlar of overwrought merchandise for Saudi Arabians or women of the Cosa Nostra. It was an underlying grievance in his relations with the Charlies that they had always backed away from the facts of how he earned his living, much as if he'd been a shyster lawyer or a moneylender. Every marketing detail of every book they'd ever written he'd lived through with them – titles, covers, reviews, awards. 'Look, what do you think?' Charlie used to come charging down the stairs to cry, holding aloft the latest volume, before the Kreitmans had even got their coats off. 'New illustrator. Yes or no?' But if Kreitman so much as mentioned briefcases the Merriweathers would suddenly smell something burning in the kitchen, or remember a stranded child they had to pick up. Don't get him wrong – he didn't *want* to talk shop, he wanted to talk *Kultur* – that was the whole point of dining at the Merriweathers once a fortnight – but a little quid pro quo wouldn't have gone amiss. Once in a while they might have expressed concern that a consignment of hand-painted lipstick cases from Gujarat had gone missing in the earthquake, or bothered to remember that Kreitman had launched a new line of mobile-phone cases in the finest kidskin, designed exclusively for his shops by him – 'So how are they going, Marvin?' they hadn't asked. He wasn't looking for a major conversation, just the small change of amicable enquiry. Nor was he looking, quite, for social acceptance – unless he was.

The one exception to this blanket distaste, ironically enough, was trade fairs. Kreitman had only to say he was off to a trade fair and Charlie Merriweather's face lit up. 'Full of carbuncled rogues and louche auctioneers, will it be?' he asked.

'It's not that sort of a fair,' Kreitman told him. 'Forget Smollett and Surtees. It's not a horse fair. It's not a carnival of the picturesque trades. It's just a thousand stalls with hard shell suitcases on them and a bunch of dead farts taking orders.'

'Clerkly types? I love those. Brown overalls and pencils behind their ears?'

'Those are cheesemongers, Charlie.'

'Lots of roistering?'

Kreitman sighed. 'The major manufacturers usually offer you a small drink and a crisp. And the people at the glamour end, if they're there, as like as not have a dozen fridgeloads of champagne on their stalls, though I wouldn't call what they do roistering – more falling asleep.'

'What about at night? Do you all stay at the same hotel?'

'Usually at the same nine or ten hotels. You do the rounds.'

'And what happens?'

'There's a great dealing of eating, much adding up of order forms, usually under the table, and some modest wife-stealing, but not enough to get excited about.'

'Sounds riveting,' Charlie enthused. 'I do wish you'd take me with you.'

But because he didn't appreciate being the Merriweathers' day at the races, the channel through which the raw sewage of human vitality flowed into the Merriweathers' cautious lives, Kreitman never did take Charlie along. Now here he was, taking Charlie's wife.

Was life strange or was life strange?

'What you'll find,' he told Chas, 'is that the wider the gap between the actual value of the object and what it fetches, the nicer to be with those who sell it. If you ask me who I really look forward to seeing up here it's the boys who sell sunglasses. How much do sunglasses cost to manufacture? Not a brass razoo. What do they sell them for? A king's ransom. And like it or not, the size of that discrepancy lifts a burden from the personalities of people in sunglasses. No bitterness, you see. Potters and woodcarvers on the other hand, whose margin is their labour, are the least amicable souls here. Shouldn't be so but is. It goes against everything I've been taught. And against everything I believe in. But there you are. Nothing smooths the path of social intercourse like easily won prosperity.'

'Is that your motto?'

'No. My motto is life is cruel. But we're here to enjoy ourselves.'

'I thought we were here for you to buy bags.'

'Same thing. Follow me.'

They were in a grand floral hall, of the sort Chas remembered skipping through as a girl, holding her mother's hand, and, once in a blue moon her father's, wondering what made one onion arrangement win first prize and another identical onion arrangement win no prize at all. She had tasted cheese in a room just like this, and pulled a face after sipping elderflower wine. And later, in similar halls in Frankfurt and other cities of the children's book, she and Charlie had been trailed round foreign publishers, made a fuss of and quizzed greedily on future projects. (Ah, Charlie!) But for those memories, she could take such a space or leave it. It was a big room, that was all. Kreitman, on the other hand, was enchanted by it. 'Stuff as far as the eye can see,' he marvelled. 'Don't you love it? Heaven will be piled high like this. Maybe with handbags and purses, maybe not, maybe leather goods are kept in hell, but lobbied and full of light just like here, high-domed with metal girders and glass roofs, with lots of little tables to have sandwiches at, and all the inexhaustible plenty of paradise laid out on stalls in numbered avenues.' She felt she was with a small, hungry boy. 'Were you denied presents as a child?'

she wanted to ask him. 'Were you forced to go without?' But she didn't dare. And in the end didn't want to. Why break the spell? This was a side of him she hadn't expected to find. Marvin Kreitman, verdant! Sometimes, she was sure without his even knowing he was doing it, he squeezed her arm. *Look, Chas! Look!* Look at what? Quantity, that was all. Sheer volume. She was astonished by him. Who'd have thought it? Marvin Kreitman, as fired up by simple abundance as a kid in Santa's grotto!

And he was the same when he was buying, too. No shrewd reserve. No horse-trading or circumspection. Simply – 'Love those, love those, not so keen on those, love those, how soon can you deliver?' – and that was that. On to the next treat.

Was he doing it for her? To show her he wasn't Flash Harry? To show he had a heart? No, he was doing it for him. She had never seen him so happily engaged in anything. Normally, if there was a normally now that she and Charlie weren't Mr and Mrs Merriweather, but normally in the sense of previously, Kreitman would burst upon them in Richmond like a change in the weather, looking for some social fix, itching for trouble, vexed and vexatious. She would never have guessed he had it in him to enjoy something so lacking in disputatiousness as placing an order for wallets. Since he enjoyed it so much, and enjoyed the intercourse that went with it – stockist to supplier, leatherman to leatherman – she was at a loss to understand why he was always looking elsewhere for his satisfactions, why he wasn't content to do the thing he did, instead of semi-professionally upsetting women. But then Chas didn't know the father of whom Kreitman was the son.

And how otherwise had Chas imagined the afternoon going? What had she pictured – Kreitman counting notes out of his briefcase and tormenting unpractised artisans with the smell of city money? 'Never mind what's on the price list, how much to *me*, sunshine?' Something more *businessy*, was that what she'd been expecting? Something that smacked a little more of the cold mercantilism of Saudi Arabia, say? – though that hardly made any sense, did it, since Saudi Arabia was hot. What then? She knew what she'd expected and wouldn't name it. Shame on me, she thought.

That she could paint herself the villain helped her face the night. He wasn't the evil one, she was. In which case, if one of them had the right to second thoughts, it was him. Nothing had been said about – she made mental quotation marks – 'the night'. They had dropped their bags off at the hotel without registering, then walked straight over, through the gardens, to the exhibition rooms. She had thought the hurry was to postpone embarrassment. Or even to bamboozle her. Night, what night? Now she knew it was simply because Kreitman couldn't wait to get over there and breathe in Elysium. But did that mean he was not calculating on any embarrassment, that it was all dusted down and sorted, he and she a couple – Mr and Mrs Marvin Kreitman! – sharing the one room, the one toothbrush mug, the one bed? Had they had that conversation? If so, she hadn't been listening. Anxiety about the arrangements had been plucking at her peace of mind – ha! her what? – ever since she'd met him on the station platform that morning, looked him over in his over-lapelled Italian suit, stared into his too avid eyes and wondered what the hell she was embarking on. By mid-afternoon her understanding of who was arranging to do what to whom – an understanding that had stopped at fluttering heroines and bad-faced villains – had undergone a quiet revolution. Let's look at it this way, she thought: it was she who had first invited him to meet her at the gym; it was she who had accepted, with what was beginning to look like unseemly alacrity, an offer to accompany him on a buying trip to Harrogate which really was *a buying trip to Harrogate*; and it was she who was wandering round the fair a picture of world-weariness and cynicism, while the heart of the scoundrel bent on seducing her was pounding like a ten-year-old's. If anyone should be wondering whether this excursion, or whatever you were meant to call it, was the right thing, shouldn't it be him?

Well, he's big enough to tell me to push off, she decided. But by God it helped her, when Kreitman had seen and bought enough, and the hour for sorting out 'the arrangements' – the hour she'd been dreading – struck, to think of him as the innocent and herself, if not exactly as the abductress, at least as a force, and maybe even the instrumental force, in whatever happened next. It only needed the receptionist to hand her a key to her own room, a room not immediately adjoining Kreitman's at that, not in the same corridor, not on the same floor – briefly, she expected to hear, not even in the same hotel – for her to wonder whether she wasn't the blackguard in this relationship, and furthermore to wonder whether the very word relationship wasn't itself an imposition of impurity on the snow–white blamelessness of Kreitman's intentions.

'I'd have expected you to be hairier than you are,' she told him, making absent circles with her fingers on his chest, trying to remember girlish ways.

She was in his arms, not easy for her as a non–collapsible woman, but she had found a way of folding down her shoulders and introverting her elbows, which was more comfortable than it ought to have been.

He looked down at himself. 'I seem hairy enough,' he said, in a voice so gentle he barely recognised it.

'That's my hair you're looking at, you fool,' she laughed. Her voice had come down off the high wire and was warm and deep again, like turned earth. 'And I'm not talking about the amount of hair you've got, anyway. I mean I expected it to be more like you, spikier and more aggressive. Your skin, too, is softer than I imagined.'

'Remembered,' he corrected her.

She knew which word she wanted to use. '*Imagined*,' she insisted, warning him off.

But Kreitman knew which word *he* wanted to use. 'Remembered,' he repeated. 'Except that it would appear you haven't.'

'Haven't what, Marvin?'

'Haven't remembered the feel of me.'

She made a movement to sit up, but he held her to him. 'You're the one who hasn't remembered,' she said. 'I haven't ever touched you. Not touch touch. I grabbed you. That was all. Once upon a time, before I was a respectably married woman, I made a grab at you in anger, but of course a man never minds that. I sometimes think you could grab a man's cock off in rage and he'd take it as a sexual compliment.'

'Try me, Charlie.'

'I don't feel any rage right now.'

He knew what he could do to change that. He could ask her to describe to him the spirit in which, on the very same spot, and *after* she was a respectably married woman, she had made a grab at Nyman. But why go looking for trouble? Don't spoil it, he told himself. Don't rub at an old itch. Isn't this lovely enough for you?

It even crossed his mind that if this *wasn't* lovely enough for him, he was as good as done for, a dead man.

Fortunately, it *was* lovely enough for him. The pair of them drifting about like ghosts lost in an unknown room, coming in and out of sleep, cautious of each other, watchful of the abrasions which a sudden movement or a false note could cause – abrasions to the body, wounds to the soul. It was what she had dreaded, the whole performance of getting to know another person intimately again, making sure your spirits didn't clash, that your knees didn't bang, that you didn't speak over each other's words, what's your star sign, what's your favourite colour, if there's a God how do you explain Auschwitz, oh sorry, have I already asked you that. That was the reason everybody their age always gave for not embarking on an affair even when an affair beckoned – who could face the getting-to-be-acquainted ritual one more time. It was what baffled people about Kreitman, how he could go on and on doing that. Without doubt it helped in this case that they already knew each other, but knowing as a friend, more specifically knowing as a friend of your husband, was not the same as knowing as a . . . well, knowing as a lover, was it? Yet here she was, here *they* were, encased in darkness, feeling their way around each other's hearts, daring to risk questions, only half noticing the answers, making gifts of revelations so tenuous they floated off into the night, finding a whole hidden history of the self here and now in the cradling of foreign arms – in short, doing everything the no-longer young said they never wanted to do again, except that it seemed they did, else why did it feel so heaven-sent.

'Is this what's always in it for you?' she asked.

He didn't stir. 'I don't get any part of that question,' he said. They had left the bathroom door ajar and by the faint yellow light coming in from the street he could just make out their distorted reflections in the chromeware, some of him in the taps, some of her in the towel rail, come together more astonishingly, if that could be, than even in their actual conjoined flesh.

She took her time. Infinity was all around them. 'Is this the reason you go from woman to woman?'

This? Well, he couldn't pretend he didn't know what *this* meant. '*This*, Chas, is the reason I'm going nowhere.'

'No,' she said. 'It isn't necessary to palm me off. I'd actually prefer to hear it from you that you go from woman to woman in order to keep on feeling this. I can see how it could become compulsive. Looking to be reinvented, again and again, remade in another person's appreciation of you. I can forgive that sooner than some heartless, accumulative thing.'

'I'm not heartless, I'm humourless. I can't do casualness.'

'I thought casualness was exactly what you did do.'

'I know that's what you thought. You were wrong. I do solemnity. I make a wake out of everything. That's to say I *did*.'

'But I'm not talking about the spirit in which you do numbers, I'm just asking why you do numbers at all.'

'I don't. Just because they accumulate doesn't mean I'm an accumulator. They accumulate in the course of my trying to pin them down.'

'But why do you want to pin women down, Marvin? Listen to your own language. Why must they be *down*, and why must you *bring* them down?'

She was disappointed in herself. She had meant to be subtler. He had not acted – so far, so far – as she had expected him to act, yet here was she asking precisely the questions which he must have known she'd ask.

Listening to her, Kreitman felt a fraud, and not a little sorry for them both. If he'd ever had a day as a doer-down of women, a libertine or whatever the word used to be, that day was over. There were no more libertines. The very idea was an anachronism. Only in the heart of Charlie – herself an anachronism – did the fear of libertinage still exist. Only in this bed, next to this woman, was he still a dangerous man. He thought it behoved him to tell her that.

'Listen, Charlie,' he said, 'you're fighting an enemy that's packed up and gone home. The great seducers of the past were first and foremost blasphemers and revolutionaries. They got at God and the established order through women. There's no mileage in that any more. Now the worst crime we can charge them with is misogyny. Which is not just feeble psychology – the idea that you would go through women because you hate them – it's also milk-and-water theology. What a downgrading of sin! To reduce evil to such a piddling ambition – the sexual downfall of a gullible woman.'

'It's not so piddling if you're the woman.'

'Of course it's not . . . assuming she exists any more, the poor but honest wictim.'

'It's still a question why you seek it, Marvin, even if you would rather be fighting God.'

'I don't seek the downfall of women. I just need them to stay still while I work out what I do seek. Which is more likely to be my own downfall.'

She could hardly stay still herself after that. 'No fear,' she laughed. She tried to break from his arms, but he kept them close around her, his hands locked in the fuzzy hollow of her back, a smaller space than he'd imagined, a velvety declivity like something unexpected in nature, a mouse hole on a golf course, or a tiny crater from a meteorite. In clothes she seemed all bones, a woman made of calcium and chalk, out of them she was an undulation of smooth surfaces. How this could be, Kreitman had no idea. But then she was all surprises to him.

He could have said that that was one reason why he went, in her quaint phrase, from woman to woman – why he had *once* gone from woman to woman – because you never knew what you were going to find. The ever unfolding amazement. But he was no longer in the grip of unlocated curiosity; what moved him now was the miracle of Chas: why her skin refuted chaos theory; why his own skin seemed to come off under her fingers, so unexpectedly possessive was her touch; why his body received hers as though her imprint had been on him since birth.

He kissed all around her eyes. Two perfect circles. 'I can't make it sound any good,' he told her, 'and I ask you not to ask me to name it – but here, now, with you, I have found what I want.'

She blinked something salty into his mouth. 'Will it do me any good to believe that?' she asked.

'Not for me to say. I can only tell you what I tell you.'

'Will it do *you* any good for me to believe that?'

He thought about it. Make a woman believe you and you're in trouble if you're lying. Trouble with yourself. He knew that. Every man knows that. The hard bit is to know whether you're lying or not. All he could think was that he'd come through a sort of purgatory getting to this point with her. She had been touchy at dinner with his business friends, noisy men who sold sunglasses and weren't at all, to her sense, those easygoing profiteers he'd promised her. 'I don't know where you're going, Kreitman,' one of them had challenged him, over the third or fourth bottle of champagne, 'but I'm going this way' – pointing upwards and meaning, if Chas understood him correctly, to the topmost rung of the ladder of success. Before Kreitman had found something witty to say in reply, a second sunglasses man had roared with laughter, offering it as his opinion that 'that way' – meaning up the stairs of the hotel – was exactly where Kreitman was going too. Just the coarse surmisings Chas had been dreading. God knows, in Kreitman's reading of the situation, she had fought hard to dispel any doubts that she was his tart for the night, by coming down to dinner in an appallingly ill-fitting trouser suit made of green sacking, the jacket loose on her chest, revealing altogether too much of a white armoured brassiere, and too scant behind, showing the label of her trousers, or something even worse; the trousers themselves too floppy and too long, a clown's trousers, through which, whether or not that was the label he could see when she rose to leave the room, was too visible the outline of her underwear. For desire to have got past such an outfit, what was over and what was under, some other element must have come into play. That other element could only have been love.

He buried his face in her neck and breathed in her odours. Hay and plum wine. Upsetting. God knows why. Something autumnal. She was passing and it was his job to hold her back.

'If you want to know what will do *me* good,' he said sadly, as though speaking of impossibilities, 'it's you learning to believe what I say to you.'

This time she did break from him, and sat up, pulling the sheets to her neck. She didn't like her white freckled chest, with its striations of middle age, nor did Kreitman; she didn't like her undermined breasts with their flat nipples, unpalatable even to her babies, as indeed they were to Kreitman – didn't that *prove* it was love?

'What would you think of me if I took at face value everything you're telling me,' she almost pleaded, 'and pretended to ignore that you've said it to a hundred other women?'

He sat up himself and reached for the unfinished wine by his bedside, by *her* bedside rather, for he had come to her room, not taken her to his, knocking gently, softly softly, no brusque alarms, even while she was still trying to decide whether she was a blackguard or not. The wine had been waiting, a queer-shaped bottle on a stainless-steel tray, with a card telling you the price around its neck. All part of the twenty-first-century makeover of grand hotels from chintz to stainless steel, the beds twice the size that had sufficed last century's travellers, and no more pretence that fucking wasn't the reason you were here. Gone, the old awkwardness around the signing-in – Mr . . . and Miss . . . oops!; gone the shifty expression on the porter's face and the coughing in the lift; gone the morning flurry to remake the bed so the chambermaid should never guess your secret – all gone, anachronisms, just like Kreitman, the last soldier of illicit sex. Now you fouled the sheets before you left the room, so no one should think you'd had a quiet night.

He sipped wine and listened to the silence of the room. Then he said, 'I am not irresponsible. I don't have a cruel streak.'

'I believe you.'

'I'm a softer-hearted man than you think.'

'That's exactly what I'm afraid of. Over the years I've heard Hazel say that it wasn't you following your prick she feared most, it was you following your tears.'

Prick – that word again. She made him light-headed. It was like talking dirty with a Mother Superior. But all he said was, 'Ah yes, Hazel.'

'Ah yes, Hazel!'

To change the subject, he said, 'And what should *I* fear most, Chas?'

'From me?' She laughed a bitter laugh. 'My cowardice,' she said. 'And maybe my inexperience. You have a one-man woman in your bed, remember.'

'It's your bed, Chas.'

'All the more shocking. I may wake up in the morning and regret this.'

'I won't let you.'

'You won't be here.'

'Won't I? Do you mean to expel me?'

'Well, I could go to your bed and leave you here if that would make you feel better. But I cannot wake with you. Not so soon. I might roll over and call you Charlie.'

'You have already called me Charlie.'

'Have I?'

'On the phone.'

'That's different. I haven't yet rolled over and thought you *were* Charlie.'

'I could handle that.'

'There you are, you see, I couldn't. We are incompatible when it comes to accustomedness. I'm still all shocks, Marvin.'

But the amazing thing – wonder of wonders – was that so was he.

FOUR

CHARLIE, ON A strange lavatory, hears Hazel asking for his alibi.

'Alibi? What alibi?'

'What's your alibi? Do you have an alibi ready?'

A hand rattles the doorknob.

'I'm in here,' Charlie says. 'It's me in here.'

The door is locked, but that doesn't stop her. And Charlie cannot put his weight against the door because the strange lavatory is long and narrow, almost a passageway, the rattling door at one end, he sitting, without an alibi, at the other.

One more turn of the knob and she is inside. Not Hazel – he had that wrong – but Chas, his wife Chas.

She is wearing a towel piled high around her head, a snow-white turban, as though she has just stepped from the bath. Her face is raw from bathing, too. Chas – fancy Chas being here! His instinct is to get up and greet her – Hello, Chassyboots! – but in the circumstances, lavatory and all that, he cannot. As she advances towards him, she grows. By the time she is upon him she is twice her normal height. He looks up and notices her fingernails. They are splayed, like scissor-hands, longer and redder than Chas ever allowed her nails to grow, not fingernails at all, when you really look, but proper nails, nails for hammering, each one silver, not red, and sharpened to a point. 'Your alibi,' she demands again. But before he can think of one, her nailed hands are in his eyes . . .

Until recently, Charlie was never that much of a dreamer. But he is dreaming a lot now. For him.

'Oh, for God's sake, Charlie,' Hazel said, 'you cannot still be raving over the contents of my cupboards.'

What this time?

Towels.

Lying back in her bubble bath, Hazel marvelled at the pertinacity of her lover's enthusiasms. Why had no one ever told her a man could be so easy to amaze? First it had been her perfumes, then her oils, then her moisturisers, then her soaps, then her rollers, if you could believe that – her piccaninny Molton Browners which would have thrown Kreitman, had he seen them, into a blue fit – after which her sheets, her pillowcases, her duvet covers, her throwaway slippers and this week, though he'd been drying her with them for months, her towels with the satin borders.

'Charlie, I've been to your home. You wife buys the same towels I do.'

Charlie shook his head. He was too big, really, for a bathroom. He didn't know where to put himself. But as long as she allowed him into the mysteries of her toilet, let him talk to her while she gently poached her flesh in hand-hot water, how could he take himself off somewhere else.

'Charlie never bought towels as large and soft as these,' he said. 'Charlie bought towels that scratched. I now wonder whether it was deliberate. On the hair-shirt principle – to make me bleed.'

Well, be thankful, Hazel thought. She considered telling him that it was more likely to have been a soap-powder problem in Richmond, but that was hardly her business, was it? And if Charlie believed her towels were softer and caused less pain, who was she to complain?

She called him to hose off her bubbles, then climbed out of the bath, pinker than a porcelain doll, into the marvellous towel

219

he held open for her. If she went limp in his arms, he would enfold her in them and dry her with the heat of his body. If she stiffened, he withdrew. It was like having a dog who could read every nuance of her moods.

She was beginning to tire of him, then? Not at all. She could not now imagine her life without him, or remember what it had been like to have no one there to welcome her out of her bath. But yes, she was taking him just the teensiest bit for granted. His own doing, he was so docile.

Nice sex, was that what Charlie was importing chez Kreitman? I should worry, Hazel thought. And nice sex, anyway, was sex enough for her. But it did sometimes occur to her to be concerned that Charlie was domesticating their bed to an extent that he would ultimately regret, even if she wouldn't.

Being married for so long to Kreitman had taught her some-thing – that men create the circumstances of their own dissatis-faction.

Their trouble was – and it may have been overstating things to call it a *trouble* – they didn't have enough to do. Charlie wasn't writing. She had set up a study for him at the top of the house, overlooking the garden so he could have green thoughts while he worked, but the loneliness had got to him. He was used to working in tandem with his wife. The pair of them at either end of their old pine table. She pounding at her typewriter, looking under or over her spectacles at him whenever she believed she had written a good sentence, he scratching behind his ear, coughing, getting up to make tea for them both, going for a wander down to the river, where he knew he would find someone with whom to exchange pleasantries, the time of day, anything, anything that employed the real warm words of life. When he told Hazel that the study she had put together for him was too quiet, or at least that his view was too unpeopled, she tried to make sure she was always in the garden while he was at his desk, so that she could animate his landscape, wave at him when he looked out, point to flowers that had recently bloomed, or just nod enthusiastically in response to his hand signals, which invariably illustrated some aspect of the making and drinking of tea. But that tied her to his working patterns rather, or at least would have tied her to his working patterns had he had any. He still couldn't get going. When she was there he played with her, when she was out he repined. He didn't know what to write. He wondered if there was any way he and Charlie could resume their collaboration by post, by e-mail, by text messaging even, without alluding to what had passed between them. But who was going to go first? He hadn't spoken to her since she'd sent him packing. All communications, including her demand that the C. C. Merriweather brand name revert forthwith to her, had been made through their accountants – now *her* accountants – which he took to be significant in that she hadn't yet resorted to a solicitor. Could they perhaps go on writing together through their accountants? It was when he reached that point in his creative deliberations that he got up, clattered down the stairs and ran a bath for Hazel.

As for Hazel, she didn't have enough to do either. Overseeing conversions and complaining to tradespeople had seemed a full-time occupation before. Now that she had Charlie at home with her she was less willing to have her house redesigned, let alone to open it to builders. 'Apart from anything else there's your concentration to think about,' she told him, as an explanation for why the Jacuzzi hadn't gone in.

'Yes, there's my concentration to think about,' Charlie agreed. 'Though we could go away for a week while they do it.'

For similar reasons – a relief, this, to service industries throughout the capital – her telephone complaints routine had stalled. She had other things to do with her mornings now. Nor did she dress any longer in the sort of clothes that had once made complaining easy. In a tailored suit she was not a person to be trifled with, even on the telephone; but wearing the sorts of frills and spikes Charlie liked to see her in, trifle was her middle name. The best explanation of why Hazel's phones slumbered quietly on their cradles, however, lay in the change that had come over her temper: she wasn't complaining because she had nothing to complain about. She was happy.

Of her old discontented habits only one remained – testing the returns policy of every shop in London. She had not been born a taker-back of clothes. Like kleptomania, of which it is a near relative, the taking-back of clothes is a function of despair, and despair had entered Hazel's life only when she discovered that her husband's tears were universal. He substituted one woman for another, shedding tears along the way, and she did the same with clothes. It was an addiction she could not shrug off, even though she had shrugged off Kreitman. The clothes she bought continued to look wrong the minute she got them home, didn't fit although she'd tried them on in the shop, looked different in different light, looked wrong, looked stupid, made her angry. But these days, instead of seething up and down the West End in the rain, her hands full of creaking carrier bags, she ambled in and out of her favourite New Bond Street stores with a carefree smile on her face, and Charlie on her arm.

It suited him. If he was taking back with Hazel he couldn't suffer those bouts of unproductive loneliness in his study. And if he was taking back with Hazel he could get to see her nipping out from behind curtains in her underwear. Here was another example of how his life had changed. With Chas, shopping for clothes had been one humiliation piled upon another, a saga of fluster and concealment, annoyance, embarrassment, misjudgement, despair – and that was just him. Off they'd go to get her out of her spinnaker, and back they'd come after a thousand disappointments and alarms with a spinnaker no different from all the others. 'Nothing else fits me, Charlemagne. This is all there is. Don't say anything!' For Chas, a changing room was a torment somewhere higher up the scale of mortifications than the ducking-stool, whereas for Hazel – well, for Hazel, a changing room was almost like a public stage. Back the curtains went and there she was, half naked, entirely unabashed, careless who saw her – 'Have you got this in a fourteen?'– waiting only for Charlie to leap from his upholstered sugar-daddy's chair and cry *Bravo!*

What a gift it is, Charlie thought, what a gift some women have for sensuality, for making life easy, for filling it with enchantment. And how lucky that makes me!

A gift for making life easy! – Hazel the difficult, Hazel who was courted in her early years by men leaving nuts outside her door, to see if they could tempt her out, so wild and easily frightened a creature did she seem – a gift for filling life with enchantment, Hazel the terminally disillusioned!

My lottery theory confirmed, she thought, noticing how she'd changed. You are who you fall in love with. And I wouldn't have understood that had I not fallen in love with who I've fallen in love with.

And if she hadn't? She didn't want to think about it. If she was now a lovely person only because she had stumbled upon Charlie, what would have happened to her had she stumbled upon the Yorkshire Ripper? Idle question. She had stumbled upon Marvin Kreitman and look at the sort of person that had made her. Please God don't send me back there again, Hazel pleaded. Please God let me stay happy and lovely and with Charlie.

Happy in the bath and lovely in Fenwick's changing rooms and Charlie never out of her sight.

But when they weren't bathing or taking back, they were light on what Hazel, with some recapitulated disgust, called a 'social life'. Kreitman's phrase for the foremost of a man's entitlements, and hence Hazel's bitter euphemism for the same. As a consequence of the indignities to which marriage to Marvin Kreitman had reduced her, Hazel had more or less finished with a social life. Other than the Merriweathers – and they were now off the list – she saw none of her old university chums. She had a few similarly placed women friends she met in the restaurants of art galleries and with whom she abstractly discussed castration and lesbianism and the like – the ones who'd cheered her on when she'd cropped her hair, accused Kreitman of fucking her brain and kicked him out of her bed – but they would not have approved of the comprehensiveness with which, to please panting Charlie Merriweather, she'd reverted to the bad taste of a passive wardrobe. Which left only her daughters, expected back from Thailand any day, much missed by her, but in fairness no more a diversion for Charlie than he was a diversion for them.

The staidness of Hazel's life when she wasn't in New Bond Street, the monastic quietness of her house, astounded and dismayed Charlie, who had always considered himself a social orphan but in truth lived in the centre of that maelstrom Kreitman was quick to call the *Kultur*. Publishers of presses which had been failing since the forties, biographers of Surtees and Trollope, literary down-and-outs who carried their manuscripts with them everywhere in plastic bags, men who bore the names and obscurely benefited from the estates of Gosse and de Selincourt and Quiller Couch, faded beauties who had once given their hearts to Desmond MacCarthy, rock climbers, swimmers, explorers, cads and fogeys of every description, and of course writers of children's books by the magic busload – all these were regular visitors of the Merriweathers. If they weren't all there together on the lawn at weekends, waiting for Charlie to pour them Greek wine and Chas to rustle them up fish pie while pretending she couldn't find the fish, they turned up unannounced, in dribs and drabs, on weekdays. Frequently one would come to complain about the other, though not infrequently the other would already be there, complaining about the one. Sometimes the older among them would be found exhausted on the Merriweather doorstep after getting lost in Safeway's or being savaged by rutting deer in Richmond Park – actually bearing wounds, some of them, actually pitting the steps with blood the colour of pink gin — or just as likely having blundered out of their own quarters on a quite different errand the reason for which had subsequently escaped them. Not so much the nerve centre of the *Kultur*, then, as a hospice for it? Same difference, in Kreitman's view. The *Kultur* as shaped by the British loved a hospice as it loved itself, revered infirmity and thrived in sick rooms. Old men on drips pulled the levers, while young men old before their time, like Dotty's beau, padded in and out of the wards, took down their memoirs and did their bidding. But that, of course, was only Kreitman's view. And who was he to be an arbiter of rude health? Call these gatherings what you will, the consequence was that time never hung heavy at the Merriweathers'. Whereas at the Kreitmans', once lovemaking and towelling were finished for the day, you could hear the movement of the second finger as it dragged itself across the face of Hazel's bedside clock.

Charlie mentally prepared himself for visitors, but no visitors ever came. As for inviting his own people, he remained squeamish about that on account of Chas. A tact thing. But perhaps he was nervous on his own account as well, not knowing what they would make of him looking so well.

He kept contact with those of the Richmond *Kultur* to whom he'd been closest. Phone calls mainly; inconsequential conversations which skidded away from anything dangerous; chit-chat of a literary complaining sort, stuff in the papers, gossip about what was happening in the television soaps, which Charlie and his set watched religiously, as an affront to those who inhabited a sniffier *Kultur* than they did. He did a pub lunch once with Clarence Odger, the friend who carried five hundred thousand words of manuscript with him everywhere in two plastic Waitrose bags, but that didn't work out too well. In the first place the friend couldn't concentrate on anything Charlie was saying to him because he couldn't take his eyes off his plastic bags, and in the second, when he did remember his manners long enough to ask Charlie how his new life was going, there seemed to be some gleam in his eye which, in Charlie's view, denoted salacious knowledge. Was that how his friends thought about him now – salaciously? Was that in some way how he thought about himself?

Thereafter he made no further arrangements to see anybody.

'So, apart from me, did Marvin have no friends?' he asked Hazel one evening.

Hazel opened her eyes wide at him. 'You know what Marvin had.'

'And when you were together . . . ?'

'Which wasn't often.'

'No, but when . . . what did you do ?'

Hazel shrugged. What did they do? Had she forgotten already? Had *nothing* happened?

'Meals,' she said. 'I recall a lot of meals.'

'In or out?'

'Oh, out. My husband loved being out.'

'So what did you do when you were in?'

Knowing Charlie liked looking at the arch of her throat, Hazel threw back her head. '*In?*' she repeated 'Now there I think you've finally got me.'

'You didn't read to each other?'

Hazel laughed a bitter laugh. 'Marvin spat chips, Charlie. You were his friend, you know that. He spat chips in front of the television, he spat chips when we went to see a film or a play, and he spat chips when he opened a book. Where would have been the fun of reading together? I needed to hear him spit even more chips? I once suggested he pick up his old academic ambitions and write a book of his own. Call it *Spitting Chips*. But you can imagine his reaction to that. He spat chips. Nothing he hated more than gerundival titles.'

'Don't I remember it,' Charlie said. 'Don't I remember the scorn he poured on our *Flying Away* series.'

'He would have,' Hazel said, blinking. She was inclined to forget that Charlie had once been a writer of fictional self-improvement books for young adults. *Flying Away* must have driven her husband bananas. 'Ing me no ings, he used to say. It should go on his tombstone. Ing me no ings. Cute fucker!'

So Charlie read to Hazel.

'I can't tell you where I am,' Chas said, returning Dotty's far too early Sunday phone call, 'because I don't *know* where I am. But I'll give you a clue – I got here by rope ladder.'

'Christ, Charlie, are you abroad?'

'In a manner of speaking. Though in fact I'm on Clapham High Street . . . I think.'

'You think?'

'Well, I'm brought here, like some empress on a palanquin, only it's not a palanquin it's a Smart.'

'It sounds as though you've been kidnapped.'

'It feels a little as though I've been kidnapped.'

'Sounds like you're having fun, though.'

She thought about it. Was she having fun? 'Yes,' she said, 'I'm having fun.'

'And you'll remember to be careful?'

'On the ladder?'

'No, not on the ladder. On the you-know-what.'

Chas laughed. 'I'm damned if I know what the you-know-what is,' she said, 'unless you're meaning to be crudely graphic. But no, as a matter of fact I have no intention of remembering to be careful.'

Then, because Kreitman was shinning up with a pot of coffee, she rang off.

He liked seeing her up there, high among his books, angular like the girders, a great creature, the biggest of the non-flying birds, nesting in his aviary. With her mobile phone to her ear.

'There's no good reason, is there,' he said, blowing hard, 'so long as you've got your phone to keep you nominally connected to the world, there's no good reason why you shouldn't stay up here for ever.'

'Until you get bored.'

'I won't get bored.'

'Until my children need me.'

'Have them round.'

'Oh yes. I can see that. They didn't like you very much, Marvin, when you weren't charvering their mummy.'

Kreitman shrugged. He was only trying to meet her objections. 'Then don't have them round. Just phone them occasionally and visit them a lot.'

'And my work?'

'You can dictate. I'll be your stenographer. You might find the child in me.'

'Marvin, I think it's the man in you we need to locate.'

That's how far advanced they were. They could insult each other and not expect to be misunderstood. Half the art of falling in love — attaining the foolish intimacy of schoolchildren.

Then her phone rang again. And then it rang three or four times after that. Dotty for a second time, warning against silliness. She knew her sister would like that. The other calls were from those of Chas's friends who were also members of her profession. 'Sunday morning,' she told Kreitman between conversations, pulling a contrite face, 'the Sunday-morning ringaround. You'll have to learn to live with this if you want me never to leave your bed. On Sunday morning I catch up with the general rejoicing.'

To Kreitman's sensitised ears — greedy for tidings from the *Kultur* — rejoicing wasn't quite the word for it. 'You're joking!' he heard Chas say. 'You're kidding me! She didn't! The Smarties? I'd have given her more chance of winning the Peace Prize . . .'

Sometimes she set her mouth, compressing her lips to a bloodless scar, zipped tight across her face. Sometimes she tapped

228

irritably at her temples, as though to loosen congealed matter. Sometimes, in a bound, she went from hilarity to despair.

'What is it?' Kreitman asked when she was done. 'What have you heard?'

She sat with her knees up on his bed of rugs and tapped the space next to her. Lie here, my love.

She was confident of him. Confidently possessive of him, even on his territory. Lie here, my love – and he did.

Then she told him the terrible truth, that even writers of children's stories felt bad about one another's success, begrudged each other every penny, resented every word of praise bestowed on someone else.

'I'd never have guessed it,' Kreitman said.

She made as if to push him from the bed. 'You needn't be sarcastic. I'm just trying to be frank with you. I know how much you idealise my profession. So I think it's time you heard it from my lips. I am not pleased for X. I cannot ever be pleased for X. I count every tick on her page a cross on mine.'

Tell me about it, Kreitman thought. Tell me something I don't already know. As with letters, so with love. Every tick on his page, a cross on mine.

He smiled up at her and stroked her arm. Lolloping arms, he had once thought them. Mere farmyard implements. Now, transfigured by desire, they were a warrior maiden's arms, long and tapering and strong, beautiful, victorious, the arms of Boadicea.

'It's because we die,' he said. 'If we didn't die we could afford to be more magnanimous. But we only get one shot. We can't forgive the person who shoots further.'

She patted him like a child. 'Exactly,' she said. 'We cannot forgive or bear it. So what we do in our profession is make sure that no one else can forgive or bear it either. When you hear a rumour of someone else's good fortune, you pass it on. Passing the Pain, Charlie used to call it. A parlour game for two or more writers.'

229

'Except,' said Kreitman, 'that you don't have to be writers.'

'You pass the pain in purses, Marvin?'

He winced. She could still do that to him. 'I pass the pain in love, Chas,' was his reply.

'"I shall still lose my temper with Ivan the coachman, I shall still embark on useless discussions and express my opinions inopportunely,"' Charlie read, *'"there will still be the same wall between the sanctuary of my inmost soul and other people, even my wife . . . but my life now, my whole life . . ."'*

'Lovely,' Hazel said. 'I'd forgotten how positive a book could be.'

Charlie closed the novel and kissed her. They were sitting up in bed, supported by banks of pillows, his reading light on, hers not, so that shadows kept half of her obscure from him, still so much of her he could only guess at. 'Tomorrow night we'll start *Barchester Towers*,' he said.

She clapped her hands. 'Goody, goody,' she said.

When they put out the light and finally turned aside from each other, Hazel found herself cursing her husband. What did it take to make her happy? Had it really been beyond him to read her a story once in a blue moon? Would it not have made him happy too – or at least been balm to his troubled soul, if happiness was too much too expect of him, the gloomy fucker – would it not have been preferable to all that frantic running around in erotic misery, just to have stayed in with her, fluffed up their pillows and read a book together?

This was the one canker eating away at her contentment – the sweeter it was with Charlie, the less she could for-give Kreitman for having made it so sour. What Charlie did – effortlessly most of the time – Kreitman, too, could have done.

So one doesn't escape, Hazel realised. Happiness now doesn't erase misery then. What perverseness, to be punishing now with then, almost out of jealousy of oneself, as though, once miserable, one never has the right to happiness again.

Thank you, Marvin.

And was Charlie thinking along similar lines?

Similar, but not the same. Charlie, before he disappeared into fevered dreamland, was thinking how like his new life was, sometimes, to his old.

Some of us wake well, some of us wake badly. Chas Merriweather woke in pieces. Nothing worked. Nothing was attached. Half her hair seemed to have fallen out and all colour had been bled from her in the night. 'Don't look at me,' she told Kreitman. Her face was corrugated but queerly virginal, like the soles of her feet. She woke blotched, fraught, exhausted, as though the single purpose of the day would be to get her back to the condition in which she'd gone to sleep.

But Kreitman looked at her. What is more he enjoyed looking at her.

'Why are you laughing at me?' she cried, hiding herself under the sheets.

Was he laughing? He thought he was smiling. Pleased to see her. Pleased to see her *there*, with him. Pleased to witness the morning miracle of Chas putting herself back together.

I am maturing, Kreitman thought. I am not waking desperate to be gone. I like it that she comes to looking like the Battersea Dogs' Home. I am becoming *fond*.

From either side of her fault line he was putting things back together himself, but not too tidily if he could help it. He was fonder than he had been, and also more roused than he had been: those two states could not be unconnected, of course they couldn't, but he was not going to swap perverseness for harmony quite yet. What roused him, surely, was the novelty of the fondness, and of course the novelty of its object. Sensual, overwhelming all his senses, a woman who refused sensuality, who thought it was silly, and who woke the colour of her feet – explain that!

In the matter of his touching her, what Kreitman couldn't figure out was how, even in the darkness, his fingers were able to measure a quality he had no adequate words for but which, roughly, he thought of as the underlay of her skin. He loved the deep give in her, what he would have called her substance were it not for that word's associations of stoutness and amplitude, neither of which Chas possessed in the slightest. How best to put it? A woman like Shelley had skin so fine you feared it might flake off under your caresses. A woman like Bernadette, on the other hand, seemed to be stitched into a hide. You didn't stroke Bernadette, you polished her. And then again there was Hazel, whose whole vascular system seemed to be in motion when she rolled her hips, or swung her heavy breasts above his face, first one and then another, just beyond his reach, making him search for them blindly, with frantic lips – a thing she hadn't done for twenty years or more, not with him anyway. But Chas's flesh structure was not like any of these. She didn't leave him desolate, that was the best explanation he could give. She didn't spill out from between his fingers like mercury, or crumble under them like rose petals. She wasn't too much or too little. She was just the right amount.

In the matter of her touching him, there were fewer mystifications. She touched him, full stop. Or rather she held him, full stop. She took hold. It was the taking he loved, the way her little hand claimed possession of him – his penis, he specifically meant, but the moment she took hold he was *all* penis – encircling him with the most deceptive lightness, as though she were leading him into painless but permanent captivity, her hand the collar and her arm the chain.

Where had she learned to do that?

He knew the answer. She had learned it from him. She had

listened to the silent desires of his body and discovered what to do. But then of course she had listened to her own silent desires as well.

Accord was what you called this. Though whether it comes only when you are in love, or is itself the reason you get to be in love, no one will ever know.

And she? Well, she wouldn't have taken such complete possession of Kreitman if she hadn't wanted to, would she?

'I've never spent so long in bed in daylight hours,' she told her sister.

'I'm glad,' Dotty said, 'that you've finally released the pagan in yourself.'

Chas thought about that. 'I'm not entirely sure it's pagan,' she said. 'It's very intense.'

'Oh, Charlie, you aren't going to go religious on me.'

'No, I mean intense in another way. It's almost as though I've taken up with a nervous system wrapped in tissue paper.'

'You *are* having sex?'

'God, yes, oodles of it. But he's a strange man. Not at all like Charlie. Being with Charlemagne was like being with a bear. He rolled all over me. He made me feel I was covered in honey. This one goes very still, as if he's listening for something. His body seems to think, Dotty.'

'That comes as no news to me, darling. Haven't we all always known what Kreitman's dick was thinking? Just as long as you don't make the mistake of believing you can make it think something else.'

'Dotty, you are terminally trivial. I am trying to talk metaphysics to you. You used the word pagan – I simply wish you to know that we're not just thrashing about up here.'

'I understand, darling. Your bodies are thinking together. Thoughts, I am sure, far too deep for me. But that doesn't have to preclude all fun, does it? Tell me at least that you are having fun.'

233

'I'm having fun.'

'And you promise me you are not falling in love with him . . . or his thoughts.'

'We all have fun in our own way,' Chas said, making no promises.

FIVE

Marvin Kreitman's idea of fun was different from Chas's. Marvin Kreitman's idea of fun was not to go anywhere. Climb up the magic rope ladder, pull up the sheets and snip off the rope. Chas set about changing that. Slowly at first, starting with the kitchen. She taught him to cook, showing him how to stew apples and to crumble butter and flour. She taught him how to make jam, which fruit to use, how not to be frightened of sugar, how to stop before it got to the condition known as sticky. (The way you do with me, he laughed.) She even showed him – taking no notice of any of that – how to make that miracle of eggs, lemon meringue pie, Charlie's favourite.

He'd baulked at that. 'You have thought this through?' he checked.

'What do you mean?'

'You do know you're turning me into Charlie.'

'No danger of that,' she said. 'You don't call me Mrs Chassyboots and rub your stomach and beg for seconds.'

So Kreitman called her Mrs Chassyboots and rubbed his stomach and begged for seconds.

Then they looked at each other and agreed not to try that again.

'No fridge magnets, either,' Kreitman warned her.

But how, once he'd said it, could she resist? One morning, after she'd left to go back to Richmond – work, children, all that

235

– Kreitman climbed down his ladder and found I ADORE YOU in little red and yellow letters on his Lamborghini toaster. He thought his legs would go from under him. When Chas turned up again the next evening she found BUT NOTHING LIKE AS MUCH AS I ADORE YOU in letters twice the size running diagonally across the fridge door.

She climbed up the ladder to him and they kissed. 'That's so sweet of you,' she said. 'I know how much a clear fridge door matters to you.'

But in truth clear fridge doors no longer mattered a jot to him. They had gone out the window with the rest of his prejudices. All he wanted now was to exchange nursery-letter messages of love with Chas on every appliance in his kitchen. The moral infection of nice had claimed him.

'Soon,' Chas said, 'you'll be buying me a bear.'

So he went out and bought her a bear.

He couldn't keep it up for ever, of course. One day Chas found I WOULDN'T HALF MIND SLIPPING YOU ONE TONIGHT on the stainless-steel extractor hood. She pretended to shed a furtive tear. 'I had so hoped it would stay pure between us,' she lamented. Whereupon Kreitman messed up the letters and wrote WILL YOU MARRY ME.

Whereupon Chas fell very silent.

She took him to the ballet.

'Anything,' he'd said, 'so long as it's not *Swan Lake*.'

So she took him to see *Swan Lake*.

He'd been surprised by her taste. 'I knew you wouldn't be modern-modern,' he told her when she bought the tickets, 'but I would have expected thirties avant-garde of you.'

'Are you being rude to me, Marvin?'

'Not at all. I'm a thirties avant-garde man myself. In everything but ballet, anyway.'

'And what are you in ballet?'

'Revolted,' he told her sweetly.

'It's the men's lunch packs, is it? Charlie was uncertain about those too.'

'I'm not Charlie. The men are fine. It's the dirty dresses on the women I have trouble with.'

'Where do you get the idea that the women wear dirty dresses?'

'It's endemic. It's what people go to see. Slightly grubby ballerinas in yards of discoloured tulle. Don't ask me why. You're the enthusiast. I think it's some perverted, dirty-washing thing.'

She narrowed her eyes at him. Perverted was an objection suddenly?

But what she said was that she'd chosen *Swan Lake* as the easiest place to start. 'At least with classical ballet if you can't stomach the perversion you can enjoy the music.'

'Tchaikovsky!'

In the event, he did even better than that. He enjoyed everything. The athleticism. The body as lyrical instrument, for God's sake. The poignancy. Even the dirty washing. 'But don't forget,' he said, kissing her during the interval, 'that it's because I love being with you and being seen with you.'

He meant what he said. Being with and being seen with. She attracted attention in evening dress. It suited her to be sheathed in plain black, lightly jewelled, hoisted up on imperious heels, her cornfield arms and neck out, her hair down, another of her fault lines showing – a tomboy in a glamour frock, country mouse in the arms of town mouse, and vice versa. Sometimes photographers got excited when they saw her getting out of a taxi. 'They think I'm Camilla Parker Bowles' younger sister,' she whispered to Kreitman, flushing, fearing that who they actually took her for was Camilla Parker Bowles.

'Gets something,' Kreitman said proudly. 'Mistress of a prince.'

But he knew why they were taking her photograph. It was because she gave consciousness of rude.

★　　★　　★

She felt more herself, however much he liked her glittering (and therefore half somebody else), in her spinnakers and flatties. Walking clothes. She introduced him to where he lived. 'Road,' she said. 'Pavement, strolling area, little park, Common, woods.'

'Woods my foot,' he told her. 'That's faggot jungle.'

'Grow up, Marvin,' she said. 'You'd cottage if men and women could do it standing up.'

He dared her. But she knew his game. As long as he was daring her he didn't have to walk. 'Come on,' she said. 'You have one of the loveliest commons in London on your doorstep. Look how flat it is.'

And away they went, hand in hand, arm in arm – he liked linking her, the way he'd seen old European men, perhaps even his father, linking women, hanging on to them, almost hanging off them – until she explained that it was better exercise to swing your arms. Hazel used to tell him that as well; but on Hazel's lips it had seemed a reproach – get your filthy unfaithful hands off me, Marvin Kreitman – whereas from Chas, from Chas he could take anything. Explain that.

She got him into an anorak. Took him to one of those adventure streets in Covent Garden and had him fitted up for toggles. He screamed at first, brushing something off himself with such violence that she thought a tarantula must have sidled out of one the pockets. Even the shop assistant grew alarmed. 'Is everything all right, sir?'

'Words,' he shouted. 'I've got words on me!'

And he had. NORTH FACE. POLARGUY. SCARP.

There were no anoraks without words. Elsewhere, words were vanishing. Soon there would be no words. Now he knew where they were going. On to anoraks.

'I'll unpick them,' Charlie promised.

But of course he got used to the words and in the end rather liked having SHOREWALKER written across his back.

He saw the future, saw his life extending into old age, serene and comfortable, his arm in Chas's, the Common an explosion of butterflies, he and she white-haired and zipped into matching all-weather parkas, still handsome, still smiling when they caught each other's glance.

Then, one achingly sweet penitential Sunday – the first and last warm Sunday of the year – he saw Hazel and Charlie also walking arm in arm across Clapham Common. Happy they looked, no get your filthy unfaithful hands off me, Charlie Merriweather, no, none of that, just happily talking, laughing, absorbed entirely in each other, not looking at the world. Funny – Hazel on the Common in dancing shoes, Chas in hiking boots; Hazel dressed for cocktails, Chas for pitching tents. He thought he caught the sound of Hazel's laughter, tinkling and seductive, like a glass chandelier with breezes blowing through it. Today, for reasons of her own – perhaps a consequence of the melancholy leafiness of the afternoon – Chas was ruminative. Briefly, Kreitman felt a pang for something that had never been: not quite the past, and not quite what he had ever wanted the past to be. But it was a pang of retrospection of some sorts. *We are with the wrong women*, he thought. We are with the wrong women. Then he quickly took the thought back.

He wasn't sure whether Chas had seen them. He didn't want Chas to have seen them. It would be worse for her, he believed. Pretending to be interested in whatever was happening on the bandstand, just kids doing wheelies on their bicycles, he steered her in that direction.

But he couldn't so easily steer his conscience away from what he'd thought. I owe her, he told himself. For that fleeting involuntary infidelity, I owe it to her to love her twice as hard and twice as long. But how long was twice as long when he'd already been contemplating eternity? He felt the tears squeezing into his eyes. He knew what he would be thinking next – he would be thinking that if anything happened to Chas he would not be able to survive. There was the grave, there was the coffin, and there was he, Marvin Kreitman, throwing himself down upon it.

She felt him giving way to pathos. 'What's the matter?' she asked.

'Nothing,' he said. 'I'm just thinking that I couldn't live without you.'

She threw him a half-grateful, half-beseeching look. 'Isn't it a bit soon, Marvin, to be thinking that?'

He simultaneously nodded and shook his head. Yes and no. But in the end it was all about this, wasn't it? You made the leap, or you didn't. Love was the decision to make the leap.

She put her arm round his shoulder. He liked that. He liked her having the confidence to encircle him, to take him away from where he'd been. Surreptitiously, she upped the pace; then she said, 'Right, swing your arms,' and soon she had him striding across the grass, invigorated, without a morbid thought in the world.

And had Hazel or Charlie seen *them*? Unlikely. Charlie rarely noticed anything when he was out walking and Hazel was enjoying herself too much to raise her eyes to other people. As a rule Charlie gave her good Sundays, unlike Kreitman who made a purgatory of the day of rest, whatever the weather. She could never get any nature with Kreitman, that had been her main complaint. He wouldn't allow her to forget the human world. Charlie, on the other hand, almost reminded her of a tree, so green and frondescent-smelling was he, so abundant and protective. Today he'd been making up stories for her as they walked. Nature stories, full of sap. Stories she could squeeze and which left the juice of berries on her fingers. Which Charlie could lick clean.

Once upon a time, Hazel-Mouse Hyphen Hazel-Worm was walking in the woods with Charlie Hyphen Smelly-Botty Farnsbarns when they came upon the good witch Cantilever Hyphen Thumbelina Fucklebum stirring juices in an iron pot. 'What are those juices you are stirring, Cantilever Whatever Your Name Is?' Hazel-Mouse enquired. 'Why my dear,' replied the good witch, 'these are the juices of unhappiness. Sourness, jealousy, maliciousness, regret, and not remembering to be kind to Charlie Hyphen Smelly-Botty. If I can boil all these juices away I will have made Felicity Soup. Have you ever tasted Felicity Soup, my little one?' Hazel-Mouse shook her head. 'Then you just sit here and put your arms round Charlie Hyphen Smelly-Botty and give him lots of kisses while I go on stirring, and if the angels are with us you'll get to taste Felicity Soup tonight.'

Hazel snuggled into him, for protection and shade. Who cared who else was crossing the Common that day?

SIX

S O EVERYONE ON planet Nice is happy, then?

And the children?

And Nyman, without whom, in all fairness, so much happiness might never have been spread abroad?

In the days before he was caught up quite so intimately in their fate, Kreitman had not been above firing the occasional cheap shot at the Merriweathers' example of parenting – semi-pseudonymous writers of (at one time) highly successful self-improvement novels for children age category 11–14, parents of actual children who were going to the dogs.

Like yours, Kreitman?

He wouldn't have denied it. Just like mine. Only I'm in purses, not in children's books. I *expect* children to go to the dogs.

In fact – had Kreitman been talking facts – the C. C. Merriweather books were not quite as anodyne as he imagined them. True, the *Flying Away* series of which Kreitman disapproved, all questions of content aside, purely on gerundival grounds, suffered from being too obviously post Peter Pan. It was Charlemagne who had planted the seed, telling Mrs C. C. Chassyboots during the interval of a performance of the play that he too, as a boy, had tried jumping off the wardrobe.

'To see if you could fly, Charlie?'

'To see if I could commit suicide.'

Not long after that, they together hit upon the idea of talking the world's children down from their wardrobes by reminding them that there were other ways of flying. Becoming a pilot, for example. Or an air hostess. Or an astronaut. Or a balloonist. Or First Girl on the Moon – the fastest seller of the lot.

'What about bungee jumping next?' their editor wondered. After thinking about it, they arrived at a mutual decision that bungee jumping was more about not hitting the ground than taking to the air, wasn't strictly speaking a profession, and wasn't really something they felt they ought to be encouraging their young readers to try.

In this, *Flying Away* was not typical of the C. C. Merriweather books. Normally they took greater risks. Slightly greater risks. While other children's writers were banging out their myths and fantasies, their legends of Ungala, their spook stories and sagas in the manner of *The Hobbit*, the Charlies stuck to their guns and wrote about what they called real kids living now. They tackled race, venereal disease, depression, drunkenness, drugs, Aids, illegal immigrants and even, latterly, affairs between schoolchildren and their teachers. They weren't comfortable writing about poor kids – never having met any – and they knew there was only a limited fantasy market for books about rich kids, so they pitched it somewhere in between, inventing little classless striplings who never smoked or swore but knew where smoking and swearing were to be found, and little sexless hoydens who were never once penetrated no matter how far they allowed relations with the head of geography to go. 'Goodbye,' the relevant member of staff always lamented on the last page, 'I will never forget you or what you have taught me.' Moral? Goodness is its own lesson. And you don't have to give away everything to make a lasting impression.

There was the problem: the C. C. Merriweathers weren't excessive enough for the children for whom they thought they wrote. Some critics believed they'd been losing their touch and their audience for years. Others admired them for not taking the easy route of witchcraft and horror. But all of that went for nothing anyway when, out of nowhere, old-fashioned owl-eyed boys with secret powers flew back with a vengeance on a magic broomstick.

What price depression in a suburban comprehensive now?

As for the Charlies' own real-life children, they were no more going to the dogs than anybody else's. So Tim had been on *Blind Date* and now fantasised about getting on *Big Brother*? From whom, under the age of twenty-five, did that significantly mark him out? And with regard to Kitty the bulldyke – a) she was no such thing, the bull part being a fiction entirely of her father's making, the extravagance of the word and the activities it denoted having caught his fancy; and b) a little light dykery was de rigueur, if not by now all but passé, among girls of her class and generation. Kreitman wouldn't have known because he never went to such places, but girls experimentally making out with girls was a commonplace in every clubbing venue in the country. His own daughters could have told him that.

But how far they were or were not burnt-out cases by their late teens, and how far that made them any different from their peers, is not the question. What we want to know – of the Kreitman girls as well – is how much their routine descent into young persons' hell was quickened by the recent cataclysmic events in their families. How did the sight of their several parents behaving like kids themselves, tying one another up into a cat's cradle of sexual irregularity – an all too regular irregularity – and then falling mooningly in love with the new arrangements – how did that gross spectacle strike them?

The fingers which Juliet and Cressida put to their brains on the occasion of Mummy's making a festive bonfire of Uncle Charlie's wardrobe on the lawn almost gets it. Fingers down their throats would have been better.

They were universally disgusted.

'I am too old myself to take account of the distaste of young people,' Kreitman told Chas when the subject finally climbed into bed with them.

'Where does that leave you with Hamlet?' Chas wondered.

'Wishing he were older.'

'It's all right for you,' she reminded him. 'Yours are in Thailand, no doubt having a ball and never giving you a thought. I have two going dippy on the spot.'

Not much given at the best of times to considering the feelings of people not within his immediate field of vision, Kreitman had forgotten all about Tim and Kitty on principle, neither enquiring after them nor accepting any of Chas's invitations at least to meet them for tea – though not at Kreitman's place, not under the bed – so they could judge ('Judge what, Mummy?') with their own eyes. He was determined, on grounds of fastidiousness not far removed from theirs, never to acknowledge Chas's domestic existence, the fish-pie and fridge-magnet Chas he'd known under the previous dispensation, and that meant never visiting her at home in Richmond, which anyway, by all accounts – that's to say by Chas's account – her little ones had turned into a madhouse.

'I don't know whether I can face this,' she would say some mornings, as Kreitman was handing her over to Maurice to Smart back to Richmond. 'Timmy lying in a pool of vomit with half his nose missing, and Kitty weeping in every room.'

'Stay with me,' Kreitman said.

'And do what with the house?'

'Torch it.'

'And the children?' She knew the answer.

'Torch them.'

There were times when she was tempted. They were over-egging the pudding, her children.

Yes, of course Kitty had felt betrayed by her father, betrayed on her mother's behalf and – you didn't have to be much of a psychologist to work this out – betrayed on her own. If Daddy was going to run away with anyone, blah-blah . . . Doubly betrayed both ends, remembering that Aunty Hazel was shock number two, shock number one having been Daddy's assault on the good name of Aunty Dotty. What was it with Daddy and aunties? Good question, Chas thought. 'I can't bear to look at him,' Kitty said, in the immediate aftermath of shock number one. Which turned into 'I won't forgive you if you ever see him or speak to him again,' after shock number two. 'That's a little extreme, darling,' Chas had replied, but since she was feeling pretty extreme herself, she understood. 'And I don't want him ever coming to this house, or trying to contact me, or speaking to any of my friends,' Kitty had gone on, stumbling over her tongue stud. If it's causing her so much discomfort, Chas thought, why doesn't she have the bloody thing out? But your daughter's your daughter. 'I'm sure he will be too ashamed to try,' she'd said. 'Too ashamed of me or too ashamed of himself?' 'Why would he be ashamed of you, Kitty?' 'Why does he call me a bulldyke? Why did he used to call me Kitty-Litter?' You know your father and his jokes, Chas half wanted to say. But the words choked in her throat. 'Your father is a sexually very disturbed person,' was what she chose to say instead.

All that was fine. Not fine, terrible, but as you would have expected it to be. Charlie had acted despicably and his daughter despised him. What Chas couldn't fathom was why Kitty was now feeling the same way about her. In the time she was alone, mourning Charlie and their collaboration, Chas had bowed to Kitty's taunting. 'You have been such a doormat, Mummy. You invited him to wipe his feet on you. You allowed him to believe he could get away with anything. He treated you with *such* contempt!' This didn't seem a fair description of either of them, but Chas accepted it. She too had failed Kitty in some way and this was her punishment. But oughtn't it to have followed, now that she had shaken Charlie out of her hair, now that she was mistress of her own affairs, no longer a doormat, no longer a shame to her daughter – oughtn't it to have followed that Kitty would be applauding her every inch of the way? 'Go for it, Mummy! Whoo!' – shouldn't Kitty have been shouting that?

Instead there were reproachful looks, flouncings out of rooms the minute Chas entered them, bouts of overcast moroseness so electric they fused the mains, sly expressions of regret, almost, for her father, as though Chas had become the betrayer suddenly in the revised history of why their little family was no more. And then, when Chas arrived home late one morning looking admittedly like a woman who'd been up all night wrestling with a gorilla – though the truth, as we know, was that she'd been lying quietly listening to her lover's body think – the outrageous indictment: 'Mummy, you should see yourself. You look a slut.'

Quite something, Chas didn't say, coming from a bulldyke!

And Timmy?

Somewhere in her heart Chas disdained her son. It usually happens that a mother loses all respect for her manchildren about the time they start falling for girls, their once-monastic touch-me-not sons all at once become open house for vagrants, every window in their natures banging open, fools for whoever comes knocking. Kreitman made her feel better by telling her that his mother had misprized him at the same age for exactly the same reasons. 'It improved,' he said, 'when I gave up on expectancy and settled down into unhappiness. Then she felt I was back. A verdant son is a nightmare to a mother.'

'Well, I'm not sure I'd call Timmy verdant, exactly,' she said.

Verdancy of the conventional sexual sort Chas wouldn't have minded. The trouble with Timmy was that he wasn't just open house, he was vacant house, tenantless, the windows of his nature flapping broken on their hinges.

He seemed greedy to her, without exactly having appetite. He wanted things, without exactly having ambition. He passed judgements, without appearing to have a morality. He denounced

247

his parents' sexual conduct with vehemence, obscenely, without appearing to know decency.

Kreitman had his own thoughts. Born into what should have been the advantages of a cultivated, middle-class home, with bookshelves on every wall and the *Kultur* gathered every weekend on the lawn, Tim had been permitted, with barely a demur, to embrace the culture of the council estate. Permitted? No, it was more than that. *Encouraged.* For what reason? *Nostalgie de la boue.*

'Why are there pictures of footballers on his bedroom door?' Kreitman used to enquire, preferably over dinner in the presence of the *Kultur*, when there was the chance of whipping up one of those civilised arguments he liked so much.

'He's a kid. All kids are interested in football.'

'But you're not interested in football, Charlie. You've never watched a game of football in your life. I bet you don't even know how it's scored.'

'What have my interests got to do with it?' Charlie exclaimed, cheered on by everyone at dinner. For these were the great democratising days of parenting, when nothing was feared more than the intrusive influence of parents themselves.

'Everything, Charlie. That's the point of Tim having you for a father and not someone else. You should be passing on your advantages.'

'We do. We send him to a good school.'

'Where's he allowed to do the same?'

'I don't know.'

'And when he comes home, it's to this?'

'As you know very well, Marvin, kids go their own way.'

'Not if you make efforts to save them.'

'*Save* them! This is the purest melodrama. Save them from what?' It was usually Chas who upped the tempo of the challenge at this point. Unless it was Hazel.

'Come on. You know what they have to be saved from. At best, triviality. At worst, degradation.'

'Degradation!' This ejaculation from everybody. For these were the great days of moral relativity, when whoever expressed a preference was a sermoniser.

'Commonness then, if degradation is too hot for you. Tell me something, Charlie – since I know you don't read the *Sun*, tell me why Tim has page-three girls on his wall.'

'Boys do that, Marvin. Boys like looking at girls.'

'Not girls like that, they don't. Plumbers like looking at girls like that. It's an acquired taste. Commonness always is. We glamourise commonness, thinking it's a state of nature. It isn't – nature is altogether more refined. So why, if it's acquired, are you allowing your boy to acquire it?'

Two invariable answers to that. You're a snob, Marvin. And you're making a great deal about very little, because kids grow out of their pin-ups and their football posters.

Kreitman doubted that. Kreitman believed you could always see the scars. What had he, for example, ever grown out of? (Seeking to disappoint his mother? Had he grown out of that?) But of course he did not now tell Chas what he thought – that Tim, like half the other kids in the country, was dying, if he were not already dead, of the culture of the council estate.

Chas's own view was altogether less apocalyptic than this. Timmy had been a lovely baby and a sweet child. A laugher. There were still pictures on the fridge of little Timmy stuffing candyfloss into Kitty's face and laughing. All being well he would be like that again, given time. She had made allowances, like all sensible mothers, for the spermy thing. Now she had to make allowances – extra allowances, given the destabilisation caused by the break-up of her marriage – for the sniffy thing.

'And what about the telly thing?' Kreitman asked her.

She wasn't sure about the telly thing.

Maybe from something somewhere on the telly Timmy would learn a little understanding, even compassion, if moral complexity from someone his age was too much to hope for – which Kreitman assured her it was.

And Nyman? Without whom, etc., etc. . . .

How went the world for the man with no visible means of support, no prospects and no attributes?

It was a question Kreitman was frequently on the point of asking Chas. How fares the faggot, Chas? But he had resisted, not wanting to do anything to break the spell that held them, not wanting to stir her into anger, and not wanting to hear the answer, for fear of the pain it might cause him.

Does that mean Kreitman dreaded learning that she secretly saw Nyman, or thought about him, or made efforts to hear of him? Or does it mean he dreaded luxuriating in Chas's falsity, if false she turned out to be?

Ah, if he only knew that.

But one thing he did know – Chas was a new life to him, a deliverance from his old self, and therefore he would have been as a dog returning to its vomit, had he sought to reinstitute the bad habits of earlier times.

So don't ask Kreitman about Nyman, however drawn he was to the smell.

He liked it fine where he was.

SEVEN

ALTHOUGH THERE'D BEEN nothing in her marital experience to prepare her for the perversities of a man like Kreitman – Charlie, before setting foot on the planet Wrongdoing, having been an exemplary husband of the strictly horizontal school of sexual adventurism – Chas knew to keep the stopper on Nyman. That wasn't difficult; he was of no interest to her. In extraordinary circumstances she had flirted with Nyman (the most extraordinary of the circumstances being that everybody else had flirted with him too), and then, under duress – force of events as much as any coercion coming from him – she had reverted to that queer family dutifulness which, not for the first time, had landed her in the soup. Flattering to a woman nearly twice his age that Nyman had asked for more, but not *that* flattering – every man was an Oliver Twist at heart, up for another helping whatever the dish. Quite what to make of Kreitman's interest in a piece of nonsense that didn't concern him and from which, as a gentleman, not to say as her husband's friend, he should have turned his eyes, she wasn't sure, but something told her no good could come of it. All right, simple jealousy might have heated his engines intially, but they were past that now. They were running. According to Dotty, who was no slouch herself, they were speeding. And there was nothing to be jealous of, anyway, given that what she'd done she'd done in rage. You can only play the cards you've been dealt. Not equipped to dress a man down verbally, and not strong enough to punch him in the face, Chas expressed her contempt by whacking him off. Which, even allowing that she had once done the same to him, was none of Kreitman's business.

It should follow from the above that her assurances to Kreitman, both during their breakfast of bitter herbs on Dartmoor and after – that she had sent Nyman packing, that she had refused to help him, that she neither knew nor cared anything of his whereabouts – were truthful. They weren't. When Nyman asked her for a loan she gave him one. Five hundred pounds to tide him over. The idea of *her* paying *him* for a kiss and a feel-up was so disgusting to her that she couldn't say no to it. If nothing else, it proved what Charlie had reduced her to. She had heard of betrayed women cutting off their hair, or painting their faces grotesquely, as an act of terrible submission to their debasement. Chas kept her hair intact but paid a cyclist nearly half her age five hundred pounds for having let her hold his dick. Put the hard word on my sister, would you, Charlie? Now look!

She also gave him her address and told him that though he couldn't possibly stay there at present while the wheels were coming off her marriage – no, not even for the odd night, not even on the floor, not even in the garage, no, not even in a sleeping roll at the bottom of her garden – she might be able to offer him a bed at some later date. With a view to further sex which she would pay for? Absolutely not. But if he thought that, she wouldn't disabuse him. She would be the more demeaned. Or rather Charlie, by the same logic, the more reviled.

Five or six weeks after Charlie moved out, at around about the time that Kreitman was losing to himself nightly at shove-halfpenny, she allowed Nyman to move in. That was how he saw it, anyway. He drove up in a small van, packed with his things, his bicycle on the roof. Chas sent him away. 'You can come back and stay for a maximum of two nights,' she told him, 'provided you are carrying a suitcase no bigger than this.' She opened her arms to give him the dimensions and noticed he was taking the opportunity to evaluate her chest. No one ever evaluated Chas's chest. 'A mistake,' she told herself. 'The boy is deranged.'

The other mistake, she realised, no sooner did she see him standing in her hall, gingery and denuded in brief khaki shorts and boots and flak jacket, like some lewd Boy Scout, was that she hadn't thought enough about the effect his presence would have on her children. People often stayed over at the Merriweathers' without Kitty or Timmy's feelings being taken into account. The house rambled. There was room enough to go on a ramble yourself if you didn't like who you saw at breakfast. And Kitty and Timmy were not generally fazed by their parents' friends anyway. But then their parents' friends were by and large too ancient or too out of it to faze anyone; certainly none of them turned up wearing shorts and boots, and if you did happen upon a flak jacket at the Merriweathers', the chances were it had seen service in North Africa or the Middle East and not been bought the day before at Prowler. What would she do if the children jumped to the mistaken conclusion that Nyman was here for her, a consolation, or worse, a replacement for Daddy? Oughtn't she to tell him she'd confused her diary, give him his taxi fare and send him back wherever he'd come from?

Something turned over in her stomach. She'd chance it.

She needn't have worried. No sooner did Kitty and Timmy set eyes on their new house guest than they were in love with him. 'I've been here before,' Chas thought. 'What is it with this guy? It's spooky. Is he some sort of hypnotist?'

In fact, Kitty and Timmy had an excuse, vis-à-vis Nyman, which their elders hadn't. They already knew him. Not in the usual sense of the word know, and not in the biblical sense either, but televisually, which is altogether more intimate.

'Wow!' Timmy had exclaimed, even before the introductions. 'It's Norman!'

'*Ny*man,' Chas corrected.

Nyman hung his head.

'*Norman?*' Chas laughed.

Nyman still hung his head.

'You're called *Norman?*' She looked from one to the other. 'OK,' she said, 'so what's with this Norman?'

And that was how she learned that Nyman who was no one had an alter ego who was maybe someone, a Norman who had done what Nyman had told them all on Dartmoor he was anxious to do – that's to say make a bit of a name for himself on the box. Whether he had therefore been teasing them all, getting them to guess what his forte might be, getting them to vie with one another over his prospects when his prospects were already proven and garlanded – garlanded in the eyes of Timmy at any rate – or whether he was simply schizoid, Chas didn't begin to guess. But her stomach turned over again.

She found it difficult to extract from either of them what Nyman in his capacity as Norman was actually famous for having done. Nyman himself wasn't talking, taking refuge in modesty and renewed difficulty with the English language. (No problem understanding when his pants were down around his ankles, Chas recalled.) And Timmy, unable even in his clearest moments to distinguish between success and failure on the box, or between fact and fiction, let alone between past, present and future, all of it merging into one great blur of form and a single trancelike continuousness of time for which there was no tense known in grammar, couldn't quite find the description to fit the job.

'An actor?' Chas asked.

Timmy simultaneously shook and nodded his head. 'Yeah, kind of, not exactly.'

'An actor in a soap?'

'Mmm . . . No, yeah. Depends how you define soap.'

'A presenter?'

'Nah,' Timmy said. 'Not a presenter, not as such, not exactly.'

'A contestant?' Chas felt she was getting somewhere now.

Maybe Norman had been a fellow guest of Timmy's on *Blind Date*. *Wow, you're Norman* was commensurate with that. I'm Timmy from *Richmond*! I'm Norman from *Nowhere*! Whoo!

Timmy scratched his head. Nyman went on looking between his naked knees. It needed Kitty, in the end, to come in from the kitchen where she'd been removing photographs of her father from the fridge, to clear things up. Norman had been on the box about a year ago in a reality game show which bore some resemblance, it seemed to Chas, to the old Yes and No quizzes of her youth. How long could people stand one another's company without saying anything – that appeared to be the premise; how mute, under the provocation of other people's muteness, could you remain. At the end of a fortnight in a confined space, Norman had tied, controversially, for first place. Chas wondered what the controversy could have been. You were mute, surely, or you were not. Chas's children exchanged looks. Did their mother know nothing! In order to drive other people into language, Kitty explained, you were encouraged to employ whatever subterfuge or underhandedness you chose. Some viewers, Kitty and Timmy among them, believed Norman's repertoire of social offensiveness was sufficient for him to have won outright. It was more subtle, they believed, than the other guy's, which consisted in crudities like hogging the lavatory and stealing other people's milk.

'Whereas Norman?' Chas asked.

'Hard to explain,' Kitty said. 'Just being himself.'

'And wearing these cool clothes,' Timmy added.

'I know what you mean,' said Chas.

And the prize which he fairly or unfairly shared?

The chance to host his own late-night talk show.

Chas didn't think it was seemly to probe too deeply, with the subject of their conversation sitting there, coolly clothed and saying nothing, but how did Norman's genius for verbal forbearance qualify him to host a talk show?

Her children exchanged the same looks as before. Mummy with her word fixation!

That Norman, for whatever reason, had not gone on to host a talk show, Chas deduced without asking. It explained him a bit. He was another of those to whom telly had promised the world and delivered nothing. Not unlike Timmy, never again, after *Blind Date*, to be the sweet, engaging boy he'd been.

The only thing Nyman had to say on his own behalf about the experience of being Norman was that he had enjoyed being recognised for a while, even though he wasn't strictly being recognised for himself, that's if he had a self. 'I liked it very much,' he told Chas, 'when I put my hand out to people at a party and began to say my name, and they said, "I *know* who you are."'

'You liked being famous?'

'I don't know if I liked *that*, but I liked thinking' – and here he tapped himself on the forehead, reminding Chas of the old moron joke: kidneys! – 'that they didn't really know who I was at all.'

'No, well, none of us does,' Chas said, chiefly to herself.

Because it was always a bit of a free-for-all at the Merriweathers, the question of how Chas had come by Nyman never arose. And because Kitty and Timmy saw him as belonging culturally to them – which made a change – it didn't once occur to them to think he might have been for Mummy. Chas took a few deep breaths and believed she had pulled off a lucky escape. After three nights she showed Nyman the door, slipped him a couple of hundred pounds, and warned him that he really was going to have to find himself somewhere permanent to live, because she was too distracted, as a woman whose husband had recently left her – and that wasn't an invitation – to have him here again. Though by that time, of course, he had already wangled himself the promise of Timmy's floor, whenever he wanted it.

And all this she kept from Kreitman? Yes. Even though it would have given him intense satisfaction to learn that Nyman's other name, maybe even his actual name, was Norman? Not Niemand, meaning mysterious Mittel European existential Nobody, but plain Norm, normal Norm, as like as not from Basingstoke. Yes. Mean of her, but yes.

Since they had become *they*, Chas and Marvin, Nyman had not cropped up much in their conversation. He was gone from her house, gone from her life, gone from her thoughts, and Kreitman had his own reasons for not reminding her of him. Once, on their first night in Harrogate, he had loomed and then been beaten down, and once again, weeks and weeks later, he had put in a guest appearance, Kreitman having succumbed to twinges in that part of his back which had come into contact with Nyman's bicycle. 'I don't know why I didn't kick shit out of the little arselicker when I had the chance,' Kreitman cursed, rolling on to the grass and trying to remember the muscle-stretching exercises the physio had taught him.

They'd been sitting on a bench in Regent's Park, holding hands, watching the ducks. One of the few dry days of late summer. The lake was scuffed with the scurrying of birds. A swan rose on the water and arched its neck. A home-loving heron they had spotted on previous walks — a pathologically uxorious heron with whom Kreitman had indentified — was playing pick-up-sticks to furnish an empty nest. All things that loved the sun were out of doors, even the women of the *jaballah* and the veil, their eyes dancing in the letter-box slots of their wintry yashmaks. From what place in himself, on such a benign afternoon, Chas wondered, had Marvin called up such violence?

She fancied she had dispelled all unseasonable ill-temperedness from his nature. She felt it was a mark against *her*, somehow, that it had resurfaced. What wasn't she giving him? It was in the face of this disappointment with herself that she let down her guard. 'What *is* it about that boy that galls you so much?' she asked.

Kreitman straightened himself up, stood on one foot, much like the heron, grabbed the other foot by the toe which the heron did not do, repeated the exercise, this time changing feet, shook the grass from his suit, for Kreitman would not go into so public a park as this in his cagoule, then rejoined her on the bench. 'He rode into me, deliberately. Twice in one evening. What other explanation do you need?'

'Your anger always seems over and above that, Marvin.'

'Over and above being knocked down?' He laughed. 'Measure me, then, the anger appropriate to being run over twice.'

'You know perfect well what I'm saying,' she insisted. Miffed, she jutted her jaw. 'You go looking for anger where he is concerned. You hear his name and beckon rage into your heart. I used to think it was a joke. The boy hardly merits so much passion, after all. Now I think he's a pretext.'

He stood up again, linked his hands in a double fist behind his back and breathed in. A relaxation exercise. He caught her eye and held it longer than was comfortable for either of them. 'Indeed the boy hardly merits so much passion,' his face said – 'from either of us.' But his actual words were less challenging: 'A pretext for what, Chas?'

'I don't know. I'm asking you. Violence? Unhappiness? Dissatisfaction with me?'

He went on fisting his shoulder blades. 'All right,' he said. 'The boy, as you call him, puts himself about as a faggot, and you assure me he isn't. Will that do?'

She opened her hands, as though to accept responsibility for the unpleasant topic, and in the hope that it would fly away, now she had released it. 'It will do me if it will do you,' she said. But it didn't look as though it did her.

Or him, come to that. 'If you want to know,' he relented, 'I fear him. I fear his nothingness.'

She was surprised by the confession. Relieved, too. She would have liked to hear him deny the charge of dissatisfaction with her, but failing that, leaving her out of it altogether was second-best. 'That surely is to accept him at his own valuation,' she said.

'I fear that as well. To a person as fixed as I am, even playing with looseness is unnerving. Anyone whose motives or movements I can't count on, I fear. I fear him as I fear clowns or madmen. They negate everything. They negate me, anyway.'

'But that's exactly what he wants to do.'

'I know that. It makes no difference. Faggot jokes are the same. Let's elevate trash and see if we can make seriousness lose its nerve. Nothing could be more transparent. But it works. I lose my nerve. When everything else has been destroyed, two things will be left in control of the planet – cockroaches and camp.'

'Marvin, he isn't camp,' she wanted to say. But wasn't that where they came in? Here was the perfect opportunity to tell him about Norman. Your indestructible vermin, Marvin, is actually a Norman.

But she backed off. She didn't have the words, and she couldn't claim to understand the psychology; but she had the feeling, lying listening to Kreitman's body think, that even as it thought about her it sometimes thought, and sometimes thought too long, about Nyman as well. And she didn't want to be a party to any of that stuff, whatever it was.

EIGHT

A T WHAT POINT Charlie Merriweather realised he hadn't changed his life at all – not radically changed it – and was back to having nice sex, only with someone not his wife, it is hard to say. A realisation of this magnitude does not come upon you suddenly. It creeps into your bed.

The wet weather was disagreeing with Charlie. The more it rained, the fewer the opportunities to go shopping with Hazel, and the fewer opportunities to go shopping, the fewer opportunities to go taking back. It mattered to him, this aspect of their life together, because it was one of the few opportunities the pair of them had to go public, to make any kind of show of the love they bore each other. Day after day it rained, and nobody visited. Night after night they stayed in, and no one visited. He read to her, novel after novel. 'Very soon now,' he joked, 'there won't be any novels left to read.'

'Then you'll have to write some, Charlie,' she joked. But his words struck fear into her. Were they running out of a resource already? Was running out of novels just another way of saying that he was running out of something else?

They discussed inviting some of his friends round. What about Basil Vavasor, great-nephew of Aubrey de Selincourt? What about Giles Akersham, great-great-grandson and biographer of Edmund Gosse? What about Clarence Odger? Charlie thought about each one in turn, then shook his head. They belonged as much to Chas as to him. They belonged to the family. In the earlier days, before the Merriweathers were launched, they had financed the family. Sent Timmy to school. Paid for Kitty's piano lessons. Built the extension. They would be embarrassed meeting him in another context. And maybe saddened. They hadn't financed him into another context. And he too would be embarrassed. And maybe saddened.

'You aren't ashamed of me?' Hazel asked.

Ashamed of her? Ashamed of Hazel? What a thing to ask. He'd never been prouder of any woman, and never prouder of himself as any woman's man. But it's a queer thing about that question – once it's asked, once it's seriously posed, it raises doubts and changes, ever so subtly, the balance of power. If Hazel truly feared he *could* be ashamed of her, what did that say about her sexual self-confidence – so important to him as a man who had travelled at twice the speed of sound from the planet Nice to the planet Wrongdoing – and furthermore, what did it say about his need to make that journey in the first place? Never mind had he overestimated Hazel, had he *under*estimated himself?

The rains fell and Charlie burned off the pages.

' *"But, in spite of these deficiencies, the wishes, the hopes, the confidence, the predictions of the small band of true friends who witnessed the ceremony, were fully answered in the perfect happiness of the union . . ."'*

Next –

' *"But I know that my dearest little pets are very pretty, and that my darling is very beautiful, and that my husband is very handsome, and that my guardian has the brightest and most benevolent face that ever was seen . . ."'*

Next—

' *"L—d! said my mother, what is all this story about? –*

' *"A Cock and a Bull, said Yorick – And one of the best of its kind, I ever heard."'*

261

'Not quite to my taste, that one,' Hazel said.

'Too ludic, for you?' Charlie asked.

'Too what?'

'Ludic. One of your husband's words. Playful without being funny. This was where he laid the blame for all the facetiousness of twentieth-century literature.'

'Then read it to me again slowly, my love,' Hazel, falling back on her pillows, implored sweetly.

The rains fell and Hazel grew anxious. She could count the changes. Charlie no longer marvelled over her soaps and towels. He no longer trembled when she took him in her arms. He no longer asked her to 'do that thing' with her eyes, that 'sly peeping thing', ascertaining that he hadn't crept away and left her fatherless again. He was still attentive to her, still loved getting her to put on heels and little else, and he was still generous with his weight, climbing on top of her on the sofa or the floor, letting her feel the full length of him, the moment she requested it. But attentiveness and responsiveness were small potatoes compared to that feast of demandingness and initiation, of watching and waiting, of desperation and gratitude, which in their early days he was up and about preparing, before she had even opened her sly peeping eyes. Funny: there was a time – long, long ago it seemed – when she saw Charlie as the very antithesis to her husband – a man to be avoided at all costs because it would be impossible to be rid of him. A puppy-dog man – shoo! Charlie, shoo! – whose rump sank lower and lower in puppy-dog gratitude the more you kicked it. Now, suddenly, she caught herself wondering what she would have to do to stop him from leaving. She had no instinct for any of this. There was demeaning oneself and there was demeaning oneself. To a fault she had been a pleaser, brought up to go along with whatever a man wanted, but trying to *work out* what a man wanted, giving your every waking hour to anticipating his desires, to pre-empting or quickening his appetite, to creating novelties for him every time he walked into the house, no, no, that was too low even for her. She remembered her girlfriends at university publicising their stratagems for keeping men simultaneously satisfied and hungry – never wearing pants, dyeing your pubic hair, always being certain to be caught sitting on the edge of the bed playing with yourself when he arrived back from work or from being with his wife. But as Hazel was keeping company with Kreitman for most of her university career, she was never reduced to the vulgarities of second-guessing: Kreitman *commanded* her not to wear pants. All that had changed since, of course. Now if her daughters second-guessed a man it was in order *not* to give him what he wanted. Allowing that Charlie was of an older time, Hazel wondered if she shouldn't be lending an ear to some of the older teaching. It was hard to imagine what, of the basics, they were missing. The pants thing she already did, even though what she wore was so scant Charlie generally preferred her with them on. He had her nipples jutting night and day. He had her teetering on stilts. He had her painting her nails purple. As for playing with herself on the edge of the bed while waiting for Charlie to get back, that was not going to work for the reason that Charlie never went out.

She supposed she could always try incorporating it into their readings. ' ". . . *for the growing good of the world is partly dependent on unhistoric acts; and that things are not so ill with you and me as they might have been, is half owing to the number who lived faithfully a hidden life, and rest in unvisited tombs . . ."*' Oh, Charlie, Charlie, oh, oh, Charlie, ohhh . . .

And throw in the odd 'sweet Jesus!' Wasn't that what women at their most irreligious, were meant to cry? Oh, sweet Jesus!

Can't see it, Hazel thought. Can't see Charlie appreciating my vying with him for climaxes, however low on titles we're running.

Bizarre, but the person she might most have benefited from a word with was her husband. What would keep you here, Kreitman, if you were him? But where that was bound to lead she definitely *could* see. First, whisper in my ear, Hazel, everything

263

you have been doing for him so far. Be conscientious. Don't leave out any detail, no matter how apparently significant. I'll decide what's important and what isn't. My ear is open. Start.

So prolix, her husband, even in his curiosity. Such a dirty-minded prolix bastard. The dirty-mindedness she could almost forgive. But the prolixity!

As for her daughters, who would no doubt have advice of their own to offer – along the lines of 'Don't wait for him to go, you be sure to give him the shove first, Mummy' – they were back, but keeping their distance. They had brought Charlie a beautiful tie-dyed kaftan back from Thailand. And matching slippers so that he should get the message it was for wearing around the house. It did no good. He tried it on once to great applause, decided it was too lovely to wear except on important occasions, and reverted to his blue candlewick dressing gown, bare feet and general air of obscene imminence.

'What if I asked Uncle Charlie to lend me his dressing gown for one of my sculptures?' Cressida proposed to her mother.

'Don't you dare,' Hazel warned her.

'Even if I could promise him it would eventually hang in the Tate?'

'Leave Charlie alone,' Hazel said. 'He makes an old lady very happy.'

'What about you, Mummy?'

At which Hazel laughed, until her laughter turned to tears.

Shocked to see her cry, for Hazel had always been a dry-eyed woman, especially with her children, Cressida put her arms around her. 'Is something wrong, Mummy?' she asked softly, for all the world a mummy herself. Ironic about everything else, they were infinitely patient with grief, artists of Cressida's generation. In their line of work they had to handle lots of upset.

Hazel let herself go limp in her daughter's arms. It was the nearest she had got in years, she thought, to knowing who Cressida was. So she was capable of doing this! Wasn't that extraordinary! She had a daughter who could give comfort. Wouldn't it be wonderful if Juliet too was capable of taking her in her arms and making her feel well.

All at once her spirits roused. She was the mother of a line. A matriarch. In her veins the future throbbed. Of what earthly significance, compared to that great fact, was Charlie Merriweather's cooling ardour?

'I'm fine,' she said. 'Someone must have walked across my grave.'

But in the night, sleepless, watching Charlie labouring at his dreams, she succumbed again to sorrow. Was his ardour really cooling?

And this time she walked across her own grave.

Not on the same night, for that would be altogether too neat, even for an entanglement made of neatness, but on nights not far apart in time, Charlie and Kreitman dreamed a similar dream. Charlie's dream concerned Chas, though by implication it also concerned Hazel. Kreitman's dream was the purer in that it concerned only him.

In Charlie's dream, Chas came out of the pumping darkness, not looking or behaving much like herself, and straddled his chest. Her hair was long and in his face, but she did not smell of anything. She put her hand behind her back to find his penis which she tried in vain to force inside her. In vain because the position was altogether wrong. Oh, brave new Charlie's penis, but it wasn't so brave or so new that it could stretch that far, even in a dream and no matter who was pulling it. But also vain in that his penis was limp. Chas recognised her mistake and shifted her body so that it was better positioned to take his. Again she reached for his penis, but it remained resolutely limp. In her desperation to force him inside her, Chas began to perspire and then to cry softly. How am I going to tell her? Charlie thought. How am I going to break it to her? But when he awoke, in great distress, he wasn't sure what news he had to break, or who the person was he had to break it to.

In Kreitman's dream the person lying on the breast was him. The person weeping was him too. He was trying to say the words, 'It's a mistake,' but his weeping wouldn't let him. The arms around his neck were very soft. Not clinging, protective rather. Arms of understanding. Except that he was sure she didn't understand or, if you like, that she misunderstood, that she mistook him, which was why it was a matter of such great urgency to him to say the words, 'It's a mistake.' 'Hush,' she said. 'It's all right. Hush.' Then he realised the weeping he had been listening to was not his but hers. *That* was the mistake. The cause of this great convulsion of sadness was her not him. And then her weeping grew so inconsolable he knew his heart would break if he didn't force himself to wake.

So who was she? Kreitman didn't know. Or if he knew, he wasn't letting on. This is the sense in which the dream concerned only him: it was a dream of grief but the only party to the grief he recognised was himself, Marvin Kreitman. Was the weeping woman in whose arms he nearly died simply every woman he had ever slept with? Was she the continuum that stretched the whole way back to his mother, the first cause of all love and discontentment in him? She wasn't Chas, he was sure of that. She wasn't either of his daughters. She wasn't Erica or Bernadette or Shelley or Vanessa. Nor was she Hazel, though it took him a little longer to rule her out. No, she wasn't Hazel. She wasn't. Hazel didn't weep like that. But she coincided with a sudden burst of longing for his wife, an ache for her physical presence, which he thought would shatter the insides of his brain.

'He's missing her,' Chas phoned her sister to say.

'Missing the tub of lard? You're joking. He never took the slightest interest in her. Are you sure it's not me he's missing? Are you sure he's not missing a broken toenail?'

'No, he's missing her. I can hear it.'

'Oh, darling, you aren't still listening to his body? This is Marvin Kreitman we're talking about. His body is certain to be lying. If it says he's missing her I shouldn't worry – it means he isn't.'

'I appreciate your words of comfort, Dolly, but I know what I'm talking about. I am beginning to understand him. He's all about loss. I don't mean the usual sexual thing about only wanting what you can't have. To my surprise, he isn't like that. He isn't losing interest in me because I'm available. Quite the opposite. On that score I have no complaints to make . . .'

'Don't boast, darling.'

'I am allowed to boast, Dolly. I only wish I could boast that he thinks only of me. But he doesn't. He'll think only of me when he's on to the next one. First he has to lose me, then he'll love me.'

'Well, for your sake I hope that isn't soon,' Dotty said.

'Hope it isn't soon he loves me?'

'Hope it isn't soon he loses you.'

'Same thing,' Chas told her.

'Well, you know what I think,' Hazel's mother told her.

'Mother, if the Palestinians haven't shot him or he isn't in prison for selling secrets to the Iranians he'll be wearing ringlets down to his knees.'

'Hazel, you are always at least twenty-five years and a dozen sentences behind me,' Hetta Nossiter said, adjusting the dimmer slightly on the lamp beside her.

Although her mother had all her faculties about her, Hazel noted she had been growing tetchy recently with the light. Either there was too little of it coming in from Great Russell Street, dying in the courtyard and finally smothered by the classical façade of the British Museum, or there was too much coming through the worn parchment lampshades. Was this what became of you when you lived alone? Was nothing ever exactly the way you wanted it?

'Are your eyes all right, Mother?' Hazel asked.

'Ha! You should have eyesight as good as mine. Between the two of us, my dear, there is only one set of eyes, and they belong to me.'

'*It* belongs to you.'

'Don't cheek your mother. My grammar was never any disappointment to Cabinet ministers. It's you who's the disappointment, not me.'

Hazel shrank from these words as though they were missiles. 'Mother!' she cried.

'Well, I'm sorry, but I have to be cruel to be kind with you. You're so prickly. How many times have I had to tell you – you don't keep a man by making his life a hair shirt. When you find a man, Hazel, you feather-bed him.'

'The way you encouraged me to feather-bed Marvin?'

Hetta Nossiter turned up the dimmer on her lamp. 'Ach, Marvin.'

My own fault, Hazel thought, looking out at the touristic dismalness of Bloomsbury, busier than when she'd grown up in it, but more aimless, no longer a place for people on some errand of the mind – my own fault for coming here.

Her mother had met Charlie Merriweather once, quite recently, in this very room, and liked him. Hazel had brought him on a hunch – correctly guessing that Charlie would be amused by her mother on account of her faded fifties associations (Charlie loved faded), and that she would be taken by him partly because his own deportment had something of the fifties about it, partly because he was tall, but mainly because he wasn't Marvin. 'An agreeable change to see you with someone whose father didn't sell purses on a market,' she whispered to Hazel, while Charlie was looking round the little flat. 'A nice build on him too. He'd look good in uniform. Is he too young to have done national service?'

'Wonderful woman,' Charlie had said after meeting her. 'I love the smell of gin around women of that era.'

This was news to Hazel. 'Does my mother smell of gin?'

'Not so much her as the apartment block,' Charlie said quickly. 'A lot of secret tippling goes on in Bloomsbury. Always has. It's either that or they blow their brains out. It's my favourite stratum of English society, what's left of it, ex-civil servants and fallen gentry, antiquarians and owners of military bookshops, all coming apart at the seams but still managing to keep going on boiled cabbage and iced gin and bleary recollections of buggery . . .'

'Buggery, Charlie? My mother!'

'The men, Hazel. The men.'

'And the women?'

He thought about it. What recollections were the women living on? All the women Charlie knew were living on recollections of being in love with V. S. Pritchett and Geoffrey Grigson. Broken hearts of another age. Was that the universal fate of women? Was it caused by men like him? 'I like your mother very much,' was all he'd say. 'She's a dear.'

So it seemed to Hazel that with so much instantaneous affection between them they amounted to a sort of alliance or network – could she actually mean a bulwark? – which she could count on in her heart. No reason, now he liked her mother, not to take Charlie round to meet her again. And no reason, now her mother liked Charlie, not to tell her that she sometimes feared her life with Charlie was built on sand.

'But I don't think,' she said, 'that I could make things any more comfortable for him than I already do.'

'Do you cook exotically for him? Do you serve him sweet-breads? Men love entrails, you know.'

'I cook as exotically as is consistent with the tastes of a man who puts tomato ketchup on his kedgeree and whose idea of a treat is a fruit scone.'

'Do you remember to put cream on his scone?'

'Double cream. And jam.'

'Marmalade's better.'

'Charlie's a jam man.'

'What about your clothes?' Without appearing to, she surveyed her daughter, not disapprovingly. She was less tailored than she had been. A good sign. 'Are your clothes feminine enough for him?'

'Mother, look at me. If I went any more feminine I wouldn't be able to stand up.'

'There you are,' her mother said. 'What are you doing wanting to stand up with a man?'

Hazel looked around the room, decorated in pink and gold, with portraits of statesmen (one of them her father) on the walls and figurines of shepherdesses (one of them her mother) on the mantelpiece. She shook her head. She had been born here. Grown up here. Educated into womanhood here. 'You know, sometimes,' she said, 'I think it's a miracle I've achieved even the little I have. A husband, for a time. A lover, for a time. Two daughters, I hope, for ever. How, given the example you have shown me, have I managed that?'

'Well, you haven't managed a sense of humour,' Hetta Nossiter replied.

'No,' Hazel said. 'No one can accuse me of managing one of those.'

And not for the first time she trudged out of Bloomsbury like a heroine in one of those great novels of humourlessness Charlie had been reading aloud to her – that's when they weren't great novels of facetiousness – footsore and weary, determined to put the shames of her past life behind her, but uncertain where her future was to be found.

Kreitman knew the longing he was feeling couldn't be for Hazel. It made no sense. He *had* longed for Hazel, first when he was very young and she had gone off to see a school friend for the weekend, leaving him weeping like a baby at the railway station, wondering if he would ever see her again, praying no accident would befall her, longing for her, actually longing for her presence, within minutes of her being gone; and then, an older man, when she had had enough of his delusive tears and turned her back on him, denying him anything that would remind him of their earlier days, no reminiscent smile, no recapitulations in the voice or retrospection in the body, nothing, stone dead nothing – then he would go out walking on his own, and *long* for her, quite simply and disconnectedly yearn, as for a person who was no more, with that same chasm in the heart the bereaved know, long, *long* to have the space left by that one shape filled by that one shape – until maybe he would meet some girl and postpone the longing for another time. Yes, yes, he knew how that was judged. Some man of feeling you are, Kreitman, to be deflected from your feelings by any trull that passes! Well, first of all hold with the trull. You haven't met her. And don't suppose that a capacity for deflection only ever denotes callousness or coldness. We are many-chambered creatures; the squishy-hearted, the inconsolable weepers at railway stations, having maybe a chamber or two more than most men. And full of longing though we are in one chamber, we are fitted with the means to be full of something else in another. Yeah, full of shit, Kreitman! Suit yourself. But the truth's the truth: they did not console him, the other women, whether they were women for five minutes or a fortnight or for life, they did not console or compensate or distract him, they simply existed concurrently. They *also were*.

Shouldn't it then follow that Kreitman's longing for Hazel had never gone away but *also was*, perhaps for all time, in the chamber where his longings were stored? Asked that question a week before, Kreitman would have pooh-poohed it. Longing for Hazel had died. She'd killed it. He'd killed it. Vicissitude had killed it. Sadness was another thing. He would always be sad about Hazel, sad for Hazel, sad *from* Hazel. But longing was of another order. Longing was as tangible as touching. What you longed for you as good as held, except that you didn't, which was why your heart broke. And he didn't feel that way about Hazel. Hazel he did not want to hold. But here was the mystery – if he didn't want to hold her, why was he imagining her in his hands, and if he wasn't longing for her, why did his heart break when he realised his hands were empty?

The afternoons were worse. At the best of times Kreitman was not good at afternoons. Work helped as a rule. A shop to go to helped. But the habits of non-attendance which Kreitman had acquired in the weeks waiting for Chas to make her mind up and materialise had stayed with him even now that they were palpably a pair. Most mornings, Chas left him in bed and went to Richmond where there was room at least to swing a cat and write children's stories. Since Kreitman wouldn't hear of it that she went home by any method but the Smart, he was Smartless for several hours himself. By the time the Smart was back, Kreitman had lost the will to do anything with his day but wait for it to return to Richmond and collect Chas. 'I should just give you Maurice,' he said. 'That way you'll end up resenting me for ruining your business,' she said. 'Do I have a business?' he asked her. 'It was your business that made me fall for you, remember,' she reminded him. 'It was your business that showed me you didn't have a heart of steel.'

So between kissing Chas goodbye and waiting for her return, on those days when she *did* return, Kreitman idled through his afternoons. The rain hammered on his roof. There was nothing to see from his windows but the tops of umbrellas and the amphibian feet of uncomplaining Londoners. Bizarre to him, the patience of these people. Did nothing stir them to revolt? By three o'clock, flamenco was on his record player and the smell of Moorish dust was in his nostrils. Whereupon the longing started.

Ridiculous, but there was nothing he could do. Anyone seeing me, he thought, would say I have finally got my comeuppance.

But then if that's what I have got, that's what I have got. It's not within my power to do anything but suffer it. You can't get up, pull yourself together and walk away from your comeuppance.

Tears poured down his face. He would walk around the flat to keep his circulation moving, smiting his chest an inch or two above his heart, great thumps with a clenched fist, as though he meant to knock himself off his feet. Maybe a bottle of red wine, maybe not. Occasionally a cigar. He did not want to become a creature of habit. By four he was too upset to trust himself to his feet and had collapsed on his desk, his forehead on his gouging knuckles, the longing banging in his ears.

But tell him this: if the longing *was* for Hazel, how come it was sparked off by flamenco – music for which Hazel had never expressed the slightest enthusiasm nor shown the remotest aptitude. Had Hazel been a flamenco dancer – no mystery. Had she loved the guitar even – no mystery. But the brutal truth was that Hazel hated flamenco with a passion and, in the days before Kreitman moved his enthusiasms to his den on Clapham High Street, had never missed an opportunity to deride his devotion to it. 'Finding the gypsy in your soul, Marvin?' she would call when she caught him with his ears to his speakers, crouched like a beast in pain. In more playful moods she would imitate the castanets, making sluttish expressions with her mouth, as though to imply this was music for the sort of tramps in whose name he had trashed their marriage. On the blackest days she would simply yell, 'For Christ's sake, Marvin, will you turn that crap down!'

You see his quandary. How could flamenco move him to yearnings for a woman to whom flamenco was crap?

What he decided was that he was in mourning for companionship, for the companionship of just one woman, and was yearning to be happy. Flamenco reminded him of all the ways a man could be unhappy. Stop playing it. Chas was all set to be the companion of his heart, but she was out of his sight too often. Stop letting her go.

Of course, the way things stood, she had to go. There was no room for her here. To get into bed she had to perform a manoeuvre of which an SAS man would have been proud. To get out of it, especially in the middle of the night, was more perilous still. There was nowhere for her to write. And she had a pair of children growing loopier by the hour to keep an eye on. There was only one resolution to this. He would buy a house for them both. In Richmond if that was what she wanted, though not on the same side of the street as the house she already had. He would get down on one knee, ask her to marry him and buy them a house.

What was wrong with that for a plan? He was obviously in love with Chas – there could be no other explanation for his missing Hazel, assuming for the moment that it was Hazel he'd been missing. He knew himself. In the process of his affections passing from one woman to another, he suffered. Something in the brain: the migrating affections, crushing over the pons Varolii, pressed upon a cranial nerve. That was how he knew, definitively, he was in love with woman Y – the agonies he suffered remembering woman X.

Not that he lacked the proof he needed in his feelings for Chas herself. The old fault-line appeal hadn't led him astray. He continued to marvel at how unlike herself she could be. He loved the surprisingness of being with her. He believed she loved the surprisingness of being with him. The sex, to isolate a single component at random, was extraordinary, by virtue of how her skin felt under his fingers – neither flaking nor about to spill – and by her virtue of how his felt under hers – her hand the collar, her arm the chain. That would change, of course, he knew that. One day his fingers would not feel what they felt now and one day the collar at the end of her chain would loosen. Infinitessimally on both counts, but that's all it takes. No matter.

They would have the continuing unexpectedness of each other. You and me, *us*; who would ever have thought *that* when you stole my cat Cobbett from me?

And who would ever have thought *this* – you and me, us – when you picked me up at a party all those years ago, taught me the Bump, and then handed me over to Charlie?

Nice, wasn't it, when life turned out so differently from the way you expected it?

Very nice.

And very nice back at the Kreitman residence where Charlie was waiting for Hazel, out visiting her mother, with a big bunch of red roses, a lemon meringue pie in a pretty cardboard box tied with violet ribbon and what looked suspiciously like a complete set of the novels of P. G. Wodehouse.

He leapt at her like a labrador when she came in. 'I've missed you,' he said.

'I've missed you,' she told him.

Then he bent to her and they kissed, balancing to perfection, you would have thought, sensuality and affection.

Maybe, thought Hazel, I don't have anything to worry about after all.

BOOK III

ONE

I F A PERSON is happy for the first sixty-nine years of his life and unhappy for the last one, does he die an unhappy man?

When is it reasonable to call 'Time' on happiness? Think no man happy until he's dead and you save yourself a lot of bother. But that's routine pessimism, and routine pessimism is merely a sort of showing off. It also dodges the question. As a young man Kreitman liked saying that you should call no man dead until he was happy – but that too was only swagger.

The trouble is that happiness, as a summation of an observable condition of life, is arbitrary. It all depends where you decide to stop. Cut the deck here and you draw happy, cut it there and you draw sad.

This might be why we like to have a painting above our mantelpiece. A painting freezes time, offering the illusion that a loveliness of nature, or an expression of human contentment, can last for ever. In the best paintings you can feel Change breathing just beyond the canvas, panting to be let off the lead. But look again the next day and he is still where he was, still eager, still chomping, but still restrained.

Someone should have painted Hazel and Charlie just before Charlie cut into the lemon meringue pie.

Or Kreitman on his knees to Chas.

★   ★   ★

'I wish I had a camera,' Chas laughed, flushing, flustered even, 'but haven't you forgotten something?'

'What's that?'

'That you are already married.'

'Oh, Hazel will be glad to be rid of me,' Kreitman said.

'Is that a recommendation?'

'Do I *need* a recommendation?'

Chas thought about it. 'And the other thing you've forgotten,' she said, 'is that I too am already married.'

'To which I cannot, with any gallantry, reply that Charlie will be glad to be rid of you.'

'No,' Chas laughed, 'you can't.'

It made her sad, suddenly, to hear the words that Kreitman couldn't say.

'Leave it,' she said, helping Kreitman to his feet. 'This is very sweet of you and entirely unexpected, but let's leave things as they are for the moment, eh?'

She was surprised how disconsolate he looked. 'Come on,' she said, taking him by the shoulders and straightening his back. It was like cheering up a child. She felt she had to put the briskness of hope back into him. 'Come on,' she said again, kissing him. 'We're all right as we are, aren't we, eh? Eh, eh?'

It had been her great thing as a wife and mother, instilling briskness. Let's go for a walk, let's buy an ice cream, let's bake a cake. She had excelled at it. But she had never been a wife or mother to Kreitman, from whose eyes the tears rolled inconsolably, like a baby's.

The moment Charlie cut into the lemon meringue pie his heart crashed through his stomach.

He had been here before. Once before or a hundred times – it didn't matter. There was the lawn running down to the river, and there were the children – his darling Kitty-Litter, his laughing boy Timmy Hyphen Smelly-Botty – doing what children do, and there were the de Selincourts and the Gosses sipping Charlie's Greek wine, and there, viewed through the kitchen window, was Chas in a comically harassed turban rolling pastry or boiling gnocchi or stringing beans – and there in the sky was the sun, and there on the river were the rowers, and there, just there, in the middle of it all, was Charlie himself standing at a trestle table, shouting 'Yummy!' and slicing lemon meringue pie for everyone. There'd been a discussion about clothes lines – when wasn't there, on the Merriweather lawn, a discussion about clothes lines, given Charlemagne's queer predilection for them? – in the course of which everyone had agreed that the clothes line, however useful, was a social menace and an aesthetic blight, and Charlie in a fit of lugubrious self-denial had made a face and said, 'Oh, all right then, I'll wear wet chinos from now on,' and to everyone's delight had taken the rusted garden shears and with an exaggerated grunt had snipped the clothes line in the middle, sending a solitary wooden peg flying into the air, where it triple-somersaulted like an acrobat before landing to great applause in Chas's homemade lemon meringue pie.

Were the Kreitmans there? Charlie couldn't see them. Let him close his eyes however many times, he could just about make out Marvin on the lawn, but not Hazel. Had she never been there, or had he never noticed her? Funny, because he had noticed every other woman. His own wife he had not, of course, *noticed* in that sense. Chas was just Chas, not there to be noticeable in *that* sense. Even as his heart was crashing through his stomach his memory did not rearrange her to be a visual stimulus to him. What he missed, with an ache like a wound, was the familiarity of her – however *un*familiar that was now, after all the months he hadn't clapped eyes on her – and that included, as a matter of course, the dissatisfactions which had driven him to look too closely and with too much undisguised desire at every other woman on the lawn. Every other woman excluding Hazel, that is. Without a doubt, she had been there. Coldly, he could enumerate the occasions on which she was bound to have been there. So why couldn't he *see* her there? He could come up with only one rational answer to that – he didn't *want* to see her there. You don't wipe a person out of your visual history unless your eyes reject them.

She had refused pie. She had her figure to think of. Something annoyed Charlie about her employment of that word. *Figure.* His mother had been fond of the word figure. On his mother's lips the shape it had made was formal and cold. On Hazel's it was voluptuous. More voluptuous, all at once, than he cared to make mental room for.

As an atonement for not being able to find her on his lawn he made himself look at her arranging the flowers he had just bought her. She was still wearing the clothes she had been to visit her mother in, a too short Whistles skirt with a too deep slit, extravagantly decorated with pretend-old buttons and lace, a sexy play on the idea of old-fashionedness, soft on her hips, and a lovely bloody maroon flesh-responsive cardigan he had helped her choose, through which he could watch her nipples breathe. Ten minutes before, the sight of her had filled him with love. Desire, too, yes. Her legs so strong in those high strappy heels. Her prodding chest. Eyes in the wrong place. But first and foremost love. 'I've missed you.' There was the problem, right there! 'I've missed you.' He had forgotten what all this was supposed to be about. He hadn't originally gone to her for love. He hadn't originally been looking for love. *He already had love.* Love was what he'd swapped with Kreitman, who had something else. If he'd merely swapped love for love, he had let a few people down, had he not? In the time it took him to revisit his garden, in less time than it took him to finish his pie, he had come down from love to fondness – another commodity he hadn't been in the market for – from fondness to consideration, and from consideration to pity.

No sight in creation looks more dolorous to a man than a woman in the fullness of her sensuality and glamour, once you have allowed pity to play a part in your appreciation of her. In restitution for which dishonour – and this explains the terrible spiral of the sexual affections once they start to tumble – you can do nothing except pity her some more.

This will pass, Charlie told himself. Don't give in to this. But he was filled with an unassuageable yearning to be back on his lawn in Richmond, bouncing his children who were no longer children on his knee, telling them mad stories, pouring lukewarm retsina, and Chas in her comical turban, up to her elbows in flour.

'One of the nice things about the relations between our familes,' Charlie had once said to Kreitman, in the days when they lunched together in Soho, 'is that our children get on so well.'

'You think so,' Kreitman had replied. He had always hated this kind of talk. 'Don't you think that's just because they're all drug addicts? In fact, they wouldn't know whether they were getting on or not. They merely supply one another.'

'Just a stage,' Charlie said. 'Like us and rock and roll.'

'Charlie, what are you talking about? You were about as interested in rock and roll as I was in motor racing. Name me a rock band.'

'I mean our generation.'

'I tell you what I don't get,' Kreitman said, 'if you're going to talk about generations, I don't get what's happened to the principle of taking turns. Rock and roll I don't remember, Charlie, but I do know that we were in awe of seniority when we were young, that however much we rebelled on the surface we deferred in our hearts, so how come, since what goes around is supposed to come around, that this latest batch isn't in awe of us? Neither on the surface nor under it. I feel cheated, Charlie. I feel cheated of my turn.'

'Try being friends with them instead, Marvin. The wise thing is to take what's on offer. We gave awe, this generation gives informality.'

'I don't want to be informal with kids. I want them to keep their distance.'

'Unless they're girls . . .'

Two old friends, one steadfastly in love with the same woman all his married life, one not, meeting regularly to decide who was the unhappier and then losing their nerve.

But Charlie had been right about what was nice about relations between the two families – the children *did* get on well together.

Back from Thailand, Cressida and Juliet Kreitman went clubbing with Kitty and Tim Merriweather even before they had that long-promised dinner with their father.

'So fill us in. Who's doing what to whom this time?' Juliet wanted to know.

'Can't we talk about something else,' Timmy said. 'Did you find the beach?'

They were in a queue on Wardour Street, waiting to pass muster, not more than a few yards, had they but known, from the place where Nyman knocked down Kreitman and did all their brains in.

'The beach is for later,' Cressida said. 'I just want to know how we can get your dad out of his shitty old dressing gown.'

'We don't have a dad,' Kitty said.

'What I just want to know,' Timmy added, 'is how we can get *your* dad out of our mum.'

'OK,' Cressida said, 'so we won't talk about it.'

And an hour later they were doing what they'd come for and wiping out every invidious recrimination, and all other invasive passions to boot, to the music of ferroconcrete robots trying to do the same.

What Nyman was hoping to wipe out in a club whose upper age limit was nineteen on an old night is harder to say. Tim had several times proposed meeting there for a Friday rave, but he hadn't really expected Nyman to show. People from the box had other people from the box to hang out with. Yet here he was, looming out of the prison-yard lighting like a fugitive, a back-to-front baseball cap on his head, a PVC rucksack on his shoulders, a water bottle with a pump and a phosphorescent straw in it round his middle, and glitter on his eyelids. 'Gotcha!' he said to Tim, catching him round the chest but not breaking the rhythm of his dance.

Timmy danced like a National Theatre production of *Marat/Sade*, the inmates of the asylum at Charenton, doubly demented. Nyman did rhapsodic – slow, corkscrew unravellings, as though confined genie-like within a narrow-necked bottle, with a touch of the shaven-headed East. Were the Dalai Lama to have danced, and upon a pinhead, he would have danced like Nyman.

'So who's your brother's spiritual friend?' Cressida screamed into Kitty's ear.

And that was how the Kreitman girls got to have their turn with Nyman, as they explained to their more than usually preoccupied father over dinner at a starry restaurant a decent distance from the Ritz.

'You know who this is you're telling me about?' Kreitman wanted to be sure.

'Yeah, we know all about the bicycle,' Juliet said. '*Alles ist klar.*'

'He told you he's German?'

'I can't remember if he did or not. But he looks German.'

'He also looks a faggot.'

'I don't think so, Daddy,' Juliet said.

'Did he squeak his eye sockets for you?'

'He hasn't so far.'

'He will. Just stay away from him.'

The girls laughed. For as long as they could remember, their father had told them to stay away from everyone. It was his idea of setting a good example and ruling with a rod of iron. Once he'd said 'Stay away' he felt he had done his duty and could get on with what interested him more.

'So you and Aunty Chas . . .' Cressida ventured, when the time seemed right.

'I know what you must be thinking,' Kreitman said.

Their conversation was interrupted when a woman Kreitman knew to be celebrated for something or other, just don't ask him what, begged Juliet and Cressida for their autographs. Not the starry thing to do, but there you had it. Today, even the famous were exercised by fame. She had seen their picture in a colour supplement. Relative Values or Sibling Rivalry – one of those. And she knew Cressida's work. Cressida's *what*? Kreitman thought. He rolled his eyes. He had famous daughters. How could this be? He had fed them warm bottles while Hazel tried to get some sleep, then he had turned away for five minutes and now they were famous. He remembered their inky fingers and their school reports, commenting on their appalling handwriting, a fault inherited from their mother. Now they outdid each other for elegant flourishes and the size of their Mont Blancs.

'We're not judgemental,' Juliet said, putting hers away in a handbag, Kreitman noticed, that hadn't come from the family business. 'It's a bit embarrassing for us, that's all –'

'And a bit naffo –' Cressida added.

'But if squeaking your sockets for Aunty Chas is what makes you happy . . .'

'. . . who are we to complain?' Cressida completed.

If I were in the market for girls today, Kreitman thought, I wouldn't succeed. They'd eat me alive. I'd have to turn faggot. 'How would you feel,' he summoned the courage to ask, 'if we married?'

Cressida hung out her tongue. Juliet made pin wheels with her eyes. 'You and Aunty Chas? Are you serious?'

'*I* am. I'm not sure about Aunty Chas.'

286

'Doesn't marriage still take two, Daddy?' Cressida wondered. 'I know we've been away for a few months . . .'

'And aren't you still married to Mummy?' Juliet enquired.

'Yes and yes,' Kreitman said. 'And for those reasons, or at least for the first of those reasons, it probably won't happen. I think Chas is worried about how Tim and Kitty will take it.'

'We can tell you,' Juliet said. 'Badly.'

'Both?'

'No,' Cressida said. 'Kitty badly. Timmy very badly.'

'You've had the discussion?'

'We've had the "Let's not even discuss it", which is more serious.'

'Is it me?'

Cressida treated her father to one of her most brilliant smiles. 'Why, is Aunty Chas seeing someone else as well you?'

Juliet laughed. 'Well, there's a thought. Our little Kraut did imply he fancied Aunty Chas was an itsy bit sweet on him.'

Kreitman stiffened, pushing his plate from him. 'How did he imply that?'

Juliet shrugged. 'How does anyone imply anything? We were talking . . .'

'*Where* were you talking?'

'In a bar, after the club. Does it matter?'

'No. It doesn't matter. Go on.'

'There's no on to go to, Daddy. We were just chatting, Aunty Chas's name came up, Nyman said something vague – you know he isn't a master of language – about how kind she'd been to him . . .'

'He used the word "kind"?'

Juliet checked with Cressida. 'Kind?'

Cressida feigned boredom. 'Kind, nice, hot, sexy, giving him the come-on – I wasn't listening.'

'And he said this,' Kreitman wanted to know, 'in front of Kitty and Tim?'

'Yeah, why not? It's some sort of joke between them.'

'The joke being?'

'Oh, come on, Daddy. Is everything sacred suddenly? Just because our parents have all decided to behave like children, does that mean we aren't allowed a bit of fun at their expense? Nyman is one of those professionally homeless people, Aunty Chas offers him a bed for a couple of nights, we enjoy jumping to salacious and I have no doubt highly improbable conclusions. Didn't we learn how to do that from you?'

Kreitman fell vacant. 'I don't know what you learned from me,' he said. 'But whatever it was I'd unlearn it.'

Had you asked him, a second later, what he had just said, he wouldn't have been able to tell you. There was no room in his head for recollection. Every spare inch was taken up by what had just flown into it. The information, and the interrogations which waited on it as inevitably as night waited on day . . . What bed, what nights, how recently, how often, to what pleasurable end . . . ? But he knew to what pleasurable end. He had the picture to go with the question. Dartmoor, Richmond – what difference?

O, full of scorpions is my mind, dear wife. That all? Cry baby! Kreitman would have killed for mere scorpions. On *his* mind fed a whole menagerie of monsters.

And they weren't only gathered there to feed, either. In the fouled corners of Kreitman's mind the world's bestiary feasted and lied and fornicated and shat.

TWO

I T SOUNDS SINISTER. A massive mechanism for spying. The London Eye.

A giant bicycle wheel, 135 metres in height, 2,100 tonnes in weight, all included, and observable just about everywhere in the city, the London Eye turns at 0.26 metres per second, just fast enough, if you draw a bead on something stationary, to discern with the naked eye. It is a marvel of modern engineering, no doubt about it. And beautiful to behold. Thirty-two luminous capsules, or pods, apparently sea green in colour with the light through them, carry twenty-five passengers apiece. So that's eight hundred of us up there, in principle, at any one time. On a clear day, we can see for twenty-five miles. Which is how many miles between us?

No citizen of sound mind dislikes the London Eye. Of those who are able to see it, or enough of it to say they see it, from their bedroom windows or balconies or rooftops, a sizeable proportion claim to have stood and watched it complete its thirty-minute cycle. You find a pod you like and then, without changing your position, you follow its painstaking revolution until it returns to where you first hit on it. You can do this alone or with a lover. With wine or empty-handed. With the radio or headphones on, or silent. Watch for more than thirty minutes and you become woozy, uncertain whether you are watching it or it is watching you. At night you can see the flashes of cameras, little light explosions, as pretty as shooting stars, coming from the highest pods. How many of those taking photographs have photographed you looking?

For some people a giant bicycle wheel, revolving high over the city, would be a nightmare. People who don't like bicycles, people who don't like wheels, people who have suffered traumas as a consequence of either, people such as Marvin Kreitman.

Yet Kreitman, too, is watching the wheel, fastening upon a pod and following its half-hour revolution. Is that how long you stay on, a half-hour? Can you pay to stay on longer, or is it strictly thirty minutes and then off? If you *can* stay on longer, do you have to make that decision when you buy your ticket on the ground – assuming that's what you do – or can you renew as an afterthought, on an impulse, on a lovers' whim, in the pod itself? Is there a limit to how many times you can go round? Is there an hour when there is so little business that you can have a capsule entirely to yourselves?

These are the questions which trouble Kreitman as he watches, human-interest questions rather than any that bear upon the weight and size of the structure, the amount of cabling needed to keep it upright, or the problems which the wind must pose.

For the wheel Kreitman watches is a wheel of fire, imagination's wheel, and the skills of engineers are irrelevant to a wheel of that sort.

Kreitman had a sighting of the wheel's upper rim from his Clapham pencil box, but nothing that could honestly be called a view. It's even possible that all he had a sighting of were cranes, swaying in the vicinity of Jubilee Gardens, helping to build the new riverside. In order to get a view proper he had to change his address. Nothing permanent. He didn't want to look at the wheel for ever, or for however long it was provisionally booked to stay up. He just wanted to look at it for a while. How long was a while? He didn't know. More than an hour, but less than a year. For the best views, in the full-on, reach-out-and-grab-a-capsule sense, there was no beating those characterless flats to which the offices of the once Greater London Council and its neighbours had been reduced. But Kreitman could find nothing rentable there on a short-term basis, nor was he convinced, once he thought about it a second time, that he wanted to be quite so unnervingly close. Seeing the wheel was the object, not the wheel seeing him. In the end he found an apartment hotel in Soho, so new it wasn't finished yet, and so bijou it made a virtue of that fact, which enjoyed the advantage of a communal roof terrace, commanding panoramic views, and what is more was situated just a collision away from the very restaurant where he and Charlie Merriweather had enjoyed their last ever dinner as good friends, proud husbands and sane men. And Kreitman was not one to look a gift horse in the mouth.

From the roof terrace in Soho, on which he has no eagerness to encounter other communal souls, the spindle of the London Eye appears to be the spire of the church of St Martin's-in-the-Field. Kreitman enjoys the prospect, out over the leaded rooftops, past the tiny attic editing suites and the neon cinemas of Leicester Square – the Odeon showing particularly well – to where the wheel turns on a needlepoint consecrated to God. Close an eye, and the golden cross of the church appears to be entangled in the spokes. In the sun, the wheel is an iridescent orb, as persuasive a covenant as a rainbow. As for distance, well, it is not exactly a handshake away, but near enough for civilities. With the use of binoculars, Kreitman can clearly make out the outlines of people in the pods, can count them, and with concentration, he believes, can even decide on the meaning of their physical dispositions, one to another.

He did not, pursuant to his glittering dinner with his daughters, confront Chas with the evidence of her double-dealing. Although incapable of taking anything lightly, Kreitman was not a man who had to get turmoil immediately off his chest. He could lie peaceably alongside a woman who had wronged him, lie folded in her arms like a vole in the embrace of a cobra, and not raise a murmur of complaint. In general this is a gift – call it a gift for quiescence – which men possess in greater abundance than women. Once wronged, most women find the physical presence of the man who has wronged them abhorrent. Fear may keep them silent, but the abhorrence remains. Perhaps because they aspire to a lesser ideal of perfection, men are better able to swallow their outrage. Kreitman was, anyway. Jealous of the very pillow on which a woman he cared for laid her cheek – a zealot of the minutiae of jealousy – he was yet able to bear it so long as the offending woman engaged him, volubly, in her wrong. Words did not have to be the medium of engagement. A look of connivance could do it. The thrum of silent confession could do it. Gross witness would, of course, do it in spades. It's a paradox, but then what isn't – the more access Kreitman was granted to the causes of his agony, which is another way of saying that the acuter his agony became, the easier he bore it.

It was not deception Kreitman found hard to take, it was exclusion.

He had not yet attained that peeled-back intimacy with Chas where he could assure her it would never matter what she did that was outside the letter of their law, provided she included him in it. In all probability he never would. She wasn't pliable enough. She preferred everything to be straight. She had come a considerable distance, for her, simply being with him at all; but he couldn't see her bending to accompany him into his spider holes and corners. What is more, he did not, in another, better part of his nature, want her to. For *himself* he did not want her to. Chas was meant to be a clean slate. She had told him she could not bear to be just another woman added to his total, and he had promised her he had stopped counting. He meant it. He had stopped counting off names and he had stopped counting off failures. And what that had to mean was that he had stopped counting off repetitions. Same spot, same sore, same itch. No more. Please no more.

What it came to was that there was nothing to be gained by accusing her of resuming old relations with Nyman, let alone, for all he knew, of instituting new ones, a) because she would never, in the only way that Kreitman craved, consider taking him into her confidence, and b) because he didn't want that craving in bed with them. Either she would have to lie, or he would have to leave. If he brought her to the point of having to go on lying, he would be the more inflamed. If he left – but he couldn't think of leaving with his mind in the state it was and his heart as pulpy as rotten fruit. Exclusion was bound to be the outcome, whatever happened. She couldn't tell him, he didn't want to ask her to tell him, but he needed to know.

Did he need to know?

He needed to know.

He was in a torment of needing to know and a torment of neither daring nor wanting to ask.

So he lay there, with Chas wound around him like a snake, saying nothing.

She, for her part, felt him drifting away.

'He's going,' she told Dotty on the phone.

'Another bulletin? You told me that last time. You make it sound as though he's dying. Stop listening and get on with it,' Dotty said.

'I don't know what to get on with. I think I may have hurt him when I turned him down.'

'What do you mean you turned him down?'

'Don't scoff, Dotty. He asked me to marry him.'

'Marvin Kreitman asked you to *marry* him?'

'It's not what you think. It was a gesture. Nothing but that.'

'And your refusal? Also a gesture?'

'I don't know what it was. But I meant it. He asked me out of desperation. I think he was frightened he was missing his wife. I think he asked me to marry him to prove he wasn't. Or maybe he just wanted me to say no so he could start missing me. Something like that. He's desperate, Dotty, and I have to ask myself what I want with a desperate man.'

'There's no other kind, darling.'

Chas thought about that. 'Then maybe I don't want to be with a man at all,' she said.

But in the meantime she tried to call him back from wherever he'd gone.

'You've left me,' she whispered one night.

'I haven't,' he said.

'You've stopped looking at me.'

'Have I? I haven't meant to stop looking at you.'

'You've withdrawn everything,' she said. 'You've stopped looking at me, you've stopped speaking to me, you've stopped kissing me.'

That was the moment, wasn't it, to challenge her with what he'd heard? It would have been a kindness. Spit it out and have done with. I know you've been seeing the faggot. Why did you lie? Why do you go on lying? What do you mean by it, and what do you intend to do with him now? Spit it all out – all of it, no matter how petty and inglorious – and give her the chance to clear the air. But Kreitman couldn't breathe clear air. Like some inverted bat in a bat cave, Kreitman needed the air fetid.

'I'm sorry,' he said. 'Take no notice. It's a man thing. Change of life. I'll be fine soon.'

Then he turned away from her so that she might hear his body and understand what it was asking for.

In the end he had to know and hang the decencies. He called Maurice up to talk to him.

Was Maurice driving Mrs Merriweather anywhere but home?

He wasn't. Other than occasionally to the supermarket, where he helped her with her trolley.

Was Maurice perhaps party to any conversations – in the driveway of Mrs Merriweather's house, say, or in the aisles of Marks and Spencer, or on Mrs Merriweather's mobile phone – which were not quite in the spirit of Kreitman's lending her his driver and his car?

He wasn't.

Would Maurice be offended if Mr Kreitman asked him to keep his wits more than usually about him, and to mention it, should he happen to be in Richmond at an unseasonable hour and see Mrs Merriweather behaving in a way that would cause Mr Kreitman concern?

Maurice knew not to bind his employer in a man-to-man smile. He inclined his head the way a chauffeur should, even though he only chauffeured a Smart. Mrs Merriweather was a very nice woman. But then Mr Kreitman was a very nice man. And Mr Kreitman paid his wages.

I am beneath contempt, Kreitman told himself, but he was quickened in every nerve.

Quickened to no end, for many weeks, to no end at all, unless you count the fraying of the nerves of his relations with Chas, until Maurice, having kept his wits about him, drew Kreitman's attention to Mrs Merriweather's having taken a taxi to the London Eye, two afternoons running.

'On her own in the taxi?' Kreitman enquired.

'On her own, Mr Kreitman. Not counting the driver. I followed her all the way.'

So that ruled out an excursion with Kitty, followed by an excursion with Timmy. But then you could say it also ruled out an excursion with anyone else, were anyone else staying over at her place.

Kreitman listened to the beating of his heart but held himself in suspense. This was the wrong way, but there was no right way. He knew himself. He knew what transfixed him. The next week Maurice reported Mrs Merriweather taking a phone call in the car and being upset by it. And the day after that Chas rang, uncharacteristically for her, to cry off an evening which they'd earmarked as romantic.

'You're tough to be with at present,' she'd said. 'I'm giving myself a little holiday from you. Be kind to yourself.'

'Tomorrow, then?' Kreitman had hoped.

'All being well. Maybe.'

A little holiday. At least she hadn't called it a sabbatical.

But that settled if for Kreitman. He put himself in her position. Where would he go to pursue an amour with a dough-faced cocksucker, *a man more rattishly and motivationally*, blah-blah, safe from the scrutiny of his children, his friends, his lover, and whoever else he did not wish to shame himself in front of? The Eye, 135 perpendicular metres beyond the reach of discovery. The Eye from which you could see trouble coming, twenty-five miles in all directions. The Eye, that great 2,100-tonne bicycle in the London sky.

Armed only with binoculars, Kreitman climbed on to the roof of the hotel and, at a cost of £290 a night, excluding breakfast, waited for the giant wheel to run over him.

THREE

'WHAT DO YOU call those holdall letters that people copy to all their friends?' Hazel asked Charlie.

'Drivel,' Charlie said.

She had brought him tea in his study. He had been sitting at his desk, writing nothing, listening to the leaves drip, watching the garden rot.

'I didn't ask you for a judgement,' she said – if I'd wanted a judgement, she thought, I could have stuck with you-know-who – 'I asked you what they're called.'

He shrugged. He had barely looked at her when she brought his tea. Once upon a time he'd have dropped to his knees and buried his nose in her belly and she'd have laughed and warned him not to make her spill the scalding liquid. 'Charlie, mind!' That was once upon a time.

'I don't know,' he said. 'A round-robin letter, maybe.'

'And isn't that something you send when you want to bring everybody up to date with your fascinating life?'

'I'd have thought so,' Charlie said, looking at the rain. 'Why?'

'I've just got one in my e-mail – and don't ask me how he came by my address – from that Nyman person.'

'Who's *that Nyman person*?'

'The cyclist who upset my husband.' She didn't add, the one whose sexual games precipitated me into your arms.

'Oh, him.' Charlie seemed in no hurry to remember. 'And?'

'And it's uninteresting beyond belief.'

Charlie put his tea down and looked at her at last. 'Wasn't that the point of him? Inverse sophistication. Wasn't he trying purposely – in a way that drove your husband to distraction – to be as uninteresting as possible?'

'Everything drove my husband to distraction. Pity he isn't here to read this.'

And she left the printout on Charlie's empty desk.

With the more than averagely inversely sophisticated bits taken out, Nyman's e-mail read:

Dearest Friends,

My twenty-sixth birthday! Another year in which nothing has been happening! How quickly the sands runs through the hourglass of our lifes! My milestones will be few compared to yours, but I tell them because they are my story.

For sixteen weeks I work behind a counter in shop in Berwick Street, selling porno things. Must I say it was the most educating time of my life? We made competitions, behind the customer's back, guessing what he was come in to buy. Or she. Oh, yes, don't be shocked – many shes too come in the porno shop! But whether a he or a she, we never guessed right. She wants whip, he wants frilly pantys. Never judge a book by its contents – that's my motto now!

As they say, one thing leads to another, and by a contact I made in this shop I am suddenly out of there and working as courier for an advertising firm. It was a lucky strike to get there. They needed a runner, but I replied only if I could use my trusty bicycle. My fingers nearly wrote 'rusty' bicycle! You may have heard I had a 'spillage' on my bike, with a captain of industry. Insignificant person, significant person – bang! How do you like that! Now I am close to the family and to friends of the family. Never look where you're going – that's my motto now!

On the future front, a fairground palm-reader has been reading my hand and prognosticating I will be famous and in love. When? Soon. But can't be certain because the lines on my hand are faint. For another five pounds she will read my personality and tell the future from that. I tell her impossible because I have no personality. Goodbye, fame! Or maybe not. But hello, love, I think.

'Nowhere Man' is a well-known song by the Beatles. On the occasion of his birthday, this Nowhere Man wishes you health and wealth.

Your friend,

Nyman

'Close to the family!' Hazel thought. 'The cheek!' Unless he was close these days to Kreitman. Which could easily mean, for she knew her husband, close to Chas.

Poor Chas! Hazel hadn't been surprised when her husband exacted his revenge, as she saw it, and squared their little circle, however an unlikely partner for him Chas was. There was no 'likely' where Kreitman was concerned. No likely and no unlikely. The idiot boy Nyman had got under his skin by finding a virtue in being no one, an almost personal affront to a man for whom being someone, for whom being distinct and aloof and outstanding, was a sort of mania. But in the end Kreitman was as much a no one as anyone. There wasn't a woman he wouldn't cry over, not a woman that couldn't disarrange him, therefore – this had to follow, didn't it? – there was no 'him' at home. Between the two – between Kreitman and Nyman – there was nothing to choose. If anything, when it came to self-possession, Nyman just edged it.

Mulling it over, she wished Kreitman were here to say it to –

299

'He just edges you, Marvin – when it comes to self-possession, he just edges you.'

Hard to believe she had cried over them both. It went to show how low a woman could be brought. Well, she wouldn't be doing that again. It was only Chas she was sorry for now. Not only on account of the wrong she had done her – though Charlie was a grown man when all was said and done, and desperate, at his wits' end with being married, a fish that was out of the water gulping air long before she cast her hook – but also because she knew how horrible it would be for Chas – if not today, tomorrow; if not tomorrow, the next day – lying by Kreitman's side. There was a subtle sisterhood of decency in these matters: you might steal another woman's husband but that didn't mean you wished Marvin Kreitman on her.

Hazel listened to the old anger welling up inside her and knew what was amiss. She was coming apart again. She was being expelled from the mother ship. Any hour now, any minute, she would be left spinning in the silent immensity, on her own.

I can't bear it, she said.

I can't bear it because I have been there before.

Better never to have been rescued? Better never to have redocked? No.

She urged herself to avoid bitterness and be thankful. Look at it like this, she said – you have had an unlooked-for holiday, a lovely time you never expected to have. Things have been said to you which you won't forget, which you mustn't allow yourself to forget. Hoard your memories. Store up treasures.

But store them up for what? Store them up for when? Her old age? Her lonely old age? Never mind, never mind. She might soon get knocked down by a bus. She might feel a stab in her chest and fold over. You never know what's waiting for you. All you can do is store. Just store.

In order to make Charlie feel that he was no fly-by-night, that Kennington was his even though none of his friends ever visited him there, Hazel had changed the message on the answering machine. Not what a modern woman was supposed to do, but she'd done it. Now it was Charlie who said, 'Neither Hazel nor Charlie is available to come to the phone at the moment . . .' She would leave the message on. Kreitman she had wiped off years ago. Charlie she would leave on for ever. She played it again. 'Neither Hazel nor Charlie is available to come to the phone at the moment . . .' In his booming voice. Falling over his own larynx. Grammatically precise. Jocular. As though the reason neither he nor Hazel was available to come to the phone at the moment was that they were lying laughing in each other's arms.

Store it up.

That's what I am now, she thought. I am like my mother. A storehouse.

She went into her office and pulled from her cupboards the plans and the wallcharts and the calendars and the timetables she had put away when Charlie moved in with her, hoping she would never have to consult them again. Then she changed into clothes more suitable for doing business and began ringing her contractors and decorators. It didn't take long before she was shouting. No need to worry about Charlie. He couldn't hear. He was sitting in the study she'd built him at the top of the house, unproductive, moving his lips like a man composing a very long letter to himself, barely aware of the rain which fell and fell and fell.

Standing in the wet didn't bother Kreitman. Ordinarily it would have maddened him, ordinarily he couldn't bear being baited by the elements, but standing watching the wheel, he didn't mind. Blow, winds, and crack your cheeks? Not exactly. He was in no fighting mood. No call to have the cocks drowned or the steeples drenched. Just himself. Dampen me, you elements. Drip, rain, and put me out.

Besides, the seeping discomfort was appropriate to the activity. Two-bit private eyes don't go everywhere in raincoats for no reason. They carry the dismal weather around with them, in their hearts.

Kreitman was amazed how quiet Soho was among the rooftops, a mere four or five storeys up. You heard the fire engines and the police cars and the occasional blood-curdling scream – usually a joke – but otherwise he felt he could have been in a suburb. Richmond, say. Even the pounding jungle music coming from car radios was no worse than you'd have got in Richmond. As for the din of the streets themselves – 'Honk, honk, urgent delivery!' – barely a whisper.

But then, as he'd have been the first to admit, he *was* engrossed. He couldn't decide whether or not he'd chosen the right location. Would it have suited his purposes better to be positioned where he could see the capsules front on, looming suddenly on the wheel's peak, hoving, hovering, then coming crashing down on him like a waterfall? Or even from behind, where he could watch their backs as they ascended from the ground, rose and arched and slowly vanished – the goodbye view? The spectacle he'd opted for, of the entire rotating wheel full-face, like the sun, all but the very lowest capsules visible simultaneously, was picturesque but less dramatic. There'd be no jolt of invidious recognition this way, no lurch of the stomach as the pod containing people you recognised, people you loved and people you hated, people you loved *with* people you hated, swung brutally into your face. Was he sparing himself, after all?

He was too far away. His binoculars were powerful, but he knew he was kidding himself if he thought he was going to distinguish any individual or individuals with any certainty among the crowds. As for whether he'd be able to make out what they were up to, paddling palms, exchanging reechy kisses, fumbling for each other's loose change – forget it. A handjob in silhouette in an empty pod, yes, he'd be able to pick that out, from Mars he'd be able to pick that out. But the pods weren't travelling empty.

On the evening Chas stood him up, Kreitman watched until

the Eye disappeared into the rain mists. Twice he thought he'd seen Chas. Her strong profile. The stiff billow of her spinnaker. A hundred times he'd seen Nyman. Insinuating as a rat. But not once together. Being discreet, were they?

Back in his flat he wondered about the logic of Chas's actions. How many times could she face making circles over London with her lover? Wouldn't that pall quickly? Silly question, since you would have thought Nyman would pall quickly, since you would have thought he'd pall immediately, but apparently he didn't. But pall or no pall, why meet somewhere so crowded, so inconvenient, for so short a time, so often? Secrecy, yes, but had Chas not heard of hotels? One possible answer was that she was tormenting Nyman by granting him the favour of her company for no longer than a single revolution of the wheel. A subtle torture, worthy of Scheherazade, that inappropriate patron saint of the children's story, and a subtle moral prevarication – driving Nyman barmy while keeping herself respectable, confining her infidelity to a single rotation in a public place, and in that way, if Kreitman could only see it, limiting the damage she was doing to him. 'I am only unfaithful to you Marvin, for the time it takes the London Eye to go round once.' Could a man who'd lived as he'd lived deny her that?

Perhaps he couldn't, but in the meantime it was himself to whom he was denying nothing.

The following day Chas cancelled again, and then again the day after that. Still holidaying. 'No need to follow her,' Kreitman told Maurice. 'Just give me a call if you see her getting into a taxi.'

And that was how, late one autumn afternoon, Kreitman came to be mingling with the crowds queuing to climb aboard the wheel. For all the world a holidaymaker himself, until you got close and smelt the agitation on him.

He had no plan of action. If he found them, would he confront them on the spot? He didn't know. Unlikely. Would he use bad language? He didn't know. Unlikely. Would he keep his distance, follow them, muffled, into the capsule, wait until they had attained the apex of the ride and unmask them in the very act? Pretty difficult to achieve, given the numbers of people and the regimented ticket-buying. And, no, not what he wanted anyway. He stood back from the mêlée, exhilarated by the machinery, the giant spokes, the great engines painted red like toy trains on their backs, the tensed cables strung very nearly as tight as his nervous system. He leaned against a sculpture dedicated to the International Brigade. THEY WENT BECAUSE THEIR OPEN EYES COULD SEE NO OTHER WAY. Him too. He was here in the same cause, a martyr to the open eye, an international brigadier of love.

Ideally, he would find them, follow them, hop into the capsule next to theirs and spy on them from there. Nothing else. That would do it. Just that. Rolled round in earth's diurnal course and never blinking an eye.

But first find them in the jostle. The fact of it was that anyone not queuing, anyone on the perimeter like him, was a thousand times more conspicuous than the funsters waiting to climb on. If they were there, they'd see him before he saw them. He decided against looking for them in the check-in lines – he hated the facetious airline vocabulary British Airways had brought to the wheel: it wasn't a fucking flight, it was a ride – and took himself instead to the disembarkation point. Never mind following them on, he'd follow them off. Catch them not *in flagrante* but *post factum, post festum, post coitum*. Not as much fun, not as much pain, but decisive. And in that way, taking the long view, maybe more extended pain eventually. Because it would mean he had allowed the thing to happen, connived at it.

And photographs too! Here was a stroke of luck. Passengers coming off the wheel – more airline talk – found their photographs waiting for them, not pinned to a board in the old innocent style of pleasure-boat snaps, but flickering on video screens. Proof, proof in the only medium that mattered, proof on the box!

Kreitman stepped up to the photograph collection point, to see if Chas and Nyman were already up there, arms about each other's waists, smiling for the birdie. They weren't. Not yet. Timed to correspond with the numbers leaving the wheel, the pictures on the video screens changed. You had to be quick. You had also, Kreitman soon realised, to have made the decision to be photographed. You weren't automatically taken. You had to go into a booth before climbing aboard. You had to mean it. You had to want it. Would Chas have done that? Too risky, surely. But then again, think of her on her knees on the croquet lawn. Hadn't that been all risk? Wasn't coming here in the first place, *all risk*?

He kept looking. Terrible fake photographs they were, super-impositions of yourself on an unpeopled pod high above the city, an artificial expression of slightly sickly suspensefulness on your face. They should have studied him before going in if they wanted to know how you looked when you were feeling vertiginous, what a sickened stomach did to your colouring, how terror pulled at the corners of your mouth, how apprehension of disaster blooded your eyes.

He went on staring at the screens, watching them change. He couldn't stop himself. It was like pornography. The same obsessional repetitiveness, on and on, page after page, hunting for that ideally disgusting image, the one that would give you everything, the one where the stranger's outlandish pose finally met, in every specific, all the prerequisites of your own deranged desires. And at the back of your mind, never leaving you free to squander yourself without reproach, the horror of waste, the sense of ruined time. Tick-tock, tick-tock, hunting for that stranger who, by the miracle of revealed porn, happened to know the very thing you wanted. Except that today Kreitman wasn't wanting anything from a stranger.

How long he'd been there he didn't know. But it was long enough to forget the wheel itself, turning and disgorging, turning and disgorging, just a few feet behind him. Something made him look round. There it was, in all its density and clarity, the over-whelming knitted mass of spokes and almost as an afterthought, a sudden flash of inspiration, those beautiful fish-bowl pods. And there, climbing out of one of them, also as an afterthought, it seemed, was Chas – in his surprise he almost called her name – and there helping her, holding her elbow, tenderly solicitous, not Nyman, no, not Nyman or anyone remotely resembling Nyman, but Charlie, Charlie Merriweather, her lawful husband.

The two Charlies, together again, looking as though nothing had ever come between them.

FOUR

'You'd be a fool,' Dotty had told her sister, a week or so before. 'You'd be going straight back into all that shit again.'

'What shit? I didn't see any shit.'

'Darling, everybody else saw it for you. Some of us were even forced to tread in it.'

'Dotty!'

'Have you forgotten already? Do you want me to remind you of the exact form of his proposition to me? The precise words, darling, were –'

'Dotty, he was distraught.'

'Of course he was distraught. He'll always be distraught. Don't agree to see him.'

'I can't. He's –'

'I know – distraught.'

'I was going to say he's the father of my children.'

'Then let *them* see him.'

'They won't.'

'Very wise of them.'

'Dotty, I've got to see him. I'm drifting about.'

'Why shouldn't you be drifting about?'

'It's not my way. I need to know where I am.'

'You're having an affair, that's where you are.'

'It doesn't suit me. I feel like someone else.'

'That's the point of an affair, darling.'

Chas fell silent. Then she repeated what she'd said before, 'I've got to see him.'

'In that case take Marvin with you at least.'

'Marvin? Don't be absurd.'

'Then take me. Maybe he'll slip in a quick proposition while he's on his knees to you.'

'Would you like that, Dotty?'

Dotty Juniper paused to take in breath. 'Ah!' she said. 'The old sisterly reproach. I'd forgotten what it was like to have the sour taste of your marital sanctimoniousness back in my mouth. Don't ask me what I think, Charlie, if you've already made your own mind up. But do yourself one little favour – he'll be all over you like a rash, so meet him somewhere you can easily pick him off you and throw him out, once you discover, as I promise you will, that you are a changed woman and don't like anything about him any more.'

With which Dotty, miffed, put down the phone.

The following evening Chas was on the wheel with Charlemagne.

It took one spin for the wife to voice her grievances – some of them going back almost a quarter of a century – and two more for the husband to admit and take the blame for everything. Almost everything. There followed a couple of necessarily stationary meetings in a coffee shop, in the course of which they had dodged, to each other's satisfaction, the more difficult implications of rhapsodic infidelity, before they went up for a fourth and final time – the time Kreitman saw them leaving – as a sort of sentimental commemoration of the settlement of their differences.

'So what was it like,' Chas had to ask, just the once, 'your sabbatical?'

To which Charlie had replied, 'I had never realised how lonely sex for its own sake gets. It unpeoples you.'

'Sex unpeoples you?'

'We never saw anyone. We never spoke to anyone.'

'Wasn't that because you were wrapped up in each other?'

Get out of that one, Charlie.

He took a deep breath. 'Sexually, yes,' he said. Charlie Hyphen Smelly-Botty Fansbarns, lost in a dark wood. 'Once upon a time,' he started to tell her, 'a very naughty man . . .'

'Don't,' she said.

'You don't want to hear about the Lilith the Night Hag, and how she made spells to entrap very naughty men called Charlie Hyphen . . .'

'Come on, Charlie,' she said, 'be honest. No one trapped you.'

'Sex can feel like that, though,' he admitted. 'You can feel ensnared in it.'

She touched his arm. 'You don't have to spare me,' she said. 'You must have been in love with her a little bit. Don't say sex when you mean love.' They were standing shoulder to shoulder, surveying like astronauts the orb of the city, both of them straining their vision towards Richmond. 'Be truthful. I can take it.'

'I mean sex,' Charlie said. 'But of course, yes, there was some affection.' He couldn't bear to say more. He put his hand in her hair, pulling her head into the sanctuary of his shoulder. He loved having her there again, but there was another good reason for holding her to him – he wasn't in control of his face, and he didn't want her to see that.

'So it was all just silliness?' she asked at last.

He nodded, not trusting himself to words. But he was just able to say, 'And you?'

She too wasn't in control of her face. 'The same,' she said, with difficulty. 'Just silliness.'

Lying in bed, Kreitman revolved the question – To whom was an explanation owing?

No words had been spoken when he saw them coming off the

wheel. What was there to say? Might not a woman go for a joyride with the father of her children, her companion for more than two score years, and her collaborator in countless stories for young people? Kreitman did not have an inflated idea of his rights. Not for a moment did it occur to him to make a scene. In one action he saw them and, without waiting or wanting to know whether they had seen him, he fled. Novel for Kreitman, this. He did not recognise himself as a fleer. He had slunk away often enough. Skulked off in hyena shame, with his feeling parts dragging in the dirt. Or even faced up to the obligations of retreat like a man, with a tear in his eye and his hand sportingly outstretched – I did you wrong, may you fare better in the future. But this was the first time he had ever turned icy cold, gathered what he could only call his aura about him, as though there were a ghost self he carried on his shoulders, like a loose coat, and *fled*.

Anyone watching would have picked him for the criminal, not the victim.

And who was to say they would not have been right?

To whom was an explanation owing?

Unable to employ his mind to any better purpose, he remained in his bed for two days, counting his books, counting out the days of his life in his books, feverishly reading their spines backwards, like a boy with the measles – ttebboC mailliW . . . lliM trautS nhoJ . . . ecalP sicnarF . . . A nice description of his condition. How did he feel? EcalP sicnarF. SicnarF to death. He didn't expect the phone to ring. If she hadn't seen him, she had no reason to trouble herself. She was holidaying from him. If she had seen him, some explanation was owing to her and she was determinedly waiting for it. Why were you spying on me, Marvin? Why were you spying on me for a *second* time? The answer ought to have been straightforward: Why were you giving me reason? But the disingenuousness of that didn't get past even him. Why was he spying on her? For the same reason that lovers have spied on one another since lovers have existed. To quiet the demons of uncertainty, Chas. Not to stir the dragons of proof, Marvin? Ah, Chas, Chas, show me the ardent lover who can tell a demon from a dragon, or who doesn't, in the end, prefer turbulence to peace. I say an *ardent* lover, Chas. Do I take it, then, that your ardour is now satisfied, Marvin? He shook his head. In bed on his own, he shook his head. Soon he would be speaking words aloud, down to only himself to talk to. Satisfied? No, he wasn't satisfied. He was as unsatisfied as it was possible for a man of exacting mental appetites ever to be. He couldn't be jealous of Charlie, or otherwise interestingly damaged by him. Rights and precedence aside, he couldn't get his stomach to turn over for Charlie. He felt disappointed and lonely, sicnarF to death, betrayed and made a fool of, but there was no accompanying kick in the gut. He considered himself doubly let down. She had deceived him to no perversely satisfying end. And whether she fairly owed him an explanation for that he couldn't decide. Probably she didn't. But she could have been magnanimous and given him something to which he had no right.

Just short of a week, he rang her.

'What's there to say, Marvin?' she asked. 'My husband has pleaded to be forgiven and taken back. And I've said yes. I suppose I've done what I always knew I was going to do.'

'You always knew that, did you?'

Her voice was back to where it had been when she'd relieved him of his cat ttebboC. All its doors closed to him. 'I *suppose* I did, yes. Surely you did too.'

He thought he might cry. It was the form of words that did it. Always the form of words.

Not the dead in their coffins, Kreitman thought, not the dead in their winding sheets in their coffins in the sodden ground are ever so finally dead as words make them.

'I didn't, actually,' he said. 'More fool me, but I didn't.'

'Well, there you are,' she said. 'We thought it would be me who'd be saying that. It should be a change for you,

Marvin, delivering a sentence you must have heard a thousand times.'

He coughed, to get the teary deposits out of his voice. 'I'm lying here,' he said, 'where we lay together, floating among my old useless books, reading my antiquated library from memory. And suddenly I'm reminded that when Francis Place lost his wife he was in such an agony of grief he was unable to attend her funeral. Instead he hid in the barn. "A mere child," he called himself, "without a particle of resolution." And he one of the most resolute men of the century.'

'Why are you telling me this, Marvin? I'm not your wife.'

'After her death he kept hearing her moving along the passages of the house. Or in the rooms.'

She said nothing. Kreitman wondered if perhaps she was listening for the sound of her own footfalls down the line.

'I hear you on my ladder, Chas.'

She laughed. 'You are one strange poet, Marvin,' she said.

He didn't laugh. 'I am one lonely poet,' he said. 'I miss you.'

'If I've hurt you,' she said, 'I'm sorry. But I doubt that I've hurt you for long, if at all. This was always a game for you.'

'It never was, Chas. It was never a game. I take responsibility for my actions. I see them through. You're the one, as you've told me countless times, and as I can now avouch with my own eyes, who accidentally falls into situations and accidentally falls out of them again.'

'I hardly accidentally fell into you, Marvin.'

'No, you didn't. But you'll think you did. At the last you'll explain me to yourself and then forget me, as an obstacle you tripped over.'

'Whereas for you it was all purpose and meaning?'

'To my shame, yes. I envy you your light touch.'

She took it. He could hear her riding with the punch. 'Well, you have your view of me,' she said. 'As for my view of what you've been doing, I'll flatter myself that the game may have got out of hand. But it began as a game. Why deny it? Charlie's told me of your dare.'

'My dare?'

'I marvel you could be so easily entertained, Marvin. It could hardly have been much of a challenge. You knew the state Charlie was in. It must have been like taking candy from a baby.'

'Charlie told you that I challenged him? Challenged him to do what?'

'Join you in one of your games. What larks, Charlie. You have a crack at the short chubby one, and I'll see what I can make happen with the long bony one.'

'He said I said *that*?'

'Or words to that effect. You'll forgive me if I'm not able to replicate the exact locution.'

'Did he give you any inkling as to why I might have issued this challenge, as you call it?'

'Idleness, Marvin. You had a wife, he had a wife – why not?'

'I had nothing better to do that night?'

'Ah, so you do remember the night.'

'I have a wife, you have a wife, let's play swaps – after all these months we've spent together my morality still strikes you as no more subtle than that?'

'You know what you did, Marvin. You're a man who prides himself on knowing his own nature. A wife has never been a sacred commodity to you. Not yours nor anyone else's. No doubt you'll be having a laugh at my expense with the next one.'

'The next one?'

'The next however many . . .'

On the spot Kreitman made a decision. He would not tell Chas what had really happened. He would not disabuse her of her regained wifely trust. Let her think of Charlie as an easily led lost lamb, if that served the marriage. That would be his second wedding present to them both. And some sort of goodbye gift to her.

Not that she would have believed him, whatever he'd told her.

The saddest part of all, for Kreitman, that. That she would never believe him.

FIVE

A ND HAZEL?
It offended Kreitman aesthetically to be thinking about Hazel now that the Charlies were back thinking about each other. There was a moral ugliness in symmetry. Kreitman believed he owed it to himself, let alone to Hazel, let alone to Chas – to everyone, in fact, except Charlie – not to be so obvious. Yet he had been dreaming about her – hadn't he? – prior to Chas giving him the heave-ho. He had been missing her well before missing her was the obvious thing to be doing; at a time, to be brutal about it, when missing her was anything but symmetrical.

He had always been a man who moved seamlessly from one woman to the next. Seamlessly but not heartlessly. If anything the seamlessness proved how much heart he had. Only another woman could put him together again, that was how hard he fell. Whether going *back* to a previous woman, if that's any way to talk about your wife, was proof of the same emotional logic, he wasn't sure; maybe it proved that this time he had fallen harder than ever.

He wasn't going anywhere else, that he *was* sure about. There was no savour in the thought of Ooshi or Bernadette. And he was too low – low in spirits, but more importantly, too ethically low in his own estimation – to have any zest for making new ground. He couldn't imagine himself polished up and ready to go. He had no shine. He had no caps in his pistol. Back was the place for him. Back made sense.

But there was a big black buzzing fly of a question in this ointment – had Charlie, out of the same mix of oafishness and unscrupulousness, told Hazel what he'd told Chas? Never trust a man who sees himself as a good husband: if Kreitman didn't know that before, he knew it now. Even Charlie, though, must have seen that telling the one was not the same as telling the other. It was one thing Charlie ingratiating himself back into the favours of his wife at Kreitman's expense. All's fair in love and war. And any insult to Chas implicit in the revelation of Kreitman's manipulative role was nicely offset by Charlie's being able to show that his defection was never really of his own doing. He pushed me, Chassyboots. You lose one, you win one back; and the one Chas won back was the one she wanted anyway. But for Charlie to have left Hazel feeling she'd been bartered, dangled as a bit of bait by her husband and snatched at by Charlie in a fit of drunken not to say desperate bravado – and for Charlie then to have left her! – that surely was something else. That surely was an unthinkable callousness.

But did Charlie know that? Buzz, buzz, sang the big black fly. Kreitman put nothing past a good husband.

Kreitman listened to the silence coming from Kennington, interpreting it now this way, now that. You can tell when a silence is going to break, what Kreitman couldn't tell was how. At last, he found a message from Hazel on his answering machine. He played it back several times with his heart in his mouth. Well? Had he or hadn't he? Hazel's voice was dark and cold, as remote as ever, and punitive – there was something he needed to come round and see with his own eyes straight away, meaning there was some misfortune he was going to have to bear the blame for. But as far as he could make out there was no reference to any new or specific misdemeanour on his part, just all the old ones.

'Go upstairs,' she told him, when he arrived. 'Go upstairs and see your handiwork.'

He had put his arms out to her, more like an old friend than an old husband. 'Good to see you,' he had said. And it was. He meant it. Having seen nothing of her in her brief frilly period under Charlie, he was not aware of the part her suit played in this latest dialogue of anger. To him she looked angry in all the former, familiar ways. Darted at the bust, scimitar'd in at the waist, creases like blades in her trousers – Hazel as she lived and breathed, and as he knew and had once loved her.

Of course, it hurt his head to see her too. Of those instantaneous comparisons which a man cannot help but make – measuring this one's figure against that one's mind, that one's freedom of spirit against this one's stately equilibrium in high heels – none made him feel good. He was still too warmed through with Chas to want to catch himself denigrating her. On the other hand he did not want to be standing looking at Hazel and wishing she were someone else. Multiply the women, Kreitman believed, and you multiply the mortifications. This was where Burns had it wrong. The illicit rove, as the poet quaintly called what Chas had equally quaintly called going from woman to woman, does not petrify the feelings; quite the opposite – it excruciates them.

Pierced in a hundred places, love-lost St Sebastian Kreitman surveyed the ruins of his wife, once his lover, and put his arms out to her.

But she'd refused them, ordering him upstairs to see his handiwork. What did that mean? He was frightened. What did she want him to see? What did she have up there? Charlie's head? Had she enticed Charlie back and sliced him up? Chas? Could Hazel have hatched a double revenge and harmed Chas? This was Kreitman's oldest fear as an illicit rover, that he would be the death of them, fuck them and find them dead. Freudian or what?

'Go where upstairs?' he asked.

'Juliet's room. And go quietly.'

A stranger in his own house, he felt gingerly for the steps. Would he remember Juliet's room? He'd better. But why there?

Was Juliet home? Juliet ill? Pregnant? Big with child? Big with Charlie's child? Was that what was waiting for him, not Charlie's head but Charlie's foetus?

Juliet's room. Ah, yes. He remembered. Bedtime stories. Herodotus. *The Autobiography of lliM trautS nhoJ*, that inspiring anti-children's story of growing up different from all other kids, and of course *every Thursday, Friday, Saturday night, come wind, come rain, small squishy-hearted Marvin Kreitman* . . . No T-shirts, no posters of footballers and hang the consequences. Once upon a time, Juliet, there was this Benthamite . . . He pushed open the door. The curtains were closed. Someone was in the bed. Too big to be Charlie's baby or Charlie's head. Too small to be Chas. And breathing too loudly, if with too much difficulty, to be dead.

'Daddy?' a voice said.

'Juliet?'

He went over to her. 'Don't kiss me,' she said.

And in the gloom he saw that her face was smashed. He thought his legs were going to go from under him. Kreitman's invariable way of signalling sympathy for those he loved: the buckling of his limbs. He had fainted when Juliet was born. Now he had to hold on to something not to faint again. There were plasters across Juliet's nose. The veins in her cheeks were broken. Her eyes were black and swollen. At least one of them was closed altogether. Yet it was she who had to say, 'Daddy, are you all right?'

'Jesus, Juliet,' he said, 'what's happened to you?'

'Collision with a bike,' she said. 'It seems to run in the family.'

He trusted himself to let go of the bedhead and knelt by her, kissing her hand. 'You don't have to be brave and make jokes,' he said. 'What happened to you?'

'I just told you. A bike happened to me.'

'What bike – ?'

But now Hazel was in the room. 'She wanted to see you,' she

318

said. 'But she didn't want to be cross-examined. If you can't sit with her quietly, I think you should leave.'

'I'll sit with her quietly,' Kreitman said. And he did, stroking her arms, tracing the length of her fingers with the tips of his, making little circles of solace round her knuckles, and saying 'Shhh.' Why Shhh? She wasn't saying anything. It discomforted him, having daughters. It always had. He couldn't blame them for anything. And he felt there was always something they were asking for, something they had a perfect right to, which he couldn't quite give them, just as he couldn't quite give it to his cat. He'd been happiest, in their early years, when they were asleep. He had loved the sound of their breathing. Asleep, he could care for them, and sometimes, with a fervency and a sort of hopelessness that baffled him, adore them. Asleep, they laid claim on him by virtue of their separateness. At last Juliet went under, lulled by his stroking fingers. He put his ear to her chest, the way he remembered doing when she was young, making sure of the regularity of her breathing. That was his idea of being a father. Waiting for them to go to sleep, then worrying in case they were dead. Not all that different from his idea of being a lover.

'Satisfied?' Hazel asked, when he finally crept down the stairs. She was waiting for him by the door, meaning that he wasn't invited to sit down, have tea, or otherwise make himself at home. Your house, but you chose for it not to be — that was what she was reminding him.

'I don't know what you mean "satisfied",' he said. He felt cornered, so he fought. 'I don't know why you invited me to see my "handiwork". What's your point, Hazel. What's happened?'

'My point is that you have brought us to this. Me a bitter hag, yourself a fool and your daughter lying upstairs like a broken doll. That's my point, Marvin!'

A terrible weariness descended on him. How old was he? A hundred? Five hundred? 'Most of this we've had out before, Hazel,' he said, measuring his words as though he had only a few dozen of them left in him. 'You're right. Right about what I've done to you. Right about what I've done to myself. But I'm fucked if I can see what I have done to Juliet.'

'You've just seen her, Marvin.'

'I didn't do that, Hazel.'

'You did it. You caused it, just as surely as if you'd raised your own fist.'

'I thought she was knocked down by a bicycle.'

'For God's sake.' For a fraction of a second Kreitman wondered whether she was going to raise her fist to him herself. 'You've just seen her. A bicycle doesn't do that. You know what a bicycle does. It makes you crazier than you are already, but it doesn't do *that*. She's been hit, Marvin. She's been beaten up. And now *you* need a chair! Look at you!'

He did need a chair. His second totter in one evening. What a pity his mother wasn't here to see it. Before his legs could go from under him, he sank on to the stairs.

'Who hit her?'

'Why, what are you going to do? Hit him back? When was the last time you hit anyone not a woman?'

He put his head in his hands. Was it all a madhouse now? Was Hazel right about what a bicycle does when you walk it into it, had it made him crazy? Had he woken up on the hospital trolley into an asylum for the insane? 'You know perfectly well, Hazel,' he said with vehemence, because a man demands justice even in an asylum for the insane, 'that I am not a hitter of women.'

'There are other ways of doing damage, Marvin.'

'Yes, there are. But we aren't talking about those. You've just told me Juliet was *hit*. Who hit her?'

'You hit her.'

'Who hit her, Hazel?'

'Who do you think hit her?'

'It wasn't Charlie, surely to God?'

'Charlie! I think, Marvin, that you and I ought not to be talking about Charlie. Before there's any more hitting, let's leave Charlie out of it. Your other friend hit her.'

'I don't have another friend.'

'Nyman hit her, you fool!'

'Nyman?'

'Nyman. What do you say to that? Faggot is what you normally say. Try it out for size. "Nyman the faggot? Nyman the cocksucker hit my daughter?" First things first, eh? First he's a faggot, then he hits your daughter. Let no one say you don't have your priorities sorted.'

Are my ears ringing, Kreitman wondered, or is this what the world is going to sound like from now on? He put the flats of his hands beside him on the stairs. He was only two steps up but he needed all the support he could get.

'Under what circumstances,' he asked, 'did Nyman beat up Juliet?'

'The usual. Boy meets girl. Girl dances with boy. Boy beats up girl.'

'Juliet's been seeing Nyman?'

'That's quick of you. Yes, Juliet's been seeing Nyman. Satisfied?'

'What is this, Hazel? What do you mean "satisfied"? Why would I be satisfied? He knocked me down. I hate the fucker. If either of us should be satisfied, shouldn't it be you?'

'You wish! You and your dirty little mind. What can I manoeuvre Hazel into this time? I know – how about the faggot I wrestled off his bicycle.'

Charlie. Kreitman heard Charlie. What really happened on that night of nights, a fairy tale for children by Charlie – one half of the C. C. – Merriweather. So what else had Charlie told her? As though it mattered! As though he cared!

He pointed his finger at her, wagged it like the moralist in all matters of sex he held himself to be. 'It was you who wanted to fuck him, Hazel. It was you who shed tears because he was showing rather more interest in other women' – he decided against saying Chas – 'than in you.'

'You found him for me, Marvin. You plucked him off his bicycle and gave him to me on a plate. And if I thought of saying yes please for a drunken minute, whose fault was that? Who reduced me to it? Who took every grain of dignity and self-worth from me, years ago . . . years ago?'

'So this is about you, not Juliet?'

'Don't dare me, Marvin.'

'I'll dare you. I'll dare you to tell me how I made Nyman hit Juliet.'

'You brought him into our lives.'

'I didn't . . .'

'You brought him into our lives after you'd made our lives shit.'

'What was wrong with Juliet's life?'

'She's your daughter, Marvin, that's what's wrong with it. You taught her to be sarcastic. You taught her to mistrust people and then to make a fool of them. You set her a cold example.'

'She's her mother's daughter.'

'And if she learned coldness from me, whose fault's that? I wasn't born cold. I didn't come to you cold.'

Kreitman shook his ringing head. 'What has this got to do with anything?'

'What do you think? She thought she could tease Nyman the way she was brought up to tease people who can look after themselves. She needled him. She riled him. She admits she did. Her idea of love talk, just like yours. And she thought he was up to it because he was a friend of her dad's.'

'She knew he was no friend of mine. I warned her to keep away from him. I warned her he was a faggot and that faggots get emotional. Let alone give you fucking Aids. Have they slept together as well?'

'What do you know, Marvin, about anything? You wound the

boy up mercilessly and thought he wasn't aware of it. You ragged him and ragged him and at the same time used him to get yourself hot. Do you think he hadn't noticed? You made a foe of him, Marvin. Is that a surprise? Did you suppose he'd love you for it? You made him your enemy. You gave him a purpose. And when Juliet treated him exactly as you'd treated him he put his purpose into action. She asked for it, she admits that. She was defending Daddy in language of which Daddy would heartily have approved. In so far as Daddy has ever heartily approved of anything, except his dick. But she didn't ask for a beating. No one in their right mind asks for a beating. You made that happen. You and your rage and your unhappiness and your greed. And that's why I ask you are you satisfied.'

He looked up at her. Was that it? Was she finished? She met his eyes. Hers were raw with tears. His too, though his tears were the dewier. He had been a weeper, Kreitman, from the cradle, but when it came to tears of this bitter sort, old worn-out encrusted tears, he was the baby of the two. How long did they look at each other? Ten seconds? Twenty seconds? Or was it twenty years? Back, back their look went, unravelling all the way to the beginning. They were so spent they could almost have embraced. Now that we know what we know, what's to stop us? Wouldn't it be the supreme act of mutual charity, me for you, you for me? Could there be a single thing nicer we could do for each other? Or for poor Juliet, the sour fruit of our union, lying bruised in her bed?

Then the look between them went out like a dead match and Kreitman rose from the stairs and left the house.

FINALE

Left from Shaftesbury Avenue into Wardour Street and then left again into the wicked warren of Berwick and Brewer and Broadwick. Round in a circle, then out via suppurating Peter Street, lined with pimps picking their teeth with old needles, and back in again through Piss and Shit Alley, where the homeless doss down and do whatever the homeless do. What does he know?

Has he come looking for Nyman? Maybe he has, maybe he hasn't. Up to the top of Dean, then right into Soho Square, then left into Tottenham Court Road, then right, following the scholars' route, in the direction of the British Museum. More Hazel's mother's beat than Nyman's. But where Kreitman's going Hazel's mother has never been. On a Liberty-print sofa in a rose-pink Bloomsbury/Weimar boudoir, the lights shaded with doilies weighted at the corners with copper coins, like an Ethiopian's headdress, cut-glass decanters on the sideboard, porno in a green Italian leather Harrods magazine rack, Kreitman outlines his desires. He doesn't have any. He wishes to be de-desired, that's why he's here.

He shakes his head to questions which he is assured are for everyone's protection. No to slave, no to submissive, no to cross-dresser, no to housework. There is a man on his knees, in woman's bloomers, circa 1935, polishing the legs of a Biedermeier rolled-top desk which could have belonged to Kreitman's father. The man is polishing it with his tongue, what else. Kreitman does not look at him. 'Just nothing absurd,' is Kreitman's only stipulation. He has done absurd.

Broken skin? Yes to broken skin.

He does not want to choose the person who will break him. He's done choosing. 'Whoever,' he says. 'But no frilly French-farce maid, and no cat-woman in rubber boots.' No role-playing, that's his other only stipulation.

Picky for someone who has come to be de-desired? Picky only in order to be unpicked.

He is led into a dungeon, which disappoints him. A dungeon is role-play. Dungeons don't figure in the real life of men like him. But what would he prefer? That they beat him in a stockroom? That they tie him to a lectern?

Undress!

So he undresses.

A hand inspects his genitals. He doesn't know what for. He isn't here for sex. He's done sex. But he submits to the inspection, looking away. He would rather not see who's handling him.

Cuffs of leather and steel go around his wrists and ankles. The old smell of leather. He sniffs.

Too tight?

He shakes his head.

There are toggle bolts or cleats or whatever – he doesn't have the language – fastened to the cuffs. With these he is attached to metal rings driven into a contraption that reminds him half of a crucifix, half of an easel for a chalkboard. Paraphernalia – why does there always have to be paraphernalia? Why can't the physical world ever match the purity of the mental? A black hole is what his mind demands.

He is facing a wall which is meant to look like dripping prison stone, but is probably wallpaper. He closes his eyes.

Spread your legs!

He spreads his legs so that the toggle bolts or cleats can be tightened. He is now an X shape, like Leonardo's Renaissance man.

A hand takes hold of his genitals and squeezes them. Crunch. His eyes water. But this is more like. He is a bullock, not a man. A Renaissance bullock. Mere meat.

It would be good if they were to turn him on a spit and roast him. Good for everybody, but especially good for him. It is turning out to be a hard thing to kill, desire.

He is offered a choice of whips. A cane, a hunting crop and something with thongs. He waves away the choice. He doesn't know which whip does what. They have never fallen within his sphere of interest, whips, not even the leather ones.

It starts with the thongs. Tickles rather than beatings. Short, insulting flicks and jibes. Derisive. Clever of her, the woman seeing to him, to know that derision will do the trick. She is a serious, faintly despairing woman. No to the frilly French-farce maid, and no to the mistress in rubber boots, so they have given him a philosopher in a straight skirt. Perhaps she is the cleaner. He would like it if she were the cleaner. When she's finished deriding him, she might flush him away.

Another crunch of his genitals. Her property, that's what her crunching fingers say. Hers to do with, or dispose of, as she wishes.

And now the hunting crop. He hears her flexing it. He arches his back towards her, inviting oblivion.

'When I say,' she reprimands him, laughing – 'not before.' Eager to be beaten, this one.

His knees go weak. *When I say*. Please God make her the cleaner.

'All right,' she tells him, smoothing his flanks like a horse's, calming him, preparing him. 'We'll start with twenty strokes. See how you survive those. That's one! That's two! Now you count . . .'

And Kreitman – alive in every fibre – counted.